# SHIFTING
# TIME

# SHIFTING TIME

*a novel*

## Kelly Bennett Seiler

INFINITE WORDS

NEW YORK LONDON TORONTO SYDNEY

INFINITE WORDS
P.O. Box 6505
Largo, MD 20792
www.simonandschuster.com

ISBN 978-1-59309-650-2
ISBN 978-1-4767-9352-8 (ebook)
LCCN 2015944348

First Infinite Words trade paperback edition September 2015

Cover design: www.mariondesigns.com
Cover photograph: © Keith Saunders/Keith Saunders Photos
Book design: Red Herring Design, Inc.

10 9 8 7 6 5 4 3 2 1

Manufactured in the United States of America

For information regarding special discounts for bulk purchases, please contact Simon & Schuster Special Sales at 1-866-506-1949 or business@simonandschuster.com

The Simon & Schuster Speakers Bureau can bring authors to your live event. For more information or to book an event, contact the Simon & Schuster Speakers Bureau at 1-866-248-3049 or visit our website at www.simonspeakers.com.

*For Rob, Jordan, Bennett and Maclain*

*In Memory of Alex*

# Acknowledgments

Becoming a published author has been my dream since I was eight years old and penned my first story, "Debbie's Magical Dollhouse." At that age, though, I had no comprehension of the long road I would need to travel to get here or the people I'd meet along the way who would assist me in achieving my goal.

First and foremost, I need to thank my agent, Sara Camilli, who has believed in me ever since I sent her my first screenplay. Her enthusiasm and reassurance that, someday, I'd be published, was the push I needed to keep writing.

I would also like to thank Zane and Charmaine Parker and the rest of those at Simon & Schuster who made my book a reality.

I find it difficult to stay focused while writing in my house—always distracted by dishes that need to be washed and laundry that needs to be folded—even TV shows that beckon to me. If Renae and Tom Molden had not offered me the use of their detached office, free of disturbances and interruptions, this book may never have been completed.

I have been a member of two writing groups over the past few years. The feedback I have received from the members—who have all become my friends—has been invaluable. And, the fact that they expected me to submit something—anything—in writing, every few weeks, caused me to get off my rear-end and get to work!

Thank you to my friend, Dr. Marty Makary, who, upon telling him

I was a writer, said, "I know some agents. Do you want me to ask some of them if they'll read your work?" His generous offer truly set the ball, for this adventure, rolling.

I am indebted to Daniel Hubbard and Amy Beres for imparting to me all their knowledge on the responsibilities of an obituary writer. I had no idea where to begin and their emails and descriptions were invaluable.

I would be remiss if I didn't thank all of my friends—both those I see in "real life" and those I only visit with on social media. If it were not for their positive words regarding my writing ability, I'm not sure I would have been brave enough to tackle an entire novel. I have felt an immense sense of love and support that has carried me through my most frustrating days.

My parents have been my writing cheerleaders ever since that first dollhouse story. Thanks to my dad, who hung a poster in my room when I was a little girl, with the words, "Girls Can Do Anything"— and made sure I believed it. And to my mom, who continually said, "Whatever it is, you can do it." And much gratitude goes to my in-laws, John and Carolyn Seiler, who always showed an interest in my writing and loved me as if I was their own daughter. I hope I've made them proud.

And to my husband, Rob, and our three beautiful children, Jordan, Bennett and Maclain—thank you for the time you have given me to write—and for the nights and weekends you have sent me away to coffee shops or hotels or resorts, alone, so I could write in peace. Thank you for all the times you let me lock myself away in my office and tolerated me saying, over and over again, "Stop talking. I'm in the middle of a thought!" I hope Rob and I have been able to instill in our children that it is vital to never give up on one's dreams.

Thanks to God for the life He has set before me. I pray I walk it with dignity and love.

# PROLOGUE

Sometimes, when the sun begins to peek over the horizon, the seagulls circle the water in search of their first meal of the day, and the tide rushes up and then slows down so as to tickle my toes, I can hear your voice. As I close my eyes and feel the salt breeze across my face, as gentle as one of your kisses, and bury my fingers deep in the sand, just the way I used to do into your thick, black curls, I feel you next to me.

"What are you doing?" you ask me.

"Missing you," I reply.

"But I'm right here," you say.

"You're not here for me to touch. You're not here for me to hold."

"I'm here in all the ways that matter. In your mind. In your heart. In your soul."

"I want you in my arms," I say, the saline from my tears becoming indistinguishable from the salt of the water, both burning my wind-blown face.

"You had me in your arms," you tell me, gently. "Remember?"

I do remember. I remember every touch. Every kiss. Every secret glance we shared. The ones I'd forced myself to remember, knowing that some-day, the memories of them would be all I had left.

"It's not enough." I cry softly. "We were supposed to have a life together."

"We did have a life together," you whisper. "Mine."

"It was too short."

"It was all I had to give you," you remind me gently.

"I wanted more," I say, the words barely passing my lips.

"So, did I, my love. So did I."

I lie back, my head resting on the soft, damp sand. I hear a foghorn in the distance and momentarily wonder if the captain of that boat has ever felt such pain. Did he plan a future with someone, only to realize his future would be spent alone? Did he wonder, as I do now, how things could go so wrong when, for a brief moment, they seemed so perfect?

"There's so much I want to talk to you about. So much I want to ask," I tell you.

"You can ask me one question. That's all. I can't answer any more," you say.

"Just one? What if that question leads to more?" I ask.

"Only one, so make it a good one," you say and then chuckle. "I know this is hard for you. You never were good at making decisions."

"I chose you," I tease. "I made a good one there."

"Touché," you say.

I hear you lie down next to me, feel the heat of your body on my side.

"One question," you remind me. "Are you ready?"

"Yes," I tell you. "I know what it is."

And, I do know. It's the one question I've held on the edge of my tongue for what seemed like forever. It wasn't if I'd been loved. I knew I had been. Completely and utterly. It wasn't "Why?" Some questions would never produce a satisfying answer, so there was no point in asking.

Delicately and carefully, I form the words. The ones I've wanted to say aloud, but never had the courage. The question I have craved an answer for and never thought I'd get.

I make my request, very softly, my question lingering in the air. I hear your deep sigh. Was it one of regret? Was it sadness?

This time, I say it more clearly. More certain than ever this is the one question I need answered.

"What if?" I ask again. "What if?"

# CHAPTER ONE
February, 1998

"When a guy says, 'I'm pretty much single,' he really means, A. I'm completely single..."

Daniel moaned and rested his head back on his pillow. "You know I hate these quizzes."

"I know," Meade replied, holding the copy of *Cosmopolitan* in front of her face so he couldn't see her smile. "B. I'm not really interested in dating you."

"Then why do you keep giving them to me?" Daniel asked.

"They're fun." Meade giggled. "Or C. I have a girlfriend, but I think you're hot."

"C. I have a girlfriend, but I think you're hot," he instantly replied, picking up the TV remote and flicking on the set.

"C?" Meade asked, marking in his answer with a pencil. "Really? That's what a guy means?"

"Yep," Daniel answered, changing the channel. "Want to watch *Judge Judy*?"

"No, she scares me." Meade picked up her feet and rested them on the bed next to Daniel's knees, slumping deeper into her chair. "Why doesn't he just say that then? Isn't honesty the best policy?"

"Not if he wants to get in your pants," Daniel said matter-of-factly.

"Daniel!"

"What?" He asked, grinning, eyes still focused on the TV. "It's true."

Meade threw the magazine at his head as he dodged to miss it. It landed, with a loud thud, on the cold linoleum floor next to the bed.

"Ow!"

"Oh, come on," Meade said defensively. "It barely touched you!"

"No, not that. The way I moved. It hurt a little." Daniel grimaced as he shifted to get more comfortable in the bed.

Meade jumped up, suddenly concerned. "Where? How much? Should I get the nurse?"

"No, silly girl," he said, reaching for her arm and gently pulling her down next to him. "It's fine. It hurt for a second. I'm okay now."

He tugged on her sleeve. "Kiss me," he said softly.

"Again?" she moaned playfully. "Didn't I just kiss you about an hour ago?"

She giggled and leaned closer, gently touching her lips to his. They tasted slightly medicinal. She would, of course, never tell him that. She did her best to make sure, while she was with him, everything seemed normal—the way it had always been. It was why she had brought *Cosmo* and *Glamour* and *Teen* magazine with her to the hospital and grilled him with the questions he despised. It's what she'd always done—since they had first fallen in love. She'd sit at their lunch table, peppering him with the silly questions as he ate his lunch, and often much of hers, complaining as he answered.

"Is there room for me in the bed?" Meade breathed into his ear.

"I think I can find some in here," he whispered, seductively, scooting over. "If you promise not to take advantage of the many slits in my hospital gown."

"I ain't promisin' nothin'." Meade giggled. "Easy access is easy access."

She lay down in the crook of his arm, resting her head on his shoulder and her hand on his chest. She could feel the beat of his heart through the thin fabric of the gown. It felt so steady. So strong. *Keep beating,* she wanted to whisper. *Please keep beating.*

"Why are you in this gown, anyway?" she asked him. "I thought your mom brought you some of your regular pj's to wear instead."

"Yeah, she did," Daniel replied, touching his lips to her hair. "But I'm supposed to have some tests done this afternoon and I have to have a gown on for that."

"Well, I find it sexy."

"Yeah?" he asked, his eyes twinkling. "If I'd known that, I would have started wearing them years ago."

Meade laughed, even though she didn't think it was funny. She couldn't bear the thought of him in these gowns years ago. She could barely stomach the thought of him in them now.

She hadn't said anything to Daniel about his attire when she'd entered his hospital room that day after school. She'd never want him to feel self-conscious. But she'd been taken aback by the sight of him in it. Usually, when she showed up, he was in sweats and an old T-shirt, like he always was when she'd go to his house to hang out on the weekends. Somehow, seeing him dressed in regular clothes made it easier to pretend everything was okay. She could tune out the medical equipment and the hospital bed and the buzz of the nurses as they made their way up and down the hallway and into his room every twenty or so minutes. She could ignore the wires he often had on him and the tubes that were taped to various parts of his body. If she set her mind to it, she could even pretend they were just hanging out, after school, catching up on their homework, as she filled him in on the latest gossip she'd heard from all her girlfriends.

But the hospital gown—that had thrown her for a loop. She'd paused at the door before entering. Fortunately, he'd been deep in discussion with one of his nurses so he hadn't seen her arrive, and never saw the expression of shock she was sure must have been on her face.

He looked so frail. So thin. So...she hated to say the word...*sick*.

There was that word again. *Sick*. It was never far from her mind and it made her stomach do somersaults. As a child, she'd kind of liked the word. When she was eight, it meant staying home from school and watching TV in her mom's bed and drinking ginger ale while munching on saltines. But now, the word had a whole new connotation. It was scary and full of uncertainty and sadness. It meant watching Daniel be pricked and prodded while he did his best to keep a smile on his face for her sake. It meant no longer being able to make plans to go to a movie together because they never knew if Daniel would feel well enough to sit in the theater without running to the bathroom to throw up. It meant watching Daniel's olive skin turn a pale color she couldn't name because it had never been in any of her crayon boxes as a child.

"What are you thinking about?" Daniel asked her, running his fingers through her long, brown hair.

"What?" Meade said quickly, embarrassed to be caught daydreaming. She shouldn't let that happen. She needed to stay present when she was with Daniel. There was plenty of time to worry about the future when she lay in bed, alone, at night. She needed to focus on only him when they were together. Their time was precious. Not because she thought they wouldn't have much more of it. No, she wouldn't let herself go there. She *couldn't* let herself go there. Daniel spent his whole day waiting for her to get out of school and show up at his hospital room door. He deserved her undivided attention for the few hours she could give him each day.

"Oh, I was just thinking I'm kind of hungry. Did they bring you anything good for lunch today?"

Daniel shrugged. "I don't know. You can check. The tray's over there," he said, lifting his chin to indicate he meant the side of the bed.

Meade eased herself out of his arms and sat up, reaching to pull the portable bed tray over to them. She lifted the lid on the lunch plate.

"Your entire meal is still here," she said, looking at the untouched grilled chicken sandwich, mashed potatoes and green beans. "You didn't eat a thing!"

"I wasn't hungry," he said, once again picking up the TV remote and flipping to a new channel.

"Daniel," she said sternly. "You have to at least try to eat something. Anything. You'll get weaker if you don't."

"You think I'm weak?" he shot at her.

Meade sighed. She wanted to snap back at him, but knew better. It had never been like this before. They'd never argued before the cancer, and he'd certainly never been short-tempered with her. But it was so much easier to offend Daniel these days. So much more common for them to have a spat or a disagreement over something that, before his diagnosis, would have caused them both to giggle at the ridiculousness of it. But now, even the smallest issue could turn into an all-out fight, and she hated that. Part of what she loved about the relationship she'd always had with Daniel was the easiness of it. There was no drama. No game playing. It was simple and fun, but still deep and sincere.

"That's not what I meant, and you know it," Meade said evenly. "You need to keep up your strength so you can fight this thing." She peeled back the top of the applesauce she found on the tray and stuck a spoon in it, handing it to Daniel. "Here. Eat," she said firmly.

He looked at the cup disinterestedly, but took it from her and stuck a spoonful into his mouth.

"How does it taste?" she asked him.

"Great," he said sarcastically, wrinkling his nose. "Just great!"

Meade ignored his tone. "I can always stop and get you something at Merchants of Venice on my way here after school if you'd like that better." Merchants was their favorite Italian deli, owned by a guy from New York, and known for making the best subs in Texas. Before Daniel's illness, the two of them would go there every Friday after school, when Daniel wasn't in the middle of basketball season, and get a large ham, salami and capicola sub, which they'd split and rapidly wash down with Cokes, as if they were famished and hadn't eaten all week.

"No, that's okay," he said, and then seeing the disappointment on Meade's face, recanted. "Actually, that sounds great. I'm not sure I'll be able to eat the whole thing, but a few bites would be good. You can eat the rest. For once, you won't have to fight me for the bigger half."

Meade smiled, happy he'd agreed to her bringing him some food. It wasn't a big victory, but it was something, and if the past few months had taught her anything, it was to appreciate the triumphs when they came around, because they were few and far between.

"Okay, I'll bring one tomorrow."

She quickly took a few bites of the cold chicken sandwich, before placing the lid back on the plate. As far as hospital food went, it wasn't too bad. But, she did realize, it wasn't like home cooking, or even their favorite restaurant's entrees.

"Do you want to watch a movie?" he asked. "My mom dropped off a whole bunch of tapes. They're on the windowsill. I think she purposely threw in a few chick flicks, just for you."

Meade smiled. Daniel's mom was so sweet to her—always had been, ever since they were little kids. Daniel was an only child, his mom's pride and joy. It didn't take a genius to recognize Daniel was the sun and moon and stars for his mom. It was right there in her eyes every time she looked at him.

"Can't," Meade said apologetically. "My mom's picking me up early. I'm going for my senior pictures."

"Sounds positively dreadful." He rolled his eyes.

"That's because you don't like having your picture taken. Girls find things like that fun. We get to do up our hair, our makeup, smile pretty..." Meade crossed her eyes, scrunched up her face and stuck out her tongue at Daniel.

"Make sure you take a photo looking just like that. I'd love a poster of that for my room."

"The real me?" Meade said, giggling.

"Definitely, the real you," Daniel replied, a smile on his face.

Meade again lay down next to Daniel and reached over his chest for his opposite hand, pulling it toward her and interlocking her fingers in his. His hand was enormous—a trait that served him well on the basketball court. Daniel was the team star. Or, at least, *had been*. Before the leukemia. Meade closed her eyes and remembered what it was like to watch him on the court. She'd never missed a single one of his games. Even before they were officially a couple. Watching Daniel gracefully make his way up and down the school gym floor evoked images in Meade's mind of a gazelle running through open fields. Daniel was in his element on the basketball court and it was a joy to behold.

Meade's mind traveled back to the last game Daniel had played. They'd won. Of course. The school team had pretty much won every game since Daniel was chosen for the varsity team. He was just so good. And such a team player. That was the thing about Daniel. It was hard to hate him. Even the guys on the team who were secretly jealous of him couldn't find a reason to dislike him. Daniel was never cocky about his extraordinary abilities. He shrugged them off and Meade had seen him blush, on more than one occasion, when praise for his talent was showered upon him. After each game, as the students would rush out of the stands onto the court to high-five or slap Daniel on the backside in congratulations of the win, he would be loudly praising his fellow teammates.

*"Did you see how many solid assists Greg had?"* or *"We could have never won without Mac's layup at the end of the game."*

As a result, no one begrudged Daniel his success. If anything, the team, and the entire school, was rooting for him to do well—in high school and beyond. That was why that last game had been so exciting.

The recruiter from Duke had been in the stands and there wasn't a single person at Larrington High who didn't know it was Daniel's ultimate dream to play basketball at Duke. Ever since his cousin, Mike, had graduated from Duke, when Daniel was ten years old, and Daniel and his mom had driven all the way to North Carolina in their bright yellow, '78 Nova for Mike's graduation, he had set his sights on one day attending there himself. And, by the looks of his academic grades and his skill on the court, it seemed like his dream was about to come true.

Meade had spent as much time during that game, watching the recruiter, as she had watching Daniel. *Was he impressed? Did he think Daniel got control of the ball fast enough? What did he think of that mid-court shot?*

Meade sat on her hands, feeling as if her heart might pound out of her chest. She was on pins and needles for Daniel. She knew how much he wanted this and she wanted it just as much for him. For them, really. They had already planned it all out. He was going to go to Duke. She was, hopefully, going to attend Wake Forest. Her early decision application was in and she would be hearing, any day now, about their decision. They didn't want to attend the same college, recognizing they should each have their own independence for a few years, but they wanted to be close. And Duke and Wake Forest were only an hour and a half apart. Close enough to attend each other's school dances and Daniel's games, but far enough away not to distract each other from their studies. And studying was important to both Daniel and Meade. They had big dreams for their future — and, in their minds, it was a singular future which they would share. Meade wanted to study English, and had dreams of someday being the editor of a big magazine in New York City — or maybe working for some big publishing company. And Daniel had his sights set on becoming a doctor. A pediatrician. Daniel was incredible with little kids and Meade never tired of watching him chase her little cousins around her back yard at all of her family picnics.

That was the only good thing that had come out of this cancer. Daniel was having a great time learning the never-ending stream of medical lingo. Meade sometimes wondered if he drove the doctors and nurses nuts with all of his inquisitive questioning. Daniel couldn't have a single medical test done without grilling the technician about why this was necessary, what they were looking for, how the technology worked...it made Meade weary listening to his questions. But, that's who Daniel was—always eager to learn and, as he saw it, what better way to learn about the human body than by learning about one's own?

Daniel had always been very attuned to his own physical being and, even when they were young, made it a point to take care of it by eating healthily, exercising and getting plenty of sleep. That was why, the week before the big game, Meade had been surprised to hear Daniel complain he wasn't feeling very well.

"I think I'm getting sick," Daniel had told her, as they sat together in the cafeteria during lunch.

"Oh, no! Of all weeks!" Meade said, truly concerned. Daniel never got sick. *Never.* In fact, Meade couldn't even remember him ever having a case of the sniffles since she'd known him. "You'd better start drinking some orange juice and go to bed early tonight. You need to be feeling better by Friday night."

"I know," Daniel said. "I told the coach I'm gonna skip practice today and head home to get some rest."

*Skip practice? Since when did Daniel ever skip practice? Never. That's when. Never.*

Something poked at Meade right then. She wasn't sure what it was, exactly. A nagging feeling that something wasn't quite right, but she pushed the thought away as soon as it surfaced.

*He's got a cold. People catch colds.*

*Daniel doesn't.*

Meade shoved that notion back down as fast as it popped up. "Okay," Meade said, sticking a French fry in her mouth. "I won't call you tonight so you can get your beauty sleep."

And they hadn't spoken that evening, which was really unusual. The last person Meade talked to every night was Daniel. It had been that way since they'd both gotten phones in their rooms in junior high. But she recognized that he needed to be well-rested for the big game and the Duke recruiter and, though it nearly killed her, she fell asleep without picking up the phone and dialing his number.

As she sat watching Daniel play that Friday night, she was happy she'd let him rest. He was playing great. If he'd been catching some sort of cold, there was no sign of it as he ran up and down the court, making every shot he took.

How could the recruiter not be impressed?

The crowd cheered loudly as Daniel made his final basket, just as the buzzer sounded. As the fans swarmed onto the court, congratulating Daniel and his team, Meade remained in the stands. This was Daniel's moment. They'd share a private one between the two of them later. She wanted him to enjoy the glory. As she watched the mayhem beneath her, she saw the recruiter make his way over to Daniel. Daniel turned to greet him. The two of them exchanged a few words and then shook hands, as the recruiter patted him on the back. He was all smiles—as was Daniel. Meade had a good feeling that things were about to become very bright in their lives.

On the way home, she told him. "He loved you. I could tell. He loved you." Meade beamed as she drove Daniel back to his house.

"You think so?" He sounded tired. Meade glanced over at him and saw that his head was back on the headrest and his eyes were closed.

"Yep, I do," she said distractedly. "Hey, are you okay? You seem really tired. Usually, you're on such a high after a big win that I can't bring you back down to earth. Still not feeling so hot?"

"No, not really," Daniel said, eyes still closed. "I think playing tonight took everything out of me."

"Okay, well, I can drop you off if you want. I don't need to come in tonight."

As she said it, Meade found herself a bit disappointed. She and Daniel had a tradition of making ice cream sundaes at his kitchen counter, with his mom, whenever he won a game.

"Of course I want you to come in, silly," Daniel said, opening his eyes and putting his hand on her leg. "I'm just a little tired. It's not like I'm dying or anything. Let's have some ice cream and then I'll crash on the couch while we watch some TV."

"Okay," Meade said, relieved, but hesitant. She was starting to get worried about Daniel. If anyone ever complained of being exhausted, it was her. It was never him.

His mom was beaming as they walked in the door. "Did you see my boy?" she asked Meade, hugging Daniel extra hard. "Did you *see* him?"

"Mom..." Daniel was embarrassed. "Of course Meade saw me. She was there."

"He was amazing! Amazing! I have never been so proud of him."

Meade smiled at Mrs. Spencer. Her love for her son was so evident. From her hugs to her smiles to the way she clearly put huge amounts of love in any meal she prepared for him. It was touching to see. Meade's own mom had never been like that with her. Oh, her mom loved her. She never really doubted that. But, her mom didn't like to show it in any demonstrative way. Mrs. Spencer, on the other hand, oozed affection for her son.

"It smells really good in here, Mrs. Spencer," Meade said. "What's baking?"

"Brownies!" his mom said enthusiastically as she hurried over to the oven and opened the door. "I rushed right out of the gym after the game—which wasn't easy seeing as everyone was stopping me and congratulating me as if *I'd* just won the game! And, I came home and stuck some brownies in the oven. I figured our sundaes deserved something extra special tonight, don't you think?"

"I sure do," Meade said, smiling. "Don't they smell great, Daniel?" Meade turned around and was surprised to see he wasn't in the kitchen. "Daniel?" She went off in search of him.

Meade found Daniel sprawled out on the couch. His extra-tall body was too long for the furniture, so his feet dangled off the end. His eyes were closed again.

"Hey," Meade said, sitting down next to him. "You okay?"

Daniel nodded, his eyes remaining closed.

"Want me to bring your sundae out here to you?"

He nodded again.

"Okay..." Meade said slowly. "I'll be right back."

Meade returned to the kitchen and helped Mrs. Spencer scoop three huge scoops onto three even larger brownies. Meade topped hers off with chocolate syrup and sprinkles and then fixed Daniel's the way he liked it—with caramel sauce, M&M's and whipped cream.

When she walked back into the living room with Mrs. Spencer, she saw that Daniel was sitting up and he looked a little bit better.

"Here," she said, handing him his bowl as she sat down on the couch next to him.

Mrs. Spencer entered the living room and sat on the chair across from them. Her face was still aglow from the team's win, and Daniel's part in that. Meade was surprised she didn't seem to notice how exhausted Daniel was. If she was anything, Mrs. Spencer was an attentive mother. When they were in elementary school, Mrs. Spencer was always the parent setting up all of the class parties and chaperoning every single field trip. She was room mom and PTA president.

If her son was involved in an activity, you were ensured Mrs. Spencer would become a part of that activity, too.

As they got older, Meade used to wonder if Daniel got annoyed that his mom was always around. After all, most boys she knew tried to get as far away from their parents as possible—and their folks weren't nearly as ever-present as Mrs. Spencer. But Daniel never seemed to mind his mom being there. He never seemed embarrassed to see her. It wasn't that he was a "mama's boy"—at least, not in the pathetic, needy sense of the term. Meade figured that, ever a team player, Daniel and his mom had become a team years ago, when Daniel's father died in a car accident.

Meade had never met Daniel's dad. He'd passed away two years before Meade showed up at school in the second grade. By the photos Mrs. Spencer still had around the house, though, Meade could tell Daniel was the spitting image of his dad. Long and lanky, always with a mischievous smile on his face. It made Meade sad to look at those photos. She didn't know why. It's not as if he'd been *her* dad—she'd never even met the man. But the thought that he'd been gone so quickly–taken from Daniel and his mom at such a young age—seemed so unfair. She couldn't imagine what that pain must have been like for Mrs. Spencer, and especially for Daniel. He'd been only six when his dad was killed, and whenever Meade thought about the sad, lost, little boy Daniel must have been when his dad was taken from him...well, it ripped her heart out. Sometimes she wondered if Daniel had ever really recovered from that loss. Daniel was happy and fun and always easy to make laugh. But sometimes, when they were quiet and she stared deep into his dark eyes, she saw a sadness there. Was that because of his dad? Would that look, which sometimes haunted Meade at night, be there if his father had lived? Then again, if Daniel had never experienced such a crushing loss as a child, would he be the young man he was today? Meade knew very few boys who were as compassionate and caring and sympathetic to the pain of those around them. Maybe it wasn't so much that he was sympathetic as it was that he was *empathetic*. He didn't only try to understand the pain of those around him—he *knew* the pain. Knew how it felt. Knew how it hurt. Knew how it knocked you to the ground and stomped on you so hard you felt you couldn't get back up again. That keen ability Daniel had, to feel the pain of those around him, as he did the day he met her, was one of the things she loved most about him.

"Thanks for the brownies, Mom," Daniel said. "They're really great in the sundae."

Meade glanced over at Daniel, next to her on the couch, and noticed he'd barely touched his ice cream, let alone the brownie. He was moving what was now merely a gooey mess around the bowl with his spoon.

"I'm so glad you enjoyed it, sweetie," Mrs. Spencer said, still beaming from Daniel's performance on the court. "I wanted to do something special for you."

Meade turned her eyes to Mrs. Spencer. Again, she was surprised his mom didn't seem to notice how pale Daniel was and how he'd barely touched the dessert. She was usually so tuned into her son and his well-being.

"Okay, kids, I'm going to hit the hay," Mrs. Spencer said, still smiling, as she wiped her mouth on a napkin and got up from her chair. "Are you going to watch a movie?"

"Maybe a little TV," Meade said. "I have to get home early tonight. My mom wants me to go to the farmer's market with her in the morning."

Out of the corner of her eye, Meade saw Daniel smile. He knew how much she hated going to the farmer's market, especially at the crack of dawn. Meade's mom was...different, for lack of a better word. At least, any better word Meade could come up with. Her mom tended to get on kicks for periods of time, dragging Meade along with her.

At the moment, she was all organic. All the food she bought had to be locally grown and pesticide-free. A noble cause, of course. But then, so had been the period of time when Meade's mom was involved with Habitat for Humanity and had awakened Meade every Saturday morning for six months, at the crack of dawn to go swing a hammer and hang sheetrock. Before that, they'd spent most weekends at dog shows, up and down the East Coast, as Meade's mom had been certain their Sheltie was destined to take Best in Show at that year's Purina's National Dog Show. The year prior, the two of them had spent every waking moment at the gym, where Meade had sat at the edge of the pool, timing her mom's backstroke. Meade had lived through dozens of her mom's crazy hobbies: origami, culinary classes, photography, trapeze flying. (Yes, her mom had momentarily courted the idea that she and Meade and her brothers could join a circus after the family won tickets from a local radio station to see Barnum & Bailey when they came to town.) Her mom had even convinced herself she could win the Mrs. America Pageant—if she could only find one of those pesky husbands. Thus, she joined a local dating service and went out with a myriad of men, a different one nearly every night. None of those evenings had ever led to a husband. Most didn't even lead to a second date. And so her mom had eventually moved on to dance, where she removed all the furniture from their living room and forced Meade to be her partner as the two of them would tango and salsa and jive across the faded carpet where their TV used to stand.

The good news was, none of the phases lasted very long. Six months was usually the max. Unfortunately, the organic one was only coming up on six weeks, so Meade figured it would be awhile before they moved on to something new.

Meade fully realized this was one of the reasons why she loved being at Daniel's house so much. Though also a single mom, Mrs. Spencer was so *normal*. And Meade craved normal.

"Night, Mom," Daniel said.

"Night, baby. Sleep tight."

Meade leaned into Daniel's chest as Mrs. Spencer left the room. "You stink," she said, holding her nose for emphasis.

"I know," Daniel said, grinning. "I can smell myself."

"Yuck," Meade said, sitting up. "Go shower. I can't snuggle up with someone who smells like an old gym sock."

"You're so demanding." Daniel grinned as he stood. "What I don't do for you. By the way," he said, giving Meade a knowing look, "you'd better not hijack the remote while I'm in the shower. I'm not going to watch an episode of *Seventh Heaven* when I get back."

"You're no fun," she said, a teasing pout on her face. "Hurry up. The air is becoming toxic in here."

"Oh, yeah?" he said, the mischievous expression Meade loved so much upon his face. "How's this for toxic?" And, in one swift motion, he ripped off his shirt and threw it at her, landing it perfectly on her head.

"Ew!" she said, yanking it off and shivering in disgust. "That's repulsive!"

He laughed, as he turned to leave the room. "I'll be right back; and remember, no crappy TV. I'm also not watching *Dr. Quinn*."

Meade giggled as she threw the shirt on the ground. "Yes, sir," she said, turning her eyes back to Daniel.

Then she saw them.

Months later, lying in bed alone, she would look back at that moment and realize it wasn't so much that time had stood still. It was more that Meade had suddenly felt as if she were under the ocean, slowly moving her mind toward a thought she knew was under there with her, but the resistance of the water kept her from reaching it quickly. A thought about a book. One she'd read in the backseat of her mom's car on a family trip down the coast of California. In it, a mom was putting her young children in the bathtub, and as they got into the warm water, her little boy pointed out some bruising on his sister's back. Bruising the mother had never seen before. Bruises that hadn't been caused by a fall or a bump. The mother was at a loss. *Where did they come from? Why were they there?*

But Meade had finished the book and as her mind finally reached that section of the story, she knew. She stared at Daniel's back. The bruises were all in a line, reminding Meade of the rocks in the river behind her house that she and her brother used to hop across when they were kids. As surely as Daniel loved her, she knew where those bruises had come from. She knew what they meant. She'd read the entire book and knew how it ended.

*Badly.*

And as she stared at Daniel's back, and saw those same bruises going up his spine, she had a sick feeling in the pit of her stomach that this time it was going to end badly, too.

Meade felt something jostle her slightly, and she closed her eyes tighter.

"Wake up, sleepy head. It's almost time for you to go."

"Huh?" Meade replied. "What's going on?"

Daniel shook her again, lightly, and planted a kiss on her forehead. "You fell asleep. Your mom's going to be here any minute. Don't you have senior pictures you need to look beautiful for tonight?"

Meade's eyes flew open. She was in the hospital, in Daniel's bed, still snuggled up next to him. How had she fallen asleep? She'd never done that before. She sat up quickly. "I'm so sorry! I didn't mean to fall asleep like that," she said, rubbing her eyes. She felt bad about it. And guilty. She'd wasted their afternoon together by sleeping and now, looking at the clock, she realized she'd have to leave in a few minutes. Damn it.

"I'm sorry. I didn't want to sleep away our time together," Meade said, apologizing again. She could kick herself.

"It's fine, babe," Daniel said, rubbing her arm. "Really. I'm not upset. I'm actually surprised you don't fall asleep here more often. You have a crazy schedule, with school and your debate tournaments and then you're here every day. You must be exhausted. It's fine." He moved his hand up her arm and began to gently massage her shoulder. "Besides, I liked watching you sleep. Your nose twitches. It's cute."

"My nose does not twitch!" she said adamantly, more than a little embarrassed. She didn't really like the idea of him watching her while she was unaware.

"You need to relax," he said, a soft smile on his face. "It does twitch and that's fine. I like it. You also talk in your sleep. I happen to like that, too."

*Oh, heavens. This was getting worse.*

"I don't talk in my sleep either!" Meade hopped off the bed and looked around the hospital room for the sneakers she'd kicked off when she'd entered. Finding them under the chair next to his bed, she sat down, slipped them on and bent over to tie the laces.

"Okay...if you say so. I guess since you don't talk in your sleep, then I imagined what you said, too, huh?"

Her head shot up. "What did I say?" she asked, a worry line forming on her brow.

A coy smile on Daniel's face, he picked up the TV remote and flipped the channel again. "Nothing. You said nothing. Remember, you don't talk in your sleep."

"Ugh!" Meade said in frustration, yanking her backpack off the floor and swinging it over her back. "I need to go."

Daniel looked up at her and, though he was smiling, Meade sensed a melancholy behind the grin. "Thanks for coming."

Her expression softened. How could she stay frustrated with him when he looked at her with those deep, dark eyes? And, she realized, she wasn't frustrated with *him*. After all, who cared what she did or said in her sleep—she had no secrets from Daniel. She was frustrated with herself for falling asleep during the short time they'd had together. She couldn't let that happen again.

"I love you."

"I know," he said, smiling as he stared at her.

"Behave yourself for all those tests. And, don't moon the nurses in this sexy gown. They don't want to see your lily white ass."

Daniel laughed. "Not even if they ask me sweetly?"

Meade bent down and planted a soft kiss on his lips. "Not even if they ask sweetly."

"Okay," he whispered, kissing her back. "Not even if they beg."

Meade stood up reluctantly. She didn't want to leave. She would've liked nothing more than to take her shoes off again and climb back in that bed with Daniel, but she couldn't. She had promised her mom she'd be waiting outside for her when she got there. Her mom hated to have to wait on her. Which, in Meade's mind, was quite ironic because Meade had spent her entire childhood waiting on her mom. She was always the last child picked up at school. Always the kid who had to hang around, long after a friend's birthday party had ended and the clown had packed up all of his balloons and headed home, because her mom still hadn't shown up. She was the kid who sat nervously in the choir bleachers during the Christmas concert, searching the crowd as she sang "Winter Wonderland", wondering if her mom would get there before the show ended.

But, her mom promised she wouldn't be late today and Meade believed her. Not because she'd worry about keeping Meade waiting, but her mom was teaching yoga tonight and couldn't risk being late for her class. Even her mom realized there were only so many jobs one could get fired from in a lifetime before it became downright embarrassing, and Meade's mom was teetering at the precipice of mortification.

"*Ciao, Bella,*" Daniel said, as Meade walked to the door. Freshman year, Meade and Daniel had taken Italian together, and sometimes she wondered if that phrase was the only one he remembered from the entire year.

"*Ciao,*" Meade replied softly, as she pulled open the heavy wooden door and slipped outside.

The hallway was abuzz with people. A few nurses chatted outside patients' rooms, while others stood by the nurses' station, clearly flirting with the handsome doctor leaning against the counter, clipboard in hand. Another cancer patient, this one an elderly gentleman, was being walked by a young woman, whom Meade figured to be his daughter. He was moving his feet so slowly, though, Meade wondered how much progress they could possibly be making

*At this rate, they won't get to the next door before visiting hours are over.*

Glancing up from the man's feet, Meade caught the eye of the daughter and blushed. The woman smiled at her as she ever so slowly pushed her dad's IV pole behind him. Meade smiled back and then turned away. She felt bad for the woman. She felt bad for the man. Hell, she felt bad for herself.

Hurrying to the elevators, Meade let out a sigh of relief when one of the doors opened the moment she pushed the down button. Once inside, and alone, she leaned against the wall and closed her eyes. She hated it there. Hated the hospital. Hated how it smelled. Hated how cold it always was. Hated why she'd come there.

She thought back to when she was a kid and her mom used to tell her it was bad to use the word "hate."

"We don't 'hate,'" her mom would say, reprimanding her. "We *don't like* things. You may not like homework, but you don't hate it. We may not like that Daddy didn't show up to take you this weekend, but we don't hate him. 'Hate' is a very strong word. You should never use it."

Even then, Meade was pretty sure her mom was wrong. There were some things in life that were so horrible that "I don't like it" or "That makes me mad" didn't quite describe them. Meade may not have hated her dad, but she certainly *hated* when he promised for six months straight to take her to Six Flags on the weekend after she graduated from the fifth grade and then, not only didn't take her, but didn't even call to say he wouldn't be coming. She'd waited for him, on their front steps, from seven in the morning until eight that night. She wouldn't even go inside to pee, in case he drove up while she was gone and thought she might not still want to go if he didn't see her ready and waiting. If Daniel hadn't walked up her street, at 8:12 p.m., and offered to buy her an ice cream cone at the corner store if she gave up her vigil—and, she had to admit she was pretty hungry by that point—she might very well still be sitting there today.

"I *don't like* my dad standing me up" didn't seem to cut it. She hated it. H-A-T-E-D it. And, leaning against the paneled elevator wall, she had to admit there were a bunch of other things in her life these days she hated, too. The hospital was at the top of that list.

The elevator doors opened as the first tear fell out of the corner of Meade's eye. She quickly wiped it away with the back of her hand and hurried outside. Her mom would flip out if Meade cried before her senior photos. Puffy eyes were not acceptable. Especially not with how much money her mom was having to fork over to the photographer for these shots.

"It seems kind of ridiculous to me that you're paying all this for photos," Meade had told her mom over breakfast that morning. "I know there are better things you could spend it on."

*Like a new dishwasher.* The old one had broken eighteen months ago and Meade was tired of being the new one.

"Don't be silly!" her mom had said to her as she placed Meade's breakfast down in front of her. Curried tofu and spinach scrambled eggs. Meade moved the meal around with her fork and longed for an Egg McMuffin.

"You are only a senior in high school once. We need to document this time."

Meade sighed. This time of her life was not one she wished to document. She wanted to forget it. Move out of it. Quickly.

But, Meade also knew her mom, and when she was stuck on an idea, there was no talking her out of it. Meade would have to find something to smile about when she looked at the camera. It was getting harder and harder, though, to come up with something that made her grin.

"Besides, I'll bet Daniel would like a photo of you to put next to his bed," Meade's mom said, as she sat down to eat her own breakfast, a knowing look on her face.

She had Meade there and she knew it. Daniel *would* like to have a senior photo of Meade for his room. Daniel loved all photos—especially ones of Meade. He always had, ever since they were kids. He had a whole bulletin board in his room, of photos of the two of them. Some were shots from when they were a couple, but many were ones that had been taken in elementary school and junior high. Birthday parties. Track and field day at school. Field trips to the zoo and the planetarium and Washington, D.C. Daniel was much more sentimental than Meade. He saved everything that reminded him of the two of them.

And Meade's mom knew the way to get Meade to do anything these days was to convince her that it would somehow benefit Daniel.

"Okay. Okay," Meade said. "I'll take the pictures."

"Happily," her mom said.

Meade paused and then conceded. "Happily," she agreed.

"Great!" her mom said. "I'll pick you up at the hospital at five. Don't be late coming downstairs. We're going to hit rush-hour traffic."

Meade glanced at the hospital clock as the automatic doors opened and she walked outside.

Five o'three.

She smiled to herself. It served her mom right to have to wait three minutes after all the times she'd kept Meade waiting.

Meade glanced out at the hospital driveway and her smugness disappeared. Her mom wasn't even there yet.

*It figured.*

As she reached the curb, a car skidded to a stop right in front of her.

"Come on," her mom called through the open window. "Hurry up! We're gonna be late."

As if that was Meade's fault.

Meade sighed and opened the back door, throwing her backpack inside before climbing in the front.

"How was Daniel today?" her mom asked.

Meade's eyes filled with tears.

"Never mind! Never mind!" her mom said, frantically grabbing the box of tissues from the center console and throwing them on Meade's lap. "No crying before pictures! We can't have puffy eyes! No crying! Let's talk about something happy!" Her mom paused, as if deep in thought. "I know! I saw a poster that they are doing ghost tours of the old, historic buildings in town. Doesn't that sound interesting? I've always wanted to learn how to talk to the dead..."

Meade rested her head back on the seat and, despite herself, had to smile. Organic living might have been on its way out sooner than she'd thought.

# CHAPTER TWO

"Pantera!" Meade called out, as she frantically searched the piles of books and papers covering her desk. "Have you seen Ian's latest manuscript? It was right here before I went home last night. Right *here*. And now, I can't find it!"

Of all manuscripts to lose, Ian Cooper's was the absolute worst. Not only was he Brownsbury's best-selling author—by a couple of million books—but he was also the most high-maintenance writer Meade had ever met. Whenever he came into the office for a meeting, which was rare these days, nearly the entire staff, including Meade, herself, was on edge. More times than not, though, he requested— *demanded* would be a more accurate term—Meade come to him. In all fairness, the locations he selected—The Four Seasons or the Peninsula hotels—were much more luxurious than her stark New York City office. She didn't mind going to them. In fact, getting away from work—even if it was to *do* work somewhere else—was a nice break in her day. It was the way he asked her to meet him somewhere. Didn't ask her. That's what the problem was. He *didn't* ask her. He simply announced that's where they would be meeting. And so she went. Meade Peterson, executive editor at Brownsbury Press—the largest, most respected publishing company in the country—came running when Ian Cooper beckoned. And she hated herself for it.

"Pantera!" Meade called again, becoming more frantic, as a stack of papers and books she'd delicately balanced on the edge of her desk, crashed to the floor. She fell to her knees, scrambling to gather up the items, simultaneously cursing herself for being so careless as to not keep Ian's latest work within reach at all times. "Where is that manuscript?"

"It's right here," a calm voice said from the door. "And you'd better get up or you're going to break the heel off your Manolos."

Meade pushed away a strand of hair that had come loose from her chignon and was now tickling her eyelashes. She'd have to run to the ladies' room to fix her hair before she met with Ian. She couldn't let him realize he flustered her. It was bad enough she realized it.

Standing carefully—Pantera was right about her not wanting to break a heel on the shoes she'd given herself as a present to celebrate her thirtieth birthday—and grabbing a few folders on her way up, Meade gave her assistant an enormous smile. Even in Meade's frazzled state, it was hard not to smile at Pantera. Besides being Meade's lifesaver at all times—Meade had lost count of how many times the young girl had found something Meade had lost, reminded Meade of an appointment she was about to miss or brought Meade lunch when she'd been too preoccupied to hear her own stomach grumble—Pantera was a breath of fresh air in the all-too-stuffy publishing world.

Never one to bow to current fashion trends, Pantera had a style all her own. If Meade had to put a name to it, she'd call it "nerdy goth." Meade was sure Pantera dyed her jet-black hair—surely no one was born with hair as dark as a moonless night in Texas. She had a tendency to wear it in pigtails on either side of her head. Meade didn't think she, herself, had worn pigtails since she was about eight, but somehow, on Pantera, the look seemed trendy, not childish. Pantera's signature look included a short, plaid skirt, which always reminded Meade of the school uniform she'd had to wear in first grade when her parents had sent her to parochial school for a year.

Today, Pantera had topped the skirt off with a black sweater vest that had a tiny skull and crossbones on the breast pocket. Meade inwardly chuckled. Somehow Pantera always managed to add that insignia to her outfit, whether it be on a necklace or earrings or a bracelet or on her socks. Oh, yes. Pantera's socks. Knee socks were essential to the look. Often black, but sometimes striped. Always unique. That's what Pantera was. *Unique.* And Meade loved her for it. Some of the other editors had thought she was nuts when she first hired Pantera from the sea of qualified applicants. They'd all filled their positions with Ivy League grads Meade felt were as boring as watching a banana take a nap. Stepford Wives. All of them. Except that none of them were actually wives. Only ambitious young women, and one or two men, whom Meade felt were secretly waiting for a chance to pounce on their bosses at the slightest whiff of weakness. But Meade knew, the moment Pantera walked in the door, wearing a tight black band around her neck, causing Meade to do a double-take—*was she wearing an actual dog collar?*—that this was the woman she'd hire. Meade was usually not one to take chances. At least, not in her professional life. She recognized right away that taking on such an eclectic assistant was a bit like going out on a limb. But it was there one found the best fruit. And Pantera had proven to be an exotic mango, whereas she, herself, tended to stick with plain apples. It was nice to venture out of her comfort zone every once in awhile.

"Where was it?" Meade said, slightly out of breath.

"On the edge of my desk. Right where you left it." Pantera gave Meade a bemused smile. "I don't know why you let him do this to you. He's just another author."

"Our best author."

Pantera rolled her eyes. "We have lots of good authors. Great authors. You never let any of the others get you all hot and bothered."

Pantera was the only person in the entire office who would dare speak so bluntly to Meade. And she was also the only one who never seemed phased by Ian's demands or impressed by his good looks.

Oh, yes. Ian was good-looking. Shockingly good-looking. That was another problem Meade had with him. It was hard to concentrate, let alone tell him, "No," when he stared at her with those piercing blue eyes. And, for some reason, she found she had no more will power on the phone either. She tended to think it might have to do something with his sultry voice.

And those looks and that voice didn't hurt any whenever it came to promoting his books. Ian was gold on TV. A pure television jewel. The camera loved him. The TV hosts loved him. America loved him. Meade...well, she didn't exactly love him. But, she was a bit smitten.

She hated that about herself, too.

Meade was a professional. She always behaved in a professional manner. To her credit, that didn't change ever. Even when dealing with Ian. No matter how hard it was.

"Okay," Meade said, walking through her office door. "I'm out of here. I'll be at the Ritz-Carlton if you need me."

"Oooh. Fancy schmancy," Pantera said, as she plopped down into her desk chair. "Have fun. Stay out of trouble."

Putting on her coat, Meade glared at Pantera, who stared back, un-blinking, a teasing sparkle in her eye.

"We are meeting to discuss his last few chapters."

"Uh-huh," Pantera said, laying some paperwork on her lap and pretending to file her nails. Meade wondered if she was about to throw her feet up on the desk, too.

"I'll be back around two. Can you have the new Stevens manuscript ready for me when I get back?"

"The one about the woman who finds out, after her husband dies, that he was really a woman who was wanted for a murder in another state..." Pantera's voice quickened with each word.

Meade smiled. She loved the way Pantera became so enthusiastic about the books they published. It not only made her job more fun, but it tended to pump up the writers when they knew their "number one fan" was sitting at the front desk in the publishing office.

"Yes, that's the one."

"I LOVE that story. The way she pretends she's really a transgender woman so she can go undercover in his old life..."

"Okay, okay, I get it. You liked the book." Meade laughed. "I need to go. See you in a bit."

Meade tied her scarf around her neck, pulled her hat below her ears—it had been snowing when she'd come to work today—and threw the manuscript into her bag.

*"Adios!"* Pantera called out cheerfully as Meade walked out the door.

Meade ducked her head as she stepped out onto the icy New York City sidewalk. The wind was brutal. In the few places where Meade's skin wasn't covered by her hat or scarf, it felt like tiny pins being thrown into her face. Meade loved Manhattan. It had always been her dream to live there and as soon as she finished graduate school, she'd hopped on the train, two suitcases in tow, and headed that way. She loved the sights, the smells of the food vendors, especially the chestnuts roasting—if not on an open fire—at least on the stove atop a small, metal cart. She enjoyed the business professionals as they rushed from the trains to their offices and then back to the trains again. She loved the tourists who blocked your way on the sidewalk so they could look up and gape at the Empire State Building. She adored the Theater District, where she never seemed to spend enough time those days, and Chinatown, where she had purchased her first knock-off Gucci purse as a young publishing intern. She remembered walking down a narrow flight of stairs which descended into a teeny-tiny room full of every counterfeit brand imaginable, not sure if she was more afraid of being arrested or of the building going up in flames and her being trapped in that basement. She'd been so sure no one at her new job would be able to tell the difference between her bag and the real thing. That is, until her second day, when one of the other interns called her out on it. She loved Bryant Park's carousel and the sidewalk artists in Union Square and the guy who played the most beautiful saxophone she'd ever heard inside her subway station. She loved New York City and she didn't need a T-shirt to prove it.

What she didn't like, however, was the cold weather. Growing up in Austin, Texas, Meade had never experienced much of a winter before. Oh, they'd had the occasional "snowstorm" — or at least, Austin's version of a snowstorm, which consisted of thirty-two snowflakes, school being closed for the day and building a snowman the size of a Smurf, and then taking photos of it to send to everyone you knew up north so that they could see that you, too, had truly experienced winter. Meade hadn't experienced her first "true" winter until her freshman year at Wake Forest. Winston-Salem, North Carolina, though south, was also known for some pretty cold winters and Meade had been in for a rude awakening when, during her first December in college, she'd realized the coats and sweaters she'd brought from Texas, though incredibly stylish, were hardly functional in the bitter cold.

And somehow, winters in Manhattan seemed even colder. Maybe it was because all the tall buildings shaded the sidewalks and blocked the sun from shining down. In any case, it was cold today and spring was a long way off.

Keeping her head down, she made her way to the Ritz-Carlton. In this weather, she probably should have grabbed a cab. After all, it wasn't as if she couldn't write it off as a business expense, but she hadn't been to the gym all week and was feeling the need for some exercise. And, with the memory of the stacks of manuscripts and paperwork she had waiting for her back on her desk, she realized she wouldn't be working out anytime soon.

By the time Meade reached the hotel, however, she was wishing she'd given up the exercise in lieu of a taxi. Even with warm gloves on, her hands had frozen into a claw position and her cheeks were raw and red. The wind had caused her eyes to tear and she was pretty certain the salt water had frozen in long drips on her face.

The heat of the hotel lobby came as a sweet release. Meade stood just inside the doorway, and soaked in the warmth for a good five minutes. She couldn't even bring herself to sit on one of the lobby's luxurious couches. She needed to warm up, and frankly, until she did, it hurt too much to move her limbs even a few more feet.

When Meade finally felt her stiff body relax as it warmed, she quickly found the restroom. She was pretty sure, after that walk, she now needed to do more to her appearance than push back a loose strand of hair. After one glance in the mirror, she knew she'd been right.

Pulling off her gloves, she rustled through her purse for her make-up bag and brush. Her appearance needed immediate attention. She'd be mortified if Ian saw her this way. Frankly, she'd be embarrassed to have anyone lay eyes on her. Her hair had come undone, her nose and cheeks were bright red from the wind, and her mascara was smeared down her face. Fortunately, Meade had always been the type of person who could get ready in a hurry. Unlike most of the professional women she knew in New York, Meade was low-main-tenance. It never took her more than five minutes to "put on her face"—as all the women she grew up with in Texas called it. And, most days, if Meade wasn't at work, she left her face off altogether, so to speak. She preferred being foundation and mascara-free. And, thanks to her mom and the good genes she'd passed on to her, Meade could get away with it. Though thirty-three years old, she didn't look any older than the day she had graduated from high school. Her skin was virtually wrinkle-free; her figure was still as slim as ever. Most days, when she wasn't at work, Meade could be caught with her long, chestnut hair pulled back in a ponytail that still reached half-way down her back, like it did during her teen years. Many women chose to cut their hair as they aged—perhaps thinking it gave them an edge of maturity—but Meade had never been one who wanted to look her age, let alone older. She looked very young and she wanted to ride that wave as long as she possibly could.

Glancing in the mirror, even as she wiped away the mascara and reapplied her foundation, she knew she looked good. Maybe even better than good. Good enough for Ian Cooper to find attractive. And she knew he found her attractive. How could she not? He told her every time he saw her. Meade often thought that was the reason he selected these luxury hotels for their meetings. Not because he liked the room service and the couches you sank down into the minute your bottom touched the cushion. No, Ian Cooper was hoping that, during one of these meetings, he'd be able to coax her away from the formal area of his suite and into his bed.

So far, he hadn't been successful.

Meade was banking on that always being the case.

It wasn't that Meade didn't find him handsome and sexual and intriguing. She was intrigued. Very, very intrigued. Ian Cooper was a bad boy. His fans knew it. The press knew it. She certainly knew it. And, Meade liked bad boys. They, as a cumulative group, were her weakness. When it came to her dating life, Meade tended to shy away from the "good guys"—the ones you could bring home to Mom—if she had a mom she'd want to bring anyone home to, that is. The more mysterious and risky and, if she were to admit it to herself, unreliable, a man was, the more likely she was not only to accept a date with him, but fall head over heels for him in the process.

It hadn't always been like that. There was a time when steady and solid and good—yes, pure, unadulterated goodness—were what she cherished in a partner. But she'd been burned by that. Scorched. And she'd shied away from it ever since.

Nowadays, Meade liked her men to be a bit elusive, with a hint of danger. Tall, dark, handsome and perilous. Sometimes, it seemed the more fraught with danger, the better. Meade liked a challenge. And bad boys—such as Ian—were the best kind of challenge. You never knew what to expect. Whether it be where he'd take you on a date or how he'd respond to a question or—and this was the best part—how he behaved in the bedroom. Meade loved to be surprised. She'd risk most anything—and had—for a fabulous and sensual rendezvous with the right (or maybe, *wrong*) man.

But even Meade had her limits. And she wasn't about to risk her career on a fling with an author. She wasn't about to jeopardize her career for anything. She'd worked too hard to get where she was and nothing...*nothing*...was going to take that away from her.

And that's exactly what she told herself...again...when Ian opened the door to his hotel room wearing nothing but a pair of form-fitting, ripped jeans.

*Heaven help her, those jeans were tight.*

"Hi, Ian," Meade said, dragging her eyes up to his face. "Missing a piece of clothing? Or two or three?"

Ian laughed. That delightful, salacious laugh which made places deep inside her quiver.

"Come on in," Ian said, taking a step back so she could walk past him into the suite. She felt him close the door behind her more than heard it.

"Drink?"

"Now, Ian," Meade said, doing her best to keep her tone playful, yet firm, "you know I don't drink during working hours."

"I've never seen you drink."

"That's because, when you and I are together, no matter what time of day it is, it's always 'working hours.'"

"Suit yourself," Ian said, as he made his way over to the thin bar along the far wall. Even the way he walked...no, it was more like a slow swagger...had her mesmerized.

Shaking her head, trying to jolt improper thoughts—and the image of his ass—out of her mind, Meade reached into her satchel and pulled out the manuscript.

"I don't think it'll take long to go over the changes. There aren't too many. I also want to discuss the PR tour. Pantera mentioned you weren't happy about a few things?"

"Meade...*Meade.* Why do you like to work so much?" Ian asked, as he made his way toward her, a drink in each hand. He handed one to her, clearly ignoring that she'd told him she didn't want to drink. That was another facet of the men Meade tended to choose. They did what they wanted. When they wanted. Regardless of objections. Their world. Their rules. Professionally, Meade hated people like that. Personally, it intoxicated her.

Meade carefully placed the drink down on the table and faced Ian, holding the manuscript to her chest, consciously putting a barrier between them, even if it was merely 436 pages of white computer paper.

"Funny question, Ian. Hmmm...let's see. Well, I like to pay my bills, for one."

"I have a lot of money," Ian said. Was it Meade's imagination or was his face getting closer to hers? Still, she didn't back up and stood her ground. She looked at him, unblinking.

"Yes, I am well aware of that. In fact, if I'm not mistaken, without me, you wouldn't have most of it."

Ian laughed, and not the sensual laugh that made Meade's body weaken. This was a deep, heartfelt laugh and Meade could see his body relax as he stepped back.

"Touché," Ian said. "Touché."

He placed his drink down on the table as he plopped into the chair across from her. He slumped down a bit and crossed his legs, grabbing his naked foot with his hand.

"You, Meade Peterson, are a challenge," he said with a grin. "I like challenges. I'm not used to them. They enchant me. You enchant me."

"Yes, I know," Meade said coolly, as if none of his words were penetrating her ears and making their way into her body. *Was it hot in here? It was feeling really hot all of a sudden.*

"I enchant most men. It's a curse. Just something I have to live with. It's not easy. But, I do my best. I hope you won't find it too distracting," Meade said, trying to appear nonchalant as she dug through her bag and pulled out a pen.

Looking up at him, she had to force herself not to smile at his expression. He was amused. And surprised by her laissez-faire reaction to his advances. She was certain that indifference was not the response he was used to getting from women. It made him want her even more. She could tell by the way his eyes penetrated into her skin. He desired her desperately. And he couldn't have her. It was killing him.

To be honest, it was kind of killing Meade, too.

"Are you ready to get to work?" Meade asked him, professional to a fault. "We have a lot to cover in a short period of time."

Ian said nothing for a moment and then, finally, sighed. He seemed resigned to the fact that, for now, work was all they were going to accomplish.

"Sure, why not?" he said, casually picking up his copy of the manuscript. "What cha got?"

Meade stepped out of the elevator, into the hotel lobby, and breathed a sigh of relief. Her meeting with Ian was finally over—and not a moment too soon. She didn't think she could have sat in that hotel suite—with the enormous king-size bed taunting her from the doorway—for one more minute. It hadn't helped that Ian had never gotten up to put on a shirt. *Who attends a business meeting without a shirt?* Ian, that's who. And he did it purposely. *Well, of course he did. Who in their right mind forgets to put on a shirt before getting to work?* But he did it because it got to her. She might have been victorious in the war today, but he'd won that battle, and he knew that she knew it.

"Argh," Meade said to herself, whipping out her cell phone. Her sexual frustration was at an all-time high, thanks to Mr. Ian Cooper.

The phone was answered after one ring.

"Hey," Meade said, speaking softly. She didn't need everyone at the Ritz to know her business. "Are you free?"

Thirty minutes, and a worth-every-penny cab ride later, Meade stood in front of a large, mahogany door at an uptown townhouse. She'd barely knocked when the door swung open.

"Hey, sexy," a deep voice greeted her. "I'm glad you called."

Meade said not a word, but threw herself into his arms, her mouth ravenously finding his. He kicked the door closed behind her and pulled her toward the stairs. They ripped off one another's clothes as they went.

"I have to be back at work in an hour," Meade said, quickly removing her mouth from his.

"So do I," he said, unsnapping her bra. "But this is going to be one hell of a lunch break."

Meade put both her hands on the elastic of his boxers and pulled them down, her body aching as he sprung out of them.

Ian Cooper may not have gotten his needs met today, but that didn't mean she couldn't satisfy hers.

Meade turned on the light switch as she put her mail down on the table near the front door. Shivering, she closed the door, careful to lock it. She lived in a safe neighborhood. That was one of the things that had drawn her to this apartment building in the first place. That, and the fact she could afford it. Not always an easy task in Manhattan. But, it was New York City, after all, and one could never be too cautious, so she was always careful to lock and bolt the door.

She made her way over to the thermostat. Sixty-four degrees. No wonder it was so cold in here. She tapped the temperature up eight degrees. She rubbed her hands together, hoping the room warmed up quickly.

Despite the chill, Meade removed her coat and hung it in the closet. She had to force herself to do this every night. By nature, she was not a neat person and her urge to throw the coat across the couch was strong. But from past experience, once she allowed herself to relax her organization, things would quickly spiral out of control. It might start with a coat on the couch, but before she knew it, she'd have empty pizza boxes on the coffee table, laundry piled on the kitchen table and dishes overtaking the kitchen sink. No, Meade couldn't let that happen. Her life was so hectic and crazy and unpredictable, she needed her home to be her solace—a place that relaxed her, not caused her to have heart palpitations the moment she walked in the door.

And, glancing around, Meade saw that the place could use a little bit of straightening up. Not messy, by any means, but a few things were out of place here and there. Knowing she should pick them up now, before going to bed, she sighed, and then promised herself she would do it first thing in the morning, before she headed to work. She was so tired. Today had been a long, long day.

She went into the bathroom to brush her teeth. Flicking on the light, her eyes caught the photo taped to the mirror. No matter where she lived, no matter how many times she'd moved over the years, the first thing she always did in any new home was tape that photo to the direct center of her bathroom mirror.

Despite her exhausting day, Meade smiled when she saw the photo. Daniel. Beautiful Daniel. Beside him, stood a young, smiling Meade. They'd taken the photo in his hall bathroom when they were seniors in high school—Daniel holding the camera above his head and shooting into the mirror. They'd smiled at their reflections, their arms wrapped tightly around each other, as if they didn't have a care in the world. Except, of course, they did.

Kissing the tips of her fingers, she softly touched them to Daniel's face and let them linger there.

"Night, babe."

And somewhere, deep inside her, she felt him whisper back to her, "Good night."

# CHAPTER THREE

M eade could tell something wasn't right the moment Daniel's mom opened the door. Usually, when Meade showed up, whether she'd been invited or not, Mrs. Spencer's face lit up at the sight of Meade standing on the other side of the screen.

"I just took some cookies out of the oven," she'd say, as she'd open the door to let Meade in. "How about I pour you and Daniel some milk to go with them?"

Mrs. Spencer always seemed to be baking cookies or brownies or bread or cake. With the amount of delicious desserts the woman spent her time preparing, Meade often wondered how neither Daniel, nor his mom, weighed 500 pounds, seeing as it was only the two of them living in the house. But, they didn't. In fact, not only were they not overweight, they were both quite thin. And tall. Very, very tall. Mrs. Spencer was easily six feet and Daniel had a good four inches on his mom. They both made Meade feel, at a mere five feet six inches, extremely tiny.

But today, Meade barely noticed the way Mrs. Spencer towered over her as the older woman led Meade into the house. Meade was too distracted by the look of complete and utter pain she saw in her eyes.

"What's wrong?" Meade said. "Is everything okay? Where's Daniel?"

Mrs. Spencer's eyes filled with tears and, for a moment, Meade wasn't sure she going to answer Meade's question. Daniel's mom merely stood in front of Meade, tears rolling down her cheeks. If the woman hadn't let Meade into the house, herself, Meade would have wondered if she even knew Meade was there.

"Where's Daniel?" Meade asked again, a little more urgently this time.

Mrs. Spencer glanced at Meade, as if seeing her for the first time. She paused and Meade wondered if she truly was not going to tell her where Daniel was, but then his mom nodded toward the stairs.

Meade rushed over to the staircase and bounded up the steps, taking two at a time—not an easy feat with her short legs.

"Daniel," Meade called out softly. Though she felt like screaming his name, something told her that what she was about to find was sacred and called for her to be calm. "Daniel," she said again. "Where are you?"

The silence was frightening. Daniel was not a quiet person. He was loud and boisterous and full of life. Though an only child, he filled this house with the chaos and vibrancy of a dozen kids.

Meade peeked into Daniel's room at the top of the stairs. It was a mess, as usual. The sheets were a tangled ball, with the comforter falling off the side of the bed. Meade noticed a stack of plates, most likely from the meals Mrs. Spencer was taking to Daniel, on the side table. Navigating the staircase was becoming more and more difficult for him and he tended to eat in his room these days. Daniel's clothes from the day before—perhaps from the week before—were in a pile on the floor. Meade often wondered why he even bothered to keep the hamper in his room, seeing as nothing ever actually went in it.

A quick scan of the room, though, revealed no Daniel. Meade glanced down the hallway and noticed the bathroom door was closed. She approached it and gently knocked on the wood.

"Daniel," she said softly. "Are you in there?"

There was no response.

"Daniel?" she said again, a little louder.

This time, Meade thought she heard a noise from inside. She rested the side of her head on the door.

"Daniel, come on. I know you're in there. Are you okay?"

Though there was still no response from within, Meade was now sure she could hear someone behind the door.

Meade twisted the handle and saw it turned in her hand.

"Listen, babe, I'm about to come in," she said gently. "If you're on the toilet or something, you'd better let me know before I walk in on you doing your business."

Meade took Daniel's silence as a sign that it was safe to enter and pushed the door open.

She wasn't sure what she expected to find, but the reality of what she saw stopped her from stepping past the doorframe.

There on the floor, in front of the sink, sat Daniel. His giant frame, appearing so small, was huddled into a ball, his knees tucked against his chest and his forehead resting upon them. Meade couldn't see his face, only his mop of dark curls.

"Daniel," she said, her voice coming out as a whisper. "What's going on? Why are you in here?"

Daniel made not even the smallest movement to indicate he'd heard her.

She stepped slowly into the bathroom, scared to enter, fearful of what she might discover, but too worried about Daniel to turn around and leave.

Kneeling down next to him, she put her hand on his back and lowered her head until it was right next to his.

"What is it, babe? What's going on?" she asked, gently stroking his back as she spoke.

Daniel's body shuddered as a sob burst out of him.

"Daniel!" she said, suddenly alarmed. "What is it? What's wrong?"

Daniel's movement was so tiny, she almost didn't notice it. Slowly, he turned his hand over, palm facing up. His fingers were clenched so tightly against it, Meade was certain he must be cutting into his hand with his own nails. Slowly, he opened his fingers and, as he did, tears sprang to Meade's eyes.

Resting in the center of his large palm was one perfect black curl.

"Oh..." Meade said, letting her bottom fall to the ground, her knees falling to the side. "Oh."

They had both known this day was coming. Every cancer patient knows it's coming. And Meade had really thought Daniel, and she, were prepared for it. They'd discussed it a hundred times.

"I've always had a thing for bald men," she'd told Daniel, as they sat on the couch in his living room, eating sea salt potato chips out of the bag.

"Oh, yeah?" he'd said, rolling his eyes. "Since when?"

"Since...um...forever."

Daniel tilted his head and gave Meade a look that told her she was totally making that up.

"Okay...since I knew you were going to become one," she said, laughing, munching on a chip. "Bald is beautiful, you know."

"Bald is the new hair?" He laughed. "Is that what you're telling me?"

"Bald is the new hair!" Meade said, jumping onto his lap and hugging his neck. "I love it. We'll get T-shirts made up."

She remembered he'd kissed her then. Hard. Passionately. She'd giggled at first, and then became lost in his salty lips.

But she wasn't giggling now. And the only thing his lips were doing was quivering.

Taking a deep breath, Meade chose her words very carefully. "It's okay, babe. It's just hair."

Daniel shook his head, but kept it down on his knees. "It's not just hair," he said, his voice hoarse with tears. She'd never seen him this way. Not even after the diagnosis. Not even after the first chemo treatment had made him so sick he'd thrown up for three days straight. "It means I'm dying."

"It does not mean you're dying," she said adamantly, sitting up straight. "It means the drugs are taking effect and doing their job. It's the first step toward living."

Daniel didn't move. He didn't even acknowledge she'd spoken.

"Come on, babe. Let's get up. You want to go lie down? We could watch a movie. Or how about I read you some more of that boring book Mrs. Abrahamson insists we read for AP English this month?"

Daniel remained motionless. Meade sighed and leaned back against the bathroom cabinet.

"Or, we could sit here all day...your call."

The two of them sat in silence for what, to Meade, felt like hours, though she realized it was merely minutes. This wasn't Daniel. Not the Daniel she knew...the Daniel she'd loved since second grade. She'd been new to the school that year. Her parents' divorce had been final the summer before and, because her mom could no longer afford to stay in the town and home they'd lived in when they were still a family, she, her mom, and her two brothers had moved to Austin. Meade had been terrified on the first day of school.

"What if no one likes me? What if I have no friends?" she'd asked her mom, as they drove to school on that first day.

"Oh, Meade. Don't be ridiculous," Meade's mother had said curtly. "Stop acting like such a baby. I have bigger things to worry about than whether or not you have friends."

Even at eight years of age, Meade knew her mom was right. She did have bigger things to worry about. Like, how she was going to feed and clothe three rapidly growing children without the support of a husband. Still, her mom's words cut deeply into Meade's small chest. She wanted her mom to care. She wanted her mom to worry about whether or not she'd have friends. *She* was certainly worried enough about it. She'd stayed up all night, huddled deep under her covers, panicking over the way the next day would play out.

And, as it turned out, Meade had a right to panic. Making friends at the new school, where everyone seemed to know each other since preschool, wasn't easy. None of the girls wanted to play tag with her on the playground during recess, or push her on the giant swing set behind the school. By the time lunch rolled around, Meade was close to despondent, certain she'd have no one to sit with at the lunch table. She shuffled into the cafeteria, her Strawberry Shortcake lunch box swinging by her side, her head staring down at the pink stars on her sneakers. She sat at the end of the table and opened her lunch, wondering if she'd have to eat alone every day for the rest of her school career.

"Why you sitting all the way down here?" a voice interrupted Meade's internal monologue of misery.

"Huh?" She looked up quickly.

"Why are you at the end of the table all by yourself?"

Meade blinked at the boy standing in front of her. She'd never seen anyone so beautiful. His hair fell below his ears and down his neck in beautiful, dark curls. The kind of curls she'd imagined to be on the heads of angels—except, for some reason, she'd always thought angels had blonde hair. And, he had the darkest brown eyes she'd ever seen. They reminded her of the Hershey chocolate bars her daddy used to bring home to her after he'd been away on a business trip. She'd always thought her dad had gotten the candy from wherever he'd just traveled to...Florida or France or Bermuda. It wasn't until she was about fifteen, and wandering the aisles of the local Tigermart, that it dawned on her he'd probably purchased the chocolate at a local gas station on his way home each time.

"Do you talk?" the boy asked.

"Oh," Meade said hurriedly. "Yes, I talk."

Shifting the cafeteria tray he was carrying to the other hand, the boy looked at Meade quizzically. "Then why aren't you answering my question?"

"Your question?" *Shoot. What was his question again? Oh, yeah. Why was she sitting here?* "Where am I supposed to sit?"

"Down there, with the other kids." The boy gestured with his chin to the far end of the table, already packed with students from her class.

"I don't know any of them. I'm new."

"I'm Daniel. What's your name?"

"Meade."

"You can sit with me."

"Really?" Meade hesitated. "The other kids don't seem to like me too much."

"Don't worry," Daniel said, giving her a goofy smile. "I got your back."

Meade couldn't help but return the smile. And, since that day, Daniel had always had that effect on her. No matter how terrible a situation, Daniel could find a way to brighten her day, with a wink or a joke or a comforting hand on her shoulder. Where others saw the glass half empty, Daniel had the ability to find a reason to declare it not just full, but overflowing.

And yet, here they were, she and Daniel, hopelessly sitting side by side on the floor of his hallway bathroom. Where was her old Daniel? The one who would have made a wisecrack about how all women seemed to like Mr. Clean. Or, how he's so thankful the local elementary school is performing the musical *Annie* this year so he can march down there to audition for the role of Daddy Warbucks. Where was *that* Daniel?

*Gone.* Gone with the thick, black curl that had fallen out of Daniel's palm and was now lying sadly on the ground between them.

Meade picked up the curl and rubbed it between her fingers.

*So beautiful.*

"What do you want me to do, Daniel?" Meade said softly. "What can I do for you?"

For a moment, Daniel didn't reply. Meade was about to ask him again when he said softly, "Maybe you should leave."

*Leave?* Was he kidding? *Leave?* He'd never asked her to leave before. Never. *Ever.* Not when he'd lain, for seventy-two hours, on this very same bathroom floor, puking his guts out. Not when his mother was crying so hard, the day after the diagnosis, Meade had spent the entire day consoling her, instead of Daniel. Meade had been there for all of it. For the initial diagnosis. For the mountains of tests and injections and X-rays and IVs. For all the waiting and waiting and *waiting* on doctors and nurses and technicians and results. Meade had been there, holding Daniel's hand, and often his mom's, too, for all of it.

And now, because of a little bit of hair on the ground, he wanted her to leave?

"You're kidding, right?" Meade said in disbelief.

"No." Daniel shook his head while still resting it on his knees. "I think you should leave."

Meade sat still. *Leave?* She'd never even considered that to be an option. Of course, she wasn't going to leave.

"Daniel, I don't want to go."

"Meade, just go."

"But, Daniel..."

"Meade!" The tone of his voice surprised her and she recoiled slightly at the sound of it. In all the years she'd known Daniel, she'd never heard him raise his voice to her—or anyone, for that matter.

Daniel must have sensed Meade's shock; he softened his voice.

"Meade..." he said quietly, still not looking at her. "I'm not mad at you. I love you. I just think you should leave."

Meade jumped to her feet. "No."

"No?" Daniel's voice was full of surprise.

"No," Meade said. "I'm not leaving. If you don't want me to sit on this floor with you, then fine. I'll go wait for you in your room. Or, I'll go downstairs and cook dinner with your mom. But I'm not leaving. You can't push me around like that, Daniel—only want me when it's convenient for you. Then, kick me out when you don't feel like dealing with me. You're not the only one who has feelings here. You're not the only one this cancer is affecting. It's hard for me, too—and sometimes I think you forget that. I know this sucks for you. I do. But it sucks for me, too!"

Meade sucked in her breath. Her outburst had surprised even her. She'd never gotten mad at Daniel like that, as he'd never gotten angry with her before. Today was full of firsts.

Daniel remained silent on the floor. Meade waited to see if he responded. He didn't.

"Okay, then. I'm going to go see if your mom needs help with dinner. I'll bring it up to you when it's ready."

She turned to walk out the door. Actually, she was pretty sure she was about to stomp out of it.

"I'm sorry."

The voice was so quiet—so tiny—Meade almost wasn't sure it was coming from Daniel.

She paused at the door, her hand on the frame, and didn't turn back to him.

"I'm sorry," he said again. "I know this is hard for you, too."

Meade took a deep breath and turned back to Daniel. "Then why don't you want me here?"

Daniel sighed deeply and slowly raised his head. At first, he didn't turn to face her. He merely stared straight ahead, not blinking. Then, with purposeful and steady movement, he turned his head and looked deep into her eyes.

Meade regretted the gasp immediately. But Daniel...*oh, Daniel*... her beautiful Daniel.

On the right side of his head, the side that had been opposite her as she sat on the bathroom floor, was a large bald spot marring the perfect flow of his black curls. The empty hollow in his hair seemed so out of place. So distorted. So *wrong*.

"I look like a freak," Daniel said. "I didn't want you to see me like this."

*Oh, Daniel...*

"I've been sitting here, trying to get up the courage to shave it all off. It's coming out in chunks. If I let it fall out on its own...I'll look like...well, I need to shave it off myself."

Daniel's voice sounded tired. And wistful. And so very, very sad.

Meade knelt down, again, next to him. She lifted her hand to run her fingers through his hair, a gesture she'd done a thousand times before, and then stopped herself, instead resting her hand on his neck. What if she did that and a handful of hair fell out? Daniel wouldn't be able to handle that. She wasn't sure she would either.

"But why didn't you want me to see you? You're not embarrassed when I hold your head as you throw up. Why is this such a big deal?"

"Because everyone pukes. It's not exactly romantic, but it's a natural part of life—especially for teenage boys who drink too much, I guess." Daniel cracked a small smile, and then it vanished quickly. "But, how many eighteen-year-old girls have to look at their boyfriend missing half his hair? That's not very sexy. And, it doesn't really make for a normal relationship."

Meade giggled in spite of the situation. "A normal relationship? When have we ever had one of those?"

Daniel gave a half smile as he shrugged.

"How many people find the love of their life before they can multiply?"

"Well...you do have a point there..." Daniel said, his grin getting bigger, though his dark eyes still looked so terribly sad.

"I know this sucks. It really, really, really, really, really, really, really, *really* sucks."

Daniel nudged her with his shoulder and shook his head. "Okay. I get the point," he said, the smile nearly reaching his eyes.

"But, the thing is, we can do this. You and I. We're tough. Hair. No hair. It doesn't matter. You're still you. *You.* And I love *you.* If your hair never grew back, I'd still love you."

"You would?"

"Sure," Meade said, grinning. "And then we'd invest in a whole lot of baseball caps."

Daniel laughed. A real laugh this time.

"Come on, let's get up. I'm gonna be the one who shaves your head."

Daniel hesitated. "Are you sure?"

"Of course," Meade said. As she stood, she grabbed Daniel's hand and helped pull him to his feet. "I got your back."

Meade tilted her head back to look up at Daniel. She'd almost forgotten how much taller he was than she. In recent months, Daniel hadn't spent much time standing. He always seemed to be lying in a bed or sitting. It had actually done wonders for the kink in her neck, and Meade felt a tad bit guilty even thinking that.

"I'm thinking we're going to need to get you a chair," Meade said, a big smile on her face.

Daniel leaned down and kissed the top of her head. "I love you, Meade Peterson."

Meade snuggled deep into Daniel's chest and closed her eyes as his arms wrapped around her.

"I love you, too, Daniel," Meade whispered. "I love you, too."


Bald Daniel was something to get used to. It wasn't that Meade completely disliked it. He didn't look *bad*, per se. He looked...well, bald.

And, a little bit sick, but Meade pushed that thought out of her mind whenever it tried to wiggle its way into her consciousness.

The first swipe had been the hardest. Meade had stood, clippers hovering like a helicopter over Daniel's curls, for a good five minutes.

"Just do it," Daniel had said firmly. "Let's get this over with."

"What if I cut you?" Meade asked hesitantly.

"You won't," Daniel reassured her.

"Okay..." Meade said. "Here I go."

But then she simply stood there. She couldn't bring herself to begin. To wipe out those precious locks.

"Meade!" Daniel was half frustrated, half amused by her hesitancy. "Do it!"

Meade sighed deeply and closed her eyes.

"Not with your eyes closed!" Daniel said, laughing. "Do you want to cut off my ear by mistake?"

Meade opened her eyes again. She caught Daniel's gaze in the mirror. "Okay, eyes open," she said resolutely. "Let's count."

"One..." Daniel began.

"On the count of what?" Meade interrupted him.

"Three!" Daniel said, laughing. "Three! Geez, Meade. Aren't you supposed to be making this easier on me?"

Meade glared at him through the mirror. "I'm doing my best," she hissed. "This is a lot of responsibility for me...what if I mess it up?"

"Okay, that's it," Daniel said, and, before she realized what he was doing, he'd yanked the clippers out of her hand, flicked the "on" button and taken a swipe at the side of his head. The curls fell, like the feathers from a pillow, covering the toes of Meade's sneakers.

Meade gasped. "Daniel!" she cried, shocked by his sudden gesture.

And then she saw the huge grin on his face. He was finding it amusing. He was finding *her* amusing. She remembered the pitiful sight she'd encountered when she'd first entered the bathroom an hour ago. That pathetic Daniel was gone. *Her* Daniel was back.

"Give me those," she said, grabbing the clippers back from him. And then, without missing a beat, she quickly ran them across the top of his head, leaving him with a reverse mohawk.

"Now, *that's* sexy," Meade said, laughing.

"Let's take a picture," Daniel said. "Go get the camera. It's on my dresser."

Meade hurried to his room and was back in a few seconds, with the Nikon that had been a present from Daniel's mom on his eighteenth birthday.

"Say cheese!" Meade called out, as she walked in the door and began clicking away.

He gave her a big, toothy smile and then spent a few moments striking various silly poses for the camera.

"Work it, baby. Work it," Meade said, giggling as she moved around the tiny bathroom, like a seasoned photographer, taking photos from various angles.

"Come here," he said, pulling her close to him. "Let's get one of us together."

Taking the camera from her with one hand, he pulled her down on his lap with the other.

"Look in the mirror," he said, as he put his head next to hers, their cheeks touching. He reached above his head with the camera and took a photo of the two of them smiling into the mirror.

"Kiss me," he said. Meade obliged and, as her lips touched his, she could hear the click of the camera.

"Now you'll always have a photo to remember this day," Daniel said softly.

"As if I'd ever forget it," she whispered back, her lips a breath away from his. "It's not every day I get to shave my boyfriend's head. Speaking of which..." She pulled away from him. "I think I should finish the job."

Daniel reluctantly let go of Meade. She reached for the clippers and began to shave the remainder of the curls, giggling as they floated to the ground, but inwardly, desperately sad to watch them fall.

*It's only hair. It'll grow back.*

At least, she hoped it would grow back. But, what if it didn't? What if Daniel never got better and this is how he'd looked for the rest of his life? And, how long would that life be?

Meade caught Daniel staring at her, quizzically, through the mirror.

"What's wrong?" he asked. "Changing your mind about my sexy bald head?"

Meade forced a smile onto her lips. "Nope," she said, pushing back the bleak thoughts of a moment ago. "I'm wondering what your mom's going to say when she sees you."

Daniel nodded solemnly. He was concerned about that, too.

"And, worse yet," Meade said, knowing she needed to reset the tone in the room to a lighter one. "What is she going to say when she sees this mess on the floor?"

Daniel grinned at Meade's reflection in the mirror. "Frankly, my dear," he said, with his best Rhett Butler impersonation, *"That* is something worth worrying about..."

# CHAPTER FOUR
## July 2013

**M**eade glanced at her watch. Her date was late. Of course he was. Hector was always late. Normally, that didn't bother her. She wasn't interested in him for his promptness—or his lack thereof, as it turned out. She was interested in him for the things he did to her. In bed. Things at which he was very good. And his innate nature of taking his time served him well when it came to that area of their life.

But this wasn't bed. This was dinner. And he was thirty-seven minutes late, which really irritated Meade. He was an artist who worked from home and had no schedule. Hector came and went as he pleased. If he had to keep others waiting in the process, so be it. It was hardly his concern.

Meade looked down at her watch again. Thirty-eight minutes. She was beginning to remember why they rarely went out together. Hector wasn't at all reliable. And Meade was nothing but. She didn't like to spend time with people who didn't value her time as much as she respected theirs. So what was she doing with Hector?

The blush that crept onto her face was all the answer she needed. She didn't spend time with Hector for his witty and stimulating conversation. He wasn't even her intellectual equal. Truth be told, they didn't have a whole lot to say to each other. But between the sheets, he was her teacher. A master at his craft. Second to none when it came to physical prowess and his ability to use it to fulfill every physical need she possessed.

And truly, Meade recognized that this relationship was, at the very least, ninety percent physical. Maybe ninety-three percent. No more than ninety-five. Usually, this didn't bother her. She wasn't looking for a husband. She wasn't even looking for a boyfriend. Just someone she could crawl into bed with on occasion. Someone who was familiar. And, on the nights when she needed an escort, someone she could bring to a charity event or business dinner and not worry he might embarrass her in front of her colleagues.

For the past six months, Hector had been that person. Handsome. Charming. All the wives of her fellow editors loved him. He had the ability to make any woman feel like she was the only one in the room—that she was mesmerizing and captivating and alluring. And what woman didn't want to feel that, even if for a moment?

Usually, Meade had no qualms with the relationship being the way it was. There was no commitment. No promises of a future. No exclusivity. Minimal dinners out, in fact. If they ate, it was usually in his bed after a passionate night of heated sex. They never went out on regular dates. She and Hector had never been to a movie together... never been to a museum...never even walked through a grocery store with each other. Theirs was not a relationship of substance. But it was satisfying in the ways Meade needed it to be.

At least, it had been...until recently. And she wasn't sure what had changed for her. With any of the men in her life—and there had been many—she liked to keep it simple. Sex—often on her lunch break. Dinner on occasion. A date when she needed one. The sex was always at the guy's place—or at a hotel. Never in her home. In fact, she'd never even had a man in her apartment—other than family members and a few close male friends. Over the past few weeks, though, Meade had begun to think that maybe she should be trying to experience more with Hector. She wasn't getting any younger. Perhaps she was too old to be having such superficial relationships. She wasn't looking for a husband. But maybe a companion?

Thus, she had asked him to have dinner with her tonight. In public. It wasn't much, but it was a first step. The two of them had also made plans for her to visit him in Chicago while he was there for a few months in the fall, teaching an art course at the University of Chicago. That was a big step for her—traveling to visit a man. Meade rarely did anything for a man. Anything other than a few sexual favors. But, he'd suggested she come visit and she'd never been to Chicago. It seemed like a fun experience—and a big step for her. Truth be told, she was looking forward to it.

"Can I get you anything?" the waiter asked Meade. He might as well have said, "Order already or get up so a paying customer can sit here."

"I'm sorry. My friend should be here in a minute." Meade picked up the menu and glanced at the appetizer. "Can you get me the spinach artichoke dip? Thanks."

The waiter seemed momentarily sated with her order as he walked away.

"Hey, darling." Hector kissed Meade on the cheek. "How are you this evening?"

Meade took a long look at her watch as she held her wrist in the air.

"I know. I know. Sorry. I got held up." He sat down across from Meade and picked up his menu. "So, what looks good here?"

Meade sighed. This was as much of an apology or explanation as he was going to give her. Hector marched to the beat of his own drum—and that drum was often several beats behind everyone else's.

"The steak is great. So's the salmon."

They decided to get one of each and put down their menus. Meade stared at him across the table. He was gorgeous. Put together in just the right way. From his dark, Latino skin, to his silky hair, to the stubble on his straight jawbone. Handsome didn't even cover it. Breathtaking was more like it. And she knew, for a fact, that what was under that tight shirt was even more intoxicating.

"So, I've been thinking," Meade said. "When I come to Chicago, how about we go to see Frank Lloyd Wright's home and studio? I hear it's incredible. And I read there are some great restaurants and shops at the Navy Pier."

"When are you coming again?"

This was so typical Hector. They had discussed the dates of her trip at length—purposely picking the school's fall break, when he'd have a few days off from his classes so they'd have time to tour the city. She'd just bought her plane ticket last week and emailed him the confirmation with a smiley face at the top.

Meade smiled at him and tried not to seem irritated. It was a simple question. He was as bad with dates as he was with time. Meade realized that. But, it annoyed her that he didn't seem to realize what a big deal this was for her. She never traveled anywhere with a man. Certainly not to *visit* a man.

"October twelfth."

Hector took out his phone and tapped the screen a few times, presumably pulling up his calendar. Meade figured he was going to make sure to add the trip to it.

"Damn. I thought you were coming later in the month." Hector took a sip of his water. "I was sure of it. I'm going to be in France."

The waiter chose this inopportune moment to return to the table for their order. Meade placed hers quickly, her heart racing.

*Was he kidding?*

"Are you kidding?" she asked when the waiter walked away.

"Actually, no."

Meade stumbled over her words. "I don't even know what to say. I checked with you three times before I booked my flight."

Hector shrugged and leaned back in his chair. "I honestly thought you were coming later in the month."

"So that's it? You can't change your plans?" Meade couldn't believe he could have made such a mistake. It was one thing to be inconsiderate with promptness, but this was completely something else.

"I can't change them. I'm really sorry."

Meade could barely catch her breath. *Sorry? He was sorry? She'd already bought her ticket.* And then something flickered across her mind. Why was he going to France? Was it for work? She could almost excuse it if he was, but...

"Are you going by yourself?"

Hector blushed a bit. "No."

"Are you going with another woman?"

His nod was so tiny, Meade wasn't even sure she saw it at first.

"Are you kidding me?" Meade said, again. Surely this must be a joke. No one could be this inconsiderate and heartless. "You scheduled a trip to France with another woman on the week you had me buy my plane ticket to come visit you?" She threw her napkin down on the table. "You are unbelievable."

People at the surrounding tables began to look over at them. Meade realized her tone was escalating, which, under normal circumstances, would embarrass her, but not tonight. She was furious. Livid. *How could he?*

"I got my dates mixed up. It wasn't intentional. I made a mistake. I'm really sorry about it." Hector picked up a piece of pita bread and scooped up some dip.

*Sorry?* He was *sorry?*

"When did you book your flight?"

"A few days ago."

Meade stared at him incredulously.

"I seriously don't even know what to say. We've been talking about these plans for over a month."

Hector popped the bread into his mouth and chewed. "I'm really sorry," he said, wiping his mouth with the napkin. "I really thought you were coming later in the month. It's not personal. I made a mistake in calendar management."

And that did it. A mistake in *calendar management?* Is that what they were calling it these days? Not rude. Not inconsiderate. Not a complete jerk of a human being. Not "Please forgive me; I'll change my plans."

*Poor calendar management.*

Meade stood up, removing her purse from the back of the chair. "Have a nice trip to France.

"You're leaving? I just got here."

*Exactly.*

Meade turned and began to walk away.

"Does this mean you're not going to come to Chicago a different week?" Hector called after her as she strode toward the door. Meade didn't even look back. She kept walking. Out of the restaurant. Onto the streets of New York. Back to her apartment.

There was a reason why Meade never let things get more serious than a romp in the hay with a man. Tonight, she remembered exactly why.


"I brought slushies." Pantera stood at Meade's door, one slushie in each hand. And a paper sack tucked under her arm. "A cherry-lime-ade slushie fixes everything."

Meade smiled at her friend and stepped back to let her into the apartment.

"Did you go out looking like that?" Pantera said, looking Meade up and down. "No wonder he's going to France with another woman."

Meade looked down at her attire. Old ratty sweatpants that sagged at her rear, a Wake Forest T-shirt that had seen better days, and giant, rabbit-head slippers. She had to smile. She didn't exactly look desirable.

"No, Ms. Smarty Pants. I did not go out looking like this. I changed when I got home."

In fact, Meade had slipped into the comfortable, if unattractive, outfit the moment she walked in the door and then crawled into bed.

She wanted to pull the covers over her head and sleep until next year—and might have if Pantera hadn't called. How could she have been such a fool? She knew better. She was not a relationship girl. Intentionally.

She should never have planned a trip with a man. That bordered on turning something into a serious relationship and that was never her intention.

Pantera handed Meade her slushie as the two of them sat down on the couch.

"Look what else I brought!" Pantera reached into her bag. "Devil Dogs!"

"Wow. You are just full of sugar tonight, aren't you?"

"Comfort food."

"I thought meatloaf and mashed potatoes were comfort food."

"Not my kind of comfort." Pantera ripped into the box and began to unwrap one of the cakes. Pantera had an enormous sweet tooth. Sometimes Meade wondered how she stayed so skinny with all the crap she ate.

Meade took a sip of the slushie. It was really good. She didn't usually indulge in this much junk food. She didn't have Pantera's incredible metabolism.

Pantera held the box out to Meade. "Come on. I know you want one."

Meade looked at the box, then at Pantera, then back at the box again. She sighed. "Okay." She reached inside and grabbed a Devil Dog. They didn't have them in Texas—at least not near Austin—which was probably for the best. Meade couldn't imagine how much she would have weighed by eighth grade if she'd grown up eating these every day in her lunch box. She took a bite. Boy, were they good.

"Calendar management?" Pantera said with a giggle.

"Calendar management."

"Wow. That's a new one. He's *good*."

Meade shook her head in disbelief. "I didn't even know what to say. What do you say to that?"

"*Adios. Sayonara. Arrivederci.*"

"*Au revoir.*"

"Exactly," Pantera said, opening another Devil Dog. "You are much too good for Hector. Don't give him another thought."

"I know. You're right. It's not like I saw us having a future together. And, I never thought we were exclusive. But still..."

"Can I ask you a question?" Pantera's voice turned serious.

"Sure," Meade said, putting her feet up on the couch. "You can ask me anything." And she meant it. Pantera was one of her closest friends—if not her closest. Their relationship had grown almost immediately after she'd hired the young woman. At first, Meade had worried about becoming such good friends with her employee. It wasn't really the professional thing to do. But, it never seemed awkward with Pantera. The two of them had worked out a system where work time was work time and friendship time was friendship time—and the two never seemed to cross. Meade never felt as if Pantera was using their friendship to get away with things at work— to work less because Meade wouldn't get mad at her. If anything, their relationship seemed to encourage Pantera to work harder. She loved Meade, like a big sister, and wanted Meade to be successful. Thus, she did her own job to the best of her ability so Meade could be effective in all of her work. It was an odd partnership—Meade in her tailored suits and stiletto heels and Pantera in her black lipstick and corsets—but it worked.

And, truth be told, Meade needed a good friend. She hadn't had a close girlfriend since Lori back in high school—and that hadn't exactly ended well. Meade still felt a pang of sadness when she thought of Lori. They'd been like sisters, too. Other than Daniel, there'd been no one she loved more than Lori. And, in a heartbeat—literally—she'd lost both of them.

Meade shook that thought out of her mind. She couldn't think about Lori. That was the past. This was the future. And she had new problems.

"Why do you always pick such losers to date?" Pantera asked her. "It's like you have radar for the worst men on the planet. Remember the one who wanted you to sign the sex contract?"

Meade chuckled. "What? You don't think I was excited about having to call him 'Master' and kneel in front of him?"

"I particularly liked the part where he said he owned your orgasms."

"Yeah...I guess he wasn't a winner." Meade sighed.

"Or how about the one who got so drunk on your first date, he puked in your car?"

"It took forever to get that smell out..."

"Or the one who was so poor he expected you to pay for all of your dates."

"Which one was that? I've had a few of those," Meade said, grabbing for the Devil Dog box and eating another one. It was definitely a two Drake's cake night.

"Precisely. Have you ever looked at your track record? I hate to say it, sweetie, but it's not very good."

"I have picked some duds."

"Yes, you have. Why do you do that? Maybe you should go to therapy to figure it out. You're a beautiful woman. Smart. Successful. Normal. No odd quirks—at least, no outward ones..."

Meade threw the plastic wrapper she was holding at Pantera.

"I'm just saying...you should have great, eligible men lined up around the block trying to get a date with you." Pantera popped up from the couch and looked out Meade's window. "All I see is the homeless guy holding up the sign, 'My liver is a terrorist. Please help me kill it.' I'll bet he's available. Should I go down and ask?"

"Very funny," Meade said as Pantera returned to the couch. "I'm not that bad."

The look Pantera gave her said, *"Yes, you are."*

"Okay. Okay. I get the point. I don't know." Meade shrugged.

Pantera's voice softened. "Does it have anything to do with that handsome boy whose photo's taped to your bathroom mirror?"

Meade looked away then. She didn't like to talk about Daniel—not even to her best friend. The pain was still so raw—even after all these years. It was ridiculous. She was sure that to Pantera—or anyone else, for that matter—the concept of moving on was so obvious. It had been teenage love. A first love. Nothing more. But to Meade, he'd been everything. He was still everything. And there was no point in looking for more when she knew the chance of something like it— something that incredible—existing again was highly unlikely. And besides, she'd made a promise to Daniel—and she had no intention of breaking it.

"He was someone I loved very much," Meade said. "One-of-a-kind, you know?"

Pantera smiled and nodded like she knew—but Meade wondered if she really did.

"You know what your problem is?" Pantera asked her, taking a sip of her slushie and kicking her feet up on the coffee table. "You have a bad picker."

"A bad picker?"

"Yep. A bad picker. Your picker's broken. You pick bad men. Continually. You need to get your picker fixed."

"And how do I do that?" Meade asked.

"By letting me pick them for you."

"You've got to be kidding me."

"Nope. I, unlike you, have an excellent picker."

"You don't even have a boyfriend."

"Of course not. My picker's so good, it's weaned out the losers and so far, I've mostly only found losers. But...," Pantera said, raising a finger in the air to stress her point. "When I find a good one, I know it. Unlike you, who not only doesn't recognize a loser, she sleeps with him on the first date. You don't even Google him first. Who, in her right mind, doesn't *Google* a guy before going out with him?"

"Me," Meade said, raising her hand meekly.

"Exactly," Pantera said. "Thus, the next man you go out with will be handpicked by me and only me."

Meade rolled her eyes. She could only imagine the type of man Pantera would pick out for her. "Can I at least limit the number of piercings and tattoos he has?"

"You can have no restrictions whatsoever. I do the picking. You just show up." Pantera opened another Devil Dog.

"How do you even eat with that tongue ring in your mouth? Doesn't it hurt?"

The glimmer of the ring caught Meade's attention every time Pantera opened her mouth. As her assistant, Pantera never wore it, so when she and Meade were together outside of work, the balled stud always caught Meade off guard.

"You're changing the subject."

Meade yawned. Tonight had worn her out. She was even finding herself too tired to argue with Pantera.

"Okay. Fine. I'll go out with someone you pick. But just *one* someone. If I don't like him, I'm going back to my old—albeit broken—picker. Got it?"

Pantera smiled from one fish skeleton earring to the other.

"I have someone good in mind for you," she said, rubbing her hands together as if she was cooking up a magical potion.

"Great. Just *great*," Meade said, standing. "Want to spend the night?"

"Of course," Pantera said. "I threw my pj's in my bag, in case you didn't want to be alone tonight."

"I know the couch is not as comfortable as that coffin you sleep in at your place."

"I do not sleep in a coffin!"

Meade laughed and shrugged. "If you say so." She gave her friend a big hug. "Thanks for coming over tonight. I needed a friend."

"And some Devil Dogs," Pantera said, hugging her back.

"Definitely some Devil Dogs." Meade grabbed one more from the box. "I'll take this to bed with me."

Pantera snickered at her. "Night, friend."

"Night," Meade said, turning toward her bedroom. She might have a broken picker when it came to men, but she had an excellent one when it came to friends. She'd done an exceptional job when she'd decided to hire Pantera—and even a better one when the two of them became so close. Meade couldn't imagine a life without Pantera in it. She was essential to Meade's world.

Tongue ring and all.

"Oh, Meade! You look stunning!" Meade's mom gushed. She placed her hands on Meade's shoulders and spun her daughter around so she could catch a glimpse of her from all angles. "Just stunning. I think I'm going to cry."

Meade looked at herself in the mirror, critically, and frowned. "I look ridiculous."

"No you don't! You look beautiful," her mother insisted.

"Nah...she does look kind of ridiculous," Nick called out from across the room. Meade turned and glared at her twenty-year-old brother, who was sprawled out on the couch, a bag of chips in one hand and a two-liter bottle of Coke propped up between his legs.

"Don't you have somewhere you need to be?" Meade hissed at him. "Don't you have class or something? Or better yet, don't you have a *job?*"

Nick shrugged and shoved a mouthful of chips inside his mouth, wiping off the crumbs with the back of his hand before he wiped that same hand on the side of the couch. "Nope."

"You need a life," Meade spat at him.

"Look who's talking, Miss I-Don't-Want-To-Do-Anything-But-Hang-Out-At-The-Hospital-With-My-Bald-Boyfriend."

Before Meade's mom could get a good grip on her, Meade lunged at her brother, knocking over the Coke and splattering the sticky substance all over both them and the living room floor. She'd gotten in one good punch, right below Nick's ribs, before her mother pulled her off her cowering brother and the now-messy couch. Nick might have been bigger than Meade, but even he knew if you got her mad enough—which he seemed to have a talent for doing—she'd fight until the bitter end, holding nothing back. He'd gone to school many times, over the years, with a black eye or bruised ribs because of the wrath he'd incurred from his sister. Nick knew he should have probably resisted provoking her, but gosh, it was so much fun.

"Meade! Nick! Stop it!"

"He's a jerk."

"She's insane. I wish I had a picture of you barreling toward me. You look like a crazy person, jumping on me in that dress. What kind of *lady* does that? No wonder you don't have a date for the prom!"

As soon as the words were out of his mouth, the room fell into complete silence. Neither Meade, nor her mom, nor Nick, said a word. He'd gone too far with that last comment. Even Nick recognized his mistake, but he wasn't the type of brother to take things back, even if the tears that swelled in Meade's eyes made him feel like a first-class jackass.

"Come on in the kitchen," Meade's mom said, breaking the tension in the room. "I have some club soda under the sink that should be able to get that Coke out from the front of your dress."

"I don't want to go," Meade said. "I told you that. I've been telling you—and everyone else—for weeks that I don't want to go."

"Of course, you want to go," Meade's mom insisted. "It's your senior prom. Everyone goes to their senior prom."

"Daniel's not going."

Meade's mom sighed. They'd been down this road before, many, many times over the past month.

"Well, no, he's not. And we all know why. But he'd go if he could. You know that."

Meade grabbed a tissue from the table beside the couch and blotted her eyes. Glancing back in the mirror, she could see her mascara had begun to run and her hair, which only five minutes earlier had hung in beautiful ringlet curls, now looked like a wild mess. Her appearance made her want to cry even more.

"More importantly, he wants you to go."

And there it was. The truth beyond all of this primping and planning. Meade's mom was right. Daniel did want her to go.

"You're going," Daniel had insisted, two days earlier. "You're going and you're going to have a good time and that's the end of this discussion."

They'd been sitting in the pediatric recreation room, playing a game of Monopoly. Daniel was winning. He pretty much always won. Whether it was Monopoly or checkers or Operation, Daniel was competitive, like he'd always been on the basketball court. Sometimes Meade was surprised at herself that she didn't get weary of losing to him—and on occasion, was irritated with him for never letting her win—but mostly, she was so relieved to see Daniel become passionate about something, even if it was how carefully he could remove the wishbone from the belly of the chubby guy with the red nose, that she never complained.

"Why? What's the point? You won't be there. I won't have any fun. I'd rather be here with you."

"Doing what? Watching another rerun of *Matlock*?"

Meade shrugged. "Maybe a new *Home Improvement* will be on."

Daniel rolled his eyes at her and shook his head. Neither said a word as he threw a six with the dice.

"Nice! Two hundred dollars, please," Daniel said, holding out one hand to Meade, the banker, and moving his top hat past "Go" with the other.

"Ergh," Meade growled. "This isn't fair."

"Hey! It's not my fault I'm a natural real estate mogul."

"Not the game. The prom! How many times do I have to tell you that if you don't go, I don't want to go."

"Well, babe...I won't be going. So, that just leaves you."

"Couldn't we spring you from this joint? For one night?" Meade practically whined. No matter which way she cut it, she could not imagine attending her senior prom without Daniel. Ever since freshman year, when she'd listened to the senior girls talk about their prom dresses and shoes and the limos that picked them up, as she sat at the next table in the cafeteria, Meade had dreamt of the day when she and Daniel would go to their prom—together. Of course they'd go together. Even as a freshman, before she and Daniel were officially a "couple," she knew he'd be her date. The thought of going with someone else was inconceivable to Meade. She and Daniel did everything together and everyone in school was aware. *The prom without Daniel?* It was too horrible a thought.

"No."

"Did you ask your doctor? What does Nancy think?" Nancy was both Meade's and Daniel's favorite nurse. In fairness, all of the nurses on the pediatric floor were incredibly kind and loving, but Nancy had a spark that both Meade and Daniel adored. She was about the age of Meade's grandma, but had the energy of the most rambunctious eight-year-old. Her skin was the blackest Meade had ever seen and her body consisted of rolls and rolls of fluff. Perhaps some people would call her "fat," but when Meade saw her, all she could think of was that she bet a hug from Nancy felt really good—like falling into a pile of feather pillows. Sometimes, when Nancy would get off her shift, she'd come into Daniel's room, plop down on the chair next to his bed and hang out with Daniel and his mom or Meade or whoever was in the room at the time. She wasn't required to stay past work hours, but she did. And, many times, Meade arrived in Daniel's room to find Nancy had baked some sort of delicious goody and left it on the night table by his bed. Today, it'd been pumpkin bread. Daniel hadn't had much of an appetite for it, but Meade had gobbled it down after school.

"I didn't ask them. I don't want to go."

"Oh, so you don't want to go and it's fine, but I have no choice in the matter? I still have to go."

"It's different and you know it," Daniel said. "It's your turn to roll the dice."

Meade picked them up and blew on her hand, for good luck. She needed it—in this game and life. Then she flung them across the board.

"Twelve!" he said gleefully. "That lands you on Park Place and guess who owns Park Place?"

"You do," Meade bemoaned. "Maybe we should quit the game now and crown you the winner."

"'Quit'? What does that word even mean? Of course we're not going to quit!" Daniel said, more animated than Meade had seen him in days. "We're going to play until the bitter end."

"Great," Meade said sarcastically.

"Don't be mad," he said, his tone softening. "It's just a game."

"I don't care about the stupid game! I care about the prom. Or should I say, I *don't* care about the prom, but I do care that you and my mom are insisting I go."

"Who would've thought your mom and I would ever see eye to eye on something?" Daniel said, grinning. "It's rather shocking. Besides, you won't be on your own. Lori will be there."

Lori. Thank heavens for Lori. Meade didn't know how she would have survived the past few months without her closest girlfriend. Daniel and Meade and Lori had been friends since Lori transferred to their school in the fifth grade. Before that, Meade's closest friend had always been Daniel—and in many ways, he still was. But, by the age of ten, Meade was really craving a best *girl*friend—someone she could confide in about the changes in her body and the way her hair never did what she wanted it to and how she couldn't get rid of the zits on her chin. And she needed someone to talk to about the crushes she was developing on certain boys...especially Daniel.

Lori's appearance in her class on the first day of the fifth grade had been like a blessing straight from heaven. The two girls had been assigned seats right next to each other and when they realized they both still played with Barbie dolls—something many of the kids in their grade thought was dumb and babyish—their friendship was sealed.

Meade had been so thankful Daniel had become friends with Lori, too. It wouldn't have changed how much Meade liked the other girl, but it would have made life more difficult, considering the huge role Daniel played in her life. Oftentimes, the three of them would hang out after school or go to the movies on the weekends or help each other study for big exams. People at school knew that, where one of them was, the other two were sure to be there, too.

Meade had worried, when she and Daniel had started dating during their sophomore year of high school, that things would become awkward with Lori. Neither she nor Daniel ever wanted their friend to feel as if she were a third wheel. She meant too much to both of them. And so, they'd both been relieved when Lori had not only taken their dating in stride, but had been extremely happy for them.

"I knew the two of you would get together!" she'd cried, pulling both of them into a giant bear hug the moment they told her they were now an official couple. "No two people were ever meant for each other more than you!"

Lori had been devastated by Daniel's diagnosis, as Meade knew she would be, and she made a point to spend as much time with Daniel at the hospital as she could. Sometimes she drove Meade there, when Meade, who didn't have her own car, couldn't get a ride. And, on the days when Meade had something she had to attend after school, Lori made sure to be at the hospital so Daniel wouldn't be by himself all afternoon. Lori was a great emotional support to Meade and Meade was truly thankful for her.

And Daniel was right. Lori would be at the prom. The prom was all Lori could talk about these days. For months, Lori had been praying that Brandon Keller would ask her to be his date. He was the star of the football team and Lori had been secretly in love with him since the ninth grade. It appeared, though, that Brandon was unaware Lori was alive and thus, Lori had finally consented to attend with Tim Eisner from their physics class. Meade had no doubt Lori would do her best to make sure Meade had a fun time at the prom, but it wouldn't be the same without Daniel.

"Why won't you go with me?" Meade asked Daniel as she rolled the dice. "If the doctors say it's okay...it'd be so much better if you were there."

Daniel sighed and put down the dice he was about to roll. He sat, silently, staring at the board for so long that Meade wondered if he'd forgotten her question.

"Daniel?"

"I can't go like this."

"Like what?"

"Oh, please, Meade. Don't insult me. You know exactly what I mean."

"Bald?"

"Uhm...yes, for starters...bald. Weak. In a wheelchair."

The wheelchair. It had been around—a presence in their life—for about two weeks now, ever since Daniel had been readmitted to the hospital for an infection. Daniel had resisted it at first, saying he didn't need it, that he was fine and could walk anywhere he absolutely needed to go. For about a week, Meade and his mother had begged and pleaded with him to at least consider using one—for trips down the hall to the rec room or to the nurses' station when they needed a break from the monotony that was his hospital room. They told him it didn't mean he was getting sicker and that it would help him conserve his energy. But Daniel had been insistent he didn't need it and when Daniel put his mind to something, well, Meade and his mom knew it was pointless to argue.

Meade hadn't even realized, at first, that Daniel had fallen. She'd run a bit ahead of him, rushing to the floor's small kitchen to try to grab the last chocolate pudding out of the fridge for him before that new kid, Sammy, down the hall got to it. The pediatric floor always seemed to be running low on pudding—no surprise, really, when it was full of young children and the only other options available were peach yogurt or grape Jell-O. It wasn't until she popped out of the kitchen, victorious with not one but two puddings in hand, that she heard the commotion and saw the nurses huddled around Daniel on the floor.

He was okay—barely even bruised, if you didn't count his pride, which he, of course, did. The nurses had helped him back to his bed and Meade had peeled open his chocolate pudding and handed it to him in silence. Neither of them said a word as they ate their small dessert cups in peace. But, the next day, when Meade arrived, the wheelchair was in the room, and when it was time to head off on their daily walk around the hospital floor, Daniel asked her to help him get into it.

"We don't have to dance…"

"Then what's the point of going if you don't dance?"

"Precisely! What's the point of going? If you're not there, I won't have anyone to dance with anyway!"

"Come on, Meade. Don't be an idiot. Of course you will. There are dozens of guys at school who've been waiting for the chance to get their arms around you. This is their big chance—and I won't be around to punch their lights out!"

"I don't want to dance with anyone else," Meade said stubbornly. "I'll just sit at a table and have a terrible time."

"No you won't," Daniel said firmly. "You're going to go with Lori and all your girlfriends. You're going to laugh. You're going to dance. You're going to take lots of pictures and then you're going to go get them developed and bring them to me the next day so I can see and hear all about the night. I won't be there with you, but I'll be anxious to hear all about it."

Meade folded her arms in front of her and leaned back in her chair.

"What? Are you pouting now? That's what you're going to do? You're going to pout?"

"Yes."

"Fine," Daniel said. "Pout all you want. It doesn't change the fact that you're going. Every girl should go to her senior prom. I am not going to be responsible for you not having pictures of that big night to show to our kids someday."

Meade's shoulders relaxed at his words. She always calmed down when he talked about their future together. The fact that he still believed they had one gave her hope that they truly did.

And so, she'd relented. She'd agreed to attend the prom—without Daniel. He'd told her he didn't mind if she went with another date; she'd been asked by a variety of boys at the school who knew her situation. But she felt too disloyal to Daniel to do that, so she would go alone—and hope Lori and Tim didn't feel like she was too much of a tagalong. The only thing Daniel had made her promise was that she would stop by the hospital, before the dance, so he could see how she looked and she'd, of course, agreed.

This led her to why she was standing in her kitchen, allowing her mom to scrub Coke off the front of her turquoise gown. Luckily, the dress was a dark color and the stain barely showed.

"I'm going to get the hairdryer to dry it off and then we'll head out," her mom called, as she ran out of the room and up the stairs.

Meade opened a kitchen cabinet and took down a glass, filling it with water from the sink. As she sipped the water, she wondered if she should take some Tylenol before she left. She had a feeling this evening was going to be nothing more than one big headache.

"You look really pretty," a voice from the door said softly.

Meade put down her glass and smiled. Of her two brothers, her youngest, Benjamin, was by far the sweetest.

"Ya think?"

"Yeah. Everyone's going to think you're the prettiest girl there."

Sometimes Meade wondered how her two brothers could be so different. While Nick was constantly getting under her skin, pushing her buttons—poking the bear, as he liked to refer to it—Benji was as kind and loving as they came. Meade knew a bunch of freshman boys from school and none of them had the sweet heart her little brother did.

"I don't want to go, but no one will listen to me."

"I know. But you'll have fun. And it's one night."

"Yeah...I guess. I feel bad that Daniel will be hanging out all by himself on a Saturday night. All his buddies will be at the prom. Even the junior guys on the team got dates with senior girls and will be going."

"Want me to go hang out with him tonight? I've got nothing to do. I could bring over that movie Mom just got me from Blockbuster. It's an action flick. I know Daniel loves those."

Meade thought for a moment. Her first instinct was to turn down Benji's offer, but why not bring him with her when she stopped by the hospital? Daniel had always liked her little brother and the two of them had formed a special brotherly bond of sorts.

"Sure. That sounds great. And I'd feel a lot better knowing Daniel had someone to hang out with tonight."

"Great!" Benji's face lit up like a Christmas tree. He'd clearly not been looking forward to spending another night home alone, either. "I'll go get the movie!"

He practically knocked over their mom in his rush out the door, as she returned to the kitchen with the hairdryer.

"What's gotten into him?" her mom asked curiously.

"Oh, he's going to go hang out with Daniel tonight while I'm at the prom. Is that okay with you?" Meade realized they probably should have asked their mom first. After all, Benji was only fourteen. But then again, Meade's mom wasn't exactly the type of mom you asked for permission to do things. For the most part, she lived her life and the kids lived theirs. If Benji hadn't decided to go hang out with Daniel, he would have been home alone because her mom had to be at work in an hour and Nick was certainly never available to pal around with his kid brother. Benji spent a lot of time on his own and that bugged Meade. He was too good a kid to be forgotten. When Daniel had been healthy, she and he'd made a point of, at least once a week, inviting Benji to go out for ice cream with them or to a movie or even down to the park where he and Daniel would shoot hoops together while she'd swing on the nearby swing set and watch. But, ever since Daniel's illness, Meade had been spending most of her time at the hospital and she hadn't had as much time for Benji.

"That's nice," Meade's mom said absentmindedly, as she glanced at the clock. "We'd better hurry up and get going. I need to get to work."

The plan was for Meade's mom to drop her off at the hospital entrance. As it turned out, "throw her and Benji out of the car" would have been a more accurate description. Her mom was always running late and prom night was no exception. And then, after Daniel got the chance to see Meade in her dress, Mrs. Spencer was going to drive Meade to the prom. Some of the other kids had asked Meade if she'd like to go with them in their limo, but she'd declined. Seeing Daniel first was too important to her. And, it seemed, extremely important to him, too. Daniel had called her, no less than three times that day, to make sure she was going to stop by his hospital room before she left for the dance.

That was why, when she and Benji reached Room 212 and pushed the door open, she was surprised to find Daniel's bed empty. A quick glance into the bathroom showed Meade he wasn't there, either. That was odd. *Where could he have gone?*

As Meade was about to plop down in the side chair to wait for him to come back, the door opened and Nancy walked in. Meade almost didn't recognize her. Instead of her usual nurse's attire, she was in a pale-pink pantsuit. And, whereas she usually had her hair pulled back in a tight bun, tonight she had it down, curled, and pinned back on one side in a pretty comb.

"Oh, hey, sugar! Are you looking for Daniel?"

Meade was never rude to Nancy—the woman was too kind—but a part of her wanted to say, "Who else would I be waiting for in this hospital room?"

"Yeah..." Meade said uncertainly. "He knew I was coming. He wanted to see my dress."

Nancy smiled at Meade, and her eyes sparkled as she looked the girl up and down.

"My, my...you are a picture!" the older woman exclaimed.

*"A picture of what?"* Meade wondered, but didn't ask. She also wanted to ask why Nancy was dressed like that, but she refrained. She was too distracted by how badly today was going and realized she really didn't care. She was too consumed in her own misery.

"Your young man is in the rec room. I think I saw him playing a game of Battleship with Sammy."

Battleship? What on earth? Couldn't Daniel have waited until she left to begin playing a board game? It wasn't like he didn't know she was coming.

"Why don't you head on down there?" Nancy said. "And who are you?" she said, turning to Benji.

"I'm Meade's brother, Benji. I'm gonna hang out with Daniel tonight."

"Well, I bet he'll be right happy to have you here!" Meade heard Nancy say, as she walked out of the room and down the hall. She'd hoped to make a grand entrance into Daniel's room—in her dress. She'd even imagined the look of awe on his face when he'd see her for the first time. It wasn't often she showed up wearing much more than jeans and a T-shirt—and certainly, never a ball gown.

But now she'd have to walk into the rec room and show off her new look to not only Daniel, but all the preteens hanging out in there, watching *The Simpsons. Could tonight seriously get any worse?*

Meade walked down the long hallway, past the nurses' station. Only one nurse was seated at the station and she looked up from her computer screen, and smiled, as Meade walked by.

"You look beautiful," the young nurse, whom Meade did not recognize, said to her.

"Thanks," Meade said unenthusiastically.

Meade reached the door to the rec room and was surprised to find it closed. Usually, it was open and the loud chaos of all the kids—especially on a Saturday night—came tumbling out into the hall. Tonight, though, the hall around the room was empty and both doors were closed. Meade was about to push down on the handle of the first one when it suddenly opened in her hand.

Confused, Meade paused. *What was going on?* She looked inside the room, but saw no one. In fact, she pretty much saw nothing at all. The rec room, usually bright from the fluorescent lights and the glow of the TV on the far wall, was dark and quiet.

"Go on in, sweetie," a voice behind her said. Meade turned to find Nancy standing behind her.

Meade looked at her, unsure of what to do. The older woman put her hand on the small of Meade's back and gave her a gentle shove. Meade walked into the room.

When she was fully inside, she realized the room wasn't completely dark at all. There were white Christmas lights strung along the walls, around the doorframes and on the edges of the tables. And, it wasn't actually quiet inside, either. Now that Meade was beyond the door, she could hear soft music playing in the background. Neither of those things, though, were what made her gasp. No. There was something much more surprising.

Sitting in the middle of the room, in his wheelchair, was Daniel. And he was wearing a tuxedo.

"What's going on?" Meade asked, not so much to him as to the air around her.

"It's our prom night," Daniel simply said. "Welcome to our prom."

Tears sprung into Meade's eyes and she put her hands to her mouth. "You did this? All of this? For me?" She couldn't believe it.

"Well...I didn't exactly do all of it myself," he said bashfully. "In case you haven't noticed, I don't have the easiest time getting around these days. But yes, I did it. And Nancy did it. And a few of the other nurses. And my mom. And your mom. And Benji."

"Benji?" Meade asked, startled. What did her brother have to do with this?

"Yes! Me!" a voice from behind Meade called out. "I helped plan this whole big thing! Good thing you agreed to let me come along tonight! If you hadn't, you would have been out one photographer!"

Meade turned and saw Benji standing behind her with Daniel's Nikon around his neck. And in the doorway, behind him, were Lori and her date, Tim.

"What are you guys doing here?" Meade asked in disbelief.

Lori ran up to Meade and gave her a big hug. "We're here to take prom pictures. We're not staying the whole time, but how could we not take pictures together on such a special night?"

Benji put Daniel's camera up to his eye and pointed it at Meade and Lori.

"Say *queso!*" he said.

The girls put their faces close together and cried out, *"Queso!"*

"Go get by Daniel," he barked, as if he was the official prom photographer. "It's time to take your prom pictures!"

Meade laughed and nearly skipped over to Daniel. Bending down, she kissed him, hard on the lips.

"Is this okay?" Daniel asked timidly. "You're not mad to be missing the real prom, are you?"

Meade nearly laughed out loud, having never heard a more ridiculous question. *Was she mad?* This was the best surprise anyone had ever given her.

"Of course I'm not mad," she said, gently lowering herself onto Daniel's lap as he wrapped his arms around her. "This is going to be the best night of our life."

And it was. Meade, Daniel, Lori and Tim smiled for the camera as Benji took what seemed like 500 photos. Meade was thankful that Tim, who really didn't know Daniel all that well, had agreed to stop by the hospital before he and Lori headed out to the school's actual prom. He seemed like a nice guy, though it was clear Lori had minimal feelings for him.

Once Lori and Tim left, Meade and Daniel ate sugar cookies and tea sandwiches that Nancy had prepared at home and brought to the hospital for this special night. She even stayed, on her night off, to serve them punch and Meade realized their special night was the reason Nancy had dressed up so beautifully. The effort she—and everyone else—had clearly put into this prom touched Meade's heart.

Once the shock had worn off, and Meade got a chance to really look around the rec room, she realized all the children's toys and games had been pushed aside and covered by white tablecloths, so as not to be eyesores. The food table was covered in a pale-pink cloth and two floral displays adorned either side of the punch bowl. Mrs. Spencer had walked in, a few minutes behind Benji, to hand Daniel a corsage for him to carefully slide onto Meade's wrist. Jerry, the physical therapy guy from the fourth floor, stood in the back corner, manning the boombox.

"Don't you worry," he called out to Meade, as she waved to him. "I made some great mix tapes for tonight!"

Meade had laughed and kissed Daniel again. Tonight was special. And she was going to make sure she paid attention to every single detail so that she'd never forget how wonderful their night had been.

Even Meade's mom surprised her, running into the rec room, once she'd found a place to park her car, to get in on a few of the photos with Meade and Daniel and his mom.

"I love you, baby," she said, kissing Meade, quickly on the cheek. "Have a good time. I'm really late for work now!" And she bolted out the door.

For once, Meade didn't blame her mom for not getting somewhere on time. Tonight, the woman had a great excuse. She hoped her mom's boss saw it that way, too.

Dancing had been a bit of a challenge. The slow dances had been the easy ones. Meade sat on Daniel's lap, her arms around his neck, as he used one of his hands to roll the wheelchair back and forth to the rhythms of the songs. They'd had to be creative, however, for the fast dances. For some songs, Meade stood and danced in front of Daniel—sometimes holding his hands as he did his best to shimmy and wiggle to the beat in his chair, and sometimes she danced alone in front of him as he laughed and clapped, never taking his eye off of her. Meade was beautiful tonight. It was obvious in the way Daniel kept staring at her. But, more than beautiful, she was happy. Joyfully and gleefully happy. She couldn't remember the last time she'd smiled so much. Her face practically ached from the grin that never left her face all night. And it felt great.

"Okay, lovebirds," Jerry called out to them, as Meade stopped dancing to grab her and Daniel cups of punch. *This dancing thing was exhausting.* "This is the last song. Let's make it a good one."

Meade and Daniel quickly downed their drinks as the first few bars of "You're the Inspiration" began to drift through the room. Though an older song, it was one of Meade's favorites. It always made her think of Daniel when it came on the radio. He truly was an inspiration—not only to her, but to anyone who knew him.

"Hey," Meade said, gently pushing Daniel's arm. "Did you pick this to be the last song?"

Daniel grinned up at her, handing her his empty cup. "Of course I did. I knew it would make your night!"

"And you were right," she said, as she placed their cups on the table and then went back to Daniel to sit on his lap. He put up his hand, though, to stop her from sitting.

"No, wait," he said. "For this song, I'm standing."

Meade looked at him with concerned eyes. Of course she wanted to dance with him —one dance —with him standing. *But, was it safe? Would it be too much of an effort for him?* She didn't want to cause him any more pain or problems than he already had.

"Are you sure?" she said hesitantly.

"Yes," he said firmly. "I'm sure. Help me up."

He placed one hand steadily on the armrest of the chair and put out his other arm to Meade. She gripped his forearm tightly as he shifted his weight and began to lean on her and the chair, evenly. It took a moment, and a couple of deep breaths, but faster than she thought he'd be able to manage it, Daniel was on his feet. Nancy came behind him to roll the chair off the makeshift dance floor. Meade gratefully smiled at her, and momentarily realized she'd forgotten the older woman was even still in the room. She and Daniel had been focused on no one but each other all evening long.

"Now, that wasn't so bad," Daniel said, a little out of breath. "Though, you might have to prop me up a bit for this one."

"No problem, babe," Meade said, wrapping her arms around his waist as he put his own around her. "I got your back."

"Literally," Daniel said, chuckling.

And then he rested his chin on the top of her head, as the two of them swayed to the music. Meade closed her eyes and breathed in his scent. He even smelled like Daniel tonight. Not like the hospital and its food and all his icky medicine. He smelled like Daniel. Her Daniel. She sighed as she inhaled.

*You bring meaning to my life, you're the inspiration...*

"I know you always tell me that this song is about me," Daniel whispered into her hair. "But really, I think of you every time I hear the words."

"Me?" Meade whispered back, startled. "Why me?"

"Because you inspire me. You motivate me to keep fighting. No matter how scary things get, I never worry that you won't be by my side. I need you, Meade. I couldn't handle all of this without you. You're the strength behind all of this—not me."

Meade lifted her head, so she could see into Daniel's eyes. He was looking down at her, lovingly.

"I love you, Daniel. I'll never leave."

"I know. I love you, too."

Neither one spoke for the rest of the song. They held each other and danced slowly, both lost in the memory of a perfect prom night. Neither of them would have changed a thing. Sure, it wasn't the same as going to the prom with all their friends. And, there would be no late-night after-party or weekend down at the Gulf Coast with the basketball team and their girlfriends, but it didn't matter. Not one bit. Tonight had been about Meade and Daniel and no one else. That truth, alone, made this night the best of either of their lives. And both of them knew they'd never forget it.

The last bars of the song faded away and Daniel bent down to kiss Meade one more time.

"Thank you for tonight," she said sincerely, as she helped him back down into his chair, which had somehow mysteriously appeared behind him by the song's end. She didn't know how he'd pulled it off or how any of the people involved had kept such a big secret, especially with all of the complaining and whining she had done in the preceding weeks. But everyone had and Meade would be eternally grateful to them for all they had done.

"You're welcome," Daniel said, beaming. It was clear he'd not only had a great night, but was really proud of himself, too—as he should have been. He'd pulled off a great prom, despite the circumstances. "You deserved a really great prom night."

"And I got one," Meade said, smiling.

The only part of the night that Meade didn't enjoy was that Daniel had asked her to say goodnight to him in the rec room and not follow him back to his room. He'd told her he didn't want her to have any hospital memories tonight, only prom ones. She'd protested, but he'd been insistent and, with all the effort he'd put forth, Meade didn't think it'd be fair of her not to obey his request. So, she'd kissed him goodbye at the door and then she and Benji had followed Mrs. Spencer out to her car so she could drive both Meade and her brother home.

"You and Daniel made a beautiful couple tonight," Mrs. Spencer said, as the car pulled onto the highway. "I wish his dad could have been here to see the two of you. He would have been so proud."

Meade smiled sadly at Daniel's mom. "I bet, somewhere out there, he saw us."

"I hope so," Mrs. Spencer whispered. "I really do."

Meade glanced into the backseat. Benji was already asleep, his head thrown back, his mouth open as he snored softly. It wasn't going to be fun trying to get him out of the car and into the house. Still, she couldn't help but smile when she looked at him. For a fourteen-year-old, he'd done a great job keeping such a big secret. He was truly a fantastic brother. In fact, Meade was surrounded by great people—

both in her family and Daniel's. She had great friends at school and, though she never would have guessed it, she and Daniel had made some incredible friends at the hospital, too.

As she rested her head on the car window, feeling the cool glass along the side of her happily flushed face, she realized how lucky she was. Life wasn't always easy these days. Sometimes, it downright sucked. But she was fortunate in many, many ways, and tonight—this most perfect of prom nights—was one evening when she realized she needed to sit back, relax and count her blessings. And, as she gazed out the window, into the star-filled Texas sky, Meade realized she had nearly too many to count.

# CHAPTER SIX
## July 2013

"You really should eat something," Ian said. "These Danishes are amazing."

Meade looked up from her book just in time to see Ian take an enormous bite out of a cherry-filled pastry, leaving some of the jelly on the side of his mouth.

"I'm not hungry," she said. "And you should probably go look in a mirror soon. It's almost time for your segment."

Ian sat back on the couch, propping the side of one of his ankles on the opposite knee. He took a sip of his coffee as he looked around. "Why do you think they call this the green room? I mean, it's kind of stone. Not even a real paint color. Definitely not green."

"I have no idea," Meade said, looking back down at her book. In the hour they'd been there, she hadn't even read a single page. To be honest, she hadn't really expected to get any reading done. She'd brought the book more to prove a point—that she wasn't needed there. This wasn't her job. Ian had a publicist for things like this. And, if his publicist was too busy—let's say, booking him on national television shows—then surely he made enough money to hire a babysitter to accompany him to his media appearances.

But Ian liked when Meade came with him. He more than liked it. He pretty much insisted on it. With any of her other authors, she would have delicately pawned them off on to a junior editor at the company, but Meade found she always made exceptions for Ian. There was something about him. It wasn't only his good looks and his charm—or the way he had become increasingly demanding of her time over the years. There was something more in him. She'd seen it the first day he'd walked into her office, when she'd asked him for a meeting after she'd read his first manuscript. Deep beneath the brilliant smile, the sparkling blue eyes, and the dimple that melted every woman in America, he was a little boy. Oh, he did a great job of hiding it. He was manly and muscular and sexual. He exuded self-confidence and security. But Meade knew something about him that she wasn't even sure he realized she recognized. He was insecure. Maybe not about the effect he had on women. He seemed to have full security in that fact. But, when it came to his writing, he was a bit unsure of himself.

As Ian got up to grab a chocolate chip muffin off the table, Meade thought back to how they'd first met. She hadn't been with Brownsbury for long. Less than a year—maybe a little bit longer. And she was trying to make a name for herself. Each night she'd take home stacks of manuscripts and stay up until just before dawn, reading and reading and reading. All the while she was praying that, somewhere in that pile, was the gem she was looking for—the book that would catapult its author—and her—to the pinnacle of the publishing world. She found some rough jewels along the way. No one could complain Meade Peterson wasn't pulling her weight and signing some really great authors. But, until then, no one had lit a fire in her belly. She hadn't found the manuscript that, no matter the hour of the night, she couldn't put down. Even the good ones—the ones she eventually published—were missing something. A spark. A hook. Some substance that went beneath the words.

She'd come home from another horrible date. The guy, John Smith, had been as bland as his name. She'd spent the night doing her best to conceal repetitive yawns, all the while wondering who, in their right mind, would name their child "John" when their last name was already "Smith." Creativity obviously didn't run in that family.

And it was apparent that trait hadn't fallen far from the proverbial apple tree. An accountant, he'd spent most of the evening explaining tax law to her. The most interesting thing John Smith said all night was that he collected bottle caps.

*Didn't someone on* Sesame Street *collect bottle caps?*

"I bet those are interesting to see," Meade said, perking up a bit. She wasn't really into collections—had never collected anything herself, not even in childhood—unless you counted the thirty Smurf figurines she'd gotten when she was in fourth grade. But, she thought the bottle caps might be interesting to look through—all the various pictures and designs on each one.

"Oh, well…" John Smith said, fidgeting in his seat, and suddenly visibly nervous. "I couldn't actually show them to you. I never show them to anyone."

"You don't?"

"Oh, no…I have some very valuable ones. I wouldn't want it to get out there that I owned them. Someone might hear about it and rob my house. Or worse, try to become my friend so they could have access to them."

*Was this guy for real?*

"You think someone might become your friend so they could have access to your *bottle caps?*" Meade said. She tried not to sound like she was mocking him, but inwardly, she really was doing just that.

"Oh, yes," John Smith said, shaking his head fervently. "People will do most anything to get their hands on something so valuable."

Meade would have done almost anything, at that moment, to get out of this date. She was sorry she hadn't asked a friend to call her in the middle of her evening so she could pretend there was an emergency she needed to get to immediately.

By the time she'd gotten home, Meade was exhausted. It had taken a lot of energy to hide her boredom with John Smith. She was dying to get in bed and forget about tonight altogether. She almost cried when she saw the stack of manuscripts that awaited her on the coffee table.

She was too tired to begin reading tonight.

But no one ever got anywhere in life without sacrifice. The thing she sacrificed most of all, these days, was sleep. Most nights she got only about three or four hours; sometimes it was less than that. Meade fondly remembered life as a high school student, when she would get ten hours minimum and maybe more on the weekends. Those had been the days and she hadn't even realized it.

Meade walked into the kitchen and turned on the tea kettle. While the water heated up on the stove, she took a hot shower and got into her warm flannel pajamas. Twenty minutes later, a mug of steaming herbal tea in her hand, she sank down on the couch and picked up the manuscript on top of the pile. *The Life I Once Had.*

By page five, she was no longer tired. She was wide awake. More than awake. Elated. Exuberant. Euphoric. She'd found it. She'd found *it*. The book she'd been looking for—night after night, month after month. The reason she could barely keep her eyes open in meetings all day long and why she turned down dinner dates and weekends away with her friends more times than not.

She'd found her book. The one she'd been dreaming of since she'd begun to imagine entering the publishing world. She looked back at the title page.

*Written by Ian Cooper.*

This Ian Cooper was hers and he didn't even know it yet.


The moment Ian Cooper walked into her office, taking her breath away with his good looks, Meade began to wonder if she was actually his and not the other way around.

How could such intelligent thoughts circulate in a head that exquisite? It almost wasn't fair. Most people had either one or the other—brains or beauty—if they were lucky enough to have one at all. Rarely did a human possess both.

But Ian Cooper did. And Meade had the evidence sitting on her desk. All 460 pages of it.

"Your book is exceptional," Meade said, as he took a seat in her office.

"Really?" He seemed stunned by her words, as if he'd expected her to tell him she thought it stunk.

"Yes. Really," Meade said. "That's why I called you in here." She rarely called an author into her office to deliver the good news. For one reason, the telephone usually sufficed. And secondly, most authors didn't live in the Tri-state area. Many were from the center of the country or the West Coast. A brief, in-office meeting wasn't exactly feasible. But she'd really wanted to meet Mr. Ian Cooper—not only call him on the phone. She wanted to meet this author—the one she knew, deep in her soul, she was going to have a strong partnership with—in person. And, luckily, it turned out that he lived in New York. It had been an easy meeting to set up. "We'd very much like to publish your book."

Ian jumped out of his chair. "You're kidding!"

Meade smiled. This was the best part of her job. Telling an author that he or she was about to become published for the first time. It never got old.

"I'm not kidding. We loved your story. It was so original. So intelligently written. So universal. I hope you'll agree to sign with us."

"Agree?" For a moment, Meade wondered if Ian might do a jig right there in her office. For a man who had walked into the room as cool as a cucumber, looking as if he owned the place, he was beginning to resemble a small child at a carnival for the very first time. "Of course, I'll agree. What do I need to do?"

"Well, we'll need to go over the contract. I could send you down to our legal department. They can go over it all with you this afternoon if you have some time."

Ian looked at his watch. "I can't do it today. I need to be at work in an hour. Can I come back tomorrow? It's my day off."

"Sure," Meade said. "Tomorrow's fine." And it was fine, but she would have felt better having the contract in hand today. She had a fear—however irrational—that another editor as hungry as she was would call him tonight and offer him a better deal. "Where do you work?"

"A bowling alley on Long Island."

"You work in a bowling alley?" Meade was startled. His book had read like poetry. She had presumed he was a professor somewhere, or perhaps, a literary student.

"Yep. Randall Lanes. If you come in, I can get you free shoe rentals."

"Thanks. Maybe I'll do that sometime. I like to bowl." Meade smiled at him. "Have you written any other books?"

"Nope. This was my first."

"Well, like I said, it's really, really good. Did you send it to many publishers?"

She gave herself a small, mental kick. She shouldn't have been asking, but she needed to know.

"Nope. Just you. My friend, Tommy, works in your mail department here. He said he'd get it to you for me."

Meade's smile broadened. *Tommy.* Of course. She had a vague recollection of him asking her, one day as he dropped off her mail, if she'd mind looking over the manuscript of a friend of his. That wasn't really how it was done. Most books came to her via an agent. And Meade usually refused—albeit gently—to accept manuscripts any other way. She didn't really want to waste her time on writing that hadn't already been vetted by a professional agent. But Tommy was such a nice guy. He always had a kind word for her when he stopped by her office and never failed to ask about her day or her family and give her suggestions on museums she should visit or restaurants she should try out. And whenever she was in a bind, needing to get something out in the mail, even late on a Friday afternoon, he never let her down—staying late if need be to help her out. She hadn't had the heart to turn him down when he'd asked her for a favor—the only one he'd ever posed. He'd given her the manuscript the next day and she'd never thought of it again. It had simply gotten lost in the enormous pile on her desk.

"Oh, yes. Tommy. He's a great guy. I'm so glad he gave me your book."

*And so glad you don't know any other mailroom employees in any of the other publishing companies.*

"I really need to be getting to work," Ian said, looking at his watch again.

"Oh, sure," Meade said, standing. "Thanks for coming in. I look forward to seeing you tomorrow."

Ian nodded, turned to leave and then looked back at Meade. "Can I ask you a question?"

Meade looked up from the chair into which she had just sunk back down. "Sure."

"Did you really like it? Is it really good?" His insecurity was so endearing. No one who looked like that would be expected to lack self-confidence in any area of his life. And yet, he did. Mr. Ian Cooper, whom Meade realized mid-meeting, had probably never even taken a college class, was unsure of his writing ability.

"It was awesome," she said. "I loved it. Other people are going to love it, too. Trust me."

Ian sighed deeply and smiled a dazzling grin that would have knocked Meade off her feet had she been standing. "Thanks."

And he had walked out her door—but into her life.

"You never eat at these things," Ian said, bringing Meade mentally back into the green room. "You really should. They always have the best food for shows like this."

"Are you still eating?" Meade said, looking up from her book. "Seriously. Sometimes I feel like your mother."

"A very hot mother."

Meade rolled her eyes at him. "I happen to know your mother. She's a very nice woman."

"And she loves you. She's always asking me if I've swept you off your feet yet."

Meade ignored him. The flirting had begun right after Ian made *The New York Times* Best Seller List with *The Life I Once Had*. The recognition had given him more confidence around Meade. Before that, he'd been like a puppy dog, doing anything and everything she asked of him. Once the book became a success, though, and he quit his job at the bowling alley— *"Turns out, writing pays more than minimum wage," he'd told her*—he'd begun to chat her up as if he'd just met her in a bar. And he became more demanding. *Much* more demanding. Of her. Of her time. Of her attention to him and his work.

Meade imagined most editors would have gotten annoyed with Ian by now and either told him to stop or find himself another editor. But Meade never did, and she had three reasons. One, and most importantly, was, he never took the flirting too far. Ian was never offensive in his playfulness toward her. Flattering. Fun-loving. Sexy. Yes, all of those things. But he was never rude or inappropriate. Secondly, he was still, to this day, her most successful author. He might have turned into a demanding diva who needed to be coddled, but she wasn't about to turn him over to anyone for anything. And thirdly, she enjoyed it. And him. She cared about Ian. She'd never date him or get involved with him emotionally. There was too much at stake to risk something going wrong in that department. But it never hurt to have one of *People Magazine*'s Most Beautiful People desire you and let you know it. What woman wouldn't appreciate that?

"Do I have to get a napkin and wipe your mouth myself?" Meade asked him.

"No, Mom. I'll do it." Ian went over to the food table and stuck the edge of a paper napkin in a cup of water, blotting the sides of his mouth with it. Turning to look at her, he asked, "Did I get it all?"

Meade inspected him carefully. She nodded.

He came over and sat down on the couch next to her. She could tell it was almost air time because his demeanor was changing. He always got nervous right before he went on camera. Not about how he looked. Even he knew he looked better on the air than he did in person—if that was possible. But, he was worried about his latest book. He was *always* worried about his latest book.

"Gail Renner said she read the book. When she came into the green room before, she said she read it last week. What if she hated it? What if her questions are about how much worse it is than all my others?"

Meade put a hand gently on his knee. "Ian, she's not going to say that. First of all, the book is wonderful. One of your best. You know I wouldn't lie to you about that. Secondly, this is a morning TV show. They aren't looking for an exposé. They aren't trying to humiliate you on national television. They want to inform their viewers of the new book out by the incredible Ian Cooper."

Ian smiled and seemed to relax.

"Ready, Mr. Cooper?" A young intern was standing in the doorway.

Meade could visually see Ian's entire persona change in front of her. While he'd seemed like an uncertain ten-year-old boy a moment earlier, the man sitting next to her was now confident, self-assured and handsome. Always very, very handsome.

"You bet," he said, standing up and winking at Meade. "Let's roll."

Meade watched as Ian left the green room. She could hear the screams, from the television monitor next to her, of the women standing outside the studio window as they panned the crowd. *"You can write my book any day,"* one of the signs they held up said. *"Tell me a bedtime story, Ian,"* another read.

Meade had to laugh. Ian knew how to connect with his audience—especially the women. And that connection meant book sales. Lots and lots of them for many years now.

Ian Cooper was the reason Meade was pretty sure she'd be able to retire early.

Meade's phone buzzed in her purse. Once Ian was on camera, she'd be inundated with texts from family and friends, saying they were watching him. Everyone, in Meade's world, at least, was aware Ian was Meade's find. And their excitement over her success always warmed her heart.

She was surprised to see the text was from Pantera. Unlike the others in her life, Pantera was not fazed by Ian or his success. If it wasn't on Meade's calendar, which Pantera ran, her assistant wouldn't even give two thoughts to Ian Cooper and his schedule. Meade was pretty sure her friend was the only woman in America who didn't swoon in Ian's presence.

*Blind date tomorrow. Ready?*

Tomorrow? Was Pantera kidding? Meade had only agreed to Pantera setting her up three nights ago.

*Uhm...no. What's the rush?*

*You're not getting any younger. Bryant Park. By the carousel. 11 am. I know your calendar is free. I'm in charge of it.*

Bryant Park? That was a weird place for a blind date. And eleven in the morning was even a stranger time.

Meade had a few friends with small kids who always talked about going on "play dates" with their children and other moms. That's what this felt like. Eleven in the morning in a park? It sure seemed like a "play date" to her.

*What's his name? How will I know it's him?*
*Oh, you'll know. Be there! Leave your broken picker at home.*


Meade sighed. This had seemed like a much better idea when she was licking her wounds over the France fiasco. She hated blind dates. Loathed them. Why had she ever agreed to letting Pantera set her up?

But, she had. And Meade was a woman of her word.

*Okay. I'll be there. He'd better be worth it.*

Meade could practically feel Pantera beaming through her phone. She'd won and she knew it.

*He is! You can thank me later.*

Meade doubted she'd be thanking Pantera at all, but it wouldn't kill her to meet this guy. And then, when the date ended up being disastrous, she could tell Pantera not to set her up again.

Not that Pantera would listen, of course. She never listened. But Meade could say it nonetheless.

# CHAPTER SEVEN
*June 1998*

"I'm starving," Meade said, stumbling into the kitchen. "What do we have for breakfast?"

"Nothing," Benji said, holding the last box of Cheerios upside down over his bowl. Three Cheerios fell into his bowl. "Why does Nick put the box back on the shelf when it's empty? Is it to tease us?"

"You'd think he'd be too lazy to even get up off the couch to put it on the shelf," Meade said, opening the door to the fridge to look inside. "Wow, it really is bare in here."

"Mom said she was gonna go grocery shopping last week, but I guess she didn't," Benji said, slumping into a chair at the kitchen table.

"There's gotta be something we can eat," Meade said, moving to the pantry and scanning the shelves. "Oh, wait. There's oatmeal." She reached inside to grab the box.

"Yuck," Benji moaned. "What don't you pour wallpaper paste into my bowl?"

"I may have to," Meade said, shaking the oatmeal container. "This is empty, too. Seriously? Has no one in this house ever heard of a trash can?"

"Or a grocery store?" Benji said, laying his head down on the table. "I'm going to waste away."

"You're not going to waste away. There's a jar of applesauce in here...oh, and some canned pumpkin!" Meade said, holding up her finds.

Benji wrinkled his nose at Meade. "And what...exactly...are we supposed to do with that?"

Meade shrugged. "Uhm...I'm not sure." And then she laughed at the absurdity of it all. "I think you're right. We are going to starve." She plopped herself down next to him.

"Mom!" they both cried out at the same time.

As if on cue, their mom appeared in the doorway to the kitchen, still wearing her bathrobe—the cordless telephone in her hand.

"There's nothing to eat!" Benji complained. "You said you'd go shopping last week!"

"Yeah, Mom!" Meade said, frustrated. Meade had heard the other kids at school talk about their parents and none of them had moms who forgot to grocery shop or, if not pack them a lunch, at least give them some money to buy their meal in the cafeteria. For years, Daniel's mom had packed him a huge lunch—much more than even Daniel, the human garbage disposal, as she liked to call him, could ever possibly eat. It wasn't until a few years into high school that Meade realized his mom did so because he'd share with Meade, thus guaranteeing she'd get at least one good, nutritious meal a day. But now, with Daniel not at school, Meade often found herself scrounging through the couch cushions, or the bottom of her mom's purse, to see if there was enough change for both her and Benji to buy something to sustain them at lunchtime.

It wasn't that her mom was a bad mom, per se. She loved her kids and all three of them knew that. She told them she loved them on a pretty regular basis. Neither Meade nor her brothers ever really doubted she cared *about* them—she wasn't exactly the type of mom who was good at caring *for* them. And, unfortunately, that was a problem. Especially when your stomach was grumbling.

"What are we supposed to eat for breakfast?" Benji whined. "Saltines and refried beans?"

Meade was about to chime in on her brother's inventory of their rather bleak pantry, when something about the look in her mother's eyes stopped her. It was as if she wasn't even listening to them. Usually, when Meade or her brothers complained, her mother smiled and laughed, as if what they said was actual music to her ears instead of laments over her questionable parenting skills. Today, though, Meade's mom seemed to not even hear them. She was in a world all her own.

"Mom," Meade said hesitantly. "What is it?"

Meade's mom came over to the kitchen table and sat in the empty chair across from Meade. She placed the phone down carefully on the table and then folded her hands in her lap, as if she didn't know what to do with them. A knot began to form in the pit of Meade's stomach, overtaking the growling that had begun from the hunger.

"What's going on?" Meade said, her voice revealing her fear. "What happened?"

Meade's mom looked up from the table, as if seeing Meade for the first time. As she looked into her mom's eyes, she noticed how green they were—a sure sign that her mom had been crying. Meade's mom's eyes were hazel, but when she cried, they turned a bright green. Meade had first noticed this trait when her dad left and she would often use it as a way to gauge her mom's mood and how her day had gone. If mom's eyes were hazel, tonight would be a good night. But if they were green...well, Meade hated when they were green. And, at the moment, they were emerald.

"You need to go to the hospital. It's Daniel."


Meade ran down the hallway to Daniel's room. Mrs. Spencer had been vague on the phone—or at least, Meade's mom had been vague in relaying what Daniel's mom had said. Meade didn't know the details, but understood the gist of the message—and it wasn't good.

Daniel had started to decline not long after their prom. At first, it wasn't really noticeable. He couldn't stay awake for a whole television show or he'd suddenly break out into a cold sweat, but neither of those things was incredibly alarming to Meade. But then, his weight continued to drop and he seemed to have a low-grade fever he couldn't shake. Some days, Meade would show up at his room after school and be startled at the number of bruises he had on his arms and legs. *Where could they have come from? It wasn't like he was walking around and banging into things.* In fact, these days, he was barely moving around at all.

She hadn't been really frightened, however, until two nights ago, when she and Daniel were watching *Conspiracy Theory* together. They were both so excited to see it—having missed it in the theater last year—and it had finally come out on video. Meade even arrived at the hospital earlier than usual on Saturday night, knowing Daniel would have a hard time staying up very late to see the end. She didn't want him to miss any of the movie. They'd both been talking about it much too long to miss a minute.

They were watching the scene where Mel Gibson tries to convince Julia Roberts that a good conspiracy theory is that which can't be proven, when all of a sudden, Daniel made a funny sound. Meade thought, at first, he was laughing at the silliness of the scene, but when she glanced over at him, she jumped out of her chair. Daniel was sitting, with his hands over the lower half of his face, and they were covered in blood.

"Oh my gosh," Meade said, running to the bathroom to grab a towel and then practically throwing it at him as she raced out into the hallway to find a nurse. Daniel had bled before—from his nose and his gums, but never like this. Never in such an excessive amount.

It took close to forty minutes to stop the nose bleed and then another thirty to get Daniel and the bed cleaned up. By the time the chaos had ended, it was certainly too late to watch the rest of the movie and, in truth, neither Meade nor Daniel had the stomach or energy for it anyway. Meade had kissed Daniel softly on the forehead, as he struggled to keep his eyes open to say goodnight to her and she'd tiptoed out of his room. She wasn't sure what had shifted in Daniel's health, but something had. And it was bad.

Today, as Meade entered the room, she headed straight for the bathroom to wash her hands before even heading over to Daniel in the bed. She'd always been careful of bringing as few germs into his room as possible—his immune system couldn't handle it—but these days, she was extra cautious. She looked at herself in the mirror, over the tiny sink, as she scrubbed. Forcing herself to put on a smile, despite the fear and sadness in her eyes, she dried her hands on a paper towel, threw it in the trash and walked back into Daniel's room.

She stood quietly for a moment before moving over to him. Mrs. Spencer was sitting by his side, talking softly to him, rubbing his hand. She looked up at Meade and whispered something to Daniel that must have been, "Meade's here," though Meade couldn't hear her over the whirring of all of the machines. Daniel slowly turned his head, with much effort, toward Meade and smiled.

That smile. How could something so simple be so glorious? Even sitting in the midst of his swollen face, distorted by the chemo, Daniel still had the most beautiful of smiles. A glimpse of it caused Meade to disregard all the wires that were attached to seemingly every part of his body. *Where had they all come from?* She didn't remember there being so many of them yesterday afternoon when she'd hurried in to say hello to him before heading to take Benji to his swim team practice. But today...Daniel was covered in wires and tubes. Meade wondered how she was going to get close to him without risking pulling one out.

"Hey, babe," Daniel whispered as she sat down next to him, taking his other hand in hers. "Fancy meeting you here."

Meade kept the fake smile on her face, though it was killing her. Daniel looked so pale. He was full of blood. She'd seen how it could pour out of him, so why did it seem like none of it ever reached his face anymore?

"Hey," she whispered back. "I hear you're not feeling so hot today."

Mrs. Spencer stood up and excused herself. She said while Meade was there with Daniel, she was going to go get herself something to eat and try to rest a bit. She'd been spending every night at the hospital with her son and, as Meade turned to watch her go, she saw that the stress and sleepless nights were taking a toll on the older woman. She'd always stood tall, showing all of her six-foot height proudly, but now Meade noticed how hunched over she looked as she practically shuffled out of the room.

Meade turned her attention back to Daniel. "Do you want some water? Ice chips?"

He shook his head, very slowly, as if the very effort hurt. He closed his eyes.

Meade stroked up and down Daniel's arm, gently. Too much pressure had become quite painful for him so she was always mindful to make her touch soft. She looked across the room at the window. The large ledge in front of the glass was full of floral displays, all from students and teachers and families at the school, wishing Daniel the best. Alongside them were dozens of get well cards. Sometimes, when the shelf became too full, Meade would take down the older cards, in order to make room for the new ones. Early in his illness, she'd started a scrapbook for all of the well wishes, where she neatly glued each card inside. She'd thought it might be something Daniel would like to look back on someday, to remember his struggle and how he'd persevered. As his illness progressed, however, and seemed to turn for the worse, Meade had stopped the scrapbook and instead, threw the older cards in a shoebox on the floor. She wondered if someday she and his mom would throw them out altogether.

"The bone marrow drive is going on right now," Meade said, trying to make her voice sound as light and carefree as possible. "Lori called me from school, before I left to come here, to say there were hundreds of kids and parents in line to get tested. We're gonna find you a match. Hang on, okay?"

Daniel didn't move, but Meade was pretty sure he was still awake and listening to her. This bone marrow drive was their last hope and both she and Daniel knew it. Daniel needed a bone marrow transplant. He had needed one for months, but so far, they hadn't been able to find a match. The fact that Daniel didn't have any siblings was a problem and his mom's marrow had proven to not be compatible. Meade and Nick, even her mom, had been tested, but no luck. Benji, who wasn't yet eighteen, had been devastated he couldn't even be tested. And Lori...Meade felt a tinge of annoyance when she thought about her friend, but pushed it back down again. Lori had agreed to be tested, too. But, on the day the test was supposed to be done, Lori had called Meade to say she couldn't make it.

"You're never going to believe what just happened!" Lori nearly had shrieked into the phone.

"What?" Meade had said, searching the house for the car keys as she listened to Lori.

Meade's mom had lost them—again. She was always losing things—her keys, her purse, important phone numbers. It was a wonder she'd never lost any of her three children when they were growing up.

"Brandon Keller asked me out!" Lori nearly had screamed into the phone. "Do you believe it? He knows I'm alive!"

Meade had to smile at Lori's enthusiasm. A part of her wanted to tell Lori she was overreacting—that, of course, Brandon Keller knew she was alive. But, to be honest, Meade was kind of surprised he did. She, like Lori, had thought any chance of him even talking to Lori was slim to non-existent.

"That's great!" Meade had said, pulling up the couch cushions. "When's the date?"

"In thirty minutes!"

That stopped Meade from reaching her hand down into the back of the couch. "Now? But, you're supposed to be meeting me at the hospital to get tested. We have an appointment in the lab in less than an hour."

"I know. I know. But, he invited me to go with him and some of his friends boating on the lake. He's picking me up in a half hour."

"But ..."

"Listen, ask the lab if I can come in on Monday. Or another day next week. I promise I'm going to get tested. And besides, the chance of me being a match are so slim anyway...I don't want to miss out on this. What if he never asks me out again?"

Meade's shoulders dropped. She didn't know what to say to Lori. She understood her friend's point-of-view. Lori had waited years for Brandon to ask her out. But Daniel needed a bone marrow transplant. Desperately.

"Okay," Meade had said quietly. "But promise me you'll get tested."

"Of course I will!" The glee had been apparent in her voice. "I wouldn't let you and Daniel down. Just not today. Wish me luck."

"Good luck."

That had been two weeks ago. When the results came back that no one in Meade's family was a match, the school had decided to hold its own drive this weekend. Lori, who was now spending nearly every waking moment with Brandon, had said she'd wait until the drive to be tested. Something about that irked Meade. Lori was her best friend. It wasn't that Meade wasn't happy for Lori, but Meade felt Lori owed it to Daniel, if not her, to get tested sooner. But all Lori was thinking about these days was Brandon Keller. And in the end, even Meade realized it probably wouldn't matter. Lori being a perfect match was such a long shot. A one in twenty-thousand chance. She might as well have her fun with Brandon. After all, the odds of him asking her out had been as bad.

"Someone in that crowd has to have the same type of bone marrow as you, right?" Meade said, gently rubbing the back of her fingers on Daniel's cheek.

Meade thought she saw Daniel nod slightly but wasn't sure. She'd become attuned to looking at him for the slightest of movements, or shifts in expression, in order to understand and meet his needs. She felt she was actually quite good at it. After all, no one—maybe not even his own mom—had spent as much time, over the years, studying every inch of Daniel—as he sat, or studied, or walked to class, or held her hand as they watched TV. If Meade knew anything, she knew Daniel. But these days, it was getting harder and harder to read Daniel. And, as for the needs he had, Meade had no idea, any longer, how to meet them, and it frightened her.

She let go of his hand and rested her head on the bed next to it, closing her eyes. She'd never been a very religious person. Her mom had never bothered to take her and her brothers to church over the years, and so, Meade didn't know much about God and how He worked. But, these days, Meade found herself praying a whole lot. *Please, God. Please let him get better. Please let us find a match. Please don't take him away from me.*

Meade felt a gentle touch on her head as Daniel began to stroke her hair. *Did he know what she was praying? Was he praying it, too?*

"Lie with me?" Daniel asked, his voice a hoarse whisper.

Meade sat up slowly, wiping away her tears before she lifted her head toward Daniel. He knew she cried. How could he not? But she still tried to not let him see her do so if she could help it. It wasn't that she didn't want him to know she was scared. Gosh, they were all frightened to death. It was that Daniel was such an empathetic person, especially when it came to her, that she didn't feel he needed to worry about her—or feel her pain—on top of his own.

"How am I supposed to do that?" Meade said lightheartedly, as she surveyed the dozens of wires and tubes that protruded from Daniel and lay across his bed. "It looks like it's pretty crowded in there already."

"Yeah," Daniel said, each word an effort. "And these wires are pretty sexy. You should be worried."

Meade smiled at his joke. If he could tease, he was still her Daniel.

"Okay, then..." Meade said, carefully lifting a few of the cords up that were on his left side and sliding her head underneath them, maneuvering until her body was horizontal with his. She placed herself carefully next to him, lifting her feet onto the bed, and then rested the wires back down on her hip. She wished she could rest her head on his shoulder, with his arm underneath her, as they'd done a thousand times before, but the pressure of her head would hurt him too much, so she settled with resting it on the pillow next to him.

The two of them lay next to each other, in silence, for a long time. Meade wondered what Daniel was thinking. *Was he even thinking or had he already fallen asleep?* She wasn't sure. All she could think about was how good it felt to be next to him—to hear each of his breaths, to know he was still with her.

"Will you always love me?"

Daniel's question caught Meade by surprise. She had thought he'd been snoring softly, though perhaps the noise she'd heard was the wheezing from his labored breathing.

"Of course," she replied.

"No," Daniel said carefully and deliberately. "I mean, when I'm gone. Will you still always love me?"

Meade caught her breath. "That's not going to happen."

For a moment, Daniel was completely silent, but he hadn't fallen asleep this time.

"I think it is, babe," Daniel said sadly. "It is."

Meade couldn't stop the tears that began to pour out of her eyes onto the pillow. It wouldn't be long before Daniel felt them reach the side of his face, but this time, it was okay to let him see her tears. There was no longer any hiding them. Though she wanted to protest again and again to tell him to stop talking such nonsense, she also was aware if they didn't have this talk now, they may never again have a chance to have it. And it was one she recognized, deep in her soul, both of them needed to have.

"I will always love you, Daniel. Nothing will ever change that," Meade said, a tear running down her face.

Daniel reached over his body, gingerly, with his right hand, and put it on Meade's shoulder. She snuggled her face closer to his, until her forehead and her nose touched the side of his cheek.

"Will I always be the love of your life?" he asked. Meade hated to hear the sadness in his voice.

"Yes. The love of my life."

"Promise me."

It was an easy promise to make. The "I promise" simply fell off Meade's lips. Of course he would always be the love of her life. The thought that she could love someone else—even a tenth of how much she loved Daniel—well, it was inconceivable. There would be no other loves for Meade. No other men who would make her heart spin and her eyes glow and her breath catch. Daniel was it. Her one and only. She knew that. He needed to know that, too.

"Daniel Spencer," Meade said, lifting her face so her lips could whisper directly into his ear. "I will love you, with all my heart, until the day I die. You and me, we're going to be together again someday. I don't know how Heaven works, but I know you're going there, so wait for me, babe. Wait for me. And I...will wait...for you."

Meade could barely get the last words out—the thought that there would come a time when she and Daniel were no longer together. It broke Meade's heart into a million pieces. But it was coming. And by the deep, though shaky, breath Daniel took when she stopped speaking, he knew it, too.

Daniel opened his eyes, but didn't turn them to Meade. He looked up at the ceiling of the room, as if there was a bug crawling on it or a photo taped up there, but Meade sensed he wasn't seeing the ceiling at all, but something else.

"I'll be waiting," he said softly. "I promise, too."

And then he closed his eyes again. Meade lay next to him for the next few hours, though it felt like merely minutes. A few times, she poked him lightly and said, "Daniel?" but he didn't reply. By the time his mom came back in, Daniel had been sleeping for quite a while and Meade carefully extracted herself from his bed and the wires.

"I'm going to get a drink," she told his mom, who nodded to Meade as she once again took up her vigil at her son's bedside. Meade looked over at them—mother and son. They were a team and had been for many, many years. It had always been only the two of them. Meade sadly wondered if soon, Mrs. Spencer would be all alone.

Meade had been sitting at the cafeteria table for about forty minutes, playing with the wrapper of her straw, when Nancy came downstairs.

"Sugar," the older woman said gently. "You need to come upstairs now. It's almost time."

*Time for what?* Meade wanted to ask. But she didn't. She knew. For a moment, she wondered, if she refused to leave her seat, if she continued to sit there and make spit balls with the paper from her straw, would it cause time to stand still? Would the inevitable never come because she refused to make room for it in her life?

But that wasn't how life worked. Daniel was going to leave them. Very soon. And if she didn't get up right now, and grab onto Nancy's hand as the older woman led her through the hospital corridors, she would lose her chance to say goodbye.

Meade rose and, holding tightly onto Nancy, made her way to Daniel's room. Mrs. Spencer was crying—not as softly as she usually did. Meade could hear her the moment she pushed open the hospital door. Daniel's mom looked up at Meade, as she walked in, and then back at her son again.

"The nurses say we should tell him it's okay to go," she said to Meade, never taking her eyes off her son. Meade saw his breathing had become much more labored in the short time she'd been gone and he was giving off a rattling noise with each intake of breath. "But I don't know how I can..."

Meade had imagined this moment. A thousand times, though she'd never admit to Daniel or his mom or even her closest girlfriend that she'd ever even contemplated it would ever come to this. But she had. She'd wondered what she'd feel. *Would she sob? Would she scream and grab Daniel and beg him not to leave? Would she collapse on his bed?*

But standing there, looking at him, and then looking at her mom, she knew she'd do none of those things. Oh, there would be a time for all of that. She couldn't say for certain she wouldn't be able to resist throwing herself into the grave with Daniel when the time came. But, now...here...in this room...she had a job to do. Daniel needed her. And his mom did, too.

"It's okay," Meade said calmly, her eyes brimming with tears, but not overflowing with them. "It's okay." Meade sat down next to his mom and put her hand on the woman's back.

"We can do it," she told the woman who had become like a mom to her. "We need to do it. He needs to know we'll be okay. You know he won't leave us if he thinks we won't be okay...and we can't keep him here like this."

Daniel's mom nodded as the tears poured down onto her corduroy slacks. She sobbed softly. "He's my baby."

"I know." Meade said gently. "I know."

"You do it. You tell him. I can't."

And so, Meade did. She stood up and put her hand gently on the side of his face. She leaned down next to him and kissed his cheek and then his lips. She ran her hand over his head, wishing there were still curls there for her to stroke, remembering all the times she'd thought he looked like an angel. And now, soon, he would be one.

She told him how much she loved him and how his mom thought he hung the moon. She told him there had never been a better or kinder or more loving man on this earth. She told him he would live in their hearts for the rest of their lives and that not a day would go by that they didn't miss him and love him and wish he were there. But...it was time to go. He needed to go. And he didn't need to worry—not about her or his mom or about anyone he was leaving behind. They would be okay. They understood. They didn't blame him. They felt nothing but love for him.

As Meade stroked Daniel's face, she wondered if he even heard her. Nancy had said he could, but Meade wasn't so sure. She was about to tell him, once again, that it was okay for him to go, when Daniel suddenly opened his eyes. He stared straight ahead, and for the rest of her life, Meade would never forget the look of peace—and joy—that filled his face. *What was he seeing? Was it his dad?*

And then, as if breathing a deep sigh of relief, surrounded by his mom and Meade—the two people who loved him most in this world—Daniel took his last breath and was gone.

As Meade and Daniel's mom sat in silence, trying to make sense of what they'd just experienced, Nancy came up behind them. Meade hadn't realized the woman was in the room. She'd been so consumed with Daniel and giving him peace.

Meade looked up at the nurse, assuming she was approaching to check Daniel's vitals, to make sure he was really gone. But, instead, Nancy walked over to the window and opened it.

And though Meade wasn't certain, she thought she felt Daniel's spirit gently brush the skin of her cheek as he passed by and into the night.

# CHAPTER EIGHT

July 2013

It took Meade thirty-eight seconds to spot her date. He was standing by the carousel, watching the kids go round and round. He was clearly out of place. Black leather pants, Metallica T-shirt, long, greasy hair down to his mid-back. As Meade got closer, she noticed that he, like Pantera, had a tongue ring, though his looked a whole lot pointier. The holes in his ears were disproportionately large, since he was wearing those enormous round earrings that stretched them out.

*What were they called? Gauges?*

Pantera knew Meade hated those and felt faint when looking at those massive holes.

*Was he wearing black eyeliner?*

She could see the moms, standing nearby, giving him nervous looks.

*Seriously, Pantera? This is what a non-broken picker picks?*

Meade had to fight the urge to take out her phone and peck into it, "You are out of your mind!" But, she loved Pantera and didn't want to hurt her feelings. After all, her friend was trying to help.

Meade walked up to the man and tapped him on the shoulder. He turned and looked at her.

*Yep. He was definitely wearing eyeliner.*

"Hi," she said. "I think you're looking for me."

"I am?" He seemed confused.

"Yes. I'm Meade. Pantera said to meet you here."

The man opened his tongue-ring-filled mouth to say something, when a little girl, dressed all in pink, ran up to them.

"Daddy! Daddy! Did you see me?" she squealed in delight.

*Daddy? He brought his child on the blind date?*

"I did see you, sweetie. You went around so fast! Was it fun?"

"Yes! Yes! Can I go again?"

The man shrugged his shoulders. "Sure. Let's go get you another ticket."

He turned back to Meade. "I'm sorry. I think you have the wrong person."

Meade could feel her face flush. "So, you're not here for a blind date?"

"No. I'm here to hang out with my daughter."

Meade glanced down at the little girl who was clearly getting impatient with this woman taking up her dad's time. Meade looked back at the dad. This was clearly one example of how you could never judge a book by its cover. Never, in a million years, would she have thought this heavy metal dad belonged to the pretty-in-pink little girl. She could imagine how back-to-school night went for them.

"I'm so sorry. How embarrassing."

"No problem," he said, as he took his daughter's hand and they walked away, toward the ticket booth.

Meade turned around and scanned the crowd. If Mr. Marilyn Manson wasn't her date, then who was? She didn't see any obvious choices from the crowd and no one seemed to be walking around in search of her. After a moment, she went and sat down at one of the little café tables.

Meade loved Bryant Park. Many New Yorkers were partial to Central Park, but to her, Bryant was so much more enticing—so charming—with its carousel and street performers. She loved, on a Sunday morning, to go there and grab a coffee or an ice-cold lemonade and read the paper, right at one of the small tables, looking up every once in a while to watch the carousel go round and round.

Her date couldn't be all bad if he'd picked Bryant Park to meet.

"Is this seat taken?"

Meade looked up to see a well-dressed man, in khakis and a light-blue, button-up shirt, standing in front of her. "Well…" she hesitated. "I'm sort of waiting for someone."

"Someone handsome?" he asked with a grin.

Meade shrugged. "Highly unlikely," she mumbled.

The man laughed. Not a chuckle, but a deep laugh.

Meade gave him a quizzical look. For a moment she wondered if he was mentally ill. Despite his clean-cut look, you never knew these days.

"Well, I hope I'm ugly enough for you," he said.

"Excuse me?"

"I was going to sit down next to you and pretend that this was a chance encounter, but to tell you the truth, I'm your blind date."

"You're my date?" Meade said, looking him up and down.

"Not what you were expecting?"

"I didn't know Pantera knew anyone who looked like you."

"Good point. Then again, you don't look that much different than me—other than you're a woman and much, much more beautiful, of course."

"I'm her boss," Meade said, as if that explained it all.

"Well, I'm her guitar teacher."

"Aaaah…her guitar teacher. You're a *musician*."

"Do you mind if I sit down?" he asked. "Or, I could keep standing here, if you like, until you decide if I pass muster."

Meade shrugged. "You can sit."

"So, I pass?"

"Sure, I guess."

"What does that even mean, anyway?" he asked. "Pass muster."

"I have no idea."

"So, do you not like musicians?"

"They're okay. Why?"

"The way you said it. You're a *musician*...like you were really say-ing, 'Oh, you're one of *those*...'"

Meade blushed, embarrassed. "I'm sorry. Musicians are fine."

"Just not your thing?"

"They're not *not* my thing."

"A double negative. I didn't know book editors used those."

"You seem to know a lot more about me than I know about you."

The man smiled. He had a nice smile. Not stunning, but nice.

"I do, don't I? It's kind of fun that way."

"Fun for whom?"

"Me, of course. After all, isn't this date all about me?"

Meade wasn't sure at first whether or not he was serious. He must have been able to tell what she was thinking, though, as he burst out laughing.

"I'm kidding. I'm not that big of a pompous ass."

"How big of one are you?"

"Big enough to get me in trouble every once in a while." He smiled again. "By the way, I'm Tanner. Tanner Dale." He put out his hand and Meade shook it.

"I'm Meade."

"I know."

"Apparently, you do. How did you know which woman I was?"

"Pantera told me to find the most beautiful woman in the park and that would be my date. I did and you are."

"She did not."

"She did!" he said, his hand in the air as if he was about to take the stand in a trial. "And she also texted me a picture."

Meade chuckled.

"Do you come here often?" Tanner asked.

"That's quite the creative pick-up line."

"Thanks. I wrote it myself."

"I actually do," Meade said, looking around the park. It was getting more crowded. There were people sitting on the grass. Kids running around, playing tag. She could see a yoga class on the far side of the lawn, lying on their mats. "I love to come here to be alone."

"Oh no! I guess I ruined that for you."

Meade put her hand to her mouth in embarrassment. "I'm sorry. I didn't mean it that way."

"Listen," Tanner said, leaning in closer to her. "This is awkward and uncomfortable. I get it. The beginning of any first date is painful and when it's a blind date...well, that takes on a whole new level of agony. Can we skip straight to the middle?"

"The middle?"

"Yes. The middle. Let's pretend we already talked about where we're from and what we do for a living and where we went to college. By the way, I did go to college, in case you're worried."

"I wasn't."

"Yes, you were," he said, with a knowing smile.

"Okay," Meade said, blushing. "Maybe a little."

"And let's move to the middle of our date."

"What happens in the middle?"

Tanner looked around him, biting his lip, slightly, as if he was deep in thought. Suddenly, he snapped his fingers. "I've got it. I'm going to walk over to that stand and get us something to drink—something cold, okay? It's getting pretty warm out here. And then, let's go for a walk."

"Where to?"

"Nowhere. Anywhere. You decide how far you want to walk with me. If you've had enough of me by the time we get to the other side of the park, then tell me. Or, we can walk to Brooklyn. Your call."

"Brooklyn!?"

"Sure. Why not? I have nowhere else I have to be today. Do you?"

Meade hesitated.

"Never mind. Don't answer that. If you decide you don't like me, then you can tell me you have somewhere else you have to be."

"But that's awful! What if I do have somewhere I have to be? When I tell you, you'll think I'm blowing you off."

"Nope. I promise. I won't. I'll believe you with all of my heart."

Meade looked at him suspiciously. She wasn't sure if he was charming or a smart ass, but she was willing to give him some time so she could figure it out. "Okay, you have a deal."

"What do you want to drink?"

"Surprise me."

"Wow. A woman who lives on the edge. I like it." He stood up. "I'll be right back."

Meade watched him walk away. She didn't quite know what to make of him. He was attractive. Pantera hadn't let her down in that department. He wasn't her "type," exactly. Generally, Meade was drawn to more exotic types, with dark skin and eyes. Tanner was fair in complexion and his hair was a dirty blond. She'd had a hard time not staring into his eyes as they chatted. Not that she was lost in them— she was worried he might think that—but they were such a bright blue. She wondered if that could be his real color or if he was wearing some sort of bright contact lenses. She stared at his back as he ordered their drinks. He wasn't exceptionally tall, but still much taller than she. She estimated him to be at least five ten. All in all, Pantera had done a pretty good job. He wasn't hard on the eyes.

But he wasn't the easiest person to read. She hadn't been sure, during their brief conversation, if he was teasing her or serious. With most people, that would annoy her. Meade was a pretty straightforward person. She liked to know what she was getting right from the start—whether it be a pizza or a man. Even allowing him to choose her drink had been out of her comfort zone. She didn't like surprises. And she had a feeling Tanner Dale was a man full of the unexpected. It intrigued her. But it also made her a bit nervous.

"Pick a hand," Tanner said, suddenly standing in front of her. His arms were behind his back.

Meade pointed to his left and he brought it around, revealing a frozen lemonade.

"What's in your right hand?"

"Not satisfied with your beverage choice?" he teased. He brought his other hand forward. "An iced coffee. Which would you like?"

"The lemonade."

"Good choice." He handed her the frosty drink. "Ready to walk?"

Meade nodded as she stood. She took a sip of her drink. "Ow!"

"Brain freeze?"

Meade nodded.

"Put your tongue on the roof of your mouth and hold it there."

Meade did as he said and within a few seconds, she felt the pain begin to subside.

"Better?"

"Yes. Thanks. How did you know to do that?"

"I'm partial to the Slurpees at Seven-Eleven. I've had my share of brain freezes over the years."

"How's your iced coffee?"

"Great. But we're done with all that."

"Done with what?"

"Small talk. It's time to delve deeper."

"Deeper into what?"

"Each other," Tanner said, gently holding onto her elbow as they crossed Forty-second Street. "So, tell me. What's your worst habit?"

"Seriously? That's the first thing you want to start with? My worst habit?"

"Let's get all the bad stuff out of the way right from the start. That way, we don't have to worry about it popping up later."

Meade took another sip of her drink. "Hmmm..."

"Okay, I'll go first. It's only fair. I still suck my thumb."

Meade stopped walking and nearly got run over by the man behind her. Tanner grabbed her arm to pull her out of the way.

"You can't just stop walking in the middle of a New York City sidewalk. How long have you lived here that you don't know that?"

"Are you serious?"

"Yes! You could get caught in a stampede!"

"Not about stopping. About thumb sucking!"

*What kind of weirdo was he?*

Tanner gave her a big smile. "Okay, I may have been exaggerating that one. Though I have been known to rip a hangnail off with my teeth every once in a while. Come on." He motioned for Meade to start walking again. "I have a sweet tooth. A horrible diet. It's terrible. I would prefer to eat a Pop Tart over an avocado any day."

Meade looked up and down his slim figure. "You don't look like you eat Pop Tarts."

"I am deceptively fit. Thanks to my parents, I have a great metabolism. I also don't work out all that much, but I never seem to gain weight, no matter how many Ring Dings and Twinkies I consume."

"I'm beginning to see why you and Pantera are friends."

"We have been known to hang out over a box of Ho Hos."

Meade had to smile.

"Okay, now your turn. Bad habit."

Meade thought for a moment as they walked. Coming up with a bad habit—one that wouldn't completely embarrass you on the first date—wasn't easy.

"I'm a little bit addicted to reality TV."

"A little bit?" Tanner eyed her, carefully, as they walked up the street.

"Okay. A lot addicted."

"Give me an example of a show you might watch."

"Well...I like *Survivor. And Millionaire Matchmaker. The Biggest Loser. Shark Tank. The Bachelor.* Uhm...let me think . . ."

Tanner laughed. "There's more? How could there be any more? I thought you were some big-shot editor. How do you possibly have time to watch all of those shows?"

"I DVR them. Usually I watch them around two in the morning, when I can't sleep."

"Okay, tell me...let's take one...how about *The Bachelor.* What could you possibly find redeeming about a show like that? They never find true love."

"They do! Well, not all the time, but sometimes they do." Meade found herself becoming animated as she spoke. "Take this one bachelor, for example. I don't remember his name. But he chose one girl and then, in the time between him proposing to her and the final show airing, he realized he'd made a mistake and picked the wrong woman! So, on national live TV, he dumped her and then professed his undying love to the other one. America was horrified, though he and the second woman did end up getting married, I think."

"*America* was horrified?" Now it was Tanner who stopped walking. "*America?* Please tell me you didn't just say that!" He began to laugh. Not a small laugh, like he found her slightly amusing, but a deep laugh. The kind of laugh that might eventually lead to tears pouring out of your eyes.

She lightly slapped him on the arm. "What? I'm serious!"

"I know!" he said, laughing even harder. "That what's so funny about it."

"America *was* horrified!"

"Whose America is that?"

"Well...mine, I guess. The America that watches reality TV." She was beginning to see the absurdity in what she'd just said. "Those people were horrified."

"And those people represent all of America?" Meade smiled then and, though she tried her best, she couldn't help laughing, too.

"Okay...okay. I may have exaggerated a bit. Come on." Now she was the one to motion him to keep walking. "You're going to get run over if you keep standing there, laughing at me."

"I'm not laughing at you. I'm laughing..."

Meade gave him the evil eye.

"Okay. I'm totally laughing at you. I'm sorry." Tanner appeared to attempt to stop laughing. "That's really rude of me on a first date. I'll stop."

Meade tried to look as annoyed with him as possible. It was rude to laugh at your date in the first twenty minutes you met her. But he was also right. What she had said had sounded a bit silly.

"It's okay. I forgive you."

"Thanks," Tanner said, wiping the corner of his eyes. "Okay, your turn. Ask me a question."

"Tell me an embarrassing story from your childhood," Meade said, sipping on her drink.

"An embarrassing story...are you going to tell me one first?"

"No. Why would I?"

"Well, I told you one first with my question."

"This is your game. You always go first."

"Oh...I see how it is." He winked at her. "Okay, give me a second to think." They walked in silence for a few minutes. "Got one. When I was a kid, my dad would sometimes get to travel for work, to really nice hotels and he'd take all of us with him."

"How many is all of us?"

"Me, my mom and my four siblings."

"Wow, big family."

"Tell me about it," Tanner said it like they overwhelmed him, but Meade could tell, by the twinkle in his eye, he was extremely fond of his family. "Anyway, we didn't have a whole lot of money. My dad made a good salary, but five kids is a lot. And so, we never seemed to have extra money for vacations or anything like that. But if my dad had a business trip, and we could all cram into his hotel room, then we'd get to tag along."

"So, it was embarrassing to all squish into a hotel room?"

"No, smarty pants. I'm getting to the embarrassing part. Because it's expensive to feed seven people—or, I guess six, since my dad's meals were covered by work—my mom would pack food for us to eat in the hotel room so we wouldn't have to eat out in restaurants. Cereal, fruit, snacks...things like that."

"And that embarrassed you?"

"You are a very impatient woman!"

"All right! All right! I'll shut up."

"The embarrassing part, Ms. I-can't-wait-for-the-climax-of-the-story, is that we'd all be walking into the fancy hotel lobby, carrying our suitcases and the bags of food my mom had packed, and my dad would follow us in, carrying a toaster oven, right through all the people in the lobby."

"No! He did not."

Once again, Tanner put up his hand as if he was making a pledge. "Honest to goodness. A toaster oven. And, when we were kids, toaster ovens were huge! Not like the small one I have on my kitchen counter now. It was like carrying in a whole kitchen stove."

Meade tried to contain her laughter, but she couldn't. "Oh, that's bad."

"Mortifying."

"I don't think I can beat that one."

The two of them had been walking aimlessly down the city streets.

It didn't seem like they were moving in any particular direction. Every once in a while, Tanner would motion for her to cross a street or turn a corner, but other than that, they seemed to be walking for the sake of walking. They had no destination.

"Want to sit?"

Meade looked up and saw that they were on the sidewalk in front of the New York Public Library. "Sit where?"

"On the steps." Without waiting for her to reply, he began to walk up them. Meade followed behind.

When they got near the top, Tanner sat down and tapped the spot next to him. Meade sat down and leaned her elbows on her knees.

"This is a great place to people watch," she said.

"It sure is. You could sit up here for hours and watch all of New York pass in front of you."

"Oh, look! A wedding!" Meade pointed to the street where a bridal party was carefully piling out of a limousine. The bride was the last to step out, as her bridesmaids delicately held her train.

Meade and Tanner watched as the group made their way up the steps, while the photographer posed them.

"What a beautiful place to take wedding photos," Meade said.

"How about when we get married, we come back here and take our pictures on these steps?"

"When we get married? Aren't you jumping the gun a bit?"

"I don't know. I've seen how you've been looking at me today. I think you're really into me."

"First of all, we've been walking," Meade said, doing her best to sound indignant. "I haven't been looking at you at all. I've been looking straight ahead."

"I don't know," Tanner said, a glimmer in his eyes. "I saw you peeking over at me a few times."

"Are you always this sure of yourself?"

"Nope. Usually I'm more cocky. I'm trying to play it low-key for our first date."

Meade didn't want to, but found she had to smile. There was something so outrageous about Tanner. If you simply read the words coming out of his mouth, you might think he was a complete jerk. But with his contagious grin and the sparkle in his distractingly blue eyes, it was difficult to not smile along with him.

"You still haven't told me your embarrassing childhood memory," Tanner reminded her.

"Oh, haven't I?" Meade said, her voice fading off. "Really? I thought I did."

"Nope. I'm still waiting."

Meade sighed dramatically. "Okay. Fine. Here it is. When I was in high school, I went on a field trip with the debate club."

"You were in the debate club?"

"Yes. Don't argue with me. You'll never win."

"I wouldn't think of it," Tanner said.

"Anyway, the coach decided we should bring a picnic lunch, but instead of everyone bringing their own separate lunch, he had a sign-up sheet and we were each supposed to volunteer to bring something off the list—fruit, cookies, drinks, etc. I signed up to bring the sandwiches."

"Why do I have a bad feeling about this?"

Meade gave Tanner a knowing smile. "I got up early that morning to prepare the food. We had a lot of cold cuts in the fridge, so I got out the Miracle Whip and spread it on all of the pieces of bread. I added cheese and lettuce and, I thought, by the time I was done, they looked really good.

"When it was time to sit and eat, we went to a local park and I started handing out what I'd made. Everyone took a bite about the same time—except for me. I was helping the teacher pass out everything. All of a sudden, all the kids started screaming that their mouths were on fire and spitting the food out of their mouth onto the grass. I couldn't figure out what had happened!"

"Oh, no. What had you done?"

"The teacher picked up one of the sandwiches and smelled it. Apparently, what I thought was Miracle Whip was really creamed horseradish."

"No!" Tanner said, leaning back on the library steps and putting his hands on the top of his head.

"Yes! It was awful! The kids were so annoyed with me, because not only were their mouths on fire, but they had no lunch for the rest of the day! It took the rest of high school to live that down. I was awarded 'Worst Cook' in the yearbook and they even mentioned it at my tenth high school reunion!"

"Remind me to do the cooking when we move in together."

"Oh, now we're moving in together? I thought we were getting married."

"Don't want to rush things."

"Of course not. Moving in together would be playing it much slower."

"See. You're starting to see things more clearly."

Meade smiled—again. It seemed she was doing that a lot on this date. She looked over at Tanner. She liked his face. It wasn't beautiful, in the way that many of the men she'd dated in the past were. It was unlikely he would ever be on the cover of a magazine. But, she liked staring at him. She liked the freckles on his nose and the little wrinkles on the sides of his eyes when he smiled and the way he winked at her when he was teasing her—he seemed to be doing often.

"Want to continue to sit here or walk around some more?" Tanner asked. "Or, maybe you have somewhere you have to be?" He said it expectantly, like he thought she might be ready to end their date. And, when they'd first begun to walk, that had actually been her plan. She hadn't really wanted to go on this blind date and was only doing it because it seemed important to Pantera. She'd decided, within the first block that, after a little while, she'd tell him she needed to go into work to catch up on some things. But, somewhere between block five and nine, she'd decided that maybe work could wait. Maybe she'd take her time with this guy—and enjoy his company.

And, for the next three hours, that was exactly what she did. They began to, once again, walk around the city. They made their way to the Theater District and talked about the shows they'd seen—her more than him because, as he said, "I am a straight man, after all." They bought pretzels and hotdogs from a street vendor and ate at the little tables in the middle of Times Square. She told Tanner that, in all her years in New York, she'd never been to the top of the Empire State Building.

"Never?" he asked, clearly in disbelief.

"Never."

"Well then, it's time to change that."

"Now?"

"No time like the present!" Tanner stood and picked up their hot-dog wrappers and cups, throwing them in a trash can. "Let's go."

Meade followed him and he grabbed her hand as he pulled her across the street. She was tempted to pull it away, but then decided to keep it tight in his palm. It felt nice to have someone else take charge of something, even if it was simply making their way down the street and buying their tickets for a tour. In all of her relation-ships—since Daniel, that is—she'd been the one to make the plans, to organize the events, to schedule the dates—if she and the men even went out on any. And, more times than not, she was the one who'd paid. But Tanner had bought everything today. Even though nothing they'd done had been truly extravagant, it was still nice to not once feel like she had to take her wallet out of her purse.

They laughed their way up the elevator to the eighty-sixth floor. It wasn't crowded today and so the wait to go up hadn't been long. The view was breathtaking. Meade pointed out her office building to him, from high above, and Tanner told her a story about how he'd brought his five-year-old nephew to the top a few years ago, and the kid had puked the minute they stepped off the elevator.

"Oh no! What did you do?"

"I swooped him up, cleaned him up and pretended I had no idea how that vomit got all over the floor!"

"Did you really?"

Tanner smiled at her and winked. Part of her was pretty sure he wasn't kidding. "I wasn't taking responsibility for that!"

They stayed on the observation deck for over an hour, talking about the places they'd been in New York and the things they'd seen. Meade told him about the dog she'd had until she was thirteen and how she'd been devastated when it was hit by a car because her brother, Nick, forgot to close the gate to the backyard fence. Tanner had Meade doubled over with laughter with his story about how he and some of his college friends were arrested for stealing a street sign one night when they were juniors. They were too embarrassed to call their parents, so they'd all spent the night in jail.

"You're on a date with a convicted felon. Just thought I should warn you."

"What was the street sign?"

"Camel Toe Drive."

"You're making that up."

"Honest! I couldn't make up stuff like that!" Tanner said, laughing himself. "Now, come on. Admit it. That is too awesome of a street name not to have the sign hanging in your dorm room."

Meade couldn't remember the last time she'd laughed as hard as she had today. And, she was pretty sure she hadn't talked so much about herself to another person—and learned as much about them—since, well, Daniel. It had been refreshing. Not at all like her typical dates in New York City, which usually involved alcohol, tight clothing and minimal conversation. Neither she nor Tanner had consumed a single alcoholic beverage all day, yet she was pretty sure she'd never felt more relaxed.

"Hey," Meade said, looking up. "This is my office building." They'd been walking for hours and she almost hadn't realized they were so close to work. "I should probably go in and get some work done. I promised myself I would spend a part of this weekend catching up on the things that can never get done when everyone is in the office."

"So, I shouldn't take it as a blow-off?"

"Absolutely not. I had a fun time."

"Me, too," Tanner said. "I'd like to see you again."

Meade hesitated. She'd enjoyed Tanner's company. There was no question about that. But she wasn't exactly sure she wanted to go out with him again, either. Though it was hard to remember, while staring into those sky-blue eyes, why she might not want to see him again. Still, she was pretty sure a second date might be a bad idea.

"How about this?" he said, sensing her hesitation. "We'll exchange numbers. You call me. I'll call you. We'll text. You think it over. Deal?"

Meade remained silent for a moment. Phone numbers were no big deal, right? She wasn't giving him her first born or anything.

"Okay," she finally replied. "Here's my number." She reached into the side of her purse and pulled out her Brownsbury Press card.

Tanner handed her a pen. "I'm sure that's your work number. I don't want to have to make an appointment. Can you please put your cell on the back?"

She shook her head at him. He was a persistent little bugger. But, she took the pen and wrote, handing it back to him along with the card.

"Thanks." He took a card out of his pocket and jotted down his cell number on the back. He picked up her right hand and placed his card carefully in her palm. "You can call me. Anytime. But know that if you don't, I will be calling you."

"Are you already stalking me?"

"Stalking sounds so sinister. I prefer to think I'm pursuing you."

Meade looked down at his card.

*Tanner Dale*

*Attorney-at-Law*

Her head popped up. "You're a lawyer?"

"Guilty as charged."

"You told me you were a musician!"

"No. *You* said I was a musician. I said that I teach Pantera guitar—which I do. On the weekends. I'm not sure if that makes me an official musician though. After all, I'm from Texas. Everyone plays the guitar down there."

Meade gaped at him. "I'm from Texas, too. Did Pantera tell you that?"

Now it was Tanner's turn to be surprised. "Actually, no. She didn't mention it."

"From Austin."

"I'm from Katy."

"Near Houston. I know it well. Wow. Small world. Two Texans in the Big Apple."

Tanner smiled down at her. For a moment, she wondered if he might kiss her, but he didn't. Instead he asked if he could give her a hug. Meade nodded.

Later that night, when Meade was in bed, she looked back at the hug and decided it was the best one she'd ever had. He hadn't simply hugged her. He'd gently rested his cheek against hers. It had been a simple touch—not sexual in the slightest. But Meade found the feel of his skin on hers had sent goose bumps up her spine. She'd suddenly had an extreme desire to touch him, to hold him, to feel him next to her. Instead, she'd backed away.

"Thanks again for today," she said.

"I'll be in touch."

Meade nodded and then turned and walked up the stairs and to her building. She was tempted, as she reached the main doors, to turn around again. She had a hunch he was still there—watching her. She also had a feeling that if she were to turn around, he might try to convince her to not end their date, but instead, go out to dinner with him.

She was surprised to realize the idea was tempting. She liked him. A lot.

But she also knew better. She was walking in dangerous territory. Meade wasn't looking for a relationship—at least, nothing serious and long-term.

And Tanner Dale had serious and long-term written all over him.

It was better to put an end to this before it got out of hand.

So, instead of turning around, Meade pushed opened the door to her building and continued walking, straight through the lobby and to the elevators, forcing herself not to look back.

# CHAPTER NINE

Pantera was sitting on Meade's desk when Meade got into the office Monday morning. Meade was almost surprised the woman could find anywhere to perch her bum considering the mess and stacks of papers Meade had left there after working for the rest of Saturday and a good part of Sunday. The work was endless. Meade sometimes wondered if, on her death bed, she'd be worrying about all the manuscripts she still had to go through, telling the nurses, "I have no time to die!"

"So..." Pantera said expectantly. "How was it?"

Meade closed her door behind her and put down her bag on the chair, pulling out even more manuscripts she had taken with her. She dropped them on Pantera's lap as she made her way to her chair.

"It was fine," Meade said, sitting down in her leather office chair. She loved this chair. It had taken her months to find the right ergonomic seat that saved her back from aching continually with all the hours she'd spent hunched over in it. Brownsbury might have been one of the best publishing companies in the world, but the office furniture they provided their employees should have come with chiropractic gift certificates attached. "I liked him. He was nice."

Pantera picked up her legs and spun around on Meade's desk, somehow not knocking a single paper to the ground, despite the enormous black combat boots she had on today.

"How nice? How much did you like him? Are you going to go out again?"

Meade thought back to their date. It had been wonderful. And she'd barely been in her office for an hour after they'd parted when she'd gotten a text from him.

*Tell me the most interesting thing you've done since you left me.*

*I heated up a Lean Cuisine meal in the microwave..*

*I can see how that would be more appetizing than dinner at Le Cirque.*

*Oh? I missed dinner at Le Cirque? I didn't know! For that, I would have hung out longer.*

Le Cirque was one of New York's most legendary restaurants. Meade had only dined there twice and both times it had been phenomenal. It was also one of the best places in the city to spot celebrities. The first time she was there, Michael Douglas and Catherine Zeta-Jones had been at the table next to her. The second time, both Howard Stern and Martha Stewart were dining there—not together. Though that would have been more interesting.

*You snooze, you lose.*

She'd smiled and had to admit, she was flattered he'd contacted her so soon after leaving her. In her experience, when a guy says, "I'll call," it meant, "I probably won't." The sun hadn't even gone down on the day of their date and Tanner was texting her. And she was writing back.

*I think you were just looking for a reason to contact me so soon.*

*In this instance I would plead "no contest" which in legal parlance means that although I'm not pleading guilty, I'm acknowledging that the prosecution has sufficient evidence to convict.*

Meade hadn't written back again that day. She'd become immersed in her work and lost track of time, not heading home until close to midnight. On Sunday, she'd come back into the office by noon and stayed until dinner. Hers was definitely not a nine-to-five type of job, which, for the most part, suited her lifestyle. There was no one waiting at home for her. No husband who expected her to be home for dinner. No kids to tuck in at night. It wasn't the life she'd thought she'd have when she was a teenager, but it was the life she led. And, it wasn't a bad one. She had money. She had friends. She had men— many men. Just not one special man. But that was okay. She'd loved a man. And been loved in return. She'd meant it when she'd told Daniel she would never love anyone the way she had loved him. She would never even look for that type of love again. She'd promised Daniel her heart would remain his and it would.

"Meade! Are you listening to me? Earth to Meade!"

Meade looked up. She'd been so lost in thought, she'd forgotten Pantera was still sitting on her desk.

"You need to get off my desk so I can get to work."

"But you haven't even given me the scoop! I want details! Details!" Pantera huffed, hopping off Meade's desk and into the chair in front of it.

"There's not much to say. He was nice. I appreciated his lack of tattoos and piercings. We had a lot in common—at least a lot to talk about. I enjoyed my day with him."

"Day? Did you spend a whole day with him?"

"A few hours. The afternoon."

"Not the night?" Pantera asked, winking.

"No, Ms. Nosey. Not the night. We didn't even have dinner together. I came back to work."

"You came back to *work?*" Pantera nearly screeched. "Why would you do that? It was a Saturday!"

"Because I had a lot of work to do. I spent most of Sunday here, too."

Pantera sank down in the chair, as if all the life was sucked out of her. "What am I going to do with you? You only give me so much to work with here!"

"You did great. And I'm fine. I met a nice man. We had a good time. End of story."

"You're not going to see him again?"

Meade's mind drifted back to the texts she and Tanner had exchanged last night. They'd been so funny. She had reread them this morning and had literally laughed out loud at their dialogue. If nothing else, she and Tanner had great banter. She wasn't sure she'd ever enjoyed the verbal back and forth so much with any other man.

"Probably not."

Suddenly, there was a knock at Meade's door. Pantera jumped up to open it. Tommy, from the mailroom, stood there holding a gift basket.

"Hey, Tommy," Pantera and Meade said in unison.

He said hi to both of them and then walked over to Meade's desk, placing the basket on top.

"Cedric in the lobby said this was delivered for you. I told him I'd bring it up."

"Thanks, Tommy. I appreciate it."

"Any time," he said and walked back out the door.

Meade wasn't overly surprised to be getting a gift basket. Authors sometimes sent them to her to thank her for all the hand-holding she did during the publishing process. And sometimes, businesses they worked with would also send her something, to get her attention or show their appreciation. But one look at this basket told her all she needed to know. This basket wasn't from any company or author.

"What kind of basket is this?" Pantera asked, taking the items out, one by one.

Mayonnaise. Horseradish. A miniature statue of the Empire State Building. A DVD of the best moments from *The Bachelor.* And a box of Pop Tarts.

Meade didn't say a word, but Pantera could clearly read her face.

"It's from Tanner, isn't it?" Pantera nearly skipped for joy around Meade's office. "I knew the two of you would hit it off. I knew it!"

"Calm down. We had a nice time. We're not getting married."

"Not yet!" Pantera said, a big, wide grin across her face.

"You can wipe that smile off your face."

"Oh, no! I'm going to be smiling all day. This is fabulous!" Pantera said, holding onto the door frame and kicking up her leg behind her. "Fabulous, I tell you!"

"Get out of here!" Meade resisted the urge to smile at Pantera's enthusiasm, no matter how misguided. She liked Tanner. She couldn't deny that. But she certainly wasn't going to let this turn into something serious.

"Ta ta for now!" Pantera said, as she made her way back to her desk.

Meade looked at the items in the basket one more time and had to chuckle. Tanner was creative, if nothing else. She picked up her phone and typed a quick text.

*I don't eat Pop Tarts.*

*Those aren't for you. They're for me to eat for breakfast when I stay over your place.*

*I don't have a toaster oven.*

*Well, funny thing! My family has a great big one I can bring with me!*

Meade laughed out loud. She saw Pantera spin around in her chair outside her door and glance back at Meade.

"Have I mentioned how excited I am?" she called into Meade's office.

Meade got out of her chair and walked to the door. "I have work to do."

"Uh-huh!" Pantera said, winking at Meade. "Tell Tanner I said hi."

Meade slammed her door. Not so loudly that anyone else on the floor would hear her, but strong enough so Pantera knew she was making a point.

Though, what point she was making wasn't all that clear to Meade. Pantera was right. She liked Tanner. Quite a bit. And that might prove to be a problem.

Meade threw her mail onto the coffee table as she plopped down on the couch. Resting her head on one of the decorative pillows she had bought last year at the Pottery Barn outlet she'd visited in New York State, Meade closed her eyes. Today had been exhausting. Work was never-ending. It always seemed like there was more to do. It was hard to feel like you were making any progress in accomplishing things when more tasks kept getting stacked on top of the ones that still weren't done. It wasn't that she didn't enjoy her job. She did. She loved it. Meade couldn't imagine doing anything else. She merely wished it would let up every once in a while so she could catch her breath.

Meade put out a hand and grabbed the letters off the table. Holding them up, she flipped through them. Bill, bill, advertisement, bill. Nothing exciting. Another bill.

*Oh, wait. Ann Taylor was having a sale.*

Meade nearly dropped the envelopes when she saw the return address on the last letter. *L. Young. Austin, TX.*

Lori? Why would she be writing to Meade? The two of them hadn't spoken in over fifteen years. Not since the day after Daniel's funeral. Not since Meade had told her they were no longer friends—would never be friends again.

For a moment, Meade wondered if maybe Lori was writing to tell her about a death in her family. Meade was no longer in touch with Lori's parents or her sisters, but she wouldn't want any harm to fall on them, either. They were nice people and Meade had loved them like her own family—maybe more so—when she was growing up. She would hope someone would tell her if something happened to any of them, though she wouldn't expect it to be Lori.

Meade had burned that bridge, and all the construction workers in North America couldn't rebuild it.

Meade slowly ripped open the seal and took out the folded piece of stationery. She recognized Lori's handwriting immediately and was filled with a sudden sense of sadness. The curves were so familiar to her—even all these years later. Meade had a sense of déjà vu as she remembered all the secret notes she and Lori had passed in classes—about the boys they had crushes on, how much they disliked their math teacher in ninth grade, what they were going to wear to the prom. They'd been close. Extremely close—like sisters. Meade would've thought nothing could tear the two of them apart.

But that was before cancer. Before Meade had learned the harm it could inflict—not only on Daniel's body—but on everyone and every-thing in its wake.

Meade began to read Lori's letter. It wasn't long. A few lines.

*Dear Meade,*

*This letter is long overdue. I have thought about what to say to you nearly every day for the past fifteen years, but the words would never come. I'm sorry does not encompass the lifetime of regret I've led. Every morning, I wake wishing I could turn back time. I was a selfish teenage girl who didn't understand what was truly important in life. I know it's unlikely you'll ever forgive me for all you lost, but I'd like to try to make amends.*

*I know you'll be home next week for the scholarship program. I'd love it if you'd agree to let me buy you lunch while you're in Texas—maybe at the Salt Lick—so we can speak in person.*

*Lori*

She'd written her phone number under her name. The Salt Lick was one of the most famous bar-b-que places in the Austin area and had always been a favorite of hers and Lori's and Daniel's. The three of them would get the "family style" portions—all you can eat—and had eaten themselves sick more times than Meade could count.

Meade read the letter one more time and threw it on the ground. *Forgive her?* Not a chance. Fifteen years later, one might forgive a former best friend for stealing her boyfriend, but not for killing him. And truly, that's what Lori had done—as equally as the cancer cells had robbed Daniel of his life, Lori had done the same.

Meade had no intention of seeing Lori when she went home— and not all the brisket in Texas could change her mind.

# CHAPTER TEN

M eade sat on top of her suitcase, begging it to close. She always overpacked and really had no idea how that happened. After all, it was hot in Texas. Uber hot. She'd barely be wearing any clothes while there and the items she did pack didn't have much fabric to them. So what was taking up so much room in her suitcase?

She reached down under her legs and snapped the latches shut. Success! Now, all she had to do was load up her carry-on bag, but she had time for that. Her flight wasn't until tomorrow. However, she felt better knowing that, at the very least, her large suitcase was ready to go.

Her phone vibrated on the nightstand next to her. *Tanner.* It always seemed to be Tanner these days. The two of them had become quite the texting buddies. He'd like to be more than that, of course. He was constantly asking her out to the movies or to dinner or to museums, but Meade hadn't actually seen him since their date two weeks ago. It wasn't that she wasn't tempted. She was. She thought it best if she kept her distance from him. There was something about him that unnerved her, and Meade was the type of woman who liked being in control of her nerves at all times.

*What's cooking, hot stuff?*

Meade smiled at his greeting. Every day there was a new one. *Morning, sugar pie, honey bunch. Hey, cupcake. Bonjour, belle.* Meade wondered how long until he ran out of creative conversation starters.

*Packing.*

*What time do you leave tomorrow?*

*My flight is around noon.*

*Time for a bite to eat first?*

*I'm eating a bagel right now.*

*I meant with me.*

Of course he did. Not a day went by that Tanner didn't ask her out in some way. A part of her felt bad for him and sometimes she wondered if she should at least toss him a bone. Coffee at the corner café, maybe? But no. There was something about Tanner. Meade couldn't put her finger on it, exactly, but she had a feeling coffee wouldn't simply end with coffee. And, for whatever reason, Meade was nervous about letting whatever this was progress any further.

That wasn't to say, though, that she didn't enjoy their repartee. No. They had incredible banter. And, as Meade had learned over the past fourteen days, banter could be unbelievably sexy.

*I have a lot to do before I leave.*

*I can make it easy for you.*

*How so?*

*What if I bring dinner to you? You don't have to move an inch. You can even keep sitting on your suitcase.*

Meade looked around the room hurriedly. Was he spying on her? Before she could reply, he texted again.

*Isn't that what women do? Sit on their suitcases to get them to close?*

Phew. It had been a lucky guess. She would've hated to write him off because he was a Peeping Tom.

*No.*

One little white lie wouldn't hurt, right?

*Oh, my bad. I guess I shouldn't stereotype.* (He added a smiley face to the end of that one.)

*I really don't have time. Maybe when I get back from Texas?*

She was lying. There wouldn't be time then, either. At least, she wouldn't make any. And he knew it. And she knew he knew it.

*What if I tell you I'm standing outside your apartment building with dinner in hand. And it's beginning to get heavy.*

Meade hopped off her suitcase and went to her window. *Was he kidding?* She glanced outside and down at the front door. He wasn't kidding. She could see him texting into his phone, a brown paper bag at his feet. She typed into her phone.

*Liar. You're not even holding the food.*

Meade saw him read the text and look up. It took him a minute to find her window, but when he did, their eyes met and a broad smile crossed his face.

*So, do we have a date?*

Well, this was awkward. She couldn't exactly leave him standing out there. She sighed. One date. What harm could come of it?

Of course, it wasn't the harm that worried her.

*I'll be right down.*

Meade stuck her phone in the back pocket of her jeans and glanced in the full-length mirror she had on the back of her closet door. Ugh. This certainly isn't how she would have dressed if she'd known she was going to be on a date. She had on an old pair of jeans, with a hole in her left knee, a ratty University of Texas T-shirt she'd gotten in high school, no shoes and her hair was pulled up into a messy knot on the top of her head.

Meade quickly let down her hair and ran a brush through it. She debated changing her clothes, but on second thought, decided not to. This wasn't an actual date. He was bringing her take-out. She didn't need to impress him. Besides, if he didn't like what he saw, well...that was his problem. He was pursuing her, not the other way around. He should see the real Meade, and the real Meade looked like this. Quite often, in fact.

Deciding against going barefoot, she slipped on a pair of flip-flops and headed toward her front door. She was about to open it, when she ran back into her room and quickly applied some blush and mascara.

Sans makeup might be the "real" her, but did it need to be seen so soon?

Meade locked the door behind her and ran down the stairs of her building. Reaching the lobby, she could see him sitting on the wall of one of the flower beds outside. Meade paused. She felt her breath catch in her chest. She was happy to see him. Very happy. But, it was more than that. She barely knew him and yet...he seemed so familiar to her. It was an unsettling feeling, which was ironic in and of itself. Shouldn't the fact that she felt so instantly comfortable with him calm her? Instead, it made her feel as if she might fly out of her own skin.

Meade pushed open the door as Tanner looked up at her. Her heart fluttered at his smile and she wondered if her face showed a blush.

Doing her best to seem nonchalant, she said, "Someone is going to ticket you for loitering if you keep sitting out here."

Tanner stood up, picking up the bag. "Then it's a good thing you came to let me in."

"You shouldn't have just stopped over."

"I know," he said, shrugging. "But would you have eaten dinner with me if I had called in advance?"

"No."

"Then I was smart to hedge my bets."

"It's your dime," Meade said, doing her best to seem cool.

"Well, actually, it cost a bit more than a dime. Prices have gone up a bit since the Depression, in case you haven't heard. But that's okay. I'm a hot-shot lawyer. I can afford it."

"Gee...thanks."

"Your enthusiasm for me is underwhelming. But that's okay. I don't think you've had enough time to experience all my charm. So let's change that over dinner. Are we going inside or should I set up everything out here on the sidewalk?"

Meade looked at all the people walking around and could imagine the sight they'd make if they sat down to picnic right in the middle of all of it. Not to mention the strong language that'd be thrown their way.

"You can't come up to my apartment."

"Got another guy up there?" Tanner asked, his eyes twinkling. "Not into threesomes?"

Meade glared at him.

"Hey, me neither!" Tanner said. "At least, not ones that involve two men. I'd prefer the two-women, one-man scenario..." He caught the look she was giving him and grinned. "But that's neither here nor there."

"No, I do not have another man upstairs. I don't let men into my apartment. It's kind of a rule I have."

"That's fine. So, where should we eat?"

Meade was relieved at the ease with which he took her announcement. Some men became quite irritated when she told them she wouldn't be bringing them home with her.

"Well, there is a roof deck..."

"The roof deck sounds wonderful."

"It's not fancy."

"As long as you and I are both on it, it's perfect."

"You're good, you know that? Did you take a class on lines to give women?"

"Nope. It's a natural gift."

Meade shook her head as she unlocked the door to her building and held it open for Tanner, but he shook his head.

"Ladies, first."

Meade nodded and walked in. At least there were some chivalrous men in New York—even if they did have to be imported from Texas.

They rode up the elevator to the top of her building in silence. Meade usually took the stairs when she was headed to her apartment. She figured she needed the exercise. But she only lived on the fourth floor. The roof deck was above the eighteenth floor. No one needed that much exercise.

When they reached the top, Meade exited the elevator and led Tanner through the small hallway, pushing open the door that led to the roof.

"It's not much," Meade said apologetically. "I don't think people come up here too often. But there's a table and some chairs over there." She pointed to the far end of the roof.

"I love it."

"What do I need to go get for us? Some drinks? Silverware?"

"I brought paper plates and plastic silverware. If you want real stuff, you can grab that. I forgot drinks, though. Do you happen to have anything at your place?"

"I'll see what I can come up with," she said. "I'll be right back."

"I'll be here."

Meade hurried back into the building and down to her apartment. Opening the kitchen cabinets, she grabbed two plates, some silverware, wine glasses and the only bottle of wine she had in there—a Pinot Noir. She wasn't a big drinker, but she tried to keep something on hand for nights when a girlfriend might stop over or she'd had a particularly difficult week. She was glad she'd replaced the bottle she'd opened after dealing with Ian last month.

She made one more quick trip to the mirror and reapplied her lip gloss and then headed back up to the roof deck. She found Tanner waiting for her at the little table. He'd taken the food out of the bag, and she was surprised to see a lit candle in the center of the table. "Where'd that come from?" she asked.

"I was a Boy Scout. 'Be prepared' is our motto."

Meade laid out the glasses, dishes and the silverware. She was glad to see Tanner had brought some napkins, as she'd forgotten them.

"I hope the wine is fine."

"It's wonderful," Tanner said. "Did you bring a corkscrew?"

"Aaaagh!" she moaned, slapping her palm to her forehead. "I forgot."

"That's okay. I can probably pull it out with my teeth."

"Classy," Meade said. "I was kidding." She reached into her back pocket and pulled out the corkscrew she'd remembered at the last second. "I'm good at being prepared, too."

"Excellent! We're the perfect match!" Tanner took it from her and began to uncork the wine.

"So, what are we eating tonight?"

"Indian food. I hope that's okay."

"I love Indian food."

"I had a feeling."

"Oh, you did, did you?" Meade asked him, sitting down at the little table. "Do you mind if I begin to put the food on our plates? It smells so good. I didn't realize I was this hungry."

"That'd be great. Dish away." Tanner poured the wine into their glasses and then sat across from Meade. "So, how has your day been so far?"

"Okay. Busy. It's not easy to leave work—even for a few days. There's a lot to do to prepare for my trip before I even begin to prepare for the actual trip."

Meade took a bite of the food on her plate. Shrimp Korma. Her favorite. How did he know? Gosh, it was good. If Tanner wasn't watching her eat, she had a feeling she'd inhale the entire meal without coming up for air. She was suddenly famished.

"Now, why are you going back to Texas?"

"Well, my family is still there. I don't see them very often. But I do go back every year for an awards ceremony. I run a scholarship program for my hometown high school. I always fly to Austin for the presentation."

"You run a scholarship program? In Texas? Sounds like a big commitment."

"It's not too big. Mostly, I review the applications and make recommendations to the rest of the committee on whom I think should receive the award. I don't have complete control over it, but I do have a big say."

"It seems like this is a passion of yours."

"It's important to me." Meade stopped at that. There was, of course, more she could say, but she didn't.

Tanner stared at her, thoughtfully, for a moment. "You're a very private person. I get that. You don't have to tell me more—about anything—until you're ready. And, if you're never ready, that's okay, too. I don't need to know all the tiny details of your life—of the present or the past. Those aren't really important to me."

"Oh, no?" Meade said, taking a sip of her drink. "And why is that?"

"Because I know you."

Meade almost choked on her wine and had to stop herself from dripping it down her chin and onto her T-shirt. "You know me? We met two weeks ago. How on earth can you know me?"

He was getting a little creepy. Was he stalking her?

"Whoah! Whoah! Rein it back in! I'm not trying to freak you out."

"Too late." Meade unconsciously scooted her chair back a few inches.

Tanner laughed. "Stop it, Meade! Come back here. I am not a psycho."

Meade looked at him uncertainly. "Promise?"

"I promise. Can I at least explain before you call the cops?"

"I guess I owe you that much," she said, relaxing a bit. "You did bring dinner."

"Gee. Thanks." Tanner's shoulders relaxed and he leaned forward in his seat. "This is going to sound nuts. I know that. So, please hear me out before you send me packing."

"Okay." Meade sighed. *This ought to be good.*

"Have you ever met someone and, in the first second your eyes meet, there is something so familiar about them you're sure you must've met before...but, of course, you haven't?"

Tanner paused for a moment, as if waiting for Meade to reply, but then quickly continued when she didn't move an inch. "Never mind. What I'm trying to say is, that's what happened when I met you. I walked up to that table and you looked up at me and instantly...and I mean, *instantly*...there was such a familiarity with you. Not like I'd met you somewhere. Not like I'd seen your picture. But a sense that I *knew* you. I knew nothing about your life or your activities or your friendships. But your soul...I knew your soul."

He looked deep into Meade's eyes. "I know that sounds crazy. It sounds crazy to me, too. Nothing like this has ever happened to me before—and I tend to think it's not going to happen again. And so, even though you seem hesitant to pursue whatever it is between us, I can't let go—at least not yet. Not until you tell me, in no uncertain terms, to walk away."

Meade didn't know what to say to him. What he'd said was so insane. So ridiculous. So scary. And yet...*familiar.* Wasn't that the word that had popped into her mind when she saw him sitting outside her door thirty minutes earlier?

She hadn't been able to put her finger on it—this feeling she got when she thought about Tanner—but he'd encapsulated her emotions perfectly. She felt like she knew him, too. Right from that first day, before she learned anything about his love of Pop Tarts and his huge family and the way he was constantly grinning from ear to ear; she was so at ease with him. She felt like she knew his being. And, in some odd way, she felt he knew hers, too.

"So, that's the story. The big scoop. You're looking at a practical, no-nonsense realist who discovered, only two weeks ago, that he's actually a romantic in disguise."

"That must have been quite the revelation."

"You have no idea. It's thrown him for an enormous loop. He can barely concentrate at work."

Meade looked at Tanner with surprise. "Really?"

"Really." He nodded solemnly. "Listen, Meade. I like you. A lot. And I don't know where any of this is going. To be honest, it makes me kind of nervous. And I can tell, by the way you squirm anytime I try to broach a serious topic with you, it makes you nervous, too. But that's okay. Because, as long as you don't tell me to take a hike, I'd like to stick around for a bit and see where this might lead."

Meade sat back in her chair and stared out into the New York skyline. From her building, she could see the Empire State Building and the tip of the Chrysler Building. As far as she was concerned, it was the best view in the city.

"Is that silence I hear the sound of you not telling me to take a hike?" Tanner asked.

Meade chuckled. She glanced over at him. He had such a hopeful look on his face, like a little boy begging his mom for a Popsicle when the ice cream truck drove by.

"No hikes necessary at this time."

Tanner broke out into a broad grin. "That's a relief. I'm a terrible hiker."

"Why does that not surprise me?"

"I hate blisters. And backpacks. And I never bring enough water."

Meade rolled her eyes. Tanner's smile sparkled as he stared at her across the table.

"There's nowhere else I'd rather be, you know," he said.

Meade looked into his kind eyes. Eyes which, less than a month ago, had belonged to a stranger. Yet they looked at her with such recognition. As if she was being seen, completely, for the first time in her entire life.

"Me, neither," she replied softly.

And to her surprise and amazement, she realized she meant it.

# CHAPTER ELEVEN

Meade couldn't help but smile as she made her way through the Austin airport. In New York or New Jersey or even D.C., there was a Dunkin' Donuts and a Starbucks and a Villa Pizza in every airport terminal—businesses which seemed to have a monopoly on the food frequent fliers ate before their travels.

But not Austin. Only local businesses were able to rent a space and sell their wares or meals at Austin-Bergstrom International Airport. It was one of the things she loved about this town. It was unique. Like nowhere else in the world. And it was home.

The warm air hit Meade as she stepped out onto the curb. Actually, warm was not a term that did it justice. It was hot. Super hot. *Habanero* hot and she felt her skin began to sizzle within the first six seconds outdoors.

There was no doubt she was back in Texas.

"Meade! Meade!" She heard a voice calling to her.

She turned and saw Benji running toward her. *Ben,* as he now liked to be called. Though she could never get used to the shortened moniker. He was her kid brother. He would always be Benji. Let his medical school buddies call him "Ben." She couldn't change.

"Benji!" she cried out, rushing to hug him.

"Ben," he grumbled.

She stood on her toes and tousled his hair like he was still six years old. "Whatever."

She had to look up at him. It was such an odd feeling. He was four years younger than she and yet, here he stood, a tall six feet four inches—all muscle. Solid as the bull she'd seen him try to ride a few years ago at the county fair. He was grown up. It almost made Meade weepy to think about it.

He bent down and picked up her suitcase.

"You know, the thing has wheels. You can roll it."

Benji shrugged. "Wheels are for wimps."

She put her arm around his waist and hugged him again as they began to walk to the parking lot. "It's so good to be home."

"It's good to have you here. I've missed you."

"Tell me everything. How's school? How's your new apartment? How's your love life?"

"You sure do know how to cut to the chase."

"Of course I do! We only have three days. I have to get everything in as fast as I can."

They reached Benji's car, a red VW bug, and he opened the trunk to throw Meade's bag inside.

"You drive this little thing?" Meade asked, startled. "What happened to your truck?"

"Transmission. I got a good deal on this one."

"But...do you even fit in it?" Meade couldn't help but stare at his long legs and then over to the tiny compartment calling itself a driver's seat.

"I make do."

Meade looked at him skeptically.

Benji laughed. "The women love it. They think it's cute."

"Oh, do they now? Tell me. Tell me," Meade said as she folded herself into the passenger seat. Even for her tiny body, it was a tight fit. She was impressed to see the ease with which Benji slid himself into position behind the wheel. Granted, the seat was pushed back so far she couldn't be sure it wasn't technically in the trunk.

"There's not too much to tell. I go out on some dates here and there."

"I'll bet the women are all over you."

Benji couldn't hide his grin. "I do okay."

Meade slugged him in the forearm, the way only a sister can. "I knew it. You're a stud."

Benji laughed a good, hard laugh. "Yep. I admit it. I'm a stud."

"But no one special?" Meade wanted Benji to find someone and settle down. She wanted a sister-in-law and she knew Nick wasn't about to provide her with one. Any woman who stole Benji's heart would steal hers, too.

"No way. I'm too young!"

"Too young? You're twenty-nine! Mom had all three of us by the time she was your age."

"And we were practically grown by the time she was *your* age."

"Very funny."

Benji glanced over at Meade and then back at the road as he began to merge onto the highway. "It wouldn't kill you to meet a nice guy and give me a little niece or nephew."

Meade sighed. This was a discussion she often had with her little brother. He wanted her to fall in love. He had only her best interest at heart, but she also knew that love—and a family—weren't in the cards for her.

"How's Mom?" Meade asked.

"I know what you're doing. You're changing the subject."

Meade smiled. "I am merely concerned about the well-being of our dear mother."

"Our dear mother? Now I *know* you're trying to change the topic."

Meade leaned over and flicked on the radio. The cool sound of country music filled the car. She leaned back and closed her eyes. "Ah... Now that's music."

"Not like that rap crap you have in New York City?" Benji was a Texan, through and through. He'd been to visit her a few times in the Big

Apple, but always began to go a bit stir-crazy after the first thirty-six hours. He needed open spaces, despite the size of his car. New York City was too cramped for his taste.

"I'm not even sure we have a country station there anymore," Meade said.

"That's wrong."

"So, seriously, how is Mom? I need the low-down before I walk in the door. What's the latest? What disaster am I walking into this time?"

"Actually, it's not too bad. She and Jimmy just got back from Costa Rica."

"Costa Rica? What were they doing there?"

"Vacationing. Jimmy says he's always wanted to go there. And you know Mom, she read somewhere that in Costa Rica they have some great zip lining over a big waterfall and some jungle...and so, she had to try it out."

"Mom went zip lining?"

"Yep. Wait till you see the pics. You won't believe it."

"Oh, when it comes to Mom, I'll believe most anything."

"Ain't that the truth? Thank heavens for Jimmy!"

Meade picked up an empty soda can she found on the floor and raised it up as if she was making a toast. "Thank heavens for Jimmy!"

The year after Daniel died, their high school had started the scholarship fund in his name. Every year, one high school student from their hometown received a college scholarship. The amount varied from year to year, increasing in value over time. Meade had begun to head the committee when she was in college and she made it her mission, each year, to fundraise and contact local businesses, requesting they make donations toward the scholarship fund. Meade had a way with words, both in person and in writing. She rarely had anyone turn her down.

The scholarship awards ceremony was one of the highlights of her year. She never failed to return home so she could be the one to present each eager and bright-eyed student with a scholarship check. This year, the amount was $40,000. It was the highest yet. Meade couldn't help but smile when she thought about it.

And that's how Jimmy had come into their lives. Five years earlier, his only child, Katie, had been the recipient of the award. Meade's mom didn't attend the ceremony every year—though, she was always invited—but five years ago, she'd agreed to come. And that night had changed all of their lives.

Jimmy was a widower who was about to come to the completion of raising his daughter. Meade's mom seduced him over the punch bowl. He never even knew what had hit him. They were married three months later and, to Meade's surprise and delight, they were still going strong.

"Are they coming to the ceremony tonight?" Meade asked.

"Of course. We all are."

"We all are?"

"Okay...not Nick. But the rest of us. Even Katie's coming."

"Oh, is she home?" Meade asked with delight. She loved her stepsister. As the saying went, if sisters were flowers, she would've picked Katie.

"She is. Came in last night."

"That's awesome!"

"Mom's making a big Mexican feast."

"Please tell me you're kidding."

"Okay, she's not really making it. She ordered take-out from Maudie's Hacienda."

"Perfect! I miss me some Mexican!"

"And some grammar, apparently."

Meade laughed. You could really only get away with such terrible grammatical expressions when everyone knew you were really a grammar freak.

They pulled into the driveway as Meade's stomach growled—loudly.

"What was that?" Benji asked. "Do they not feed you in New York?"

Meade laughed. "I didn't have time to eat before my flight. And you know they don't feed you on the planes anymore. I forgot to pack a snack."

"So you're starving."

"I'm starving."

"Okay, then," he said, throwing the car into park. "Let's go eat!"

If Meade had wanted to slip into the house quietly and steal a quick taco before anyone noticed she was home, she was out of luck. No sooner had she opened her car door than the front door screen flew open and her mom can running out.

"My baby's home! My baby's home!"

"Hi, Mom," Meade said, trying not to suffocate within her mother's tight embrace.

"Hi, sweetie. We're so glad you're here. Jimmy and I were just saying how quiet it is in the house without you at home."

Meade seriously doubted anyone thought the house was quieter when Meade wasn't home. For starters, Meade had never lived in the same house as Jimmy and so her absence surely did not make a difference in the way he'd always lived. And, secondly, as far as noise level went, Meade was certainly the quietest of the siblings. She guessed the noise level didn't even go up a full decibel when she was around.

"Hey there, girl. Good to have you home." Locked into her mom's hold, Meade hadn't even noticed Jimmy coming up behind his wife. Meade untangled herself from her mom and fell into Jimmy's arms—his big, burly arms. Jimmy was the dad she'd never had. He was kind and loving and smart and *reliable*. If he said he was going to do something, he did it. Whereas, before Jimmy, if Meade's mom had told her she was coming to visit her daughter in New York City, there was a fifty-fifty chance her mom might actually get off the plane when

Meade showed up at the airport to pick her up. Actually, the odds were probably more like thirty/seventy with the seventy percent not working in Meade's favor.

But if Jimmy told you they were coming for a visit, not only did they come, he booked a hotel in advance, made dinner reservations at a variety of restaurants he'd researched online and surprised everyone with Broadway tickets he'd secretly purchased while still in Texas. You could count on Jimmy to do what he said. And more. He always went beyond what you expected from him. Meade couldn't believe how lucky they'd all gotten the day he'd entered their lives.

"The fajitas are ready. Let's go in and eat!"

Meade, Benji and Jimmy followed their mom into the house. It smelled delicious. Meade had forgotten how much she missed the aroma of corn tortillas, refried beans and spicy salsa. The only thing missing was some Mariachi music to remind her she was back in Texas.

"Meade!" Katie came running down the stairs and practically knocked her big sister over with her hug. "I'm so glad you're back!"

"I'm so glad, too! Let me look at you!" Meade held Katie back at arms' length. "You get more and more gorgeous every day. And those legs—I swear, they've grown even longer."

Katie blushed. She was such a beautiful girl, with long blonde hair and a dimple on her left cheek. She was tall—model tall—and slender, too. If Meade didn't love the girl so much, she might've hated her. No one should be that pretty.

"What are you doing home?" Meade asked.

"I'm home for the days you are. I couldn't miss seeing you. You never come to Texas."

Katie had a point there. Ever since she had graduated from college, Meade rarely returned. Usually it was once a year for the scholarship ceremony. More years than not, now that she was grown, she found a reason not to return during the holidays. It was too difficult to come back when there was no Daniel waiting for her.

It had been fifteen years since he'd died and still, the moment Meade stepped foot in Austin, she felt his loss as if he'd left her yesterday.

"Don't you have class?"

"I can miss one or two."

Katie was a graduate student at Texas Tech, studying civil engineering. She was smart. Meade had known the girl would go far when they'd awarded her the Daniel Spencer Memorial Scholarship her senior year of high school. Back then, of course, she had no idea the girl would someday become her sister. The kid was special.

"Okay, we're all here, so let's eat!" Meade's mom said.

It didn't go unnoticed by Meade that Nick wasn't there, but she didn't dare ask about him. She was sure she'd hear the good, the bad and the ugly soon enough—and she'd rather not lose her appetite before she'd even begun to nibble on some chips and queso.

"So, Ben," Jimmy said, as the crowd sat down at the dining room table and began assembling the fajitas. "Tell us about the hospital. How's it going?"

Benji smiled as he dropped a large dollop of guacamole on his tortilla. "It's the hardest and yet the most rewarding thing I've ever done."

"Do you manage to get any sleep?" Jimmy asked.

"It's minimal. Residency hours are brutal, but I'm not complaining. I'm one lucky guy to have gotten the residency I got. Most docs in my position would kill to be where I am."

Benji had attended the University of Texas Medical School in Houston and was now completing his residency at MD Anderson. It was one of the top cancer hospitals in the world. People came from all over the planet to receive treatment there. When Benji finished his residency, he'd be a sought-after oncologist. Already, Johns Hopkins and the Mayo Clinic were showing an interest in him. He'd graduated at the top of his medical school class and was making a name for himself at MD Anderson. He would have a pick of job offers from all over the country when the time came, but Meade had a feeling he'd find a way to stay in Texas, even if it meant accepting a less prestigious position. Benji was, and would always be, a Texan. And truth be told, money and status meant little to him. He hadn't become a doctor for either of those things and hadn't stayed up night after night cramming for his exams so he could someday become a famous cancer surgeon. He'd become a doctor for one reason and one reason only. *Daniel.* He might have been a young teenager when Daniel died, but he'd never forgotten it. Though overwhelmed by her own grief, Meade hadn't been immune to the suffering of her little brother when they'd lost Daniel. Benji had viewed Daniel as the big brother he'd never really had—if you didn't count Nick—which neither he nor Meade did.

For a long time, Benji searched for a way to honor Daniel's memory. He wore Daniel's basketball jersey to school, and on occasion, he asked Meade to take him to the cemetery, where he would sit right next to Daniel's headstone, with his head on his knees, and cry. It had broken Meade's heart to see him that way, as she'd waited for him in the car. Benji had needed a man in his life—someone to look up to. Without a dad or an older brother of his own he could count on, Daniel had filled that role. It wasn't fair that Benji had lost the only man—even if that man was no more than a boy, himself—who'd ever really cared about him.

It would have been easy for both Meade and Benji to pull inside themselves and away from those they loved. The heartbreak of losing Daniel had been so traumatic for both of them. They could have crawled into their separate corners and licked their wounds—alone. But the opposite happened. Daniel's death actually drew them closer. In a way, Meade felt that building a stronger relationship with her brother was a way to honor Daniel's memory. Daniel had loved Benji.

He'd told Meade over and over again how lucky she was to have such a great boy as her kid brother. Daniel would've loved to have a younger brother like Benji.

And frankly, Meade needed a distraction. For years and years, Meade's world had been Daniel. Before he got sick, Meade's life had really revolved around their relationship and his basketball games. She'd spent every day in class, daydreaming about their next date or adventure. Daniel was who she hung out with on the weekends and who helped her pass her biology class by tutoring her. She spent every Friday night cheering him on at his basketball games. And then, when Daniel was diagnosed with leukemia, his illness had been all-consuming. Meade's life had become a whirl of hospital trips and doctors' visits, constantly thinking about Daniel's blood cell counts and his lab results. She'd had very little time for anyone or anything else in her life. In truth, it was amazing she'd been able to maintain her grades. But Daniel had been the reason for that, too. He had no intention of letting his academics fall—even during his illness—and he made sure Meade's didn't suffer, either. Many an afternoon was spent on Daniel's hospital bed, while they quizzed each other on U.S. Government or sat, side-by-side, composing AP English essays. Both Meade and Daniel had plans to graduate at the top of their class. And, Meade had. She'd graduated seventh out of 300 students. Daniel would have been fifth if he'd only lived a few more weeks.

Once Daniel was gone, and the shock of that loss had begun to wear off a bit, Meade turned her focus and time to Benji. It was so clear he needed someone, and Meade decided that someone was going to be her. If her mother wasn't going to nurture him—and, by the amount of time he'd been spending home alone playing video games, it seemed she wasn't going to—then it was Meade's job to make sure he grew into a strong, independent and compassionate man. She didn't have much time. Meade was going to leave for college in a few months. But that whole summer, she invested all her energy into Benji. She tutored him in the subjects he found most difficult — which turned out to be writing and history. She took him to museums and to baseball games and out to the movies. She got to know his friends and sometimes invited them along, too. She found places where the two of them could volunteer together — handing out sandwiches and drinks to the homeless on Austin's Sixth Street on Saturday mornings and working at the local food bank. It hadn't been easy. Her pain was still so raw. But, she began to see a change in Benji. He was growing up and becoming more self-assured, more confident in himself and what he had to offer to this world.

For the next four years, while Meade was away at college, she'd done what she could to continue to build that relationship with her brother. Phone calls, letters written to him, sending him plane tickets to visit her whenever she could save up enough money from the part-time job she worked at the campus library. And summer and Christmas breaks were solely for him. There'd really been no other reason for her to go home. If it hadn't been for wanting to spend time with Benji, she would've made an excuse to stay on campus during the breaks. But she wanted her brother to be successful. Nick was already a lost cause. And her mother was in a world of her own. But Benji...there was still hope for him and she'd be damned if she was going to let him get lost in the cracks because she was too busy mourning the life she could've had.

Looking across the table from Benji now, his head thrown back as he laughed at something funny Jimmy said, Meade couldn't help but smile to herself. They'd done it. She and Benji. Against all odds, he'd come out of this crazy family and landed on his feet. His cowboy boot-clad feet, no less. He was happy and well-liked. He was living a rewarding life. And he was dependent on no one. Meade didn't know what it felt like to be a mom, but she had a feeling that if you did your job right, it was a little bit like when she looked at her baby brother.

"So, Meade," Meade's mom said, interrupting her thoughts. "Tell us about this year's recipient."

"He's *amazing!* One of our best and brightest ever." And then, catching herself, she blushed as she looked at Katie. "Except for you, of course."

"Of course!" Katie said, laughing. Meade knew, instinctively, that Katie wasn't offended. That scholarship had changed her life in more ways than one. It had helped her afford the college of her choice—something she would've never been able to do with the little money her dad had been able to put away over the years. Her mother's long battle with MS had pretty much used up any extra cash Jimmy and her mom had ever been able to save. But college hadn't been the only thing the scholarship had altered in her life. It had given her a family—one she had dreamed of for many, many years. Even before her mother's death, Katie had disliked being an only child. She'd wanted brothers and sisters—and now she had them. And she loved them with all of her heart—even Nick, which wasn't an easy thing to do. It didn't matter to her, one bit, if she wasn't the smartest or most impressive person to ever be awarded the Daniel Spencer Memorial Scholarship. If they awarded a thousand more scholarships, none of those recipients would ever earn a prize as wonderful as the one she'd been given.

"He's a basketball player, straight-A student, involved in a gazillion volunteer opportunities. He actually reminds me of Daniel in a lot of ways, though, that wasn't the only reason he got my vote," Meade said. She loved the hours she'd spent combing through the applicants' files, reading about all their accomplishments. It made her feel good about the world—and the youth who were someday going to be running it. In a way, choosing someone to receive the scholarship in Daniel's name each year, also made her feel a tiny bit closer to Daniel.

"I'm sure he's the perfect choice," Jimmy said. "It's wonderful the way you have kept up with this scholarship. Many people would have moved on by now—lost interest. But you have always been dedicated to it and have helped to change the lives of so many young people."

Fourteen young people, to be exact. Meade could remember the names of each and every one of them. Samuel Higgins. Alexandra Livingston. Jose Rodriguez. The list went on. She remembered each individual, where they went to college, what they majored in. She kept in touch with nearly all of them. They'd all graduated at the top of their classes—gone on to have good jobs. Some had families. All had become successful and none of them took any of the work Meade had done to get them there for granted. Alexandra had become a veterinarian. Samuel had become a commissioned Army officer after college and now taught at West Point. Jose was a banker on Wall Street. Their lives and careers varied, from a restaurant owner in Beverly Hills to a school psychologist in rural Pennsylvania. But all of them were very, very special in Meade's mind and held a sentimental place in her heart. And Jackson Benson, tonight's recipient, would be no different.

"Hey, we'd better get going!" Benji said, glancing at the clock. "We don't want to be late."

Everyone jumped up and began to clear the table.

"Leave it! Leave it!" Meade's mom said. "We can get it later."

Meade, Benji, Jimmy and Katie all exchanged glances and laughed. If they didn't clean up now, the table would never get cleaned. Though the type of person to put off a task until later, Meade's mom was not the type of person to actually get around to that task when later finally arrived.

"It's okay, Mom," Meade said. "With all of us, it'll just take a minute. Plus, we don't want the cheese and chicken to go bad sitting out while we're gone."

"Well, okay, if you insist..."

Meade smiled at her mom and then put her arm around the older woman's shoulders. "Thanks for dinner. It was great. My favorite. Thanks for making my homecoming so special."

Meade was surprised to see tears spring up in her mom's eyes. She was a lot of things, but weepy was not one of them.

"I'm so thankful you're home. I miss you. We all do. It's not the same without you here." She glanced over as the others carried the dishes and glasses into the kitchen. "I know why you don't come home. I really do. But because Daniel isn't here doesn't mean the rest of us still aren't. We want to be a part of your life."

For the first time ever, Meade felt guilty. Her mom was right. She didn't come home. And there was nothing she could say to dispute that. But how did she explain to her mom that coming home felt like tearing open a wound that had just barely healed?

"It's okay," Meade's mom went on. "You don't have to say anything. Like I said, I understand, but I want you to know we miss you."

Meade kissed her mom's cheek. "I miss you, too."

"Are we ready to go?" Jimmy said, walking back into the dining room. "And how are we going to get there? We won't all fit into one car."

"I'm ready," Meade said, squeezing her mom's shoulder one more time. "I think I'll drive with Mom, if that's okay with you, Jimmy. How about you and Katie and Benji go in the other car?"

Meade saw the glance that her mom and Jimmy exchanged and the small smile that passed between them. She had a feeling many conversations had transpired over the years that revolved around her. For a moment, she wondered what had been said. And then, realizing it was probably best if she didn't know, she walked over to the front door and grabbed her mom's keys off the hook on the wall. "I'm driving, Mom! I think we'll all be safer that way."

"Amen to that," Benji called out behind her.

Meade's mom shook her head, but didn't say a word. She continued to smile as she got in the car with her daughter.

The high school library was packed. Jackson was a popular kid, but she had no idea so many people would show up to see him receive this scholarship. Of course the Daniel Spencer Memorial Scholarship was the most sought-after at the school. Everyone wanted it and the presentation of the scholarship was a big deal. Local newspapers always showed up—as did most of the community. It was a time to honor a student who'd worked hard and was being rewarded for his or her achievements.

Meade spotted Mrs. Spencer the moment she walked in the door. Daniel's mom was standing off to the side, deep in conversation with the school principal, the same man who'd been principal when Meade and Daniel had attended the school. Mr. Barker had seemed old back then, though he'd probably only been in his mid-fifties. He was definitely getting up there in years now, though. Meade studied him carefully from afar. His hair was whiter than she remembered it being—even last year. And he had a bit of a bend to his back. But he still looked great. Tall and lanky, with a contagious smile. She'd always liked him and it had always been clear he loved the students at his school. This wasn't a job to him; it was his passion. Those were his "kids"—each and every one of them. Meade had also always enjoyed the easy repartee she and Mr. Barker shared—even when she was merely a student. He was strict and no-nonsense in a lot of ways, but the man had a sense of humor, too—and Meade had found, early on, she was often able to bring it out of him.

Meade walked over to them and they stopped talking the moment she approached.

"I didn't mean to interrupt," Meade said.

Mrs. Spencer gave Meade a huge smile and an even bigger hug. "You are never an interruption!" she said. "We were just talking about you. Were your ears ringing?"

Meade put her hand out to Mr. Barker.

"You want to shake my hand? Come over here and give me a hug!" Within seconds, Meade was locked in his embrace. "It's good to see you, Meade. It's always good to see you." The principal let go of Meade and she smiled at him. "You always were one of my favorites."

"Well, that's sweet of you to say. I never minded you too much, either." Meade winked at the older man.

He roared with laughter. "You've always been a feisty one, too. Kept me on my toes. So glad to have you back."

"It's good to be back." And Meade meant it. It was good to be back.

Mr. Barker's gaze fell across the room. "I'd better go talk to some of my current parents. I'll catch up with you later, Meade." He turned to Mrs. Spencer. "It was lovely to see you, Evelyn."

"Thanks, John. See you Friday?"

"I wouldn't miss it. See you then."

As he walked away, Meade turned to Mrs. Spencer—certain her jaw must be on the floor.

"Evelyn? John? See you *Friday?*"

Mrs. Spencer blushed slightly.

"Are you two *dating?*"

Mrs. Spencer giggled like a young schoolgirl. "I wouldn't call it dating. We're just spending some time together."

Meade gasped and couldn't help the smile that broke out on her face. "You're dating Mr. Barker! You have a boyfriend!"

"Now, Meade. I am too old to have a boyfriend. I have a companion."

"Oh, is that what they call men who take you out to dinner now? A companion?"

"Yes. He's a companion. I've known him for twenty years. He's been a good friend. He was very supportive when we lost Daniel."

Meade's smile softened. "You know I'm teasing you. I think it's great! Boyfriend...companion...whatever you want to call him. I'm happy for you. I love Mr. Barker. He's a good guy."

"He is," Mrs. Spencer said, her eyes on the man across the room.

"And Daniel really liked him."

Mrs. Spencer looked at Meade. "He did, didn't he?"

Meade nodded. "He did. He'd approve."

Mrs. Spencer put her arm around Meade's shoulder and squeezed it gently. "Thanks for saying that, sweetie. That means a lot." She let go and picked up her punch glass, which was sitting on a table next to her. "So, tell me, how are you?"

"I'm great. Work is keeping me busy."

"You know, I read all the books you work on. You always sign the best authors."

"Thanks. We try. It's not easy, but boy, is it a fun job. I love it."

"It's important to love what you do."

"That it is. And tell me, how's the shelter?"

A few years after Daniel's death, Evelyn Spencer had become the director of a local women's shelter. She'd been so touched by the outpouring of support and love she'd received from the community, she wanted to give back. It had taken her a few years to find her niche, but she had, with the Travis County Home for Women and Children. The shelter took in a number of women and their children, at all hours of the day and night, who were trying to escape dangerous living situations. Under her supervision, the shelter had become a vital resource to the Austin community-at-large. It was hard to know how many lives Mrs. Spencer had touched over the years—and changed for the better—but the number was significant.

"Oh, it's growing like you would not believe. We're about to open a new facility—a much larger and more beautiful one—in the hill country. The grand opening will be in the fall. I hope you can make it back for it."

"I'd love to. Email me the dates and I'll try to get it on my calendar."

"I will. It's amazing to see the women and their children come back, years later, and hear their stories of how they've triumphed and persevered and moved on in their lives. It touches my heart."

"You do amazing work there. They're lucky to have you."

"Well, we don't save all the women. Many go back into their terrible lives and can never really make a break. It's so sad to watch. But, there are some who find the strength to move on. Those are the stories I live for. And, I'm the one who's lucky. Without those women—and the incredible staff I work with—I'd be lost. It's not easy being alone at my age."

Meade sighed. Mrs. Spencer had lost so much. Her husband...her son. Before she'd reached the age of forty-five, she'd found herself all alone in this world. It would have been easy to give up. To crawl into a hole and die. And Meade was sure there were many days when Daniel's mom had wanted to do just that. Meade, herself, had wished for death more times than she wanted to think about. She'd wanted to be with Daniel so badly. And how much greater a mother's pain must be. But Mrs. Spencer had gotten up, dusted herself off, and realized there were other people in this world who were also suffering immeasurable pain, and she was going to find a way to help them as others had given of their time to help her during her suffering.

"If you have a chance before you go back to New York, stop by the shelter. I'd love to show you the model of the new facility and introduce you to some of the women. In fact, maybe we could arrange for you to give a little talk? Something inspirational about your career? It might motivate some of the women to get back into the workforce."

"I'm only home a few days, but I'll call you tomorrow and we'll see if we can put something together quickly."

"That would be wonderful, Meade."

Meade didn't really feel like fitting in a speech at a local woman's shelter. She'd have to take time to prepare what she was going to say and her time at home was so short to begin with. She was really hoping to relax and enjoy Austin. But, she would never say "no" to Mrs. Spencer. Meade loved Daniel's mom and she'd do anything for the woman.

"Dear, it looks like they want to you go up front. It's time to start the show!"

Meade glanced over and saw one of the committee members waving her forward. "Oops. I'd better get up there. We'll talk more later."

Meade hurried to the front of the room, as Mr. Barker spoke into the microphone, asking everyone to please take their seats. She took a seat off to the side of the small stage they had created in the library.

Placing her purse on her lap, she felt it vibrate. Reaching inside, she pulled out her cell phone.

*Hey, beautiful. How's sunny Tejas?*

Meade shook her head. Tanner was nothing if not persistent. She momentarily debated sending him a quick text back, but then worried if she replied too quickly, he'd get the wrong idea. She liked him. A lot. But he was the type of guy you started a real relationship with... the kind of man you fell in love with. And, despite their wonderful meal on the roof deck, Meade was not the falling-in-love type. It would be better to reply to him sporadically—at best.

"And now, I'd like to introduce to you, the chair of the Daniel Spencer Memorial Scholarship, Meade Peterson."

There was polite applause as Meade placed her purse on the ground next to her chair and made her way up to the podium. She didn't have a speech written down. She never did. When it came to Daniel,

Meade had decided, years ago, it was best to speak from the heart.

She took a deep breath as she looked out into the crowd. There had to be close to 200 people present. She briefly made a mental note to suggest that next year they move the event to the auditorium.

"Welcome. Thank you for coming. Tonight is always a special night in my life. In fact, I look forward to it all year. Not only am I thrilled to come back to Texas—I now live in New York—but it's the one time of the year when I get to talk about Daniel.

"I know to most of you who are high school students, Daniel Spencer is the name on the biggest scholarship this school has every offered. He's a photo hanging by the school office. But he was a real person. He and I used to walk these school halls, like you do. We ate lunch in that cafeteria. We sat at the top of the bleachers on the football field during homecoming. We fell asleep when Mr. Marotta showed us movies about World War II in U.S. History."

Meade heard a smattering of giggles from the crowd.

"He was real. He's still real. To me and to his mom and to all of those who loved him. He was going to be a doctor. And I know he would have been the best one to ever come out of Texas. He had a way with people. He cared about each and every person he met. There was no one—and I mean *no one*—who ever met Daniel and didn't love him back.

"This scholarship means so much to me, not because we get to present an incredible student with money that will help him succeed in college. It's not about the money to me. It's about honoring the memory of a young man..." Meade's eyes filled with tears, but she blinked them back. She would not cry. "...who used to sit over there in that chair..." She pointed to a table at the back corner of the library. "...and quiz me on the periodic table. It's about giving someone else the future he never got, but truly deserved. Daniel would love tonight— and not because his name was on the award."

There was some more chuckling.

"He'd love tonight because Daniel loved to see people succeed. Not only himself or me, but those around us. His friends on the basketball team. The kids in our classes. People we didn't even know. He loved a good success story, and that is exactly what Jackson Benson is—a success."

As Meade continued, describing all of Jackson's achievements and the difficulties he'd overcome in his life, she felt a peace surround her. This was where she was meant to be. Daniel would approve. And in a way, he was there with them tonight. Cheering her on. Proud of her and all she had accomplished in his memory.

"I'm exhausted!" Benji said, as they drove home from the awards ceremony. "Who knew there was so much to say about one high school kid!"

Meade laughed. "He's an amazing kid. I tried to limit the length of his teacher's speeches, but I guess everyone wanted to have their moment in the spotlight."

"They ran out of punch and cookies midway through the calculus teacher's diatribe. It was hard to stay awake after that."

"It is shocking how much you can eat," Meade said. "If I ate as much as you, I could take over as the UT longhorn mascot at the next game."

Benji pulled the car into the driveway. Their mom, Jimmy and Katie had decided to head over to Dairy Queen afterward—something about Jimmy wanting a Peanut Butter Bash.

"What's he doing here?" Meade said, spotting Nick's turquoise Chevelle in the driveway.

"Probably sleeping."

"Sleeping?"

"That's what he does when he's not drinking. Sometimes he's

smoking. On occasion, he's working. That is, when he doesn't get fired."

"He got fired again?"

"About a month ago."

"And so now he's here to mooch off Mom and Jimmy and raid their kitchen?"

"Amongst other things..."

"What do you mean?" she looked Benji square in the eyes. "What else is he mooching?"

"He moved in."

"He what?!"

"I know. I know. Mom didn't want to tell you. She said you'd flip out."

"I would not flip out," she said indignantly.

"Oh, no? This isn't you flipping out? That's not steam I see wafting out of your ears?" He swatted at the side of her head.

"Okay, maybe I'd flip out a little bit. He's thirty-five years old! This is ridiculous."

"It is. Ridiculous. I agree with you there," Benji said, opening his car door. "But, it is what it is. Mom and Jimmy don't know what to do about him. Mom's trying to get him to go to rehab, but you know how well that always goes over."

Meade did know. All too well. She'd initiated an intervention with Nick and the rest of the family about six years ago. She'd been certain that, if they presented him with the facts and evidence of his alcoholism—backed with their support—he'd be willing to immediately check himself into rehab.

Boy, had that plan backfired! Not only had Nick not gone to rehab, he'd branded her as Enemy Number One from that point on. While they'd never been close, he despised her now and made no attempt to hide his disdain whenever Meade was around. That was why she'd had no intention of seeing him on this trip.

"How could Mom not tell me he was staying here?"

"Because she knew you wouldn't stay here if she did."

"Of course, I wouldn't have stayed here!"

"And she wanted you here..."

Meade sighed. He was right. She would have found another place to stay—perhaps with Mrs. Spencer. And Meade's mom had wanted all of her kids under one roof, even if for a few nights.

"Come on," Benji said, walking up the stairs to the front door. "Let's go in and get this over with."

Meade sighed, got out of the car and followed her brother up the steps.

She could smell the whisky the moment Benji pushed open the door. Benji dropped his keys on the table next to the door. Meade took a deep breath and followed him inside.

They found Nick sprawled out on the couch, a bottle in one hand. The TV was blaring so loudly, Meade wasn't sure how he could stand to be in the room with the noise.

Benji walked over to the set and lowered the volume.

"Hey, man! What are you doin'? I'm watching that!"

"Good to see you, too, Nick. The rest of us would like to maintain our ear drums."

At the term "the rest of us," Nick glanced back toward the doorway, spotting Meade for the first time.

"Oh goodie. Look who's back in Texas. Little Miss Sunshine."

Nick took a swig of the whiskey and laid his head back on the armrest of the couch, his eyes once again glued to the TV.

"Hi, Nick," Meade said. "How are you?"

"Grand. Just grand. I'm always grand."

"Great." Meade looked at Benji who shrugged at her and sat down in the armchair across the room. There was only one other empty chair in the room and so she went over to sit in it. She didn't want to have to ask Nick to move his legs so they could share the couch.

"How's work?"

Benji glared at her across the room, as if to say, *"What are you doing?"* But, she couldn't help herself. Nick got under her skin. He always had. He was such a...*loser.* And why? He hadn't had it any rougher than either she or Benji. Their dad had deserted *all* of them when they were kids. Not only Nick. And they'd all been raised by the same unstable (albeit loving) mom. Nick hadn't lost his high school girl-friend—or anyone else he cared about, really—to a terminal illness. So what was the deal? Why had she and Benji turned out okay and Nick was the raging drunk of the family? Why was he living back with their mom, unemployed, without a dime to his name, at an age where he should already have a home, a career and possibly a family?

And why was everyone always making excuses for him?

"Not working these days. Times are rough. Hard to find a job."

"Really? I saw a Help Wanted sign at Target when Benji and I stopped there a little bit ago."

"Not my thing."

"No? What is your thing? Napping on mom's couch?"

She could feel Benji's eyes boring into her—could almost feel them burning the side of her face—but she was going in for the kill. She was tired of Nick and his crap. Tired of hearing everyone talk about how they didn't know what to do about Nick. Well, Nick needed to figure out what to do about Nick. He was no one's problem but his own. He wasn't a misguided teenager anymore. He was an adult and he needed to start acting like one.

"Listen, missy," Nick said, throwing his legs off the couch and sitting up straight. "Not all of us are as lucky as you—with your hoity-toity job in New York City."

"Lucky? You think I'm lucky? I have that hoity-toity job because I worked my ass off for it."

"You mean you used your hot piece of ass to work your way up the corporate ladder."

Meade jumped out of her seat. If steam hadn't been coming out of her ears in the car, she was certain it was now. "I am smart and driven. I have never used sex to further my career."

"No? Of course you don't. Because you're still crying over your dead boyfriend."

Benji stood up at this point. He wasn't sure what Meade was going to do to Nick, but he had a feeling it wasn't going to be pretty. She might be the smallest one in the family, but she was fast, with a temper that could scare grown men. Benji was glad there didn't seem to be anything too sharp in the vicinity of the couch—other than the whiskey bottle. He momentarily wondered if she might hit Nick over the head with it.

If Nick saw the glare Meade was throwing his way, he didn't seem to care. "I bet you still cry into your pillow over him every night." He began to imitate a crying sound. "Oh, poor me. My boyfriend died and my life is so horrible."

"You're a real jerk, Nick," Meade said.

Nick shrugged. "I say it like I see it. You think you're all high and mighty, only coming home when something has to do with Daniel. What about your real family? I never see you doing anything for us."

"Hey, Nick," Benji said. "That's not true. Meade's always been there for our family."

Nick snorted. "Really? When exactly would that be? She never comes home for the holidays—even if Mom begs. And I bet she's making a whole lot of money in her big fancy office in New York City." He turned to Meade. "You do have a big fancy office, don't you? And yet, I don't see you helping out any of us who are struggling back home. Not even fifty bucks here or there."

"The only person who might need money in this family is you," Meade said. "And if you would get your lazy ass off Mom's couch, and stop drinking like a fish, you might actually get a job and make your own money. It's funny how that works. You go to work and they pay you. It's a crazy concept, I know, but I'm sure even an idiot like you can grasp it."

Nick jumped up off the couch, and within seconds, was standing within inches of Meade. Though a good six inches taller than her, his height didn't intimidate her. He was glowering down at her, but she stood her ground, hands on her hips, and icy stare matching his gaze.

"You'd better watch it, Meade. You don't know nothin' about nothin'."

"I know when not to use a double negative."

Benji had to stifle a laugh, despite the tension in the room.

"Just remember that we settle things differently here in Texas than your fancy friends do in New York City."

"Oh, are you threatening me now? Nice, Nick. Threaten your own sister with violence. I didn't think even you'd stoop that low."

Nick shrugged and took a step back. "Just sayin'. You shouldn't be coming in here and spoutin' off your big ol' mouth."

"I'll spout off my big old mouth any day I like," she said.

Meade heard the front door open. She and Nick continued their menacing staring contest, each daring the other to look away first.

"We're home," Jimmy called out. "I brought you a dipped cone, Meade. You'd better eat it quickly! It's melting all over my hand."

Meade forced one more burst of invisible fire out of her eyes and into her brother's and then turned away. Jimmy was standing in the doorway, a concerned look on his face.

"Everything okay here?" he asked, as Meade took the cone from him. Their mom and Katie walked in behind him.

"Yes," Meade said. "Everything's fine. Thanks for the cone."

"I remembered it was your favorite," Jimmy said distractedly, as he stared at Nick. "You okay, Nick?"

"I'm just fine and dandy," Nick said, picking up his whiskey bottle and moving past his family and out of the room. "I'm going to bed. Make sure to wake me when *she* leaves the state."

"I'm sure it'll be sooner than when you move out and get a job like a grown-up," Meade called after him.

"Seriously, Meade? Are you like, *twelve?*" Benji asked once Nick was out of the room.

"Aaagh!" Meade cried out and plopped down on the couch. "He gets on my last nerve."

"Honey, you need to be patient with him," Meade's mom said, sitting down on the couch next to her. "He's struggling."

"Mom, he's thirty-five years old. He needs to get a grip on life."

Her mom sighed. "I know. I wish I knew how to help him. But I don't. You'll see—someday when you have your own kids. You think raising children is black and white, but it's not. It's full of gray and most things don't go at all like you thought they would."

"Then good thing I won't be having any of those," Meade said, licking her ice cream.

"Oh, sweetie, yes you will. Wait. Someday you'll meet the right guy..."

Meade patted her mom on the knee and then got up off the couch. There was no point in having this discussion with her. Especially not in front of the whole family. "I'm beat. Gonna go hit the hay. See everyone in the morning."

"Already?" Benji asked. "I'm heading down to Sixth Street. Some old high school buddies have a band and are playing at one of the bars. I thought you might want to come."

"Thanks for the offer, but I'm exhausted. Have fun, though."

"Sleep well," Jimmy said.

Meade went over and kissed him on the cheek and then did the same to Benji and Katie. "Thanks, I will."

"Big plans for tomorrow that you need to be wide awake for?" Benji asked.

"I was kind of thinking of heading down to the Capitol Building and taking a tour. I haven't done that since my third-grade field trip. Might be interesting. Plus, I have a writer working on a fictional book about the Alamo. I might come up with a few tidbits to share with him. Anyone want to join me?"

"I'm going to go for a run down by Town Lake," Katie said. "Don't imagine you want to join me?"

"Ha! No thanks. Running's not my thing. But, how about we meet at Chuy's for lunch when you're finished? Let's say noon?" She looked at her brother. "You want to come, too?"

"Sounds good to me," Benji said and Katie nodded.

"Mom? Jimmy? Up for a Capitol tour?"

The two of them exchanged a look and then Jimmy spoke on their behalf. "No thanks. If we'd wanted to go on a tour of the Capitol, we would've done it by now. But you have fun and make sure to take some pics to show us at dinner."

"You've got it," Meade said. "Okay. Night, everyone."

"Night," they all said in unison.

Meade walked down the hall and up the stairs to the guest room she was sleeping in. It was a beautiful home, she had to admit. Much nicer than anything she and her brothers had grown up in with their mom. Five bedrooms, three baths and a whole lot of space, it was the type of home they'd never even dreamed of living in as children. Jimmy had brought a lot of wonderful elements to their lives, and financial security for their mom was definitely one of them.

Just as she plopped down on the bed, she felt her phone vibrate in her pocket. She pulled it out and glanced down at the text. Tanner. Again.

*I know you'd never ignore me, so you must be super busy. Is the sky still bigger in Texas?*

Meade smiled sadly as she read the text. Being back in Texas, surrounded by memories of Daniel, she was more certain than ever she couldn't get into a serious relationship with Tanner. Despite all the things he'd said to her on the roof deck—words she'd believed at the time—she *didn't* know him. And he certainly didn't know her. She'd been known one time and one time only by a man. And that was over. Everywhere she looked when she was home in Austin drove that point straight into her heart.

She needed to have a talk with Tanner when she returned to New York. Explain to him why she couldn't get involved. It wouldn't be fair to do that via a text. For now, she'd continue the lighthearted dialogue.

*Everything's bigger in Texas. And more beautiful.*

His reply came within thirty seconds.

*I remembered the "more beautiful part" the moment I met you.*

Meade lay back on her pillow and rested the phone on her chest. It would be easy to let herself get carried away with feelings for Tanner Dale. If things were different...if her past was different...but then again, if things had turned out the way they were supposed to, she'd be married to Daniel, with a houseful of kids.

She would have never even met Tanner Dale.

# CHAPTER TWELVE

M eade couldn't believe her good fortune when she found a parking spot right on Congress Avenue, across the street from the Paramount Theater. She'd thought it highly unlikely she'd be able to park so close to the Capitol Building—especially on a weekday. Austin was growing by leaps and bounds. These days, it always seemed to be on someone's national list—the "Fastest Growing Cities" list or the "Best Place to Raise Children" list or the "Best Vacation Destinations" list. It had gotten so one could hardly turn on the news in the morning without hearing about Austin's latest honorary distinction.

Those accolades, however, did not translate into better parking. In fact, in the years since Meade had lived in Austin, the traffic had become atrocious. Sometimes she wondered if she was actually better off staying in New York City and dealing with their gridlock than fighting rush-hour traffic on IH-35. So much for her sleepy little town.

She turned off the car and opened the door. It felt like she had just entered Hansel and Gretel's oven. The heat blast was so overwhelming, she momentarily considered shutting the car door and cranking up the AC again. She glanced at her watch. Nine in the morning. If it was this hot so early in the day, she hated to think about what it would feel like by noon.

*What on earth did Texans do before air conditioning?*

Meade wiped her brow, disgusted that a sweat bead had already formed there, and headed over to the meter. After swiping her credit card through the parking meter and hoping the two hours it earned her would be enough time, she began to walk the two blocks north to the Capitol Building. Her shirt was sticking to her by the time she reached the historical iron fence that surrounded the Capitol grounds. Glancing up as she walked through the main entrance gate, she had to catch her breath. Meade never got tired of looking at this building. With a majestic dome, similar to that of the Capitol in Washington, D.C. (though seven feet taller, a fact in which Texans found great pride), the Texas Capitol Building was visible from all areas of the city. It was most noticeable, though, as you drove due north on Congress Avenue. Then the building was straight in front of you.

Normally, Meade found the long pathway from the street to the steps of the Capitol breathtaking. But today, in this heat, it seemed never-ending. She slowly made her way up the slight hill. A group of elementary school students was seated on the benches on either side of the walkway. Meade guessed them to be about third grade.

*Wasn't that the year Daniel and I visited the Capitol on our class trip?*

The kids were giggling and goofing around, while their teachers and chaperones stood by, looking worn and weary.

*"And it's only nine,"* Meade thought. *"They still have a long day ahead of them."*

"Peter!" one of the teachers called out. "Get off that cannon! They're not for climbing!"

Meade giggled to herself as she continued up the path. She was glad she'd never been tempted to go into education. She liked kids enough. Enjoyed hanging out with them from time to time. Wouldn't mind if Benji got married and had one or two, so she could become an aunt. But teaching? A class of thirty little kids all day long? No, thanks.

Meade walked up the stairs to the front door. Huffing and puffing as if she were 300 pounds and carrying another human being on her back, she paused to catch her breath at the top. This was shameful. *She was a Texan.* She needed to adjust to this heat.

Meade pushed open the ornate wooden door to the Capitol building and nearly sang with glee when she felt the cool breeze of the air conditioning hit her face. Hurrying inside, she paused in front of the security checkpoint in an attempt to cool down.

"Hotter than a pistol out there, ain't it?"

Meade looked up at the state trooper standing by the X-ray machine. She had to smile at the cowboy hat. He might as well be wearing a bandana that said, *"You're in Texas now."*

"It's awful! I might stay in this building 'til winter. I'm not sure I want to go out there again."

"Record-breaking heat, the news guys say. We're now at forty-six consecutive days in the hundreds."

Meade put her purse on the conveyor belt, along with her phone and her keys.

"You wearing a belt or any other metal that will set off the alarm?" he asked.

"No, I don't think so."

"Okay, then you can walk on through."

A female state trooper motioned Meade forward. Meade held her breath for a split-second, but no buzzers went off.

"Looks like you're good. Enjoy the Capitol Building," the first trooper said.

"Thanks. I will. Try to stay cool standing by that door."

"Will do."

Meade gathered up her belongings and walked over to the sign that said "Tours."

*The Next Tour will Begin at 10 A.M.*

Meade looked down at her watch again. Nine-fifteen. It looked like she had some time to kill.

Spotting a tour guide heading back into the office, Meade gently tapped her shoulder. "Is there a gift shop?" she asked.

"Yes! A lovely one," the woman said. "It's in the underground extension." She gave Meade directions and pointed to the staircase that would take Meade where she wanted to go. After thanking her, Meade quickly made her way through the rotunda and down the stairs. It took a few wrong turns, but eventually, Meade found herself in the newest portion of the Capitol, and it didn't take her long to locate the gift shop.

Meade loved gift shops. She always had, even as a kid. Even when she'd had no money to buy anything. Whenever she'd gone to a museum or the gallery or even the local zoo, she'd always begged her mom or teacher to please let her wander through the gift shop. She loved to look at every item in the store—most of which, of course, were completely useless to her everyday life and cost three times what they would if they were being sold at Walmart. But still, there was something about the uniqueness of them or the way they were displayed that made her wish she could buy each and every item. Even as an adult, the gift shop, be it at a hotel or a historical building, was a must-see wherever she visited.

And this one did not disappoint! No one knew how to celebrate their state like Texas. There was nothing—*nothing*—that Texas could not personalize. If there was a flat surface on a product, it would be sufficient to hold the image of a Texas flag or a blue bonnet or a lone star. Meade spotted a rack of potholders and aprons bearing the state flag, next to a shelf of Texas-themed mouse pads, key chains and shot glasses. There was even a bucket of golf balls on the floor, all carefully painted so that it looked like the flag was wrapped around them. There were Texas Christmas ornaments—*though, who thought about decorating a tree in this weather?*—and Texas baby bibs. Because, as all Texans know, it's never too early to start building a child's state loyalty.

Meade flipped through a stack of bumper stickers.

*I wasn't born in Texas but I got here as fast as I could.*

*Life's too short not to live it as a Texan.*

*Don't mess with Texas women.*

*My state is bigger than your state.*

It was hard not to chuckle. Everything *was* bigger in Texas—including its pride. She picked up one sticker that held the famous Davey Crockett quote, "You may all go to hell, but I will go to Texas."

Next to her, she heard a mother and daughter talking, in deep Southern accents. Meade liked the sound of their twangs. It was funny how so few people in Austin actually had Southern accents. Meade wasn't exactly sure why that was. Perhaps because Austin was a melting-pot type of town. Many, if not most, of the people who lived there seemed to have moved from other cities—some in Texas, but many were from all over the country. If someone had a Texas accent, they likely did not actually grow up in Austin, but rather, in a surrounding town or a more distant area of the state.

The daughter was holding a piece of paper in her hand, reading from it. "Look, Mama. You can become an honorary citizen of Texas. Know anyone you'd like to make an Honorary Texan?"

"No one deserves to be an Honorary Texan," the mother snipped. "You have to be born here."

Meade put her hand over her mouth so the laugh didn't actually exit her body. Yes, Texas pride was real and alive in Austin.

She spent some time browsing around the gift shop. She wanted to bring something back for Pantera—not an easy task. Pantera had unique taste, to put it mildly. Meade finally settled on a jar of Texas jalapeno jelly. Pantera would love that. Sweet and spicy—like Pantera.

After paying, Meade made her way back up the Capitol steps, to the front entrance of the building. A small crowd was gathering near the tour sign. Meade saw the tour guide was already there, chatting with some of the visitors.

"Where are you from?" she heard him ask an elderly couple. Their answer wasn't clear, but by the guide's response of "Oh! Are you cheeseheads?" she figured they must have said "Wisconsin."

"Did you know that the first word said on the moon was 'Houston'?"

Meade glanced to her side and noticed a little boy looking up at her. "You know, I did know that," she said, smiling down at him.

"Did you know that the word 'Texas' means friends?"

"Yep, knew that, too."

"Hmmm..." the little boy said, putting his hand to his chin, clearly thinking. "Did you know that it's illegal to milk another person's cow in Texas?"

Meade couldn't hold back the laugh. "Now that, I did not know."

"It's true!"

"I have no doubt you're right." She could not take her eyes off the boy. He was clearly very intelligent. And personable, as he had successfully struck up a conversation with a perfect stranger. But there was something else about him that drew Meade to him. He looked like Daniel. Albeit, an elementary school-aged Daniel. But, he had the same tan skin and dark hair that hung in curls, framing his face. And the eyes. Those eyes. She hadn't seen eyes as brown and bright as those since Daniel had closed his for the last time.

"How old are you?" Meade asked.

"Eight."

"Eight! You seem like you're much older."

"Most people think I'm older 'cause I'm tall. But I'm just eight."

"I was thinking you seemed closer to forty—'cause you're so smart," Meade said.

The little boy giggled.

"I get straight A's in school."

"I'll bet you do."

Right then, a woman rushed over to the little boy. She had a wet paper towel in her hand and began to wipe the side of his face, where signs of his breakfast remained. "I'm sorry," she said, addressing Meade as she wiped the boy's face. "I hope he wasn't bothering you. I went to the restroom to get a towel."

"Mom!" The boy tried to wiggle away, but his mother's grasp on his arm was firm. "Stop!"

"I will not stop. I told you to go into the bathroom and clean your face before we left the hotel. I will not have my son walking all over Austin with food on his face."

The boy stopped squirming long enough for her to finish.

"There," the mom said, standing up straight. "Much better."

The boy smiled up at Meade. "I had pancakes for breakfast."

"And the syrup got a bit messy?" Meade asked.

The boy shrugged. "I guess."

Meade turned to the mom. "He wasn't bothering me at all. In fact, he was educating me on some interesting Texas facts."

"Did you know that it's illegal, in Texas, to shoot a buffalo from the second story of a hotel?"

Meade laughed again. The mom turned a bit red.

"I'm sorry. I thought it would be fun to buy him a book that listed interesting and funny facts about Texas. I didn't know he'd recite them to everyone we met."

"I think it's awesome. Maybe someday he can get a job giving tours here. So I take it you're not from Texas."

"No. We're from New Jersey."

"Oh, really? I live in Manhattan."

"Just across the Hudson from us. We're in Hoboken. What are you doing in Austin?"

"I grew up here. Came back for a visit. I haven't been to the Capitol since I was a little kid and so I thought it might be a fun thing to do before I go back. And you? Why are you here?"

"My husband has a business trip. He's at the Convention Center this morning. Max and I thought it might be fun to explore Austin on our own."

Meade turned back to Max. "Have you seen the bats yet?"

"The bats? No!"

"Did you know that Austin is the home to the world's largest urban bat colony?"

"No!" Max nearly squealed with glee. "Where can I see them?"

"Well, you have to check with your mom and dad first." Meade looked up and smiled at the mom. "But if they say it's okay, you can all go and wait down by the bridge on South Congress Avenue. Right around the time the sun sets, the bats come out for the night. There are millions of them, and they'll fly right over your head."

"Cool!"

"Yep. It is pretty cool."

"Can we go, Mom? Can we go?" Max pleaded.

Meade mouthed the word "sorry" to the mom, but the woman smiled back at Meade.

"We'll have to check with Dad, but I'll bet we can work something out."

"Awesome!"

"Okay, may I have your attention, please? I think we can start our tour now." Meade turned toward the tour guide and saw he was trying to get everyone's attention. "It's kind of noisy in this area of the Capitol, so you'll have to stand pretty close to me and to each other so you can all hear."

The group moved in closer to the guide. There seemed to about twelve people joining the tour, including Meade, Max and his mom.

"I'd like to draw your attention to the painting behind me. It is a William Huddle painting and it depicts the Surrender of Santa Ana. In the painting, you can see Santa Ana being brought forward as a prisoner of war, surrendering to Sam Houston, who's on the ground with the injured leg. Houston had been shot in the ankle during the Battle of San Jacinto. The injury eventually healed, but caused him pain for the rest of his life.

"Now, if you'll look on the opposite wall, you'll see another Huddle painting. This one is of Alamo defender, David Crockett. It has been hanging in this foyer since 1891..."

"I'm Meade, by the way," Meade said to Max's mom. The two women shook hands.

"Rachel. It's nice to meet you, Meade."

"Meade's a funny name," Max said.

"Max. Ssh. That's not polite."

Meade bent down to whisper in Max's ear. "It is a funny name. You know how I got it?"

"How?" Max whispered back.

"Before I was born, my dad went whitewater rafting on a lake called Lake Mead in Arizona. He liked it so much and thought the lake was so beautiful, he wanted to name me after it."

Max smiled.

"That's a fun way to have gotten your name," Rachel said.

Meade leaned in close to Rachel, so Max couldn't hear. "At least, that's the story my mom tells me. My dad left us when I was a kid. I kind of think the name came from all the alcohol he consumed, but hey...what do I know?"

Meade winked at Rachel and Rachel chuckled.

"Well, however you got your name, it's a beautiful one."

"Thank you."

"Now, if you will draw your attention to two statues by the entrance to the rotunda, the one on your left is of Sam Houston. He is the only man to have been governor of two states. In 1827, he was elected the Governor of Tennessee. In 1859, he became the Governor of Texas. The statue to your right is Stephen F. Austin..."

Meade took her notebook out of her bag and began to take notes.

These were, of course, facts that her author could get in any text-book or webpage, but she was hoping to hear some unique ones he might miss out on—if not from the tour guide, then maybe from Max. He seemed to have the best facts around.

The group continued into the Rotunda where they learned about the six flags that flew over Texas and how, when originally built, there were only 300 workers in the Capitol building. These days, though, when Congress was in session, there could be up to 8,000 workers on the grounds.

"And that is why, in the 1990s, it was decided that we needed to build an underground extension to the Capitol," the tour guide said as they made their way downstairs.

"Why underground?" Max asked.

"That's a good question, young man," the guide said, turning to Max. Meade looked at the tour guide carefully. He seemed like a really nice man. Middle-aged, with graying hair, he gave off a joyful air. It was clear he enjoyed his job and he'd been nothing but patient with Max and the hundreds of questions he seemed to throw at the guide throughout his talk. No one on the tour, though, seemed to be get-ting annoyed with the young boy. If anything, he was adding levity to heavy historical stories and, by asking so many questions, extract-ing some pretty interesting facts from the guide.

"That's so as to not block the view of the capitol dome from any-where in the city. If you are at the University of Texas, you still have a clear view of the building."

"And who are those babies on the picture behind you?"

"Ah..." said the tour guide, turning to the frame behind him. Inside was a poster that showed photos of all the Congress men and women from 1967 and in the center of them were about twenty-five baby photos. "Those are the important representatives. They vote on things like recess time and lunch meals and snacks..."

"Really?" Max's eyes grew wide.

The guide laughed. "No. Not really. They are the grandbabies of the representatives and we call them our 'honorary mascots.'"

"Oh." Max's shoulders fell in disappointment.

Rachel put her arms around Max and kissed the top of his head. The group continued on through the underground extension and then back upstairs again. By the time they'd once again reached the Rotunda, Meade had filled fifteen pages of her notebook. She hoped her author would find something valuable in what she wrote.

"I noticed you taking notes," the guide said to her as they reached the top of the steps. "Are you an architecture student?"

"No, I'm a book editor. One of my authors has a story taking place in historical Texas. I thought I might learn something useful for him on this tour."

The guide grabbed onto his nametag and pulled it forward, so Meade could read it clearly. "It's Jeff," he said. "With *two* F's."

Meade laughed. "You want to be a character in his book?"

The guide shrugged. "It never hurts to ask."

The two of them had just reached the center of the Rotunda floor when Meade heard someone yelling. She looked toward the tour guide, waiting for an explanation from him. Perhaps this was part of a show performed every morning for the tourists.

One glance at his face, though, told Meade all she needed to know. This wasn't a show.

"Nobody move!"

Meade quickly looked around her for the source of the voice. Entering the Rotunda was a man about her age, wildly waving a gun.

"I said, nobody move!" the man yelled again, though Meade didn't see anyone moving. Everyone was suddenly frozen in place.

She studied the gunman closely. He looked like he belonged there. He was dressed in a suit. He was clean-cut. If it wasn't for the crazed gleam in his eyes, she would have thought he was a state senator or, at the very least, a congressional aide.

*But how did he get past security with that gun? And where were the sheriffs?*

"Now that I have everyone's attention, there are a few things I'd like to discuss."

*Discuss? What was he talking about?*

"And I expect to be given some respect. No one—and I mean, *no one*—had better move."

Meade doubted there was any risk of that. The people around her were as still as the statues of Austin and Houston they'd passed in the foyer. The man definitely had everyone's attention.

The gunman opened his mouth to speak again, when out of the corner of her eye, Meade saw Max bound up the stairs from the basement. He and his mom had stayed behind to look around the gift shop for a minute.

"Hey, Meade!" Max called out, completely unaware of the situation at hand. "Look what I got!"

Time moved very slowly from that point on. Meade saw the man turn toward Max, gun raised.

"No!" Meade screamed. Whereas a second earlier, she'd been completely unable to move, frozen in fear, a rush of adrenaline cascaded through her body. Meade took off at a sprint, lunging at Max as she reached him.

The crack was loud. Meade heard it as she landed on top of Max and wondered if he had hit his head on the ground when he fell.

"Max," she said. "Max. Are you okay?"

She tried to move off of him, to give him some air, but she felt pinned down—like someone was holding her there with a hot cattle prod, burning a brand through her back and into her chest.

"Police! Put your weapons down!"

*Good. The police are here now. I need to get up.*

Meade pushed against the floor again, but it made no difference. She felt Max wiggle out from under her.

*He's okay.*

"Max," Meade said. "Max."

"It's okay, Meade. You'll be okay," Rachel said, stroking Meade's hair.

*Okay? Why will I be okay?*

"We need an ambulance over here!"

*Was that Jeff the tour guide? Why did they need an ambulance? Had she jumped on Max too hard? Had she hurt him?*

"Meade. Meade," Max said, lying on the ground next to her, his face inches from her own. "Did you know that the Dallas-Fort Worth Airport has the largest parking lot in the world?"

*No. I didn't know that.*

Meade looked at Max's face. He looked scared. Why was he scared? The police were there now.

*Max.* She looked at him closely. Or was it Daniel?

*Daniel.*

It was getting hard to keep her eyes open.

*Daniel. Why are you a little boy again? Daniel...*

Meade looked into the little boy's eyes. They were so dark. She felt like she was falling. *Falling into them? How could she be falling into them?*

But she was. The eyes became bigger and everything around her became darker. Until there was nothing at all. Just darkness.

And peace.

# CHAPTER THIRTEEN

M eade felt the crick in her neck before she even opened her eyes. She needed to roll over to stretch it out, but it felt like she was frozen in place—as if a large garbage truck had rolled over her and then dumped its load on top of her flattened body. Even the slightest movement made the dagger—that apparently had fallen off the truck and directly into the side of her neck—pierce her skin at a deeper angle.

"Ugh..." Meade moaned, taking a deep breath. She debated not moving at all and falling back asleep, in the hopes of feeling better next time she awoke, but she really had to pee.

"One...two..." she silently counted in her head, promising herself that, on the number three, she'd begin to move. "Two and a half..."

"Chicken," she told herself. "Three!"

With as much strength as she could muster, which was pretty minimal, she flipped her body over and onto the other side. Tilting her head into the pillow, she attempted to stretch out the side of her neck. Pain shot down, through her shoulder, and up into the top of her head.

"Ugh..." Meade moaned again. She wracked her brain for what she might have done to feel so achy this morning. Maybe she'd been so tightly curled into a ball, trying to keep warm, that she'd inadvertently "slept funny." She pulled the covers tighter around her. She really needed to get up. Her bladder was about to burst. But it was so cold.

Even with an enormous down comforter on top of her, she was shivering. And the thought of putting her feet down on the cold, wood floor—*why hadn't she worn socks to bed?*—was nearly more than she could bear. She snuggled deeper into the covers.

It was mornings like these when she wondered why she hadn't moved back to Texas after graduation.

*Beep...beep...beep...*

Quickly, Meade's hand shot out from under her pillow—*wow, was it cold out there*—and over to the nightstand, patting the air haphazardly. *Where was that clock? And, more importantly, why was it going off?* Meade didn't remember setting any alarm last night. She must have done it in her sleep. She'd been known to do things like that in the past. The worst was the time she turned *off* her alarm in the middle of the night, thus causing her to miss her six a.m. flight to London. That was a memory she wanted to forget. She'd been scheduled to meet with a well-known author they were trying to sign— *actually, it was more like, steal away from their competitor before he signed another contract*—immediately after her flight landed in England. He'd been very clear with her that he could only spare an hour before he, himself, left on an overseas flight for a month-long vacation in South Africa. By the time she awoke and realized her flight had left three hours earlier, there was no point in even making the trip at all. She'd never get there before he left the country. Despite numerous apology phone calls to the writer—and one very expensive cheesecake she'd had shipped to Johannesburg—*that had been a poorly thought-out plan*—the writer had stayed on with his current publisher. He'd never said it outright, but Meade knew he thought she was a bumbling fool. His last book had sold 11 million copies, a fact which grated on Meade. She'd never before set her sights on an author and not been able to win him over. Meade was charming. And witty. People liked her. Authors loved her. They felt safe in her care. The fact that she'd let one get away—albeit, early in her career when she was still wet behind the ears—got under her skin. She never discussed it with anyone—not since she'd had to explain and apologize her way out of a very uncomfortable meeting with the senior publisher who'd told her, in advance, nothing was more important than signing this guy. But because she never said his name aloud didn't mean she'd forgotten the sting. And every once in a while—specifically when she'd meander through a bookstore and see a display for his books—it got the best of her.

Turning all the books over, so only the back covers showed, didn't affect the man's sales, of course—and she wasn't proud of herself for doing it—but somehow, it always made her feel the teeniest bit better.

Meade's hand finally found the alarm and she slapped the top of it—hard. Actually, it took about three slaps, but ultimately, the noise ceased.

She quickly pulled her hand back into the warmth of her pillow. It felt so good in her little cocoon, but the pee was about to trickle onto the bed. She needed to get up. Taking a deep breath, and once again counting to three in her head, Meade quickly threw her feet out of the bed and onto the floor, simultaneously sitting up.

The carpet was what surprised her first. It was deep and soft and warmed her feet the moment they sunk down into it. *Did I buy a rug?*

She opened her eyes to check. There *was* a rug under her feet. A dark-beige sheepskin rug. The kind she'd seen at a furniture store about two months ago, and debated buying, but ultimately decided against it. At least, she *thought* she'd decided against it.

She raised her eyes from the rug and gasped. Quickly, she scanned the room. Across from the bed stood a dark wood dresser. Photos in various frames adorned the top, though from the bed, she couldn't make out the images. She saw a hair brush and some combs in front of them. One of the drawers was partly open and a shirt hung halfway out. There was a tall ficus tree next to the dresser—the kind she hated because they never failed to get dusty and were virtually impossible to clean. *Who, in their right mind, wanted to dust each leaf, one at a time?* The pictures on the walls were all prints of modern art. Some she recognized as famous ones. Some she didn't know at all. The frames looked cheap and clearly not professionally done. The walls were beige. Plain beige. The kind of beige that comes with an apartment. Not the bright blue of her bedroom walls. Not the blue she'd spent an entire weekend painting by herself, dripping the paint so badly as she used the long roller high above her head, that she'd shown up at work Monday morning with paint specks in her hair.

Nothing around her seemed familiar. This wasn't her stuff. Not her bookshelf. Not her dresser. Not her curtains. Not her window. *That wasn't her window.* This wasn't her room. This wasn't her apartment.

Meade felt the blood rush out of her head, and she put her hands down on the mattress on either side of her to steady herself.

Not only was this not her place, it wasn't at all familiar. She hadn't woken up in a friend's house. She'd never seen this room.

"Mmmmm..."

Meade froze. *What was that?*

Her body stiffened. She couldn't move. Her hands were stuck to the bed and her head didn't want to turn. Until now, it never occurred to her she might not be alone.

She heard a deep sigh behind her. She closed her eyes, squeezing them tightly, and then opened them again. She was still here. *Damn.* This wasn't a dream.

Slowly, with deliberate moves, she twisted her body so she was facing the opposite side of the room. She covered her mouth with her hand, quickly, so as not to let out a squeal.

There was a man in bed with her. And, from the back of him, which was all she could see from this angle, he didn't look familiar.

*Did I have a one-night stand? With a stranger?*

He shifted in bed and she jumped slightly. She glanced around the room, searching for the door. It was on his side of the bed. She could make a run for it. He might see her, but she was fast. She could probably get out before he caught up with her.

And then she glanced down. She couldn't make a run for it looking like this. She was wearing nothing more than a gray tank and matching panties. They were cute, but surely not one-night-stand worthy. Meade was momentarily embarrassed that she hadn't made more of an effort to look nice for her date.

*"Slap yourself,"* Meade told herself silently. *"This wasn't a date. You don't know this man."*

Curiously, Meade took a closer look at him. Did she know him? He seemed tall, if the long lump under the covers was any indication of his height. His hair was dark—nearly black— but she could see slight flecks of gray by his temple. She couldn't remember where she might have met him.

Meade glanced down at the floor, in search of her clothes. Where were her clothes? It must not have been a wild, crazy night of passion if her clothes weren't thrown onto the floor. Maybe they were on his side of the bed?

*Did he undress me? Was I drugged?*

Meade studied him again. Did he look like the type of man to roofy a woman? She wasn't sure. She didn't know what those men looked like. *Did they have a look?*

Meade tried to remember last night. *Was* there a last night? She couldn't remember. The last thing she remembered was being in Austin. She'd gone home to see her mom. She and Nick had gotten in an argument and then Benji had asked her if she wanted to go down to Sixth Street to hear a band he liked. *Had they gone? Did she meet this guy at a bar downtown?*

She listened to the sounds around her. They were plentiful. Horns honking. Garbage trucks rumbling. Police sirens screaming in the distance. No, this was New York City. She didn't have to look out the window to know that. Even on its busiest of days, Austin never sounded like this.

*New York?* How had she gotten back here? Or, maybe she'd never left. Had her trip to Austin been a dream? But even so, if it were, how had she ended up in this apartment? And, more importantly, who was this guy in bed next to her?

Meade looked at the man again. She wondered if she should tap his shoulder and ask him his name. Or would that be too awkward?

*"Hey, thanks for last night. I don't remember any of it...and I have no idea who you are or what your name is...but I'm sure we had a great time. Now, if you don't mind, I'm gonna get dressed...if I can find my clothes...and go home...that is, if I can figure out how to get home... call me?"*

No, she definitely couldn't say that.

Meade took a deep breath. Boy, was this a quandary. She'd experienced a lot in her life, but never, ever anything like this. Maybe she should call someone. She wondered if anyone was worried about her. *Am I a missing person?*

That was a disheartening thought. *Where's my cell phone?* She glanced at the nightstand, but didn't see it sitting there. She did, however, see a tall, open bottle of Izze on a coaster next to her side of the bed. Sparkling Blackberry. Her favorite. She couldn't have been too scared of the guy next to her if she'd taken the time to drink a carbonated beverage in his bed. As quietly as she could, she reached over and slowly pulled open the nightstand drawer. Maybe her phone was inside. The drawer squeaked on its rollers. *Damn.*

"What are you looking for?" a voice said from behind her. He sounded sleepy.

Meade held her breath. Should she reply?

"Uhm...my cell phone," Meade answered, not turning around. "I can't seem to find it."

"It's on the charger in the living room," he said, yawning.

"Oh, yeah..." she said. "I forgot." She turned back to look at him. He was lying on his stomach now, his face buried in the pillow. "Okay... well...I think I'd better go..."

"Where are you going?" he mumbled into the pillow. "I thought you weren't working today."

*Not working today? He knows about my life? He knows about my schedule?*

"I...um...I think I should go home. I have some errands to run today."

"Home?" His head popped up. "Did you have a stroke in your sleep?"

And then she saw him. His face. That face. She knew that face. Not that exact face. Something was different about it. Something was off. Older? But she knew it. She knew him. But, she couldn't possibly...he was gone. But he wasn't. He was right here. In bed. With her.

Meade jumped off the bed and threw her body backward. She fell into the small bookshelf that was under the window, knocking a stack of books onto the floor. She heard the clatter of the volumes as they hit the ground, but the sound was muffled. The siren was too loud for her to hear anything clearly. Except, it wasn't a siren. It was a scream. And she was pretty sure it was coming from her.

"Meade!" The man scrambled over to her side of the bed and in two seconds he was standing in front of her. "Meade! Are you okay?"

He reached out as if he was going to put his arms on her shoulders, maybe to steady her, but she put out her hands to block him.

"Don't touch me. Don't touch me!"

Meade frantically looked around the room. What was going on? Where was she? *Was this a dream?* It had to be a dream. This couldn't be happening. How could it be happening?

206 Kelly Bennett Seiler

A million questions raced through her mind, but only one came out. "Why are you naked?"

The man looked down at his bare body and laughed. "Is this what this is all about," he said. "I always sleep naked. You know that."

No, she didn't know that. *How could I know that?* She'd never seen him fully naked. She always thought she would someday. When they were older. But they were never older. *He* was never older. Except, now he was.

Meade started to shake as tears welled up in her eyes. It was becoming very hard to breathe. She had to say something—had to know for sure. Was what she seeing real?

"Daniel?" Meade asked, her voice barely more than a whisper. *"Daniel?"*

# CHAPTER FOURTEEN

"Yes?" he said calmly, as if he heard her speak his name every day. "What's wrong? Are you sick?"

Meade almost laughed. *Wasn't that the question of the day?* She must be sick. In fact, she must be extremely ill to be hallucinating so severely. Maybe the 117-degree weather in Austin had finally taken its toll on her and she'd had a heat stroke. Or...

Suddenly, Meade was struck with a worse thought. What if she wasn't sick at all? What if she was *dead?*

Dead. That would make perfect sense. She was dead. That's how she was seeing Daniel. She was dead. He was dead. They were both dead—*together.*

She looked down at her body. Funny. She'd always thought that when she died, she'd be taller, and that the hips which had bothered her since her twenties, making finding the perfect pair of jeans nearly impossible, would be replaced with petite ones. Wasn't that the whole point of Heaven, anyway? Didn't you get a new and improved body to make up for the one you were dealt during your earthly life?

*Heaven?* Was this Heaven? Meade looked around the room again. The walls were cracked a bit, right by the ceiling. And, the lighting wasn't very good. Somehow she'd thought Paradise would be brighter. And did Heaven really have honking taxi cabs? Didn't people get around by chariot there? Meade glanced back at the nightstand. There was a long scratch in the wood. She was pretty sure the furniture in Heaven didn't look like it had been purchased on Craigslist.

But if this wasn't Heaven, and she wasn't dead, then how was Daniel standing in front of her? He was definitely dead. Staring at him, she suddenly remembered the soap opera she'd watched all through her teens and early twenties. When Meade was in college, one of her favorite characters had died in a plane crash. The woman's husband—and the whole television audience—saw the plane fall off the cliff—as the man who loved her tried to rip her from it. Meade had cried over that episode. It had been so heartbreaking. The plane had fallen into the ocean. There was no chance she'd lived. And yet, about five years later, she came back to town—having somehow miraculously survived the crash—none the worse for wear. Maybe it was like that. Except, Daniel *was* dead. She'd seen him pass away... seen him take his last breath. She'd stayed in that hospital room with him, holding his hand, until all of the heat had left his body. She *knew* he was gone.

So why, then, was he standing here, looking at her with those beautiful brown eyes?

"I think I need to sit down."

"Good idea," Daniel said.

He motioned back to the bed, as if to guide her to it, but he was careful not to touch her. Meade walked over the soft rug and sat down. She was suddenly very tired. Maybe if she were to lie down and close her eyes, she'd fall asleep...and when she woke up, she'd find this was all a dream.

*But then Daniel would be gone.*

Even as panicked as she was, and uncertain about what was happening, she didn't want that to happen. She might not know what was going on. She might not know anything at the moment, including where she was. But she did know she didn't want Daniel to leave.

Meade pulled her legs back up onto the bed and moved her body so she was now resting against the pillow and the headboard. She pulled her legs toward her and wrapped her arms around them. Daniel sat down on the edge of the bed as she rested her chin on her knees.

"Can I get you a drink?" he asked.

Meade shook her head.

"Did you have a bad dream?"

Meade wasn't sure how to answer that. *Was this a dream? Or, was Daniel dying in the dream? And, if it was, why can I remember that dream so much better than this life?*

"I...don't know," she said hesitantly.

Daniel nodded at her, as if he understood, which of course, he didn't. Even Meade didn't. She stared at him. Really looked at him this time. He was Daniel. Her Daniel. Only, he was different. He had lines in his face that hadn't been there before. He was heavier, too. Not only heavier than sick Daniel had been, but heavier than the way he'd been before the Leukemia. He wasn't fat, by any means. Not even overweight. But there were love handles where there had been nothing but muscle and the tiniest of pouches at his belly. Meade tried to not look at his stomach because if she did, she'd have a hard time keeping her eyes from going any lower. And he seemed older. This man was clearly not eighteen years old. If she had to guess, she'd say he was...well, she'd say he was her age. The age she was now. Not that age she had been when she'd last seen him. The most striking difference about Daniel, though, was his hair. For starters, he *had* hair. It must have grown back. *Or never fallen out to begin with?* She wasn't sure. But it no longer hung in the beautiful curls Meade had loved and dreamt about for years after his death. His hair was short—all over, but especially on the sides. You could see the tiniest bit of wave on the top, but no one who looked at him now would have any indication of the full head of curls he'd sported in his youth.

"Your hair..." Meade said.

"Again with the hair, Meade?" Daniel said, rolling his eyes. "I'd think after two years, you'd be used to this short cut."

*Two years?*

"It's so short."

"Yes, it is. And it shows less gray this way. You know that."

*Do I know that?*

"Are you now having nightmares about *my hair?*"

"No...I. . ." Meade was at a loss. He was looking at her, expectantly. He was waiting for an answer. Why had she screamed and jumped out of the bed, nearly falling out the window. He looked like he was worried she was losing her mind. What should she tell him?

"I dreamt..." Meade looked around the room, not wanting to look him in the eyes as she said it. "I dreamt that you...died."

"Oh," Daniel said. He didn't seem at all surprised by her answer. It was if he'd nearly been expecting it. He pulled his entire body onto the bed and moved over next to her. Lying down, he placed his head on his pillow and looked up at her. "I didn't die. I'm here. In the flesh. You can stop having those dreams. I'm here and I'm not going anywhere."

*Stop having those dreams?*

"It seemed so real."

"I know. That's what you always say. I imagine they would. We came pretty close to it being real."

*Pretty close?* She'd felt his spirit leave the room.

"But you didn't die." She wanted to pose it as a question, but given that she was lying so close to him she could smell him, it seemed a ridiculous thing to ask. *His smell*...boy, had she missed that smell. Not the smells of the hospital. Not the medicinal smells she'd inhale as she'd lie on his chest in the months before he died. The old Daniel smells—sweat and a hint of cologne and maybe a little of the chocolate he was known to sneak when he thought no one was looking.

"Nope. Thank heavens for modern medicine—and a whole lot of your TLC." Daniel smiled at her. "Want me to hold you?"

Five simple words, but they opened a floodgate of emotions and tears. Did she want him to hold her? Was that not what she'd wanted every day of the past fifteen years of her life? Had she not spent countless hours lying in bed, with a pillow propped up against her back, pretending the light pressure on her skin was really Daniel instead?

She couldn't speak, but merely nodded. She lowered her legs and moved her body closer to Daniel, resting her head on his shoulder. She lifted her right leg and gingerly placed it on top of his own, as she had a million times before. Only, he'd never been naked when they'd done this. She was still doing her best to not look down. She had enough to wrap her mind around at the moment.

She rested her hand on his chest—his very *hairy* chest. *Had he had this much hair before the cancer?* She couldn't remember. There was a strong pulsing deep in the palm of her hand. *His heart.* It was beating. Hard and strong. She began to count the beats, as the two of them held each other in silence. She stopped when she got to 300. Three hundred heartbeats...and hundreds more that followed. His heart was beating. His skin was warm. She felt his breath on the top of her hair and his lips as he kissed her forehead. If this was a dream, it was the most realistic one Meade had ever had. All dreams should be like this.

Meade closed her eyes. She didn't want to sleep. She didn't want to miss a moment of being with Daniel. She didn't want to risk that he wouldn't still be there when she woke up. Like her days in the hospital with him, she wanted to remember every moment, every touch, every smell...in case she, once again, lost them all forever.

Yet, despite her best efforts, the beating of Daniel's heart and the steady rhythm of his own breathing, as he started to fall back to sleep, were too much for her to resist. She found herself falling...not only asleep, but back in love. With a man she'd never actually stopped loving. A man she thought was gone forever. A man who actually was a man—and not the boy she had loved since she was eight years old. He was suddenly here, holding her, telling her it was all a bad dream.

It still didn't make sense. She didn't understand why she could remember none of this life, and all of a world that seemed very far away. But, it didn't matter right now. She yawned and stretched her body, pulling it closer to Daniel. She'd think about all of that later. Worry about that when she awoke. For now, she was again in Daniel's arms—and that was all that mattered.

"Night, babe," she whispered, even though it was morning. For once, she wasn't whispering it to a photo on her bathroom mirror.

And for the first time in fifteen years, she was sure the "Good night," she heard really came from Daniel—and not the longing in her heart.

# CHAPTER FIFTEEN

"Morning, sunshine."

Meade felt the whisper of lips pass over hers as she opened her eyes. Staring at her, with all the love in the world, was Daniel. It hadn't been a dream. He was really here. And so was she.

"Morning," she said sleepily. She yawned and stretched her body. "What time is it?"

"It's late. Almost eleven. I need to be at the hospital by noon, so I'm gonna go jump in the shower."

"The hospital?" Meade shot up in bed, nearly knocking Daniel backward. "Why the hospital? Are you sick?"

The thought was almost too much for her to bear. This new Daniel couldn't be sick. She'd just found him. She couldn't handle it if he was ill and she would only end up losing him again.

"No, silly. I'm not sick. I'm never sick." He tugged her hair teasingly. "At least, not anymore. My shift. I mean my shift begins at noon."

Daniel unwrapped himself from the covers and got out of bed. Meade had a hard time taking her eyes off his rear end. Somehow, thinking of it as an "ass," where Daniel was concerned, seemed inappropriate. It was nice. Really nice. She'd always imagined it would look like that.

"Your shift?" she said absentmindedly. She shook her head, trying to bring herself back to the conversation at hand. "What do you mean, *your shift?*"

"Uhm...for work. What I do for a living. I go to *work.*" Daniel looked at her curiously. "Are you okay? I mean, do you feel all right?"

*Work? At the hospital?* Was Daniel a doctor? He'd always dreamed of being a pediatrician, since they were little kids. And the cancer had reinforced that dream. But now he was telling her he actually was one? *Wow.* Based on his apparent age, it would make sense he had some sort of career. But, it was still so hard to wrap her brain around it. Meade's head was beginning to spin.

"Yeah...I'm fine. Great. Just a bit sleepy still."

"Okay," he said, his tone indicating he didn't completely believe her. "Then I'm just going to shower and get ready. Why don't you stay in bed and relax. Read a book. Enjoy your day off."

Meade nodded and smiled at him, as if what he said was a great idea and not, actually, the last thing she would ever contemplate doing today. She needed to figure out what was going on. And quickly. It was clear she couldn't ask Daniel. For one thing, it didn't seem like he thought anything was amiss at all. He was acting like they were living their normal, ordinary life together. How could she tell him she didn't remember this life *at all* without coming across as a crazy person?

"Sounds like a plan!" Meade said, a little too cheerfully. "Enjoy your shower. I'm going to chill out...right here...in bed."

Daniel raised his eyebrows a bit, but then shrugged and said, "Okay," before closing the bathroom door behind him.

As soon as Meade heard the click, she jumped out of bed and scanned the room. Where did she begin?

She vaulted over to the dresser. *The photos.* They could be a clue into this world. There were about a dozen frames, of various shapes and sizes, sitting on top. While, in her house—her *real* house, that is—all the frames were silver and organized perfectly on her shelves and tabletops, there seemed to be no rhyme or reason to this selection.

Some were gold, one had a pink floral design...one was even in the shape of a baseball. There was a photo of Daniel and Meade in that one. They couldn't have been more than ten years old. Both were wearing blue-and-white uniforms. Meade remembered the year they were on a co-ed softball team together, but she didn't ever remember seeing this picture before. Daniel's mom must have taken it. Meade looked at all the photos, taking time to study each one carefully. There was one of Daniel's dad and him when he was a child—the two of them laughing on a carousel. And a couple of photos that included his mom including one at a graduation ceremony. Mrs. Spencer was standing next to a beaming Daniel, who was decked out in cap and gown in his hospital bed. Meade caught her breath when she realized he was wearing their high school colors. Daniel had graduated from high school, even if he hadn't been able to attend the ceremony. Only, he hadn't graduated. He'd died two weeks before graduation. Meade hadn't wanted to attend—couldn't imagine going without Daniel there—but her mom had insisted. The principal had held a moment of silence in memory of Daniel. Meade had stared straight ahead, willing herself not to cry. It had been a terrible day, not the one she'd always imagined their graduation would be. Daniel had missed it. And yet, he, apparently, hadn't completely missed it. Meade put her face closer to the picture, truly studying it. Daniel was thin. And bald. He was clearly still in the middle of his treatments. But he was smiling. And his mom—well, she was grinning from ear to ear—clearly so proud of her boy. Meade gently put the frame back in its place.

The remaining photos were both startling and touching to Meade. They were all—every single one of them—of her and Daniel, at various ages. She recognized many of them. There was the day they'd gone on the fourth-grade field trip to the Alamo and they'd posed in front of the old, wooden doors of the fort. And the day when Meade had gotten her braces off and she and Daniel and Benji had made huge bowls of popcorn to celebrate that night, only to end up throwing more popcorn at each other than they put in their mouths. It had taken over an hour to clean up all the popcorn from the floor and her mom's couch. There was a photo of the two of them, at fifteen years old, making rabbit ears behind each other's heads, as they waited in line to ride a giant roller coaster at Six Flags Fiesta Texas. Meade smiled at a picture of the two of them, standing on their high school basketball court. It'd been taken after one of Daniel's big wins. Somehow, in his basketball uniform, the ball under his arm, he seemed to tower above her even more than he did in any of the other photos.

The rest of the images, though, were unfamiliar to her. She was in them. Every single one of them. But she didn't remember any of the moments captured on film. Daniel and her in her dorm room at Wake Forest. The two of them at his college graduation ceremony. Photos taken, apparently, on a trip to the Grand Canyon—both of them wearing hiking clothes as they stood next to two ornery-looking mules. There were pictures of them at dinner parties and next to Christmas trees and in a field of Texas bluebonnets. All beautiful photos. All brought a tear to Meade's eyes, but not because they were precious memories. She had no memories. None. Of any of these moments. How could that be? When clearly, she had experienced all of these special times.

Meade picked up the photo of them in her college dorm room. She could tell, by the layout of the room and the posters on the wall, it was her freshman room. The two of them were seated on her bed— Meade had a giant stuffed panda bear on her lap—and their arms were around each other. She wondered who took the photo. Her roommate, Susan? Meade looked at the bed. Daniel had never sat on that bed. She was sure of it. He'd never been to her room at Wake Forest. If he had, she wouldn't have spent night after night clutching that bear, lying on the bed, crying herself to sleep.

Meade heard the water turn off in the shower and she hurriedly returned the frame to its original location. She scurried back to the bed, pulling the covers over her, just as Daniel opened the bathroom door, dressed in nothing more than a towel.

"Not asleep yet?" he asked. "I was sure you'd be dead to the world when I came back in here."

"No," Meade said. "I'm not feeling all that tired. I think I might go out in a bit."

"What are you gonna do?" Daniel asked, opening a dresser drawer and digging around for some underwear. He dropped the towel and bent down to put them on. Meade looked away. She couldn't get used to seeing Daniel naked. She wasn't sure why. She'd seen many men naked over the years—more than she wanted to think about at this moment. But somehow, Daniel was different. They hadn't had that type of relationship in high school. Many of her friends had started having sex in their teens, and it wasn't that she and Daniel hadn't been tempted. There'd been plenty of kissing and touching—and it had all been wonderful—but they'd always stopped short of sex. They'd never really discussed it—not in any depth, that is—but they were both waiting. For the right moment. That might have been marriage. Maybe it would have been in college or right after, when they were older and on their own. She wasn't sure. But, the right time, for them, wasn't in high school—in his bed with the *Star Wars* sheets or in an electric hospital bed with nurses and doctors coming and going at all hours of the day and night.

The word "marriage" stuck in Meade's head and she looked down at her left hand. No ring. She glanced over at Daniel. His finger was bare, too. It was oddly comforting to realize she hadn't also forgotten her own wedding.

"I might go into work for a bit..." Meade said.

Daniel gave her a puzzled expression as he pulled a white T-shirt over his head. "Work? On your day off? That doesn't sound like you."

*"Doesn't sound like me?"* Meade thought. *"That sounds just like me."*

"It doesn't?"

"Uhm...no. I would have thought you and Lori would be going to some chick flick today. Or shopping away your entire paycheck at H&M."

*Lori? Did he just say, "Lori?"*

Daniel pulled on a pair of scrub pants he'd taken off the closet shelf. He sat down on the bed, next to her, as he bent over to tie his shoes.

"Lori?" Meade tried to keep her voice even. As if the mere mention of Lori's name didn't cause her whole body to shudder.

"Uh-huh," Daniel said, distracted. "Have you seen my keys?"

Despite herself, Meade had to laugh. Some things, apparently, never change. For as long as Meade knew him, Daniel had been notorious for losing things—his keys, his homework, his wallet, movie tickets, his backpack. Sometimes she'd wondered how someone so smart could be so absentminded in other areas of his life.

"Nope. Sorry," Meade said.

"I'll bet I left them on the kitchen counter," Daniel said. "Okay, gotta go. Meet you for dinner tonight around eight? At our usual place."

*Our usual place? Oh, no.*

"Sure." Meade scrambled to figure out a way to find out where there usual place was before he left the room. "Do you know their number? I want to call and ask them a question."

"A question? About what?" Daniel asked.

"Uhm...I wonder if they have any gluten-free options," Meade said, hoping that sounded reasonable and that their "usual place" was a restaurant.

"Gluten-free? Since when do you care about that?"

Meade shrugged and tried to stare back at him innocently. "I don't know. Thought I might try something new. Maybe clear up some of the fogginess I've been feeling in my brain lately."

*As if gluten was the cause of me forgetting an entire lifetime.*

"I don't know the number off the top of my head, but I think we have it on a magnet on the fridge." He bent down and kissed her forehead. "Okay, see you tonight. Love you."

"Love you, too."

Meade watched as Daniel strode out of the room, in search of his keys. "Found them!" she heard him call a moment later, right before the apartment door slammed shut.

Meade waited a few minutes, making sure Daniel was really gone and not going to rush back in the door because he'd forgotten something else. When she was fairly certain he must be on the street and headed to work, she got out of bed. It was time to find some clothes.

There was only one closet in the room. Meade poked her head inside. It wasn't very big and the clothes were crammed together on both sides of the tiny walk-in. A quick scan revealed Daniel's clothes were on the left, leaving Meade to realize those must be her clothes on the right. She fingered her way through the hangers. The blouses and jeans and dresses were all her size all right, but none — not one thing — looked familiar.

*Oh, well. I don't have time to worry about that right now,* Meade thought, grabbing the closest pair of jeans she could find and pulling them up over her gray panties. Yep, they fit perfectly. She walked back into the bedroom and headed over to the dresser she'd been standing at earlier. She opened the top drawer. Daniel's socks. Second drawer. Daniel's underwear. *Don't I get a drawer?* In the third drawer, she found some T-shirts she was pretty sure belonged to her. She pulled out one that said *Columbia* on the front. *Was that where Daniel attended medical school?* She quickly tugged it over her head and went off toward the bathroom. She'd never peed last night and her bladder was about to explode.

The photo stopped her in her tracks. It was there. On the mirror. In this unfamiliar apartment. The sight of it — its *familiarity* — brought tears to Meade's eyes. Meade had never been in this place, never before stepped into this bathroom, but she must live here if that photo—the one of her and Daniel on the day she shaved his head—was taped to the bathroom mirror. This was her home and that photo proved it.

Once she peed—*what a relief that was*—Meade found a pink brush she assumed must be hers in a basket on the shelf next to the sink. She raised it to her hair as she glanced in the mirror. As soon as she did, she gasped, dropping the brush to the ground. Quickly, she bent over to retrieve it and stood back up. With the brush securely in her hand again, she gazed back at the image in front of her. It was her. Same nose. Same eyes. Same scar above her eyebrow that made her think of her mom and all her crazy ideas every time she looked at it. But her hair. *Her hair.*

She'd gone to bed with long hair. It had been so hot in Austin—so dang *hot*—she had pulled it into a knot at the top of her head, trying to keep it, and the sweat, off her neck. And yet...Meade put her face right up to the mirror, as if getting closer to her reflection might some-how alter the version she was seeing. It was short. Super short. Shorter than Meade had ever worn it. The term *bob* popped into her mind, but she wasn't even sure it was accurate since she'd never had a reason to use that word to describe her hair. Meade reached up to touch it. It felt soft and clean. She tried to push a strand behind her ear. It stayed for a moment and then fell forward again. It was even too short to wear behind her ears. This was going to take some getting used to.

Meade ran the brush through it. It took no time at all to smooth it out. After all, there really wasn't anything to smooth. She found some mascara and lip gloss in a makeup bag and applied them quickly. She looked at herself and smiled. She looked good. Different. But good. It was reassuring to know she could get ready as quickly in this world as she could in her other one.

Meade felt her stomach growl and realized she hadn't yet gone to explore the rest of the apartment. Now seemed like a good time to find the kitchen.

The apartment was small. Smaller than Meade would have expected. *Pediatricians must not make a whole lot of money.* There seemed to be only three rooms—four, if you counted the bathroom. The living room was sparsely decorated. A beige couch stood against the far wall, with one other chair across from it. There was a coffee table—at least, Meade was fairly certain one must be under the giant pile of books and magazines scattered on top. Another one of those ficus trees stood to the left of the couch. *Seriously, Daniel?*

The kitchen was tiny—even by New York City standards. There was probably only three feet of counter space—total—and most of that was covered by the toaster oven and dirty cups and dishes. Apparently, Meade didn't make as much of an effort to keep things tidy in this world as she did in her other one. She briefly wondered how she and Daniel ever cooked anything in this kitchen, given its miniscule dimensions. Opening the refrigerator, though, answered her question. If its contents, or, lack thereof, were any indication, the two of them must go out to eat a lot. Meade wondered if that was where her paycheck must go—into restaurant meals and take-out. What she made at Brownsbury Press wasn't an enormous amount, but it was significant. More than most of her friends were making, that was for sure. New York real estate was expensive, and Daniel had always been a frugal person, but *this*...she glanced around the apartment...this was ridiculous. This place made her other one look like Buckingham Palace.

Meade stared into the fridge, deciding what to eat. There wasn't much to choose from. Three eggs. Seven bottles of Izze. Five cans of beer. Some milk at the bottom of a half-gallon container. Meade opened it and stuck her nose to the top, nearly gagging at the odor. *So much for that.* She dumped the contents into the sink and down the drain. A jar of pickles. Ketchup. Meade pushed aside three bottles of water to find a bag of Entenmann's bagels in the back. *Score!* There didn't seem to be any butter, but she did find a jar of strawberry jam in the door.

Meade slid the dishes into the sink with her forearm as she opened the door to the toaster oven. She pried open a pre-cut, cinnamon swirl bagel and put the two halves on the little shelf before setting the timer to "toast." The timer dinged just as she heard a knock on the door.

She quickly spread the jam over the top of one side, burning the tips of her finger, before she ran over to open the door. Taking a bite as she opened it, she nearly spit the bagel back into her hand the moment she saw who was standing there.

*Lori.*

She was holding up a bag of bagels in one hand and a plastic tub of cream cheese in the other.

"Bummer!" she cried. "I thought I'd surprise you! I didn't know you'd already be eating a bagel!"

Meade stood stunned as Lori walked her way past her and into the apartment, making her way to the kitchen and placing the bag down on the counter.

"Oh goodie! You're eating Entenmann's! That's not like the real thing. Nothing beats a New York City bagel, right? Why don't you throw that one out and we'll eat these instead? Do you have any coffee?" Lori began to look through the kitchen cabinets.

Meade felt the steam begin to pour out of her ears. She didn't like the feeling. Wished it wasn't happening. It wasn't a voluntary reaction. It was a metaphysical reaction. The thought—or, at the moment, the *sight*—of Lori, brought out the absolute worst in Meade. She began to sweat. Her heart raced. Her breath quickened.

Meade was a southern woman—born and raised to be polite, especially to guests in your home. But even a southern belle had her limits. Before she knew it, the words were out of her mouth.

"How dare you?" she hissed. "How *dare* you?"

# CHAPTER SIXTEEN

If Meade had actually hit Lori, she didn't think the woman could have flown back any further. And the look on Lori's face...it was so unexpected. So startling. As if Lori, herself, was surprised at Meade's angry reaction to her presence. *But of course, she couldn't be.* After all these years, Lori certainly knew of Meade's disdain for her. *Everyone,* at least, everyone in their small hometown, knew of Meade's disdain for her. That was no secret.

*Why, then, did Lori look as though she'd been punched?*

"Excuse me?" Lori said, her voice clearly shaking. "Did I do something?"

Meade nearly laughed out loud. Of all the ridiculous questions...*Did you do something? How about ruin my life for starters?*

Meade shook her head in disgust. The question wasn't even worth answering. "You need to leave."

"I don't...I don't understand. Seriously, Meade. What's wrong? Did I do something?" she asked again.

Meade still had the door handle in her hand. She motioned to the hallway with her other one—the one holding the Entenmann's bagel. *"Adios."*

Lori seemed fixated in place, her eyes darting between Meade's face and the open door.

"Is this a joke?" Lori asked, a half-hearted laugh coming out of her chest. "Am I being punked?"

"Uhm...no. You're being asked to leave. And, you're not being very gracious about it."

"Gracious?" The word screeched out of Lori's mouth. "Gracious?! My best friend is asking me to leave her home—clearly upset with me—for *what* I have no idea. And I'm not being gracious by leaving?"

"Best friend? You have got to be kidding me!"

Meade saw the color literally drain from Lori's face. The girl never did handle having someone upset with her very well. When they were kids and Lori would get picked on at recess, Meade would nearly always have to come to her rescue. If she didn't, Meade knew Lori might very well pee her pants right there on the playground. Lori could not deal with conflict. And by the transparent shade of her skin, Meade realized that attribute hadn't changed over the years.

"Yes, best friend," Lori managed to get out. "We have been best friends for over twenty years."

"No," Meade spat. "We *were* best friends. But you made sure to ruin that and you have no one to blame but yourself."

"Meade! What are you talking about?"

"Get out."

"Meade!"

"I said, get out. Now!" There was no masking the wrath in her tone.

Meade saw the tears spring into Lori's eyes and nearly felt bad about it. She hated to see people cry. But Lori wasn't just anyone. The two of them had history. What Lori had done was unforgivable. She deserved a couple of tears. She deserved a lifetime of them, in Meade's opinion, to match the ones she'd caused Meade.

"Okay. I'll go."

Meade said nothing as the woman picked up her purse, which she'd dropped on the floor by the kitchen entrance, and made her way to the door. "You can keep the bagels."

Meade rolled her eyes. *Bagels?* She nearly snorted out a laugh. As if that was going to make things better between them.

Lori stopped in the doorway, inches from Meade. Even in her fury, Meade was struck by the changes in Lori since she'd last seen her. Her hair was longer, her face thinner. She had more wrinkles, but then, so did Meade. She was still beautiful, though. Still had that blonde hair Meade had always envied. Still had the dimple in her left cheek when she smiled, which she'd been doing when Meade opened the door. Now, though, her expression was grave and clearly confused. She looked out toward the elevator and Meade thought she might make a run for it, but instead, she turned back to Meade and looked her straight in the eyes.

"I don't know what is going on," she said. "Truly, I have no idea. But I *am* your best friend. I'm sorry if I did something to hurt you. I can honestly say that if I did, I'll try my best to make it right again. You can always come talk to me."

Meade glared at her. *Leave already. Leave.*

"Always," Lori repeated.

When Meade showed no sign of being moved by her speech, Lori sadly shrugged and walked out the door. Meade slammed it behind her. The sound was so loud and so definite that even Meade jumped a little.

Lori had a tremendous amount of nerve showing up here. Enormous, in fact. Who did she think she was? Did she think she could waltz into Daniel's apartment...

*Daniel.*

Meade sunk down onto the couch, dropping the bagel to the floor and gripping the edge of the coffee table to steady herself.

This was Daniel's apartment. Maybe hers, too. But Daniel definitely lived here. He wasn't dead. In her anger with Lori—a rage she had harbored for fifteen years—she'd completely forgotten that. And if he wasn't dead—and had, instead, lived—then, did she still have a reason to be angry with Lori?

Meade put her head in her hands and slowly began to rock back and forth. It was all so confusing. So overwhelming. Nothing made sense.

A part of her wanted to rush out the apartment door and hurry down the stairwell, hoping to catch Lori before she exited the building. She could probably catch her before the elevator reached the bottom floor. That is, if they weren't too high up. *What floor were they on anyway?* She hadn't yet taken a good look out the window. If she could catch up to Lori, she could explain.

But what exactly would she explain? That yesterday Daniel was dead? And the yesterday before that...and the yesterday before that... he was dead all those days. And, he'd died as a result of Lori's selfishness when they were teenagers? And that was why Meade was so angry with her.

She could imagine the look on Lori's face as she explained it. It wouldn't be one of sadness, as Meade had witnessed a few moments earlier, but instead one of complete and utter terror over the fact that her friend—her *best* friend, apparently—was losing her mind.

No, she couldn't explain it. Not now, anyway. Not as long as she, herself, didn't understand what was going on. Once she knew and figured it all out, she'd go and find Lori and apologize. Assuming, that is, Meade had anything to apologize for—which she still wasn't certain of—though, it was seeming, with each passing moment, more and more likely that she did.

Meade took a deep breath. She needed to get a grip on things. Somehow—somewhere—there had to be an explanation for all of this. She needed to figure out what that might be. And she knew the person to ask about her situation. Of course! Why hadn't she thought of it sooner? There was only one person who wouldn't think she was insane the moment she began to explain her situation.

Meade jumped up, feeling like she had a new lease on life. No, it was more than that. It was *hope*. She felt hopeful. She knew whom she could turn to and where to find that person. A smile spread across her face.

She scurried into the kitchen, suddenly hungry for one of those New York City bagels Lori had promised her. The delectable smell hit Meade's nostrils the moment she opened the bag. *Ah*...that was the smell of New York. She'd missed that aroma during her time in Austin. Austin had great breakfast tacos, but nothing beat a New York bagel. Meade pulled out an onion one from the top—momentarily wondering how Lori, whom she hadn't hung out with in over a decade, and never on the East Coast, knew that was her favorite—and quickly slathered it with the cream cheese Lori had left on the counter. A schmear is what they called it here. A schmear of cream cheese. The first bite was incredible. Meade licked her lips as she savored it and then walked over to the fridge. If she was going to meet Daniel at their usual place, she'd better find out where that was now. She might be gone all day.

She found the number on a magnet on the fridge. It wasn't hard to locate. It was the only restaurant one there, and it was pinning the take-out menu of Wok This Way. She didn't need to look at the listed items to know what kind of food they served. She smiled to herself as she jotted the address down on a scrap of paper she found in a drawer. Tucking the paper into her jeans' pocket, she practically skipped into the bedroom in search of her shoes. She suddenly had somewhere she needed to be, and she couldn't wait to get there.

Meade wanted to throw herself onto the sidewalk and kiss the ground the moment she laid her eyes on the Brownsbury Press office building. The structure, with its steel-gray window frames and revolving doors, and the giant grandfather clock that stood in the entryway, was a sight for sore eyes. She didn't think she'd ever seen something so beautiful—and familiar. And, if she'd learned anything over the last twelve or so hours, familiarity was never fully appreciated until it was gone.

She wanted to run in the door and twirl in a circle, her arms raised, spinning and spinning until she fell to the ground. She felt like a kid in a candy store and had to stop herself from skipping up the stairs to the entrance. She was *home*. Her bed might not be in the same apartment, and she had no idea why the bag she'd found her laptop in didn't look familiar in the least—*why would she be carrying her computer in a hot-pink, floral bag instead of the sleek leather one she'd bought herself last year when she'd gotten a raise?*—but none of that mattered at this moment. She was where she belonged. Brownsbury Press. She couldn't wait to get to her desk and sink into her plush office chair.

More importantly, she was anxious to talk to Pantera. If anyone would listen to her, and not judge her, it was her assistant. Pantera believed in things—supernatural entities and unexplainable phenomena. Meade had always chuckled at the yearly trek Pantera took to Roswell, New Mexico. *Did people really believe in UFOs these days?* Meade hadn't thought so until she'd met Pantera. Pantera believed in a lot of things Meade had always thought were off-the-wall, like reincarnation and ghosts and the healing power of crystals. Meade had often shaken her head at the fervency with which Pantera professed her beliefs, but she'd never faulted the young woman for them. They'd added to Pantera's charm. Pantera was her own person and open to new ideas. And boy, did Meade have a story to tell her. She couldn't wait to get Pantera's take on what was happening. If anyone was prone to believe her, it was Pantera.

Meade hurried up the stairs, taking two at a time, and smiled as she pushed her way around the revolving door and into the lobby. Approaching the front desk, she dug around inside her bag, searching for her ID badge. Funny, she always left it right next to her computer, so she'd have it when she got to the office. For some reason, it wasn't there. She glanced up and smiled with relief when she saw Cedric was at the security post today. He'd be able to let her in.

"Hey, Cedric," Meade said, hardly able to keep the glee out of her voice at the sight of seeing someone she recognized from her old world. "Having a good day?"

Cedric looked up from the newspaper he was reading. The sports section of *USA Today*. Of course. Cedric was a huge sports fan. For Christmas last year, Meade had gotten him season tickets to the Nets. He'd practically cried with joy when he opened the envelope. "No one has ever given me such a beautiful gift," he'd told her, sounding as if she'd just given him a Ming vase. She'd loved his reaction. It was so much nicer to give someone a gift when they truly loved it and didn't give you an obligatory, "Thanks."

"Yes, ma'am," Cedric said. "Can I help you?"

"You sure can. I can't seem to find my ID badge. Do you think you can let me in?"

"I can probably do that," he said, tapping the space key on his computer to bring up his home screen. "What's your name?"

Meade blinked. She blinked again. This couldn't be happening.

"Cedric, it's me. Meade."

"Is Meade your last name?" he asked, pecking away at the keyboard with his two index fingers.

"Cedric. It's me," she said again. *"Meade.* Meade Peterson."

Cedric looked up at her and smiled. She knew he didn't know the names of all the employees in the building. It was an enormous skyscraper. But she *knew* he knew her. She'd brought dinner to his house when his wife had given birth to their fourth baby—another little girl—and he'd been invited to the surprise birthday party her office had thrown for her after work last year down at Hannigan's on the corner.

"I apologize," he said, clearly embarrassed. "I don't always remember everyone's name."

Meade smiled gently. She did look different with this haircut. Maybe that was it.

"It's okay," she said, trying to sound understanding and not hurt. "Can you let me in?"

"Sure, let's see," he said, continuing with his one-finger pecking. "P-E-T..."

"What are you doing?" Meade asked him.

"Looking you up in the records." He finished typing her last name. "You said your first name is Meade?" He put his face closer to the screen, scrolling through all the Petersons who worked in the building. It appeared to be a fairly long list. "Not Mary?"

"No, *Meade.*" It was hard to keep the frantic pitch from her voice. Her palms were beginning to sweat and a sick feeling was developing deep in the pit of her stomach.

"What company do you work for?" Cedric asked. "I don't see you here. Maybe I can look you up by company name."

"Cedric. Stop. Look at me."

He stopped scanning the names and turned to look at Meade. He smiled at her, but it wasn't a smile of friendship, one that had been built over years of working in the same building and chatting on her way in and out—about not only their jobs, but his family and her brothers in Texas and their mutual love of suspense thrillers. It was a polite smile. The one she'd seen him give to countless visitors over the years. He didn't know her. She was sure of it. And it had nothing to do with the haircut.

"You don't know me, do you?"

"I'm sorry, ma'am," he said, a bit bashful. "Like I said, there are a lot of people who work here."

Meade wanted to cry and had to take a deep breath to keep the tears from actually falling. What was she going to do? "Okay, do me a favor and look me up under Brownsbury Press. Do you see my name there?"

Cedric typed a few more things into the computer and began to scroll again. It seemed like a lifetime before he answered her. "No, ma'am. I'm sorry. I don't see your name."

Meade's heart was racing. Why didn't she work at Brownsbury? It didn't make sense. She needed to talk to Pantera.

"Okay...okay..." she said, trying to steady her breathing and compose her thoughts. "Can you do me one more favor? Can you look up Pantera Libertelli? At Brownsbury Press."

Cedric nodded and went back to his computer. "Sorry...there's no Pantera at all in the building."

*No Pantera?* How could that be? Meade was beginning to understand that things weren't the same for her in this world, but why would they change for anyone else? After all, Cedric still worked here. And, as she looked around the lobby and the people rushing to catch the elevator, they were all people she recognized, at least by face. Why would their lives be the same, but Pantera's be different?

*Unless...*

Meade quickly thanked Cedric and turned back toward the door. She dug into her bag, as she made her way out of the office building and grabbed her cell phone—the one she'd found charging in the living room, exactly where Daniel said it would be. She typed in her four-number password and then held her breath, hoping it worked. She smiled when the phone unlocked. Apparently, in this world, she still used Daniel's birthday as her code.

She ran her finger down the names in her address book. Some she recognized—like her mom and Benji and Nick—but some were unfamiliar to her. There was no Pantera. She looked in the L's, hoping she'd put Pantera in there under her last name, but no luck. Meade sat down on the retaining wall at the bottom of the stairs. She needed to think. *Where was Pantera?* It was becoming clear to Meade that Pantera didn't work at Brownsbury Press because *Meade* didn't work at Brownsbury Press. And, if Meade didn't work there, then Pantera had never been hired by her. Knowing the other editors, it seemed highly unlikely any of them would have hired her. Pantera didn't fit their mold of the perfect assistant. So, if Pantera wasn't employed by Brownsbury, where did she work? Meade wished she had access to the publisher's database of applications. Maybe she'd be able to pull up Pantera's resume—assuming she'd ever applied there for a job—and get the woman's contact information. But there was no chance of that. And, of course, she didn't have Pantera's number memorized. *Who memorized phone numbers these days when they were all plugged into your cell phone?*

Where did Pantera work before Meade hired her? Meade tried to rack her brain. They'd discussed it, but it seemed like a million years ago. *A cell phone store?* No. *Fast-food?* No, but she did remember Pantera saying something about making sandwiches. *Avocado and tomato.* Those had been the ones Pantera loved to make the best. But where did she make them? Meade tried to remember. Pantera also made a mean latte and would often surprise Meade with one on her desk in the morning. She'd said she learned that at work, too. *A coffee shop.* That was it. It was some sort of coffee shop that sold pastries and light sandwiches. But which one? New York had hundreds—if not thousands—of those places, and that was if you didn't count Starbucks locations on every corner.

A memory started to trickle into Meade's mind. Last summer, Brownsbury decided to get involved with Habitat for Humanity and each department had participated in a work day. Meade's department had spent a day building a home for a much-deserving, down-on-their-luck family. When Pantera had shown up, Meade—and all of their colleagues—had done a double-take. Instead of walking in wearing her usual platform boots, laced up her calves, lace gloves and gargoyle earrings, she was dressed...well...so normally. The pounding of hammers had literally silenced the minute Pantera strolled up the path. Meade was fairly certain she heard multiple jaws hit the ground and wondered if her own gasp was audible.

"What?" Pantera asked, looking around at everyone. "Haven't you ever seen someone in jeans before?"

Sure. They'd all seen people in jeans. They'd never seen *Pantera* in jeans. Or in sneakers—ones without heels, that is. Or white socks. Or a T-shirt. A regular, ordinary, vintage-style T-shirt. And it was *green*, no less! Not even black. Pantera had even pulled her long hair back in a run-of-the-mill ponytail, and the makeup she had on was so minimal, Meade wasn't even sure she'd applied any. Meade remembered looking at Pantera before she picked up her hammer and went back to work and thinking, *Wow. She looks so young. She even has freckles.*

But it wasn't the freckles Meade was recalling at this moment. It was that green T-shirt Pantera had worn. It had said something on it, and Meade had a feeling it was the name of the coffee shop where she'd used to work.

It was a funny name. Not typical. Nothing like Java Joe's or Heavenly Espresso. It was something unique. Something that had made Meade chuckle when she read it. And it hadn't been spelled correctly, either. It was written like a text.

*What was it?*

Meade put her head in her hands and squeezed her eyes tight, trying to envision Pantera that day. She'd been sitting on top of a ladder when Meade had read the shirt.

"We don't give you cute tees like that at this job," she'd joked.

"That is a disappointment," Pantera had said. "Maybe I should quit."

"Don't you dare!" Meade had warned her. "I couldn't survive without you."

Meade was suddenly worried that if she didn't come up with the name of that shop, that was exactly what she'd have to do. Survive without Pantera. And, in this new and rather alarming world, that was a frightening thought.

*C U Latte!*

That was it! C U Latte Coffee Bar.

Meade breathed a sigh of relief as she retyped Daniel's birthday back into her phone and began Googling the name of the shop, in search of its address. It was in the Village. Of course it was. There was nowhere in New York City more suited to Pantera than Greenwich Village. Meade glanced at her watch. It was three o'clock. She had plenty of time to get down there before having to head back to meet Daniel for dinner. She prayed Pantera still worked there. And Meade crossed her fingers that if she did, she was on duty right now.

If all went well, she might have a better understanding of what was happening to her by the time she met up with Daniel tonight.

*What if Pantera doesn't know me, either?*

The thought almost stopped Meade in her tracks, but she quickly abandoned the notion as she headed down the stairs to the subway.

She'd cross that bridge when she came to it. For now, all that mattered was finding Pantera.

# CHAPTER SEVENTEEN

The coffee shop wasn't easy to find. Meade had to walk up and down Bleeker Street at least three full times before she was able to locate the small doorway leading into C U Latte.

*How do they do any business?* If no one could find your establishment, it would seem very unlikely you'd make any money.

Meade retracted her concerns over their financial security, though, the moment she walked in the door. The place was packed. A quick look around showed Meade that finding a table—or even an empty chair—would not be an easy feat. Apparently, C U Latte was a well-kept secret that was, well...no secret to anyone in Greenwich Village.

"Seat Yourself" the sign at the entrance said. *Easier said than done.* Meade scanned the room and noticed a table with two elderly gentlemen in the back corner. Something about their body language made Meade think they were almost ready to leave their table. Meade made her way through the crowded shop, saying, "Excuse me," a number of times as she wiggled her way through tight tables and standing patrons. By the time she reached the men, she saw one was signing the check. She tried to look inconspicuous and not directly at them, hoping they didn't notice her waiting nearby, as she played with her phone and twirled her short hair. One of the men, still mid-conversation, stood up and removed his jacket from the back of his chair. He looked at Meade curiously.

"Did you want this table?" he asked her.

"Yes," Meade replied, shrugging a bit, trying to not look like she was hurrying them along. She was struck by how handsome he was, especially for a man his age. Tall, seemingly fit, stick-straight posture—a thick head of gray hair. He reminded Meade of Henry Fonda.

"Then, I don't think we're done here yet," the man said, rehanging his coat on the backrest.

Meade felt her face flush. Had she offended them by hovering over them before they were ready to part ways? She'd tried not to seem too obtrusive.

"I'm just kidding, my dear," the older man said, laughing. "We're finished. Hurry up and sit down before someone snatches the table out from under our noses."

He didn't have to say it twice. Meade slid into the chair he was now pulling out for her. The other man closed the bill folder and returned his credit card to his wallet. He smiled at her. "Tables in this place are like gold."

"I can see that," Meade said, looking around at the standing-room-only establishment. "I've never been in here before."

"My recommendation? Order the Caffé Medici. It's heavenly."

"Really? Thanks," Meade said.

"Leighton and I have been meeting here every week for five years and I don't think he's ever ordered a different drink," the first gentleman said. "Once he likes something, he's faithful to it. I, on the other hand, have tried nearly everything on the menu and you can't go wrong. Especially with the avocado and tomato sandwich."

Magical words to Meade's ears. *Avocado and tomato sandwich.* She was in the right place.

"You come here every week?" she asked.

"Yep. We're two retired schoolteachers. I never married and Leighton, here, lost his wife...what?" He looked over at Leighton. "About ten years ago?"

"Eight," Leighton said, and Meade saw a flicker of sadness cross his otherwise sparkling eyes.

"Oh, yes. Eight years ago. We meet here every Wednesday. We like to say it's for intellectual conversation, to keep our minds stimulated, but often, we gripe about the people in our lives who are driving us nuts—like Leighton's kids and my sister."

Meade smiled. It was hard to not smile. Both men must have been in their seventies, but they had the spunk of two fifteen-year-olds.

"I'm sorry about your wife," Meade said, looking at Leighton, who was still sitting across from her. "I lost the man in my life, once, too. You never get over it."

"No, you don't," Leighton said. "And you're young to have experienced that. You move on. You begin to resume your life. You spend time with those you love and you try to get back to normal. But that's never really possible. All you can hope for is a new normal."

*A new normal.* That's what she'd had in her old world. Normal had become a world without Daniel. *In this world, though?* She didn't know what normal was anymore.

"Look at us...talking away as if you wanted to spend your afternoon gabbing with two old men!" Leighton said, standing up. He was much smaller than the first man. And pudgier, too. Clearly, if the Henry Fonda look-alike worked out, he didn't take Leighton with him. "Enjoy your time here. This is a great place."

"Thanks," Meade said. "And I've enjoyed talking to you."

"We're here every Wednesday, if you ever want to come join us," the other man said. "By the way, my name is Henry." He put out his hand to her and she shook it. Meade smiled with the realization his name actually *was* Henry, like the actor she'd had in mind ever since she first laid eyes on him. She wouldn't forget it anytime soon.

"I'm Meade."

"Meade. What a lovely name. I've never heard that one before."

"Thank you."

"Well, Meade, like I said, we're here every Wednesday. We'd enjoy the company and the fresh conversation if you'd like to join us."

"Thank you. I might do that. Thanks for the table."

"Anytime." The men nodded to her and began to walk away.

"Oh, wait!" she called after them. "I have a question for you. Since you're regulars here, you might know. Is there a waitress here named Pantera?" Meade had tried to scan the room in search of her, but with the crowds, it was hard to tell if Pantera was here.

"Pantera?" Leighton asked. "Oh! Panty! Yes. She works here. She's our favorite."

*Panty?* Oh heavens. Pantera must hate that one.

"Is she here today? Have you seen her?"

Leighton and Henry exchanged glances and both men seemed to shrug.

"I don't remember seeing her," Henry said. "But that doesn't mean she's not here. She might even be in the back making the food. She does that sometimes. You should ask someone who works here."

Meade nodded. "Thanks. I will."

"Have a good afternoon, Meade," Leighton said and the two men turned and walked away.

Meade sat back in her chair as she surveyed the room. It wasn't a huge coffee shop to begin with, and it was made to feel even smaller by the number of people crammed inside. No one seemed to mind the tight space, though. Everyone was talking and laughing. A few people were working on their laptops, but it didn't seem to be that type of place. Not like the coffee shops downtown near her office. When she went into one of those, the silence was noticeable. No one was talking. People were *working*. Starbucks was an extension of the financial and publishing businesses in the area—somewhere to get a good cup of coffee and maybe a sticky bun—but a place where everyone continued on with their busy lives. This coffee bar, though, was full of life. Meade could feel the underlying vibe of inspiration. These were people who weren't only here to socialize and catch up with friends, but to share ideas and concepts. And, she had a feeling those weren't related to money matters, but rather, artistic and musical and literary topics. This was a creative group. No one needed to tell Meade that. She could tell by the way they dressed and used their hands as they talked and leaned into one another as if what the person across the table from them was saying was not relatively interesting conversation, but rather, worthy of rolling around in their own mind and pondering for hours on end.

This was the perfect place for Pantera to work. That is, if she didn't work for Meade.

The motif of the shop, if you could call it a motif, was eclectic. While Meade was used to all the coffee bars near her having the latest modern furniture and décor, this one looked like it might have been put together over a series of trips to some New Jersey flea markets. None of the couches matched. And they looked old and rather worn, though, Meade had to admit, comfortable, too. Like the kind of couch you'd find in your grandmother's living room. Tattered in the right spots—calling out to you to curl up into a ball with a good book. And a cat. That's what this place needed. A cat. It was like your local neighborhood bookstore. A bit musty. A bit overcrowded. But somewhere you wanted to spend hours, browsing and dreaming and remembering what life used to be like before things got so busy you couldn't take a breath.

"Hi. I'm Leslie and I'll be waiting on you. Can I get you something to drink?"

Meade had been so lost in thought she hadn't even noticed the waitress approach.

"Oh!" Meade said, caught off guard. "Yes. Sure. I'd like a Caffé Medici. I hear they're really good."

"They're to die for. No joke. One of the best things on the menu."

"Great. Then yes, I'd like that and...can I actually have a menu?"

"Oh! I'm so sorry," Leslie said. "I didn't realize you needed one. Most people here already know what they want. I'll be right back."

Meade watched as Leslie scurried through the crowd. She debated asking Leslie about Pantera when she returned, but then decided against it. She didn't want her to go tell Pantera. If she didn't know who Meade was—and, by this point, Meade was pretty certain she wouldn't—Meade didn't want the woman to wonder why some stranger was inquiring about her. Meade needed to handle this in the right way. What way that was, however, Meade couldn't quite figure out. *Hi, you don't know me, but you work for me—in a different universe, that is. And, we're actually really great friends. Though I know you think you've never laid eyes on me before. Anyway, I need you to help me figure out why my dead boyfriend isn't actually dead. Can I buy you a drink?*

Ha! Even Pantera, who was the best at "going with the flow," would find that one hard to follow.

Leslie seemed to appear from nowhere and handed Meade a menu. It was actually more like a single-sided piece of paper. Clearly, the selection was limited.

"The drinks are all on a board above the front counter. This lists the sandwiches, salads, and pastries."

Meade skimmed the sandwich options. All four of them.

"I'll have the avocado and tomato sandwich." *Of course she would.* Was there any doubt of that? "And I'd like to hang on to this so I can read what else you have. Maybe I'll go for a pastry when I'm done."

"Sounds good. I'll be right back with your sandwich and drink," she said, smiling at Meade. "I'd say holler for me if you need me, but I don't think I'd hear you in all this noise—so I'll come back to check on you periodically."

"Thanks. I'd appreciate that," Leslie made her way back to the front of the restaurant. Meade read through the other options. They actually all sounded really good. Especially the chocolate caramel tart. She would definitely have to order that.

"Here you go," Leslie said, returning shortly with Meade's order. "I hope you enjoy it. Like I said, I'll come back to check on you. Do you need anything else?'

"Nope. I'm good."

"Okay, then. See you in a bit"

Meade took a bite of the sandwich. For such simple ingredients, it was really, really good. She wondered if there was cream cheese on the bread or some other sort of dressing. Taking another bite, Meade looked up and there she was. *Pantera.* She was across the room and there were dozens of people between them, but it was definitely her. Meade's heart leapt at the sight of her friend. It took everything she had to not stand up and wave her arms around crazily, calling out, "Over here, Pantera! Over here!"

She watched as her assistant—at least, the woman who *used* to be her assistant—made her way around the room. Periodically, she'd stop at a table to see if the patrons were enjoying their drinks or sandwiches and to exchange a few words with them. Meade couldn't wait for Pantera to make her way over to her table.

The way she was dressed was a bit surprising. It wasn't quite as normal as that day with Habitat for Humanity. Pantera still had her black pigtails and cross-bone earrings on. Though across the room, Meade could see them dangling from Pantera's ears. And there was no mistaking those boots with the buckles up to her knees. She was wearing jeans and a Latte T-shirt, though this one was a pale blue. It was so bizarre to see Pantera in color. Almost as if she'd walked from her black-and-white house to the bright colors of Oz. Except, even in black and white—or, actually, just black, as was generally the case with her assistant—Pantera shined with the brilliance of all the colors of the rainbow. She was that kind of person. She exuded life and love and Meade found herself craving her friend's warmth.

It took a few minutes, but eventually Pantera was standing in front of Meade. It was immediately clear, by the way she nonchalantly looked at Meade, that she'd never seen her before in her life. Nonetheless, Meade couldn't contain her bright smile. She was so happy to see her friend.

"You look like you're having a good day," Pantera said. "I hope some of that cheer is a result of being here with us today."

"Oh, absolutely," Meade said. *She has no idea.*

"Is there anything else you need? How's your food?"

"It's wonderful. I think I'm good for now," she said, her brain scrambling for the right words to say to entice Pantera to want to speak with her. It was clear the woman didn't recognize her. Surprisingly, that didn't faze her. She'd already braced herself for that possibility. If Cedric didn't know her anymore, Meade figured Pantera wouldn't recognize her, either. That didn't mean Meade couldn't initiate a friendship with Pantera—a new friendship. *But how to begin?*

"No, I'm great. Thanks. But listen, I have a question for you...and this may sound crazy..." Meade said, stumbling over her words. "When do you get off work?"

Meade thought she saw the faintest of smiles cross Pantera's lips.

"I work 'til closing tonight," she said and then leaned down closer to Meade. "But listen," she whispered. "I appreciate the offer, but...I don't swing that way."

*Swing that way?* What was she talking about? *What offer?*

And then understanding filled Meade's mind and eyes. "Oh! No! *No!*" Meade cried. She didn't know if she should gasp in horror at Pantera's misunderstanding, or laugh at the very thought of it. "I'm not asking you on a date!"

"Well, that's a relief," Pantera said. "I mean, you're cute and all, but definitely not my type."

Meade had to laugh out loud at that. The thought of her and Pantera as a couple...it was too funny. She'd have to tell Pantera...the *other* Pantera...the one in her real life...about all of this. If she ever got back there, that is.

"I....Where did she go from here? How did she explain to Pantera what she wanted? Especially after the woman thought she was asking her out on a date. "I'd like to talk to you about something. Someone told me you believe in spirits and the afterlife. That stuff fascinates me and..."

Gosh. She was beginning to sound like a ghost groupie.

"I'm writing a paper on such phenomena." *What? Where did that come from?* "And so...I was hoping to interview you."

Oh, boy. Now, she wasn't only crazy; she was a liar, too.

"Wow. That sounds really interesting. Who's the paper for?"

"What?"

"Your paper? Is it for a newspaper? A college class you're taking?"

"Oh, yeah...the paper. It's for a class I'm taking. A grad school class. But I'm hoping to get it published."

"Great. In what publication?"

Boy, she was an inquisitive one, wasn't she? That was a trait Meade had loved about Pantera in her old world. It was proving to be tricky today, though.

"I'm not sure yet. Maybe you can help me with that, too."

"Okay, sure. That sounds like fun. Do you want to meet when I get off tonight? It'll be kind of late."

"Uhm...probably not. I have plans with my boyfriend." *The dead one.* "Can you meet tomorrow?"

"Sure. When I get off work. What are your work hours?"

The question caught Meade off guard. *Did she work?* She'd thought so, this morning. She'd shown up at work, only to be told she wasn't employed there. But Daniel had said she was off today. So that must mean she had a job. But where? And what were her hours? Apparently, not traditional if she was off mid-week.

"Yes. I'm not sure of my schedule yet." Meade took out her cell phone. "How about you give me your number and I'll text you to see when we can meet up."

"That works." Pantera quickly rattled off her number as Meade entered it into her phone. "Okay, then. I'll talk to you tomorrow."

"Yes! Thanks."

Pantera turned to walk away and then turned back. "Oh, wait. I don't know your name. Mine's Pantera, but then I guess you probably already knew that."

"Yes. Mine's Meade." She put out her hand to shake Pantera's outstretched one. "Meade Peterson. It's nice to meet you." *Again.*

"Nice to meet you, too. Talk to you tomorrow."

"Tomorrow."

Meade watched as Pantera walked away and began socializing with a young couple at a table a few feet away. It had felt good to speak with her old friend, even if her old friend didn't know she was such. Meade was already looking forward to getting together with her tomorrow. She'd have to spend some time figuring out how to explain everything to Pantera. It would be so much easier to explain it all if she understood it herself.

She looked down at her sandwich and drink. They looked as good as they tasted—simply delectable. And she was famished. She hadn't realized how hungry she was until her stomach began to growl at the smell of the sandwich and pasta salad accompanying it. Yum.

Yes, she was definitely going to need to spend some time thinking about how to approach Pantera on the subject of this alternative life she was living. And, she was going to have to spend even more time determining where it was she worked. It wasn't going to be easy to figure that out. She couldn't exactly ask Daniel who it was who paid her salary and where her desk was located. She'd have to be creative about it. But that was okay. Meade was a creative person. She'd figure it out.

For now, though, she was going to concentrate on nothing more than her avocado and tomato sandwich and her delicious drink. All of her problems...and they seemed vast at the moment...would still be there when she was finished. She was pretty sure of that. There was no need to worry about them at this very moment.

Like Scarlett O'Hara had said, "I can't think about that right now... I'll think about that tomorrow."

Meade might not wait as long as tomorrow to worry about it all, but she could put the uncertainty of her situation on hold for a little bit...at least until dinner tonight.

*Dinner with Daniel.* It had such a lovely ring to it. Actually, now that she thought about it, she definitely might not want to concern herself about this new world until tomorrow. What harm could come of enjoying Daniel's company for one evening? The fact that he was dead wouldn't even enter her mind until morning.

*Forget Daniel was dead?* She'd been waiting fifteen years to do that very thing.

# CHAPTER EIGHTEEN

Meade opted to walk home instead of hopping on the subway. It felt good to walk. The weather was beautiful. It was summer, as it had been in her old world, but whereas Texas had been unbearably hot when she'd left it—*vanished* from it—New York City was having a perfect day. Just the right amount of warmth with a cool breeze thrown in. If Meade didn't have things she needed to do—*figure out*—she would've enjoyed spending the whole day outside. It would have been an ideal day to hang out in Bryant Park, sipping an iced tea as she sat at a little bistro table, watching the children on the carousel squeal with delight.

Instead, she was hurrying her way through Chinatown, looking for the entrance to the staircase that led to their little apartment. Yes, *Chinatown*. Even she couldn't believe it. In a million years, she'd never expected that she and Daniel—*Doctor* Daniel—would be living in some little economy apartment in Chinatown. Granted, it wasn't as small as a studio, but surely, by this age, they should be able to afford something nicer. He was, after all, a doctor. He was in his early thirties and should have a pretty good career going. And she had a job, too. Though the exact description of that was still vague. So why were they living above the Hard Wok Café? Meade couldn't believe she'd had to walk down four flights of stairs to get outside when she'd left their place this morning.

*Couldn't they have at least picked somewhere with an elevator?*

When she'd finally reached the door and pushed her way out into the city, she didn't even need to smell the egg rolls and the chicken chow mein to know she was in Chinatown. The knock-off purse vendors working out of the trunks of their cars were a quick indicator of where she was.

At least she wouldn't have to walk far to get to their favorite place for dinner. It was down the street.

Meade took the steps, two at a time, up to the apartment and was winded by the time she got to the top. She clearly didn't work out any more in this world than she did in her last. In a pathetic, out-of-breath way, it was a relief to know she was an exercise slacker here, too. She put her key in the lock—all *four* of them—and let herself into the apartment.

*Yep, it's still as small as it was this morning.*

She closed the door behind her and relocked all the bolts on the door. Apparently, this wasn't the safest neighborhood around. Turning back to the living room, Meade surveyed her surroundings.

*Where to begin?*

She didn't see a filing cabinet or desk in this room. Had there been one in the bedroom? She couldn't remember. She'd decided, on her walk, there had to be paperwork, somewhere, documenting her employment life. Paystubs, bank statements, an old application, a contract...it was a matter of finding all of that.

Meade headed into the bedroom. Her memory hadn't been faulty. There was no desk in here. There was no *room* for a desk in here. She walked into the closet and moved around the longer items, searching for a file box that might be shoved to the back. She found an old, cardboard one, but a quick look inside revealed it was filled with old textbooks from college—and she recognized all of them. It was good to know she still had her degree.

Meade came back into the bedroom and stood with her hands on her hips. Where would she keep her papers? The dresser drawers were full of clothes. *Maybe under the bed?* Meade got down on her stomach and pushed up the bed skirt. She was momentarily filled with glee when she saw a long box underneath. Her happiness was short-lived, however, when she realized it was full of nothing more than winter sweaters and coats.

*Damn.*

She got off the ground and walked back into the living room. She opened the cabinet door to the end table, but there was nothing in there except some photo albums. She made a mental note to look through those later. There didn't seem to be anywhere else to look.

Her eyes landed on the kitchen. Maybe. Though it seemed unlikely. Meade strode the four steps it took her to get into that room and began opening cabinets and drawers. Junk drawer. Silverware. Pots. Cups. Dishes. No paperwork.

*How can two professional people live without any paperwork?* It was impossible.

The phone startled her. She hadn't even realized they had a land line in the apartment and she had to search for it, finally finding it under a bunch of take-out menus on the kitchen counter. *Who had a land line these days?* Why not throw the money directly *into* the toilet bowl instead?

She looked at the caller ID. *The New York Times.* Ugh. It was most likely a sales call. Surely she and Daniel didn't actually get a real newspaper, too. Had they never heard of reading the news online?

She almost didn't answer and then changed her mind.

"Hello?" she asked into the receiver. It was definitely more of a question than a greeting.

"Meade! Thank goodness you picked up! I've been trying your cell phone for an hour," a male voice screeched through the handset. And it wasn't familiar. No, definitely not familiar.

"Uhm...I think it might be on silent," Meade said hesitantly. "Who is this?"

"Marshall!"

"Marshall?"

"Meade, this is you, right?"

"Yes."

"It's Marshall," he repeated. When Meade didn't reply, he went on. "Williams."

"Oh. Hi." She had no idea who he was. She didn't know any Marshalls. She wasn't sure she'd ever even met a Marshall before.

"I'm so glad you picked up your home phone. Can you come in? Like...right now."

"Uhm...come where?"

"What do you mean, 'come where'? Work! Come to work!"

Oh, no. This must be a co-worker. Or her boss. He sounded really anxious.

"Oh . . .work. Uhm...why?"

"Why? *Why?*" His voice was reaching a near frantic sound. "Have you not been watching the news?"

"The news...?" Meade looked around for a TV and saw it mounted to the wall across from the couch. She hadn't even paid attention to it before. "Uhm...no. I've been out. Why? What's going on?"

"Thomas Gallagher died!"

"The actor?"

"Of course, the actor! Would I frantically be calling you about a butcher named Thomas Gallagher?"

*Boy, this guy was snippy.*

"I guess not...that's sad. How'd he die?"

"Massive heart attack, they're saying. His girlfriend found him in the tub."

"Wow." This was sad news. He was a well-known and beloved actor.

Meade was pretty sure she'd seen every movie he'd ever made. He was one of those guys who'd started out as a sidekick in a whole lot of movies and then, at about the age of thirty, he got a leading role in an action film. It had catapulted him to stardom and he'd been working steadily ever since. She was pretty sure he had a movie coming out in the next week or so—at least, he did in her other world.

*"Wow?* That's all you have to say?"

"Uhm...I don't..."

"We have a problem. The author of the advanced one was William Vogel."

"Uhm..."

"Obviously, we can't use that one since he died three years ago. How would I explain that? We're clairvoyant?"

*What the hell was this guy talking about?*

"Hold on a sec." Meade heard him talking to what sounded like another man. A moment later, Marshall was back. "You're in luck. When I couldn't get hold of you, I called Adrian. He's here now. He can rewrite it. You don't need to come in."

"Oh, that's good." Meade wished she could ask him where it was, exactly, that she would have "come" and what she would have had to do once she got there. And, what did Thomas Gallagher's death have to do with any of that? But she could come up with no creative way to broach the subject.

"So, I'll see you tomorrow," Marshall said. Meade could tell he was about to hang up.

"Wait!" She couldn't let him go—not until she asked him a few questions. "What time do I need to be there tomorrow?"

"What time? The usual time."

"And that would be..."

"Meade, are you okay? You seem a little weird today."

"Oh, yeah. I'm fine. You just woke me up," she lied.

"You're sleeping at six o'clock at night? Maybe you're getting sick." He sounded concerned. Meade wondered if they were friends in addition to working together.

"I'm okay. Thanks, though."

"I'll see you at eight in the morning," he said slowly. She could tell he was making fun of her.

"Yes. Eight o'clock, on the dot."

Marshall laughed. "When have you ever been on the dot?"

"Always?" Meade asked, confused. She was definitely not a late person.

"You're kidding, right?"

Meade forced a laugh. "Of course, I'm kidding." But she wasn't. She had no idea what he was talking about. She was pretty sure she'd never shown up to anything—at least, not anything important, like work—late in her life.

"Okay, then. See you tomorrow! Gotta get back to work."

"You do that," Meade said and she replaced the phone on the receiver. She looked at the caller ID, again, as she did.

*The New York Times.*

Did she work at the *New York Times?* She must. Marshall had said he was calling from work.

That was so awesome. She'd thought about applying for a job at the *Times* years ago, before she'd gotten into publishing. She had no regrets about the literary path she'd taken, but she was still excited at the thought of working for such a well-known paper.

She wondered if she was an editor there. Maybe a senior editor, if she'd worked her way up by now. Marshall wasn't exactly talking to her as if she was an editor. Unless, of course, he was one, too. She was curious to find out.

Fortunately, she knew where the *Times* building was on Eighth Street. She'd make sure to be there at eight tomorrow—or maybe, eight o'three, so things didn't seem at all out of place right off the bat.

Speaking of time, Meade had two hours to get ready for her dinner with Daniel. The place couldn't be too fancy—he'd be coming straight from work and probably still in the scrubs he'd had on when he left this morning—but that didn't mean she couldn't look great. After all, the two of them hadn't been on a date in over fifteen years. This was a special—no, *momentous* occasion. She needed to look hot.

Glancing in the mirror by the front door, she realized it might take her some time to figure out how to style this new hairstyle of hers and find something suitable to wear in her unfamiliar wardrobe. She'd better get moving.

She'd never been so excited about a date before in her life.

It took close to the full two hours, but Meade was finally ready. Turning on the antiquated shower had been tricky. Who knew something so basic could be so complicated? And there hadn't been a whole lot of hot water once she stepped inside. *So much for a leisurely shower.* But her quick wash and rinse had done the job.

She'd been right to worry about the hair. Hairdressers always said, "Cut your hair short! It'll be so much easier to deal with. Just wash it and let it dry."

Well, that was a load of hooey and it hadn't taken her long to realize it. She was glad that she'd had the good sense to never cut it short in her real life. She had no plans on keeping it this length in this world, either. Assuming, that is, she stayed here long enough to grow it out.

Picking out an outfit had been another difficult task. Apparently, this Meade didn't like to dress up. Her choices were mostly limited to jeans, T-shirts and work shirts. Didn't they ever go out dancing? They lived in New York City, after all. Where were her nightlife clothes?

She wanted to "wow" Daniel—and nothing she found in the closet came close to saying "wow." At most, the outfits said, "Eh."

Meade finally settled on a short black skirt and black top that draped around the neck. It was tight in all the right places, and Meade was sure Daniel would notice that. He'd always been a boob guy. She found a pair of cute, strappy sandals with a pretty high heel and after a little searching, she found some bright blue nail polish under the bathroom sink. She sat on the tub as she painted her toe nails.

Once they had dried, she slipped on the sandals. Giving herself the once-over in the mirror, she decided what she saw wasn't half bad. It wasn't her best effort, but it was still pretty dang good.

She grabbed her purse, keys and cell phone as she left the apartment, remembering to lock all the bolts behind her. She looked at the time on her phone. Seven forty-five. She should be there perfectly on time. Maybe even earlier than Daniel. If anyone was ever late, it was him. Not her.

# CHAPTER NINETEEN

Meade was mistaken. Daniel wasn't late. She walked into the restaurant right at eight o'clock, but Daniel was already waiting for her at the table. She could see him sitting in the back, hunched over his phone. She wondered if he was texting someone or playing a game. *Did he play games on his phone?* She didn't even know. The Daniel she knew had left this earth never having heard of a smartphone.

She stopped walking the minute she spotted him. It was so unreal. So unbelievable. There he was. Daniel. Her Daniel. In a restaurant. Waiting to eat dinner. With her.

How was this possible? And, would she ever be able to wrap her brain around it?

As if he read her mind, he looked up and, spotting her, broke into a big grin and waved. Her heart leapt with joy. She'd never tire of seeing his beautiful face. She began to move toward him again. He stood as she got closer. She was pretty sure she saw his jaw drop.

"Holy cow," Daniel said. "You look amazing."

*Holy cow?* It wasn't "wow," but it was close.

"Do I?" Meade said, as if she'd thrown her ensemble together carelessly. "Thanks."

"What's the occasion? Do you have an event tonight?"

"This is the event," she said as he held the chair out for her.

"Dinner at Wok this Way is the event?"

"No, silly," Meade said coyly. "Dinner with *you* is the event."

The waitress came over to their table and put down two glasses of water and a bowl of crispy noodles with a side of duck sauce. She was middle-aged, with shiny black hair and happy eyes and she seemed to be the only female working in the restaurant. Meade wondered if she was the owner.

"Hello, Meade and Daniel," the woman said with such a thick Chinese accent, Meade almost expected her to say, "Daniel-son."

"Hey, Li," Daniel said easily. "How's your week been?"

"Oh, busy, busy. Glad to see you here. You have your usual?"

Daniel nodded. "I will." He turned to Meade. "You, too?"

Meade had no idea what her "usual" was, but she couldn't say that, so she nodded.

"I be right back with your food and hot tea," Li said. She smiled at Meade. "You look very pretty tonight. Hot date?" She glanced at Daniel and winked.

"This is my hot date," Meade said, as she had to Daniel.

"She want something from you," Li said, giggling as she looked at Daniel. "You give to her. She look nice."

"She sure does," Daniel said, beaming at Meade lovingly. "I hope I can afford whatever it is she wants."

"You big doctor," Li said. "You can afford anything."

Daniel laughed. "Maybe you can ask the hospital execs to give me a raise next time they come in to eat, okay?"

"Sure. Sure. I do that," Li said. "I be right back."

Meade watched her walk away. "See?" Daniel said. "Even Li doesn't think eating here is a big event. So what's with the outfit?"

Meade was beginning to feel a little awkward with all the attention being paid to her clothes. She'd wanted to impress him, not be stared at by everyone as if she was out of place—like a circus clown in the middle of a congressional hearing.

"I had an idea..." Meade said, though until this very moment, she'd actually had no idea other than to try to look nice for Daniel. But, something had occurred to her in the last few seconds—a way to explain why she was dressed the way she was while simultaneously finding out more about Daniel and this current life.

"Oh, yeah?" Daniel picked up a few crispy noodles and dipped them in the duck sauce. "What idea would that be?"

"Let's pretend we're on our first date."

"Our first date? Did we ever have one of those? I thought we grew up dating."

"Precisely. We never really had a first date—not like most people. I think tonight should be it."

"Seems a little silly to me..."

"Does it?" Meade was actually surprised by his reaction. The Daniel she knew was always up for any crazy idea she concocted. Of course, that Daniel had been a kid—and this one was a man. People tend to outgrow things, she realized. *Maybe he'd outgrown a little of his playfulness.* The thought made her a little bit sad.

"Humor me," she said, with a smile.

Daniel sighed. "Okay...okay. What do we do?"

"Maybe I should walk back into the restaurant."

"What?"

"You know—walk back in and we can start from there. We can pretend this is a blind date and we know basically nothing about each other."

"We know every single thing about each other," he said.

"I know that." She tried to not get frustrated with him. "That's why it's a game."

Daniel chuckled. "Okay. Let's do it."

Meade smiled at him. "I'll be right back." She got up from her chair and began to walk toward the door. Out of the corner of her eye, she saw Li return to their table with the tea.

"Where she going?" Meade heard Li ask Daniel.

"Don't ask," was his reply.

Meade walked back outside the restaurant and paused. She took a few deep breaths to steady herself. She needed to figure out what she was going to ask and how she was going to ask it. It was a bit nerve-racking, but mostly, Meade had a feeling this game might be really fun.

She took one last breath and opened the door to walk back inside. Once in, she looked around the restaurant, as if she was searching for someone and wasn't completely sure what he looked like. She glanced at Daniel. He was back to playing on his phone.

*Seriously?*

After what seemed like decades, he raised his head. When he saw her staring at him and not moving, he looked at her curiously. When she still didn't move, she saw him mouth the word, "Ah...," and then he waved at her as he stood up.

Channeling her best Angelina Jolie acting skills, Meade smiled, waved at him and made her way over to him. "You must be Daniel," she said, a bit shyly, as he pulled the chair out for her. "I'm Meade."

Daniel gave her a look that clearly said, *"You've got to be kidding me."*

The look she gave him back said, as clearly, *"I am not kidding and you had better play along."*

"It's nice to meet you, Meade."

"Likewise." Meade sat and Daniel sat across from her. The two stared at each other, a bit awkwardly. Clearly, Daniel was not going to make this easy on her.

"Have you been waiting long?" Meade asked.

"Nope," Daniel replied. "Just got here a few minutes ago."

They sat in silence for another few moments.

"Do you live around here?" she asked, trying again.

"I sure do. Just down the street."

"Well, that's convenient."

"Yep."

Going out of character, Meade leaned forward and glared at Daniel. "Are you not going to play along with me?"

He sighed again. "This seems silly."

"I don't think it's silly. I think it's fun. Is having fun not something we do anymore?"

Pursing his lips and blowing air out of them, Daniel shrugged. "Okay…okay. I'm tired from work. I'm sorry. I'll play along."

Meade sat back again. "Thank you."

He sat up straighter, making an intentional effort to focus. "I live down the street. In an apartment over another Chinese restaurant."

"Did you choose to live here so you'd have fast and easy access to Moo Shoo Pork twenty-four hours a day?"

Daniel smiled. "Yes. I love Moo Shoo Pork. But more than that, it wasn't too far from work."

"Oh? Where do you work?"

"A hospital in Brooklyn."

*Really? Brooklyn?* Not that Brooklyn hospitals weren't good—actually, Meade had no idea if they were good or not. But Daniel was good. At least, she'd always figured he'd grow up to be good—the best. She'd assumed he was a doctor at a prestigious hospital like Sloan-Kettering or New York Presbyterian. Not *Brooklyn*.

"Oh…Brooklyn."

Daniel laughed. "You don't sound impressed."

Meade smiled, but looked sheepish. "No. Brooklyn is great!" she said, a little too enthusiastically. "What do you do there?"

"I'm an ER doctor."

*ER doctor?* She hadn't expected to hear that, either. Daniel's dream had always been to be a pediatrician. Or maybe a pediatric oncologist. He'd shown an interest in that field after he was diagnosed with leukemia.

"That's interesting. Why did you choose the ER?"

"I had to do a stint there as a part of my residency. I hadn't planned on staying in the ER. Always thought I'd become an oncologist. But I fell in love with the ER. I liked the fast-paced atmosphere. I liked the immediacy of helping someone and seeing the results."

"Why did you originally want to become an oncologist?"

"I actually wanted to be a pediatric oncologist. I enjoy children and I had cancer when I was a teenager. I wanted to help kids who were suffering like I did."

"Oh?" Meade felt like she was saying that a lot. "You had cancer? You seem so healthy now."

"I am. Been in remission for close to fifteen years." Daniel took a sip of his tea. "Almost died. Came really, really close. Then, when at death's door, we found a bone marrow donor. She saved my life."

"You found a donor?" She couldn't keep the surprise out of her voice. "How? Where? Who? When?"

Her surprised reaction didn't go unnoticed with him. He gave her a curious look, but kept talking. "A girl from my high school. She was actually the best friend of my high school girlfriend."

"Lori?" The name was out before Meade remembered she was supposed to be playing a role of his blind date for the night. He looked at her with a raised eyebrow, as if to say, *"This was your game."*

"I mean," Meade corrected herself, "that's amazing that you found a match!"

Li brought their food right at that moment. After telling her how delicious everything looked, and taking a few bites, Meade looked up at Daniel. She was afraid he wouldn't continue where they'd left off and was relieved when he did.

"It's actually a crazy story," he said, sitting back in his chair. It appeared to Meade that he was finally beginning to relax and get into their role playing. "When we realized I needed a transplant, my mom and girlfriend and her family went to get tested to see if any of them were a match."

"And were they?" Meade, of course, didn't need to ask the question. The day they'd found out that none of them was a match had been one of the worst in her life. She'd been so sure someone—if not her, then maybe Nick or her mom—would be able to donate bone marrow to Daniel.

"No. None of them. It was really disappointing. And I'm an only child, so there were no siblings to test. That's where you usually have your best shot. My mom was hoping it'd be her, but it wasn't."

If she was on a real first date, she'd have said, "What about your dad?" But, this wasn't a blind date and, game or no game, she saw no need to open old wounds. "So what happened?"

"Well, my girlfriend's best friend was supposed to be tested that day, too, but at the last minute, she couldn't make it."

*Couldn't make it?* Ha! That was a nice way of putting it.

If Daniel noticed the irritation that crossed Meade's face, he made no indication of it. "The school decided to hold their own bone marrow drive, but it took a little time to get it together and I was getting sicker by the day."

The memory of that time brought tears to Meade's eyes and she quickly brushed them away. Even fifteen years later, the scar was fresh and the wounds were raw. "Did they find one at the drive?"

Meade was trying to find the point where things had taken a different turn in her life. The reason she was now in this alternate world. There had to be one moment. Something that changed everything. The catalyst that had sent her into a life without Daniel, while—simultaneously—creating a parallel world where he still existed.

"I don't know," he said, shrugging. "Maybe they would've. They never held the drive."

*What?* What did he mean "they never held the drive"? Of course they did. Lori had called her from the school that day. There'd been hundreds of people who showed up to be tested for Daniel. And a match had been found. But it had been too late. Daniel had died, while Meade held his hand, as people continued to get tested, not knowing his fight was already over.

"Never held the drive?"

"Nope. No need to. We'd already found a match before then."

*"What?"*

Daniel smiled. "Lori. My girlfriend's best friend. See, my girlfriend, Mea..." Daniel mouthed the word, "Oops," when he realized he'd almost said her name. "My girlfriend..." he repeated, "got so mad at Lori for not showing up that day when everyone else got tested, they had an enormous fight. My *girlfriend* told her best friend she'd never speak to her again for letting her—and me—down."

*She did?* Meade didn't remember it going that way. She'd been upset with Lori for choosing that guy over getting tested. But she'd never confronted her about it. Though irritated, she figured the chance of Lori being a match was slim. They'd certainly never had a big fight over it—that is, not until after the results came back from the bone marrow drive—three days after they'd buried Daniel—showing that Lori had been a perfect match all along.

At that point, Meade had gone ballistic. If Nick hadn't pulled her off Lori, she might very well have killed her. Meade had never been that furious at another human being. The selfishness of Lori had appalled her. And the consequences that resulted from her actions? Unthinkable. Lori had chosen to go on a date. *A date.* With a loser. And Meade had lost the love of her life as a result of it.

Daniel nodded. "She sure did. You don't—didn't—want to mess with my girlfriend. When she was passionate about something— watch out."

"She sounds like she was a wonderful catch," Meade said teasingly.

"Yeah...she was all right." Daniel grinned and winked.

"And so what happened?"

"Lori went and got tested. The next day."

*She did?*

"And she was a match."

That was it. Meade couldn't help but hear the words to a Robert Frost poem she'd learned in high school. *Two roads diverged in a wood, and I—I took the one less traveled by, and that has made all the difference.*

It wasn't quite the same, of course. Meade hadn't made a choice to travel down the road that didn't include Daniel. But that was the moment the roads diverged. The second her universes split.

Lori got tested. In time to save Daniel. And she was a match.

And everything, from that moment on, changed.

Meade shuddered when she thought of how she'd treated Lori that morning. She'd been despicable to her old friend—the woman who had saved Daniel's life. And the worst part was, Lori certainly had no idea why Meade was so angry. Meade was going to have a lot of apologizing—and explaining—to do.

"And you had the transplant?"

"I did. It went off without a hitch. The recovery was slow and it took a long time for my body to become strong again, but I've been in remission ever since."

*I've been in remission ever since.* Those were words Meade had waited a lifetime to hear.

Suddenly, Meade was filled with an enormous desire for Daniel. She had more questions she wanted to ask. About his mom. His career. Their life in NYC. But not now. Now, all she wanted to do was put her arms around Daniel and hold him and never let him go.

"Let's go home."

Daniel looked up at her with surprise. "Now? You've barely touched your food."

"We can take it with us."

"You hate cold Chinese."

"Not tonight."

"You sure?"

"Yes." Meade stared at him intensely. There was no mistaking the desire in her eyes.

Daniel's hand shot up. "Check, please!"

Meade had to laugh. The sparkle in Daniel's eyes. The grin. The wink he gave her. She'd missed all of that so much—more than she'd even let herself believe.

And now it was hers again. And it wasn't a dream. She didn't know what she'd ever done in her life to deserve such an incredible second chance, but she wasn't going to waste a moment of it.

They practically ran back to their apartment, holding hands and giggling like they had as little kids. Daniel chased Meade up the four flights of stairs and she found her hand shaking as she struggled to unlock all the bolts on their door.

She felt like a virgin. Nervous for her first time.

Though, of course, she was hardly a virgin. She'd had many lovers over the years. More than she wanted to remember at this moment. She'd pushed down her sorrow over losing Daniel by finding attention and affection with other men. The rest of her life, she'd been able to hold together. She'd gotten numerous degrees. She had a great career. She'd built many strong relationships.

But sex? And love? There'd been much of the first and none of the latter.

More times than she could count, she'd go to bed with a man and let him take her—all the while pretending it was Daniel in bed with her.

Alcohol was often involved in those encounters. A lot of it. It had made it easier to ignore the truth about the present and get lost in the fantasy of the past.

Tonight, though? She was sober as could be. Meade was so thankful she'd only had tea at dinner and nothing stronger. She didn't want beer or wine or a Cosmopolitan to cloud her mind. She didn't want to get lost in a fuzzy haze. She wanted to remember every moment with Daniel. Every touch. Every kiss. The moment he entered her— for the first time.

She'd waited a lifetime to make love to Daniel.

And, in that way, she *was* a virgin.

She may have had sex with many men. She may have given her body to them. But, she had never given her heart...her soul...her being...to any of them.

Those had always belonged to Daniel.

She'd had sex, but she'd never made love to a man.

Tonight, though, as Daniel led her into their bedroom and slowly began to unzip her skirt, she knew that was about to change.

# CHAPTER TWENTY

As a book editor, Meade had read more sex scenes than she could count, but none—not a single one—had come close in conveying the level of passion and desire Meade felt for Daniel tonight. She'd thought yearning was longing for a man. But she'd had no clue until Daniel's body was pressed next to hers—with nothing separating them but skin. She hadn't been able to get enough of him. Her hands had raced all over his arms and chest and stomach until, ultimately, they found the part for which they were searching.

Daniel's gasp had been nearly drowned out by her own. She was touching him. Daniel. Sexually. He was hard. And he wanted her. That much was brilliantly clear. It was such a heady feeling. To be in bed with the man she loved. To be making love to him. To have his mouth all over her naked body. She'd never wanted this moment to end.

Unfortunately, as all good things do, it did eventually end. Much too quickly—at least, in Meade's opinion—Daniel rolled off of her and onto his back. His eyes closed, she heard him breathing heavily.

"What got into you tonight?" Daniel asked.

"What do you mean?"

"I mean, you were a wild woman."

"I was?" Meade opened her eyes and turned her head to the side. She'd been excited, for certain, but she didn't think anything she'd done to him warranted special attention.

"You sure were. I haven't seen that kind of passion come out of you since...um...like, never."

"That's not true!" Meade said defiantly, propping herself on one elbow, simultaneously pulling the covers up to cover her exposed breasts. "I'm always very passionate."

"Really? Name the last time you attacked me like that."

Well, he had her there. She couldn't name another time when she'd practically pounced on him, but only because she couldn't remember *any* of their times together. Surely there had to be other zealous sexual encounters between the two of them. She was certain of it. Meade was many things, but hesitant in the bedroom had never been one of them. She liked sex. A lot. And she made it known to the men she was with just how much.

In this life, though, it was likely Daniel was the only man she'd ever been with—the only one she'd ever had in her bed. Thus, he must have been the beneficiary of all the sexual need she'd had through the years. Didn't that only make sense?

"I'll have you know, I am a lioness in the bedroom!"

Daniel laughed. *He actually laughed.*

"Did you just laugh at me?" Meade asked incredulously. *You have got to be kidding me.*

"I did," Daniel said, opening one eye to look at her and then laughing again.

Meade sat up, pulling the covers close to her chest. "Why on earth are you laughing?"

"You? A lioness? I'd say you're more like a cocker spaniel."

Meade practically jumped out of bed. "A cocker spaniel?!" she shrieked.

Daniel laughed again, closing his eyes. "Yes. A cocker spaniel. You're soft and cuddly and you like your belly rubbed."

"I like my belly rubbed?"

"Well, you know. You like to be on your back. Missionary-style. That's kind of like belly rubbing, right?"

Meade wasn't sure if she should hit him with the pillow or punch him with her bare fist.

Daniel opened his eyes, wide enough to see the steely look she was giving him. "What?" he asked. "That's not an insult."

"Well, it sure as hell isn't a compliment."

"Oh, come on, Meade," Daniel rolled over and put his arm across her. "I love having sex with you. It's nice. It's comfortable. It's familiar. It doesn't have to be all crazy. That's not us."

For starters, sex with Daniel was anything *but* comfortable for Meade. Though incredibly turned on, she'd also found that a part of her had been shy with him. This had been her first time with the boy she'd known since well before puberty. Would he like what she saw under her clothes? Would they fit together perfectly? Would he desire her as much as she needed him? It may have been familiar to Daniel, but it was new and exciting and exhilarating for Meade. He may have made love to her a thousand times over the years, but this had been her first time with him and she'd wanted it to be perfect.

And now he was telling her she was like a small dog in bed and a little bit too crazy.

She'd dreamt about how sex would have been with Daniel, many times over the years, but never once did any of those fantasies involve a canine reference. They did, tonight, though. Once Meade fell asleep, her dreams were full of cocker spaniels in her bed, licking her face.

And when the alarm went off in the morning, Meade momentarily thought it was a dog barking in her bedroom. She opened her eyes and glanced at the clock. Seven o'six. *Damn.* Why hadn't she set it for earlier? She hopped out of bed.

"Where are you going?" Daniel asked, trying to pull her back, but getting nothing more than a handful of sheet.

"I have to be at work at eight. I'm going to be late."

"So, what's new?" Daniel asked sleepily, and rolled over.

*What's new?* That was the second time someone had implied that Meade was a late person. She was not a late person. Did the people in this world not know her at *all*?

Meade jumped in the shower and was washed and dried in record time. Selecting clothes to wear was a difficult task. Did people in her office dress up for work? If so, what would she wear? Nothing in her closet screamed "classy and professional" to her. She finally settled on a black pencil skirt and a black-and-white polka dot, button-down blouse with a sash around the waist. She slipped on her shoes. Flats. It seemed she had very few shoes that weren't flats. Grabbing her purse, keys and phone, she went back over to Daniel, still in bed. She bent down to kiss his cheek, inhaling his smell.

"Bye, love," she whispered. Her words were met with a soft snore.

Meade quietly tiptoed out of the room and headed to work. She had butterflies in her stomach. She didn't know what she'd find when she got there. She didn't know her responsibilities. She didn't know her co-workers. She didn't even know what floor she worked on. And she was going to have to pretend that none of that was the case. If she ever needed to draw on the one semester of acting she'd taken in college to get her fine arts credit out of the way, it was going to be today.

As luck would have it, Meade didn't need to suffer through an awkward encounter at the front desk of the *New York Times*, attempting to explain to the receptionist why she didn't remember where she worked. She'd barely stepped into the front doors of the tall building when she heard a voice behind her.

"Meade! Meade! Wait up!"

Meade turned and saw a life-size Weeble approaching her. She felt ashamed of herself for having such a thought. Her mother hadn't raised her to be so judgmental. But, that's what the man hobbling his way looked like. He was largely disproportionate—with a wide midsection that didn't match his smallish head and skinny legs. His shirt was untucked on one side and he carried a briefcase that jostled up and down by his side as he swayed. He looked to be about ten years older than her. And, as he got closer, she could see his forehead was dripping in sweat.

"Geez," he moaned, as he reached her. "It is sweltering out here." He wiped his forehead with the back of his shirt sleeve and then reached into his breast pocket to pull out his key fob. He scanned it at the door. Meade quickly realized she must have one, too, and was thankful to find it neatly tucked into the side pouch of her purse.

"I think it's only about eighty degrees outside," Meade said as the man quickly hurried ahead of her. For a person of his size, and the way he lumbered as he walked, he sure was fast. Meade had to take two steps to keep up with each of his.

"You Texans think no one has hotter weather than you!" he quipped teasingly. "But you guys don't know about humidity. It's the humidity that's gonna kill you."

Meade shrugged. Even with the humidity, it hadn't seemed all that warm outside, but she certainly wasn't going to argue with Marshall. At least, her best guess was that it was Marshall. He sounded like the voice she'd spoken to on the phone yesterday.

Marshall impatiently poked the elevator button seven times and switched his briefcase to the other hand. "You ready for your trip? Isn't it in about two or three weeks?"

*My trip?*

"I don't know why you're going back to Texas in the summer. If I were you, I'd head there when there was snow on the ground here."

The elevator doors slid open and Meade followed Marshall inside. She made note when he pushed the thirtieth floor.

"You should tell your family to come visit you here," Marshall continued. "There's more to do here. What are you going to do there? Ride a bull?" Marshall laughed at his own joke.

Meade wondered if she liked him. It was hard to tell. He was brash. Very New York. She could see how he might rub people the wrong way. But, he was also animated when he spoke and had a jolly smile. Her gut said she liked him. She wondered if he was her boss.

"I'm going to see my family," Meade said. She figured that was a safe answer, though, until three minutes ago, she didn't even know she was traveling to Texas. She wondered if Daniel was coming with her.

The doors opened on the thirtieth floor and, though Marshall motioned for Meade to step out of the elevator first, she waited for him to begin walking down the corridor before following behind. She had no idea where she was going.

Marshall greeted everyone they passed by name and many of them said, "Hi, Meade," as they walked by her. She returned each greeting warmly, if not hesitantly. How could all these people know her and yet, she'd never seen any of their faces before?

Marshall stopped at a cubicle near the water cooler and threw a folder down in the next cubicle. "That's for you," he said. "I printed them before I came to work."

Meade glanced down at the desk. Spotting a five-by-seven framed photo of herself and Daniel, she figured this must be her station.

"What are they?" she asked. Potential news stories, she assumed. After all, as a reporter, she was probably always after the best story or angle.

"The online entries. There were a bunch last night. Apparently, people are dropping like flies in this heat."

*Dropping like flies?*

"And, when you're done, can you start processing the info the homes sent over?"

*The homes? What homes? Nursing homes?* What kind of news stories could they have? *One of the tennis balls fell off the bottom of Granny's walker and she stumbled into the rose garden?*

"Uhm. Sure," Meade said, trying to sound more confident that she knew what she was doing than she felt. "I'll get right on that."

"Great. I'll be in my office if you need me."

*Guess he's my boss.*

Meade sunk down into her chair, dropping her purse to the floor. She did a quick scan of the cubicle. Besides the picture of her and Daniel on the desk, it was relatively sparse. None of the photos that graced her desk at Brownsbury were here—none of her mom and Jimmy, none of Benji's medical school graduation—not even the one of Katie the day she moved into her first dorm room.

Meade stared at the folder on her desk. She figured she might as well open it and begin to delve into whatever career she now had. She hoped the stories that awaited her would be exciting, but manageable. At this point, she was so overwhelmed, it'd nice to be able to easily slip into her job and not worry about what was going on there. She knew nothing about writing for a newspaper—other than the time she had worked on her college paper—but she figured it couldn't be all that different from book publishing. After all, they both dealt with words, right?

Meade flipped open the folder and read the top sheet of paper.

*Eleanor Sholley, 72, of East Harlem, died Sunday. Eleanor was the owner and operator of Ellie's Steakhouse, which she opened with her late husband, Gerald, in 1956. Prior to that, she was an elementary school teacher. She was a parishioner of St. Lucy's Roman Catholic Church, East Harlem. She was a graduate of New York University. Arrangements: Kremer Funeral Home, East Harlem.*

Meade had to read it again to make sure she understood what she was reading.

This was an obituary. Or maybe, a death notice? She wasn't really sure what the difference was between the two. Nor, at this moment, did it seem to matter.

*What was going on?*

Meade quickly flipped through all of the papers in the folder.

Louis Kocsis, 82.

Sandra Whittington, 55.

Nichole Molden, 26.

Meade put her hand over her mouth. These were obituaries. *All* of them were obituaries. As if a light suddenly popped on inside her head, Meade gasped.

She wasn't an impressive reporter for the *New York Times*. She was an *obituary writer.*

How could this be? In her other life, she was a top book editor. Never in a million years, had she thought she might become an obituary writer. In fact, before this moment, she was fairly certain she'd never spent more than two minutes even pondering how death notices got written and placed into newspapers.

She knew now, though. *She* did it. *She* was the one who put those obits into the paper. Her. Meade Peterson. Obituary writer.

She wanted to cry.

"Hey, Meadie-Peadie," she heard a voice say outside her cubicle, "how are the bodies stacking up today?"

Meade glanced up and saw a young man she guessed to be about twenty-three, standing in her cubicle, a cup of water in his hand. He had glasses that were two times too large for his little face and freckles up his nose that went perfectly with his bright red hair.

"Uhm...I haven't counted yet," she said. "Marshall says there are a lot, though."

"I heard on the news last night that there was a murder-suicide in Brooklyn. Two teenagers. Boy killed his girlfriend and then himself. She was an honor student—about to head to Harvard. That will probably be crossing your desk soon."

Meade felt a knot in the pit of her stomach. Murder-suicide? Teenagers?

"I wouldn't want your job," her red-headed co-worker said. "You've got the worst job around."

"Gee...thanks," Meade said, trying to sound as if she was joking, but thinking he was probably correct.

"Anytime," he said, with a grin. "I'm always here to cheer you up if you need it."

"Hey, Mark," Marshall said, approaching Meade's cubicle and patting the smaller man on the shoulder. "Listen, Meade. I'm about to train the new kid. Want to sit in and see how I do it? That way, next time, I can hand this miserable task over to you."

If ever there was a miracle, this was one and Meade knew it immediately.

"You bet!" she said, jumping up. "See you later, *Mark*."


Meade's head was spinning by lunchtime. Who knew so much went into obituary writing? As it turned out, her department had three editors, a news assistant and seven writers. She, apparently, was one of those writers. Until William Vogel's passing three years earlier, he'd been the sole writer hired to pen all of the advance obituaries. Those being the ones the newspaper kept "in the can"—all ready to go when a famous person kicked the bucket. Meade was shocked at the notion. But apparently, it made practical sense. When a well-known person passed away, every newspaper was rushing to be the first to have a story on them hit the wires. If the meat of the article was already written—all about their career, accomplishments, personal life—then all the writer had to do was add three graphs at the top—(Meade learned that was the newspaper term for paragraphs)—regarding the circumstances of the individual's death and it was ready to go to print. Ever since William, himself, died, however, all of the writers wrote a number of advance obits a month. Currently, the *New York Times* had about fifteen hundred advance obituaries ready to go.

The "new kid," as Marshall had called her, was a fresh-faced girl just out of college. Her name was Staci and she had big dreams of becoming a novelist. She told Meade she figured if she started out "at the bottom"—writing obituaries, it seemed, fell into that category— she would someday work her way up to features editor and, if lucky enough, through her various contacts and experiences, secure a book agent and be on her way. Meade wondered if that was how this job had started out for her. A means to an end. Instead, it ended up being the end.

"What about death pools?" Staci asked Marshall.

"What about them?" Marshall asked, seemingly annoyed with the young girl. He clearly had more important work he wanted to get back to accomplishing.

"Do we pay any attention to them? Do they influence who gets an advanced obit?"

*What are death pools?*

"Why on earth would we pay attention to a bunch of crazy people who place bets on when famous people are going to bite the dust?" Marshall asked, clearly getting irritated. "Okay, I think we're done here. Meade has to get back to work and so do I. Staci, I'm going to find you a place to sit and you can fact-check some stuff for us, okay?"

Meade saw Staci nod eagerly as she headed back to her own desk. Sitting down, she pulled her phone out of her purse. She'd missed a text from Daniel.

*Your brother wants to change dinner to tomorrow night. That work?*

Meade reread the text three times. Her brother wanted to have dinner tomorrow night? Where? She wasn't headed to Texas for a couple of weeks—or so she'd been told.

*Won't be in Texas for a bit.*

She was careful how she worded that message, still not sure if Daniel was joining her on the trip or when she was going.

*Not Benji. Nick.*

*Nick? We're having dinner with Nick?* Meade thought. *Why would they ever do that?*

She quickly texted back. *Where?*

*We can do the usual place.*

She assumed that meant Wok This Way.

*Okay, tell him that works.*

Boy, this new life was full of surprises. But she was glad she didn't have plans for this evening now—though fifteen minutes ago she didn't know she'd had any to begin with. The Lori situation was weighing heavily on her and she needed to set it straight. She had enough to worry about in this universe. Hurting Lori's feelings, when Meade was clearly in the wrong, should not be one of them.

Meade scrolled through her phone contacts and found Lori's number. It was so weird to see her old friend's name in her phone. She certainly wasn't in the phone Meade normally carried.

Meade hit "Send message" and began to type.

*Can I see you tonight? Need to apologize. Want to explain in person. Please?*

Lori's response was nearly instantaneous.

*Sure. What time?*

*When I get off work.*

*Okay. Come by my place.*

Well, that was a problem...Meade decided to be honest. At least, partly honest, for now.

*Sure. Can you text me your address? Long story.*

Within a minute, Lori's address popped up on her screen. No questions asked.

Marshall walked by Meade's desk and she quickly threw her phone inside the top drawer of her desk. She wasn't sure, yet, if he was the type of boss who got irritated if you took care of personal business on work time, but she didn't feel like finding out right now, either.

When he was safely down the hall, she took the phone out again. She found Pantera's number and typed a quick message to her, too.

*Hey, Pantera. It's Meade. From coffee shop. Can you meet tonight? 8 pm?*

She hoped that gave her enough time to finish up with Lori.

Pantera must have also had her phone nearby because her response came within a minute.

*Sure! I'll just be getting off work. Want to come by the shop?*

*Perfect. See you then.*

Meade made sure her phone was still on silent and slid it back into her desk. Now that those meetings were scheduled, she needed to get back to work. Apparently, a lot of people had died in New York City in the past twenty-four hours. And, it was her job to make sure their lives were acknowledged.

# CHAPTER TWENTY-ONE

Meade started in on her apology the moment Lori opened the door to her apartment.

"I'm sorry. I'm sorry. I'm sorry. I can't even begin to apologize enough for how I treated you. I can only hope you'll forgive me."

Lori rolled her eyes at Meade and moved aside so the woman could enter her apartment. "Of course I forgive you. Though I'm not sure what was up your butt yesterday."

Closing the door behind her, Lori headed into her kitchen. Meade followed behind, like a pathetic, lost puppy. "I'm so sorry. I was so rude."

"Yes, you were."

"And out of line."

"Uhm...I'd say. I brought you *bagels.*"

"I know! Good ones, too!"

"Yes!" Lori said, cracking a smile. Opening the fridge, she took out a can of Coke and handed it to Meade. "Here. You need some caffeine. I can tell by the exhausted look in your eyes."

"I need more than caffeine," Meade said, taking the can nonetheless. She leaned against the kitchen counter as she popped the top off.

"Want to tell me what's going on?" Lori asked.

Meade wanted to tell her. She desperately wanted to tell Lori. But what could she tell Lori that wouldn't make the other woman think she'd lost her marbles? Her mind raced for the words and when she couldn't find them, she started to cry.

"Whoah!" Lori said, coming over to her friend and putting an arm around her. "Let's go sit on the couch."

And so, though she hadn't intended on telling Lori any of it, Meade told Lori the entire story.

"So, wait," Lori said, a contemplative expression on her face. "You're telling me you remember nothing from your life?"

"Nothing," Meade said. "I mean, nothing from my life since the moment Daniel died—or, I guess, didn't die. Actually, I guess I don't remember things accurately from the moment you didn't get tested with the rest of us to be a donor."

"Nothing?"

"I might remember some things, but I'm not sure which ones occurred in that life and also this life and which ones happened in that life."

"That was confusing."

"I know!" Meade threw her head back on the couch, covering her face with her hands, and began to cry again.

"Stop crying, Meade. That's not like you. You're strong. Not a crier."

Meade was happy to hear such a fact come out of Lori's mouth. In her old life, she wasn't prone to tears, but who *knew* what she was like in this world?

"Have you been to a doctor?" Lori asked.

"I'm not sick."

"I know. But you have to admit, this is really weird."

"Ya think?"

"Maybe it was all a dream. Maybe you dreamt that Daniel died," Lori suggested.

"But dreams are vague. That life is specific. I can tell you anything from it. Anything. From my ATM PIN number to the bathing suit I wore when I went to the Jersey Shore last week."

"Hmm..." Lori sighed. "I don't know what to make of it."

"But you don't think I'm lying?"

Lori's head jerked up in surprise. "Of course I don't think you're lying. Why would I think that?"

"Because I sound crazy. Even to me, I sound crazy."

"We've been best friends for twenty years...though, I know you don't remember most of them. But I do. You're trustworthy, Meade. If you say you don't remember this life—but remember a whole other one—then I believe you. I just don't know what to tell you to do about it."

Meade looked at her phone. It was almost seven-thirty. She didn't realize she'd been crying to Lori for so long. *Geez.* People were right. She was always running late.

"Do you have plans for tonight?" she asked Lori, getting up off the couch.

"Just vegging on the couch, watching reruns of *Friends*."

"Great. Get your shoes on. I have to meet someone and I want you to come."

"Okay." Lori stood up without question. "Give me five minutes."

Before Lori could leave the room, though, Meade pulled her friend into a hug. "Thank you. And, again, I'm so sorry."

Lori squeezed Meade tight. "No worries. You weren't that rude to me yesterday."

"No," Meade said, releasing her friend, "Although you don't remember it, I'm sorry I haven't spoken to you in fifteen years. No matter what happened, our friendship was special. I shouldn't have thrown it away."

Lori laughed. "I forgive you," she said airily. "I hope my alter ego in your other life forgives you, too."

Meade thought about what Lori had said as she stood in her friend's living room. Would the other Lori forgive her? Would Meade even ever have the opportunity to apologize for the way she'd treated her friend?

And, more importantly, did Meade want to have the chance to return to that world to do so or was she better off staying in this one?

Pantera was taking off her apron, and hanging it up behind the counter, when Meade and Lori walked in the door. She waved at the women and motioned for them to find a seat. The shop wasn't quite as crowded as it had been the other day, but it was unusually full for any food establishment at eight in the evening on a Monday night.

Meade led the way to a table in the back. They were going to need privacy for this conversation.

Pantera came over to them a minute later. "I know I'm off duty, but do you want me to get you anything to eat or drink before I sit down?"

Meade shook her head as Lori said, "No thanks."

Meade felt too sick to her stomach to eat. Lori had believed her, but they had a history. Pantera, on the other hand, was a stranger—at least, in this world. Would she think Meade was crazy? Would she call the police and say she needed to be committed?

*Stop that. No one's going to have you committed.*

Pantera sat down across from them and Meade began the introductions. "Pantera, this is my best friend, Lori. We've been friends since elementary school. Lori, this is Pantera. She..." Meade's voice faltered for a moment. She'd been about to say that she and Pantera were also best friends. But, that of course, would sound nuts to Pantera. So instead, Meade told Lori, "She's been nice enough to agree to talk to me tonight."

"Sure. I don't know what you're interested in, exactly. But I can try to help you out. Do you want to tell me more about your paper?" Pantera asked.

Meade paused. She wasn't sure what road to take with this. She could lie to Pantera. Turn her situation into a hypothetical—or pose it as a situation that happened to someone Meade "knew." Or, she could tell her the truth.

She looked at her friend—at least, the woman who used to be her friend. She owed her more than a lie. So, with a deep breath, Meade dove right in. "Pantera, I wasn't completely honest with you. I'm not writing an article."

"You're not?"

"No. I wanted to meet with you and I didn't know how to explain to you that I needed to talk to you, so I made up that story. I'm sorry."

"Okay..." Panterea said hesitantly. She looked at Meade cautiously and then over to Lori, as if trying to determine if she was in a safe situation and Meade was suddenly glad they'd agreed to meet on Pantera's turf.

"What I'm going to tell you is going to sound totally crazy. You probably won't even believe me. And, if you don't, that's okay. I don't even want to believe me. But, I promise, it's all true. I'm not nuts. That's why I brought Lori, so she could vouch for me that I'm a sane person. And Lori is really reliable and smart. She's...." Meade stopped mid-sentence and looked at Lori curiously. She'd been about to name Lori's profession when she suddenly realized she had absolutely no idea what Lori did for a living.

"I'm a marriage counselor."

*Really?*

Lori went on, ignoring Meade's perplexed expression. "And I can tell you, I've known Meade for over twenty years. She's a good person and trustworthy. Geez. I moved to New York City on her word alone. Hadn't even ever been here before, but eight years ago, she told me I'd be happy here and could stay with her until I found my own place. And I listened to her. Do you believe that? I packed up my car with all of my belongings and no job and moved halfway across the country to an enormous city, sight unseen, where I didn't know a soul—except for Meade and her boyfriend. Just because she said I'd be happy here. And she was right. I trust her with my life."

Meade was nearly speechless. She didn't know any of this tale. Lori gave her a look that said they'd discuss all of this later.

"See?" Meade said, turning her attention back to Pantera. "I'm not a loon."

Pantera looked at Meade warily. Meade realized that if she wasted any more time, she might lose Pantera altogether.

"Okay, so here it is. When I was eighteen years old, my high school boyfriend, Daniel, died of cancer."

"Oh, I'm sorry," Pantera said.

Meade waved her off. That fact seemed so insignificant at this point, it was ridiculous. "I have lived the past fifteen years without him. But I've always loved him. He was the love of my life."

Pantera nodded and Meade could tell that this Pantera had the same empathy as the one in her other life.

"But..." Meade continued. "And this is where it gets crazy...a few days ago, I woke up in bed with him. I mean, *alive* him. Not *dead* him." Meade felt it was important to make this distinction.

"You what?" Pantera was clearly confused.

"I woke up in an apartment I didn't recognize. And, next to me, was Daniel. But not the eighteen-year-old Daniel who died. This Daniel was in his thirties. Apparently, he never died. And we've had a life together for the past fifteen years. But, the thing is, I don't remember any of it. I only remember the life I had after he died."

Pantera looked at Meade. She turned and looked at Lori. She looked back at Meade.

Before she could even ask the question, Meade answered it for her. "This isn't a joke."

Pantera looked around the café uncertainly.

"And you're not on candid camera," Lori said.

"You're not messing with me?" Pantera asked.

"Nope. I'm serious," Meade answered.

Pantera took a deep breath. "Yowzers!"

"You're telling me," Meade said.

"So, how do I play into this? Why did you come looking for me?"

"Well..." Meade said. "I came looking for you because I know you."

"You know me?"

"Yes. In my other life."

"Really?"

"Yes."

"That's a little bit creepy."

"I'm sorry."

Pantera shrugged. "That's okay," she said, as casually as if Meade had just told her she'd accidentally eaten all of Pantera's French fries. "So, how do you know me?"

"Actually, you work for me."

"I *do?*" Pantera perked up. "What do I do?"

"You're my assistant."

"What do *you* do?"

"I'm a book editor for Brownsbury Press. At least, that's what I did in my old life."

"Wow. That sounds exciting. Do I like my job?"

"I hope so," Meade said, smiling. "You're good at it."

"I am?" Pantera said, startled. "I never thought about working for a publisher before."

"And you're my closest girlfriend."

"I *am?*" That seemed to surprise Pantera more than the fact that she could possibly work for a book publisher. She looked Meade up and down and her expression said, *"You don't look like any friend I'd have."*

"I know. It's hard to believe. But trust me. We're friends."

Pantera eyed Meade suspiciously. "I don't know. This is weird."

"It is weird. It's bizarre. I get it. But, I need you to believe me."

"Why?"

*Why?* That was a good question. "Maybe because I think you can help me figure this out. Or maybe because I really miss my friend. You're the only two people I can tell. I can't tell Daniel, that's for sure."

Both of her friends nodded in agreement. Meade certainly couldn't tell Daniel that not only did she have no memory of their life together for the past fifteen years but, until the other day, she thought he was dead and buried.

No, that wouldn't go over well.

Suddenly, an idea popped into Meade's head. "I can prove it to you!"

"How?" Both Lori and Meade said at the same moment.

"I don't know about your recent life—the one here at the café—but I know a lot about your personal life. Your family. Your pets. Your hobbies. Assuming those things haven't changed—or been affected by the fact that you don't work for me—they should be the same, right?"

Pantera and Lori both nodded and shrugged. It seemed to make sense.

"Okay, so ask me a question. Something only a close friend would know."

Pantera thought for a moment, biting the inside of her lip. "What job did I have throughout high school?"

"You worked in a funeral home."

"What part of the job did I like the best?"

"Helping people pick out the caskets."

"What was my first tattoo?"

"A skull and cross bones on your bikini line. You got it in some guy's kitchen. He learned how to give tattoos in prison. To this day, you still haven't told your mom about that one."

Pantera's mouth dropped open, but she quickly closed it. "Where did I go to college?"

"You didn't."

"And why not?"

"Because your dad had a gambling problem and he blew through the money your grandmother left you in her will."

Pantera's gasp was audible. "I never tell anyone that."

"Anyone other than your best friend."

"I don't have a best friend."

"In my other life you do."

The three women sat in silence for what seemed like forever to Meade. Did Pantera believe her? What more would she have to tell her to prove that she wasn't lying?

"Well, I'll be damned," Pantera said slowly.

# CHAPTER TWENTY-TWO

M eade felt like a thousand-pound weight had been lifted off her chest when she crawled into bed with Daniel that night. She was no longer carrying this secret alone. She had friends. Two of them. And they both believed her. How did she ever get so lucky?

Of course, neither of them could help her figure out what to do about the situation. And, that was alarming. But, for now, the fact that she felt like she had people who believed she wasn't nuts really, really helped.

"Wanna do it?" Meade said, seductively to Daniel, as she shimmied her body up close to him. He was reading one of his boring World War II novels. By the stack of similar volumes on his nightstand, Meade had come to the conclusion that old war books seemed to be Daniel's "thing."

"Not tonight, babe. I'm still worn out from last night."

"Really? I think I could find a way to revive you." Meade slid her hand under the sheet, but before it could reach its destination, Daniel grabbed it with his own and placed it onto her hip.

"Seriously, Meade. Not tonight."

Meade rolled over on her back. "But why not?"

"Because we don't have to do it every night."

"Do we do it every night?"

"No. But we did it last night."

"And when was the last time before that?" She wasn't trying to prove a point. She honestly didn't know.

"I don't know? Last week, maybe."

"Last week? *Maybe?*"

"What has gotten into you?" Daniel said, resting his book on his chest.

"I find you attractive," Meade said, rolling back over and putting her hand on Daniel's chest, stroking the soft hair. "Is that so wrong?" She leaned in and began to kiss his neck.

She had an insatiable desire for him. She still couldn't believe he was here.

Almost as much as she couldn't believe it when he pushed her away.

"Meade, come on," he said, wiggling his neck away from her. "Get on your side of the bed. Read a book or something."

*Read a book?*

"Do you not find me attractive?"

"Now you're being silly. Of course, I do."

"Then why aren't you all over me? *I'd* be all over me," she said with a smile.

Daniel laughed at that. "Oh, you would be, huh?"

Meade took the laughter as a sign to move closer. "Yes, I would." She put her hand back under the sheets.

Almost instantly, Daniel removed her hand again. "Meade, I'm not kidding. I'm tired. We have to get up early. Let's go to bed."

Meade's heart sank and she rolled onto her side of the bed. She was tempted to keep trying, but it seemed like her efforts would be in vain. Daniel wasn't in the mood for sex and she wasn't in the mood to be rejected by him. She turned off the light on her side of the bed and lay down, her back to him.

"Night, babe," he said. "I love you."

"I love you, too," Meade said softly. And, though she meant it, she was surprised it was possible to feel this sad with Daniel alive and only two feet away.

"Must we go?" Meade asked Daniel.

"Yes, we must go," Daniel said, coming out of their closest wearing nothing but a pair of boxer briefs.

Meade turned her head and tried to not look at him as she lay on the bed. The sight of his bare chest was enough to make her want to pull him down on top of her. But last night's rejection was still fresh and she didn't feel like reliving that now.

"But why? I'm exhausted. Work sucked today."

"That's what you say every day," Daniel said, digging through the dresser drawers in search of a T-shirt and some shorts.

"And after today, I can see why I say it every day! It has got to be the most depressing job on the planet. For most of these people, the only time they've ever made it into the newspaper is for their obituary. Isn't that horrible? The only time you're in the news and you're not even alive to enjoy it?"

"I doubt they'd enjoy reading a news story about their own death."

Meade was silent for a moment. What would Daniel think if she were to hand him a copy of his own obituary? She didn't have a copy, of course. It didn't exist in this world. But it existed in her mind. She'd read it so many times over the years, relishing every word of his life as if reliving each accomplishment with him, she could write the entire thing down in less than ten minutes.

"Are you going to change or go like that?" Daniel was standing next to the bed, staring down at Meade. She was still in her work clothes, while he was now dressed super casually.

"I'll change," she said reluctantly, getting up off the bed. The last thing she needed was for Nick to make some snide comment about how she was dressed all hoity-toity, to show him up.

For the life of her, she couldn't figure out what Nick was doing in town. And what was equally puzzling was why she and Daniel were agreeing to have dinner with him. Did Daniel not know of Meade's complete and utter disdain for her brother?

"Well, hurry up. We're going to be late." As Meade headed into the closet, she thought she heard Daniel mutter, "Not that that would surprise anyone."

When Meade entered Wok This Way, she immediately began looking for the grungiest man in the place. When she spotted "that guy," she would have spotted her brother. After skimming the relatively packed restaurant, Meade came to the conclusion Nick wasn't here yet.

"He's in the back," Daniel said and began to make his way through the tables.

Meade tried to peer around Daniel, but couldn't catch a glance of Nick. She was nervous about this dinner and hoped they didn't have to stay too long with him. She hated being with Nick and couldn't remember the last time they'd spent an entire meal in each other's presence. This evening would be torture.

*I wonder if he'll expect us to pay for him?*

Meade almost laughed out loud. Of *course* he would expect them to pay for him. Nick was nothing if not a moocher.

Daniel reached the table first and Meade was surprised when he hugged her brother, with Nick giving Daniel a big slap on the back. Meade hadn't even seen them approach Nick's table. Daniel was so much taller than she was, it was hard to see anything when he was ahead of her.

"Hey, little sis! How are you?"

Daniel stepped aside and Meade was instantly lifted off the ground in an enormous hug.

*What the...?*

Nick put her down and Meade finally got a good look at him. What she saw almost made her pass out.

He looked so...*clean.*

Yes, that was the only word that came to mind. He was clean. Clean-shaven. Clean-cut haircut. Clean clothes. And not just any clothes. He was in a suit. And, from what Meade could tell, an *expensive* suit.

And, by the brilliant clear look in his eyes, he *was* clean. Clean and sober. She wanted to cry. But not because he upset her or disappointed her—as he continually did in her other life—but because he looked so good. So healthy. So whole.

"Dude," Daniel said, as they all took their seats at the table. "What are you doing dressed in that monkey suit?"

"I'm sorry. I just came from meetings. I had to rush to get over here. There was no time to run home to change."

*Run home?* Did Nick live in the city?

"Well, we're thrilled you're back. It hasn't been the same without you."

"I'm happy to be home, too. There's nothing like New York—and air conditioning."

"You're one lucky guy, though. Not all of us can take a month-long vacation."

"Well, a month off of work is great, but I would hardly have called it a vacation. We slept in un-air-conditioned huts and worked fifteen-hour days. But it was worth it. The school should be up and running by the end of the month."

Meade was trying to follow the conversation, but was at a loss. A school? *Huts?* Where had Nick been? And what on earth was he doing there?

Meade's thoughts were interrupted by Li's appearance at their table.

"Hey, Li," both Daniel and Nick said in unison.

"Oh! Look who back! Fancy-schmancy man!" Li said, clearly excited to see Nick. "I tell my sister you go to Africa to build a school. She want to know if you wear a suit there!"

"Ha!" Nick said, laughing. "Nope! I wore shorts and a T-shirt and a lot of sunscreen."

"We so glad you back. So proud of you! Big Wall Street man! We want to see photos of you banging hammer!"

"What? You can't picture me getting dirty?"

For some reason, the image of this made Li laugh. She continued to laugh as she put the water on their table and took their orders and then made her way back to the kitchen. In turn, Nick, Daniel and Meade started to laugh, too. Meade couldn't remember the last time she'd laughed over anything with Nick—and it felt really good.

She was dying to ask him a million questions. Starting with, "How did this happen?" and "You work on *Wall Street?*" But, she couldn't ask him that. Or anything else she wanted to know about how this transformation had occurred. That didn't matter. She had Lori now and she could ask her everything later. For now, she was with her big brother. And, from what she could see, he had turned into a wonderful person.

"So, tell me, Nick..." Meade said, speaking for the first time all night. "What about the little kids? Are they excited about their new school?"

"You can't even imagine," Nick said, his eyes sparkling as he told her about Uji, a little boy in the village who Nick would play soccer with every evening.

Listening to her brother and watching him smile and laugh with Daniel made Meade's heart soar. There would be time to find out the details of his transformation later. At this moment, she wanted to enjoy the two men in front of her—both of whom she'd thought she'd lost forever.

# CHAPTER TWENTY-THREE

"You need to tell me everything and don't leave anything out," Meade said to Lori, as she, Lori and Pantera sipped iced coffee at a back table in CU Latte. She'd waited four long days until all of their schedules were free at the same time. As it was, Pantera only had an hour break, so they had agreed to meet back at the café.

"Are you telling me Nick isn't a financial whiz in your other world?"

"Ha! Hardly! He's a loser who sleeps on my mom's couch. He can't keep a job. And he's an alcoholic. Maybe a drug addict, too. I'm not sure."

"I can't even wrap my brain around that. He wasn't the most motivated of teenagers, but he's been so successful for so long, it's hard to remember that old Nick."

"What I want to know is, how did he become this new and improved Nick?"

Lori bit the inside of her lip and thought for a moment. "I don't know. It's hard to say. I think Daniel had a lot to do with it."

Meade nodded as she took a sip of her drink. "That would make sense. The game changer had to be Daniel not dying. But what did Daniel do to influence such a metamorphosis?"

"I know that when Daniel got better, he and Nick started hanging out a lot. Daniel felt he'd been given a second chance and wanted to do something with that opportunity. I remember he told me that if he got a second chance, why shouldn't Nick get one, too? Daniel felt like, after the miracle of his recovery, anything was possible."

"And Nick went for that? He barely spoke to Daniel when we were kids. I think he was jealous of him."

"I think Daniel's illness affected Nick more than you realized. He may have seemed like a tough kid—or young man, as he was at the time—but he'd never had to deal with illness or death before. And here he was, watching his sister's boyfriend dying in front of his eyes and he didn't know how to handle it. You were too consumed with Daniel to notice it. And rightly so," Lori quickly added, clearly not wanting to make Meade feel guilty. "But, it's not like your mom was any help to him in sorting through his emotions. And, you don't really have a dad."

"I never thought of it that way," Meade said.

"You know, I don't know any of these people," Pantera added. "But it seems to me that maybe Nick really looked up to Daniel, though, it might have come across as jealousy to you. He was scared, too, and had no one to confide in, so he drowned himself in alcohol."

"And, in my other life, when Daniel died, Nick fell further and further into hopelessness."

"But when Daniel didn't die, he and Nick began a close friendship. Daniel believed in Nick and encouraged him to go to college. Nick enrolled in the community college, but did so well, he eventually got a scholarship to Wharton."

"Wharton School of Business?"

Lori nodded. "He went on to get his MBA. Graduated top of his class."

Meade couldn't believe it. Nick. Her brother, Nick. A success. It was hard to wrap her brain around it. "I hate him in my old life."

"You're kidding," Lori said. "He's one of your closest friends in this one. You tell me all the time how happy you are he lives in the city, how you don't know what you'd do without him. He's a really, really good person."

This was all almost too much for Meade to process. She was going to need to put all thoughts of Nick in a different compartment of her brain. It wasn't going to be easy. She hoped the dislike she had for him in her other life didn't show itself to him in this one. They apparently had a great relationship and she didn't want to do anything to ruin that.

"Hello, ladies," a voice from behind Meade said. "We hope we're not interrupting."

Meade looked up and saw Henry and Leighton standing next to their table. She couldn't help but smile at the sight of them. Her first encounter with the old men had been brief, but they'd made such a great impression. She'd really liked both men.

"Hey, there!" Meade said enthusiastically. "It's great to see you again."

"Hi, Henry. Hi, Leighton," Pantera said.

"Hey, Panty," Henry greeted her.

Meade glanced at Pantera's face to see if she cringed, but she didn't seem to mind their nickname for her. Maybe because both men were so old and sweet.

"Oh, this is my best friend, Lori," Meade said. It sounded so weird to say those words again, after not saying them for fifteen years. But it also felt really good. Lori shook the hands of both men.

"Ladies, I'd like to introduce my grandson to you," Leighton said. "This is Cory." For the first time, Meade saw a young man standing behind the older gentlemen. He appeared to be in his twenties and was dressed in a black T-shirt and ripped jeans. His chin was pierced and his hair was a little bit too long for her taste. But Meade knew someone who liked men who looked like that...and she was sitting right at their table.

Seeing an opportunity and grabbing it, Meade said, "Would you like to join us? Pantera has about forty-five minutes until she has to get back to work, so we'll be hanging out."

"That would be wonderful!" Leighton said, perhaps a bit too enthusiastically. Meade and Lori got up and helped the men pull another table and some chairs over to them, and when Henry orchestrated it so that Cory sat directly next to Pantera, Meade knew that the older man had been thinking the same exact thing she had.

"You sneaky man," Meade said, leaning over and whispering to him. "You're playing matchmaker."

Leighton blushed a bit. "Henry and I have been talking for the past year about how we needed to introduce my grandson and Pantera. They're the perfect match. When Cory said he was coming for a visit, I knew we needed to bring him into the coffee shop!"

"And, from the looks of it, you might be crowned Cupid very soon," Meade said, giggling. Across the table, Pantera and Cory were already deep in conversation.

Leighton winked at Meade. Meade glanced over at Pantera. It looked like her friend's picker was picking herself a good one.

"Can we pop in here?" Lori asked Meade as they walked past a bookstore. They were headed to Lori's house to hang out for the rest of the night. Daniel was working the late shift—again—and Meade didn't feel like being alone. They'd left Pantera behind at the coffee shop. Her shift wasn't over yet, but she and Cory had made plans to go out when she got off later that night. Meade had to hand it to Henry. It seemed like he'd made a good match.

"Sure," Meade said. "I'm not in a hurry."

"There's a new book out I've been wanting to read. I'll only be a minute."

"No problem. Take your time."

The two women walked into the store and Lori headed to the information counter to ask about her book. Meade leisurely strolled through the aisles. It had been weeks since she'd been in a bookstore. She missed being around so many books. At work, now, instead of books piled on her desks, she had stacks of death notices. And, instead of talking to fascinating authors and their agents all day long, she spent hours dealing with funeral directors.

Meade glanced at a bookshelf in the front of the store. The sign on top read "Best Sellers." Meade smiled as she looked at the display. She knew who'd hold at least one of the top five spots. She scanned the hardbacks and then, sure she must have somehow missed what she was looking for, she carefully checked each book again.

"I'm done!" Lori appeared next to Meade. "What's wrong? You look like someone just killed your pet hamster."

Not bothering to answer Lori, Meade made a beeline for the information desk.

"Are you sure?" she asked the employee behind the counter, after asking him to search for five different books. "Not one is available here?"

"I'm not saying they aren't available in our store. I'm saying, they aren't available anywhere. In any store. Our chain or any other bookstore in the country. Those books don't exist."

"But, of course they do. I've read all of them. I even pub..." Meade stopped herself short.

*Oh, no.*

"Do you have a car?" Meade said, quickly turning to Lori.

"Yeah. It's actually parked in a garage not all that far away."

"Good. Let's go get it," Meade said, already heading toward the door. Lori hurried to keep up. "We need to go to Long Island—tonight."


"Are you sure this thing works?" Meade asked Lori, fumbling with the GPS.

"Yes, it works!" Lori said, laughing at Meade's frustration. "Do they not have technology in your other life?"

"Well, I'm sure they do, but I don't have a car there, so I don't need to bother with these things. Okay, here we go," Meade said, finally getting the city screen to pop up. "Long Island." Meade's fingers typed out the words.

"It's going to give you some options. Click on 'points of interest.'"

"Okay, got it." Meade did as she was told and scrolled through the options. After pressing the screen a few more times, she found their destination. She hit "Go" and then attached the GPS to Lori's front window so Lori could follow the directions.

"We shouldn't be too far away at this point," Lori said. "It took you long enough to program that thing."

"Sorry! I was an English major. Not a computer whiz."

"It should be right around the corner," Lori said, leaning forward to see the road more clearly. It had begun to rain as soon as they'd driven the car out of the garage and now, the precipitation was picking up. "What are you going to say?"

"I have no idea," Meade said. She'd been thinking about it on the whole drive and still wasn't sure what words would come out of her mouth when she saw him. She had to hope that whatever they were, they were the right ones.

"Here we are," Lori said, pulling into a small parking lot. "Randall Lanes. I'll drop you at the door so you don't get too wet."

"You're the best," Meade said as Lori pulled to the curb.

"I'll wait for you in the car. Text me when you're done and I'll pull up to get you if it's still raining."

"Thanks," Meade said, hopping out of the car.


The bowling alley was dark inside, with neon disco lights flashing above each of the lanes. If Meade hadn't known better, she would've thought she'd been transported into another decade and not a parallel world where Daniel was still alive.

It didn't take her long to find him. The alley wasn't very big, with only about ten lanes and a bar in the back. The sign said the bar served drinks as well as pizza, hamburgers, fried pickles and nachos. Not exactly health food.

He was working the counter. Meade stopped walking so she could observe him without being noticed. He looked great. He always looked great. Tall and rugged. If he hadn't written so many great books, he should have, at the very least, been the cover model for them. She watched as he filled a glass with Coke and placed it in front of a little boy at the counter.

"Two bucks," she heard him say, as the boy slipped the bills onto the counter and Ian picked them up. "Bowl a strike for me, okay?"

"You got it!" the kid said, running off to find his mom.

Meade walked over to the bar. No other customers were there, though the lanes were full. If she wanted to talk to Ian privately, it was going to have to be now, before someone decided they couldn't last one more minute before clogging their arteries with some fried pickles.

"Hey," she said quietly.

"Hey, there," Ian said. "What can I get you?"

"How about Sprite?"

"One Sprite coming up," Ian said, taking a foam cup from beside the machine and pushing it into the ice dispenser. "Getting kind of nasty out there? Looked like it was gonna rain when I got into work."

"Yep. The rain's coming down. It was hard to see the road."

"You a bowling fan?" Ian asked, filling her cup with soda.

"I like to bowl. It's relaxing after a hard day of work." Meade wasn't sure this segue would work, but it was worth a try.

"Oh? What do you do for a living?"

*Bingo!*

"I'm a writer."

She knew this would get Ian's attention as sure as the fact he liked three olives in his martinis.

"Really? A writer?" he said, placing her drink down in front of her. "I'm a writer, too."

"You're kidding. What do you write?"

Ian leaned his elbows on the counter and relaxed his body. "Novels. Well, one novel so far. I haven't been published or anything, but I hope to be someday."

"Have you sent it out anywhere?"

"Nah. I hear that you can send out a hundred query letters and maybe one agent might say he might read it. It seems so futile."

"You never know until you try," Meade said, sipping her drink.

"Yeah. I guess. I did give a copy to my buddy, Tommy. He works in the mailroom at some big publishing company. He said he'd see if any of the editors would agree to read it. But, so far, no one has said they would."

*Because I'm not there.* Those other editors were a bunch of stuck-up idiots. They didn't realize that doing one favor, for the mail guy, could skyrocket their own careers.

"I don't think you should ever give up. I'll bet you're really good."

Ian's eyes brightened. "You think? Why would you say that?"

"I have a good feeling about you. I think you should send out all those query letters. Maybe only one agent will read your stuff, but I bet, when they do, they'll love it."

"Hell, maybe you're right. I can't work in a bowling alley my whole life. You gotta have a dream."

"Yes, you do. And I'm serious. Go home tonight and start sending out those letters. I'll come back here in a year and I'll bet you won't be working here because you'll be so famous. I'll have to ask where to find you."

Ian smiled—that gorgeous, heart-stopping, melt-your-entire-body smile.

"Thanks. I appreciate the encouragement. I'm gonna do that."

"Great," she said, opening her purse. "How much do I owe you?"

"It's on the house."

"Well, that's nice of you." Meade picked up a pen from the counter and handed it to Ian. "Will you sign my cup?"

"Sign your cup?"

"Sure. That way I'll have your autograph when you become famous."

Ian chuckled, but did what she asked. Meade looked at his signature, the one she'd seen him sign thousands of times at book events.

"Take care, Ian Cooper."

"Bye."

Meade took her drink and picked up her phone, texting Lori to come pick her up. The car was waiting by the entrance by the time Meade walked outside and she ran to get into it. The rain was really coming down and she was soaked after only being in it for two seconds.

"How'd it go?" Lori asked, as Meade slammed the door and put on her seatbelt.

"Well, I think." She put her drink down in the cup holder. "When I'm done with my Sprite, you can keep the cup."

"Why would I want an old foam cup?" Lori asked, pulling out of the parking lot.

"Because someday, you'll be able to list it on eBay—for a whole lot of money."

# CHAPTER TWENTY-FOUR

"Guess what I bought for us?" Meade said excitedly, as Pantera walked into her apartment.

Daniel was working late again. He was always working late. Sometimes Meade felt like she barely saw him more now that he was alive than she did when he was dead.

And so Meade had invited Pantera over for dinner. Pantera had offered to bring some sandwiches from the shop and Meade had said she'd provide the beverages and dessert.

"What?" Pantera asked, placing the bag from the restaurant on the kitchen counter.

Meade grabbed a box from the kitchen cabinet and excitedly held it with both hands in front of her face. "Cupcakes!"

"I love cupcakes!" Pantera said.

"I know!" she said. "I got your favorite. Chocolate cake and chocolate icing!" Meade picked up the can of icing she had left on the counter.

"I still have a hard time wrapping my head around the fact that you know so much about me when I know pretty much nothing about you."

"It is a little weird," Meade said. "Does it feel like I've been spying on you?"

"Maybe a little. But that's okay. I'll get used to it." Pantera was nothing if not flexible. Meade loved that about her.

"This will be the first thing I've actually cooked since I got here,"

Meade said. "And I don't know where anything is in the kitchen. I bought eggs and cupcake liners. I'm assuming we have a pan and some oil." She began to search through the cabinets and was relieved to find both.

"So, how's Cory?" Meade asked Pantera with a grin.

Pantera blushed a bit. "Good. I like him." She began to take the sandwiches out of the bag. "Do you have plates?"

"I think they're in the cabinet next to the sink. I can never remember."

"We've gone out about three times. He's thinking of moving here. I don't know. We'll see where this goes."

"But you like him?"

"Yeah."

"A lot?"

Pantera smiled shyly. "Yeah."

Meade was thrilled her friend seemed so happy. In all the years she'd known Pantera, she'd never once seen her smitten over a man. It was nice to realize she may have finally found someone really special.

Meade read the directions on the box. *Bake at 350 degrees*. She moved over to the oven and turned the dial.

"Do you think a light is supposed to go on when you set the temperature?" Meade asked Pantera.

"You're asking me? I don't cook."

"Me neither." Meade laughed. "But still, I would think something would light up to let you know the oven was on."

Meade put her hand on the oven door. It didn't feel like it was getting warm. She opened the door to see if the pilot light was lit inside. "What on earth...?" She opened the it all the way and pulled out a large plastic box. "Apparently, the oven doesn't work...so instead, we use it for storage."

"What is that?"

Meade shrugged and put the box on the counter. She opened the lid. Inside were files. Here it was. The box of papers she'd spent her first day in this world searching for.

"I guess we're not having cupcakes," Pantera said, a hint of disappointment in her voice.

"We can go down to the bakery on the corner after dinner," Meade said distractedly.

*Were the answers to many of her questions in these files?*

Meade carried the box over to the couch and placed it on the coffee table. She took out a stack of folders and placed them on her lap.

The first few files contained some important documents—her and Daniel's birth certificates, insurance plans, their passports. She momentarily wondered if they'd ever left the country on a vacation. It didn't seem as if they lived a life that lent itself to many vacations.

The second folder contained bank statements. It seemed she and Daniel had two joint accounts and the amount in each of them was so low, Meade began to worry if she could afford the cupcakes she'd just promised Pantera. Especially after finding her most recent paystub at the back of the folder. Geez. She barely made anything.

It was the third folder, though, that left Meade breathless. Bills. So many bills. Credit card statements, college loans for both her and Daniel, medical school loans, a car payment. Meade flipped to the back of the folder and found a spreadsheet where someone—either she or Daniel—had neatly typed up exactly how much they owed. The grand total made Meade blink. *Hard.* How could this be possible? In her old job, that was more than she made in two full years—with bonuses! From what she gathered about what she made in her current obituary-writing position, it would take her a decade to even make a dent in that amount. And though she was sure Daniel made more than her, it wasn't going to be nearly enough to pay this down quickly.

No wonder they lived in this crap hole. She was surprised they didn't live in a cardboard box.

"I don't understand," Meade said aloud.

"What don't you understand?" Pantera asked, bringing their sandwiches and drinks over to the couch.

For a moment, Meade debated whether to keep their debt a secret from her friend. She wasn't the type of person to discuss her finances with anyone—even her friends. But that was when she had money. Did the same rule apply when you were broke?

"In my other life, I'm not rich, but I'm doing well for myself. I have no debt. I have a pretty good-sized savings account. I paid off my student loans. I really don't worry about money. But this?" Meade held up the folders. "If this is accurate, we will be in debt until we enter the nursing home."

"Oh. That's a bummer."

"Yeah. A big bummer. I hate debt. I'm always so proud of myself that I don't have any," Meade said, closing the folders. "But, apparently, I do. A lot."

Meade tried to stuff the folders back in the box, but found they wouldn't fit. Something was in the way. She stuck her hand down inside and pulled out a small, black jewelry box.

"What's that?" Pantera asked.

"I have no idea." She carefully opened the lid. Inside was a beautiful—albeit small—diamond ring.

"Are you engaged?"

"I don't know," Meade said. "Since I've been here, Daniel has never once mentioned a wedding. I doubt we're in the middle of planning one or I think something would have come up."

"Maybe he hasn't proposed yet and was hiding the ring," Pantera suggested.

"In our bill box?"

"Maybe he knows you don't like to look in there?" Pantera giggled.

For the first time since she found the box, Meade smiled. "That could totally be true."

She pushed the box to the side of the coffee table and placed the ring box next to it. "Let's eat. I'm starving."

For the next hour, the bills were forgotten. It was so fun to hang out with Pantera. Whether in this world or the other, the woman was unique and interesting and Meade never got bored listening to her stories. Though these revolved around the coffee shop and her new boyfriend, whereas the old Pantera spent a lot of time sharing the office gossip with Meade that she could never have learned on her own.

When every last crumb of the sandwiches had been devoured, Meade hopped off the couch. "It's cupcake time!" She picked up the television remote and threw it at Pantera. "Here. Entertain yourself while I'm gone. I'll be right back."

"I like…"

"Anything that has chocolate, chocolate and more chocolate. I know!"

"It's creepy, I tell you."

Meade smiled as she headed out the door, making sure to lock it behind her. She still wasn't really comfortable with where they lived and wasn't about to leave her friend alone in the apartment without all four locks bolted behind her.

The cupcake store was a block away. The only non-Chinese establishment within three blocks. But they did offer a fortune-cookie cupcake where they hid a paper fortune inside. Meade wondered if the paper got soggy.

She pushed open the door to the store and heard the bell jingle. It was crowded, as always. *They must make a fortune.* Meade momentarily debated if she should quit her job at the *New York Times* and open a dessert business instead.

She began to read the menu on the wall. She knew exactly what she would get for Pantera. The chocolate ganache cupcake. For herself, she decided on the red velvet.

"Excuse me," a male voice said. Meade realized she was blocking the door.

"Oh, I'm sorry," she said, moving so the man could get out of the store. She took her eyes off the menu and glanced at him. Instantly, she gasped. "Tanner."

The man looked up, startled.

"Uhm...hi," he said, clearly confused. "I'm sorry. Do I know you from somewhere?"

*Damn.* Now she was in a pickle. *Why didn't she keep her big mouth shut?*

"Oh. I guess this is weird. I'm Meade." She put out her hand to shake his. "I'm friends with Pantera."

*Please, please, please let him know Pantera in this world.*

A big smile crossed his face. *Phew.*

"Pantera. The best guitar student I have!" He leaned in closer to Meade, as if to tell her a big secret. "To be honest, she's the only guitar student I have."

Meade smiled.

"How did you know who I was?"

*How did she know who he was?*

"I guess I saw a picture of you somewhere. I don't know...maybe on her phone or Facebook. Anyway, I'm sorry. I didn't mean to startle you. I saw your face and knew your name and it kind of popped out."

"No problem. It's nice to meet you, Meade. Do you come here often?"

She was flooded with a sense of déjà vu. That was exactly what Tanner had said to her in Bryant Park. "That sounds like a pickup line." Meade laughed.

Tanner shrugged. "I guess I can't help myself. It's not every day a beautiful woman hits on me while I'm buying cupcakes."

"Oh, so now I'm hitting on you?"

"Weren't you?" Tanner winked at her.

"You got me. I couldn't resist," Meade said. She couldn't help but smile. It felt so good to see Tanner. Even without him knowing who she was, she was happy to be around him. She hadn't given him too much thought since she'd gotten here—she'd been so consumed by Daniel being alive and trying to navigate this new life—but seeing him now made her realize she'd missed him. If truth be told, quite a bit.

It made her feel guilty.

"Well, it was nice to meet you," Meade said, clearly bringing their interaction to a close. "I'll tell Pantera I saw you." She purposely didn't mention she was about to see their mutual friend, fearing he might ask to join the two of them.

Tanner took her cue. "Thanks. It was nice to meet you, too, Meade. I hope I run into you again."

Meade nodded and went back to looking at the menu, as if looking into Tanner's eyes didn't fluster her in the least bit.

*What is wrong with me? I have Daniel. Daniel. He's not dead. He's alive. And I love him.*

And Meade did love him. *Tremendously.*

So why was it that seeing Tanner had made her heart race?


"You look like you've just seen a ghost," Pantera said as Meade placed the cupcake box on the coffee table.

"I think I sort of did," Meade said, plopping down onto the couch. "I ran into Tanner at the cupcake store."

"Tanner?" Pantera said, opening the box. "Yum! This looks delish!"

"Tanner Dale."

Pantera stopped the cupcake halfway up to her mouth. "My guitar teacher?" Meade nodded. "How do you know Tanner Dale?"

"Well..." Meade said slowly. "In my other life, I'm sort of dating him."

"You're *what?*"

"Dating him. I'm dating him. That is, we've had a couple of dates. Two to be exact. And a lot of texts."

"How did this happen?"

Meade gave Pantera a knowing look.

Pantera gasped. "I set you up, didn't I? I am so awesome. I totally rock. What a fantastic match."

"I'm glad you're so proud of yourself."

Pantera took a bite of her cupcake, savoring every lick. "Wow. This is amazing."

Mead picked up her cupcake and took off the wrapper. "I know. They make the best cupcakes. I'm almost glad our oven doesn't work."

"So...let's get back to Tanner. How much do you like him?"

Meade took a bite of her cupcake and avoided making eye contact with Pantera.

"You like him a lot! Wow," Pantera said. "Wow."

"I, truly, have barely thought about him since I got here. I was caught up in the fact that I now had Daniel back. Nothing else—no one else—seemed to matter."

"And then you saw him today."

Meade nodded. "And then I saw him today."

"Can I ask you a question?"

"Shoot."

"Are you happy with Daniel? You've spent the past fifteen years dreaming about what a life with Daniel would've been like if he'd lived. And really, you've been given this amazing gift—to see how life would have turned out. What I'm saying is, how is it? This life? Is it like you thought it would be?"

Meade sighed. Not a tired sigh, but a deep, thoughtful sigh. "I would think that'd be an easy question to answer, but it's not." She was surprised she felt tears springing to her eyes.

"Oh, baby," Pantera said, handing Meade a tissue from the box on the table. "I didn't mean to upset you."

"No, it's not you. It's a lot of things. I guess I'm so overwhelmed.

Nothing is like I thought it would be. I still love Daniel. That's never changed. And he's still the kind, sweet man I remember, though a little grayer." Meade smiled. "But our life isn't what I thought it would be. I thought we'd be married with kids, living in the 'burbs." She nearly said she'd thought Daniel would desire her more, but stopped herself. That was too personal to discuss, even with Pantera. "I thought he'd have a successful medical career—not that he's not successful, but I guess I should say the career is not lucrative. Not if these bills are any indication of what he's making.

"And I never, in a million years, thought I wouldn't have the same career if Daniel and I were still together. I love my job. And I miss it. Tremendously. And I really hate my new one," Meade said, wiping the tears that were falling faster now. "It's not like things are all bad. You and I are still friends. Lori and I have reconnected. And look how great Nick is doing. It's…I guess I never imagined that changing one event in my life—in this case, Daniel not dying—would change every single thing in my life."

"It's funny how that works," Pantera said. "I wouldn't think so, either."

Meade wiped the tears from her eyes. "I need to stop crying. Daniel will be home soon. I wouldn't be able to explain to him why I'm upset."

Pantera stood up, and picked up the trash from the table. "I need to get going."

"I didn't mean you had to leave because he was coming home. And you don't need to clean up. I'll do that."

"No, I need to go. I told Cory I'd meet up with him in a bit."

Meade stood up and grabbed the empty glasses from the table. "I'm so happy you're happy."

"Am I dating anyone in your other life?"

"No one."

Pantera shrugged. "That's okay. Maybe I'll meet Cory there, too. Like you met Tanner here."

*Tanner.* There he was again. She'd almost pushed him to the back of her mind. "Maybe you will."

Meade heard Daniel's keys unlocking the bolts on the front door.

"Looks like I'll finally get to meet the infamous Daniel," Pantera said.

Daniel walked into the door, looking bleary eyed. He seemed surprised to see Pantera, though Meade had told him her friend would be coming over tonight.

"Hey, sweetie," Meade said, going over and giving Daniel a kiss. "I want you to meet Pantera. Pantera, this is Daniel."

Daniel eyed Pantera's attire curiously, though, truth be told, it was rather toned down this evening. She was in black leggings, a plaid shirt and a black T-shirt with a skull and cross bones on the front. Her shoes were high-tops. She'd left the combat boots at home.

The two of them shook hands. "Nice to meet you," Daniel said.

"Me, too. I've heard a lot about you," Pantera said. "Okay, I'm outta here. Thanks for the fun time." She gave Meade a hug.

"I'll text you tomorrow."

"You got it. Bye!"

When Meade had locked the door behind Pantera, she turned back to Daniel. He was holding the ring box. Meade momentarily hoped she hadn't ruined some sort of surprise.

"Hey, you found your ring."

"Oh, yeah," Meade said casually. "It was in the bill box."

"You said you put it somewhere safe. I guess there's nowhere safer. No thief would want anything in there," Daniel said with a wry grin, placing the box back on the table.

"Speaking of which, I was looking over how much we owe. Wow. It's mind-boggling."

Daniel went into the kitchen and opened the fridge, grabbing himself a beer. "Yep."

"And, I see I still owe some money for Wake Forest. But, I don't see any bills from grad school. Did we pay that off?"

Daniel gave Meade a curious look. "My medical school loans are all in there—or, at least, they should be."

"No, I mean grad school for me."

"Grad school for you?" Daniel plopped down in the armchair and grabbed the TV remote.

"Yes. To NYU."

"You want to go to NYU?"

*Want to go to NYU?*

"How would we ever afford that with all we owe? We'd never even be able to get a loan for you. It was your idea to begin working right after college to help me pay for medical school. Are you regretting that now?"

Suddenly, it all made sense to Meade. Why she wasn't a book editor. Why she was working in a job she hated. She hadn't gone to grad school. She'd started work right after college, to help support Daniel in his dream. She'd wanted nothing more than a life with Daniel and so, of course, she'd been willing to give up some of her own dreams if it meant achieving that.

But look where that choice had gotten them.

"Oh, right. I know. I guess it's wishful thinking."

"You gonna put your ring back on?" Daniel asked her, glancing at the box on the table.

Meade smiled as she picked up the box. "Want to put it on my finger?"

"Like I'm proposing?"

Meade nodded, smiling.

"Nah," Daniel said, changing the channel on the TV, his attention already diverted. "I did that once. Wouldn't want to tarnish the memory."

Meade's shoulders fell as she slipped the diamond onto her own left ring finger. There would be no memory to tarnish. She had no memory of Daniel proposing to begin with—and that made her sad. She realized she'd never know what it felt like to have Daniel ask her those four magical words. In her old world, he was gone, and in her new world, she'd shown up too late. And he clearly had no interest in re-creating the scene.

"I'm going to bed," Meade said, standing up. "Want to join me?"

"I'll be there in a bit."

"Okay," Meade said, hesitating. Her first instinct was to go kiss Daniel goodnight, but then she changed her mind. She wasn't sure he'd even notice if she didn't. So, instead, she quietly made her way into the bedroom.

As she got in bed a short time later, and began to drift off to sleep, her thoughts weren't of an engagement to Daniel, as she imagined they'd be, but rather of Tanner. In her dreams, he was the one proposing.

And, to Meade's surprise, she was saying yes.

# CHAPTER TWENTY-FIVE

"So, you really don't want to come with me?" Meade asked Daniel, as she packed the last of her toiletries into her suitcase.

"And go back to that soap opera?" Daniel asked, as he shaved in their tiny bathroom. "No, thank you."

Meade had realized Daniel wasn't joining her on her trip back to Texas, one day at work, when she searched through her email inbox for her ticket confirmation and only found one ticket—for her. She hadn't been exactly certain why she was returning to Austin, especially in August, when it was so unbearably hot. But Lori had told her she always made a short trip back home to see her family, at this time of year. Thank heavens for Lori. Her friendship with her old friend—and all the information she could provide—had made living in this world so much less embarrassing.

"But you'll be missing out on all the fun!" Meade teased.

"That is fun I can do without," Daniel said, wiping the remaining shaving cream off his face with a towel and throwing it on the floor.

*Did he think the maid magically appeared and picked that up later in the day?*

"Okay, then. Give me a kiss and I'll be on my way."

Daniel bent down and pecked her on the lips. It wasn't the kind of kiss she'd been desiring, but unfortunately, the one she'd been expecting.

Meade was disappointed Daniel wouldn't be flying back to Austin with her. It would've been so much fun to go down memory lane with him—visit all the old haunts, so to speak. Get a big sub to split at Merchants of Venice, swim in Barton Springs, walk around downtown. Maybe rekindle some of the magic it seemed they'd lost over the years. But Daniel had told her he couldn't take the time off work and Meade could hardly argue with him. She'd seen their bills and they needed the money.

"Bye, babe. Try not to stress out too much while you're there."

"Gee. Thanks. That's encouraging."

Daniel winked at her and walked out the door. A moment later, she heard the front door open and then close again, and the sound of the bolts being locked.

Meade took a deep breath. It was now or never. She was heading back to Texas. And, though she was dreading it in a way—the way she always did—she was also curious. Life in New York was so different than it was in her old world. Would life in Austin be the same? Worse? Better? Things with Nick were already incredibly improved and Meade was enjoying rebuilding their relationship. Maybe things with everyone else in her family had transformed, too—for the better.

Meade could only hope.


As Meade walked through the Austin airport, she couldn't help but feel like she'd just done this. Of course, last time, it was in her old life. And she'd been returning to present a recent high school graduate with the Daniel Spencer Memorial Scholarship. This time, she wasn't sure what she was doing here. Clearly, there would be no awards program. If Daniel hadn't died, there was no scholarship in his name. Meade felt a twinge of sadness over that fact. The program had helped so many kids who, otherwise, wouldn't have been able to afford to go to school. Or else, they'd still go but be saddled with debt—as she and Daniel now were.

Meade walked outside the sliding doors and into the hot Texas sun. *Holy crap, was it hot!*

Meade guessed it was easily over one hundred and ten degrees—in the shade.

Last time she'd arrived, Benji had been waiting for her. This time, though, Meade saw no one she recognized. Her mom had sent her an email last night—the first one she'd received from her mom in this world—to say "someone" would be there to get her. Meade loved the vagueness of the note—as if they were drawing straws to see who got the short one and would be stuck coming to the airport to pick her up.

After ten minutes had passed, Meade sat down on one of the small ledges outside the arrivals' terminal. Waiting like this, especially in the heat, was bringing back memories—and none of them good.

If her driver was tardy, it meant only one thing. Her mom was picking her up.

Forty-five minutes later, Meade saw her mom drive up in an old Toyota Corolla. She was momentarily surprised by how run-down the vehicle was. She didn't think Jimmy would let her mom drive something so dilapidated. He was usually so particular about making sure she had a relatively new, safe car.

Her mom made a quick stop in front of Meade and jumped out. "My baby's home! My baby's home!" her mom said, rushing around the car and grabbing Meade into a huge hug. Meade looked around at the passing travelers, embarrassed.

"It is so good to see you. Let me look at you," her mom said, holding Meade at arm's length.

For the first time, Meade got a good look at her mother and was taken aback. After all, she'd seen the woman about two months ago, so her appearance was fresh in Meade's mind. But this mom looked very different from the one in her other life.

For one thing, she was thinner. But, not the healthy thin that comes from working out and eating well. She was gaunt, as if she was under too much stress and not getting enough nutrients. And her hair was long and scraggily. Meade hadn't seen it look like that since she was a kid. Nowadays, she kept it in a cute, short bob—the way Jimmy liked it. *And, her eyes.* They looked old and tired and bloodshot.

"Are you feeling okay, Mom?" Meade asked, suddenly concerned.

"I'm fit as a fiddle." She certainly wasn't acting ill. "Let's throw your suitcase in the trunk and head home. I'll bet you're hungry. I can probably find something in the fridge to feed you."

*Guess there was to be no Mexican feast on this visit.*

Meade shoved aside the empty fast-food wrappers and coffee cups on the passenger seat and got into the car. Meade didn't need to try to come up with topics of conversation with her mom. The woman rattled on and on the entire drive, peppering Meade with questions about Daniel and her job and his job and Lori and Nick. Apparently, her brother didn't make it home all that often, either.

Meade was so busy answering her mom's questions, she didn't even notice when they pulled into the driveway of a small house in East Austin.

*Where are we?* Did her mom need to pick up something from a friend? She hadn't mentioned that.

"Home sweet home!" her mom said, putting the car in park.

*Home? Whose home?*

"Let's go on in and get out of this heat," her mom said. "We can get your bag later."

Meade sat for a moment and stared at the house and the front lawn. It was overgrown and the stones on the front path to the porch were broken. The door was in terrible need of a good painting and the big bay window was missing a screen. Meade found it hard to believe Jimmy—meticulous Jimmy—would let their house get like this. She wondered if perhaps he was ill—or maybe, had somehow lost his pension.

Meade finally got out of the car and followed her mom down the uneven path to the house. She hesitantly placed her weight on the porch steps, unsure they would hold her. Her mom unlocked the front door—Meade noticed there were as many bolts on her mom's door as there were on Meade's own apartment door—and the two women went inside.

Instantly, Meade was brought back to her childhood. This home was nearly identical to every rental house and apartment she'd lived in with her mom and brothers as a kid. The furniture was worn—clearly purchased secondhand. The curtains were bohemian sheets her mom had tacked up with nails instead of curtain rods. The walls were bare. There were no family photos or decorative paintings. There was one couch and no other chairs. The coffee table was made of old wooden pallets.

*You have got to be kidding.*

"I have some hummus and pita bread. And I think there's a frozen pizza deep in here," Meade's mom called out from the kitchen. "Oh! And I found some leftover refried beans from my dinner the other night. Maybe you can put them on a tortilla?"

Meade walked into the kitchen as her mom closed the door to the fridge.

"I hope you don't mind fending for yourself tonight. I have a date."

*A date?*

And then it clicked. Meade could have slapped herself for being so dumb. Of course her mom had a date. This was her old mom. Not the mom of her other world, but the pre-Jimmy mom. Her mom had a date because she wasn't married to Jimmy. And, she wasn't married to Jimmy because Daniel had lived and there was no longer a scholarship in his name for Jimmy's daughter to win. She'd never even met Jimmy.

Meade thought she might throw up.

There was no Jimmy in their world. And that meant, there was no

Katie, either. In a matter of seconds, Meade had lost her stepdad and sister. They wouldn't even know who she was if she ran into them on the street. Two of the best members of her family and they weren't even in her family.

"I wouldn't normally go on a date while you were home," her mom continued, oblivious to the revelation going on in Meade's mind or the faint look on her daughter's face. "But, I've been hoping this guy would ask me out for months now. He's in my tantric sex class."

*Tantric sex?* Meade didn't even want to know.

"And, when he finally asked me out, I couldn't say that it wasn't a good night. I mean, what if he never asked again, right?" her mom asked, clearly looking for her daughter's approval.

"Oh sure, Mom. Go. I'll be fine."

"I knew you'd say that. Besides, Benji said he'd try to stop over when he gets off work."

"Off work? He's working around here now?"

"Well, of course he is," her mom said, looking at Meade with an odd expression. "What other town would he be working around?"

Meade shrugged. There was no point in trying to explain her question.

"Okay, then. I'm going to go get ready. You make yourself at home!" Meade's mom gave her another big hug and then headed into what Meade imagined was her bedroom to get ready.

Meade looked around the small house. She hoped Benji showed up soon. She didn't know how she was going to survive this trip without him. She was already sorry she'd come.

Benji arrived around eight o'clock. Meade had hoped he'd come earlier, but her mom was gone for two full hours before he walked through the front door. She'd tried texting him, but had gotten no response.

"Hey, sis," he said when he walked in the door. "Long time no see."

Meade was startled by his appearance, but then again, what didn't startle her these days? He was still as handsome as always—just as tall and attractive. No doubt the women loved him in this world, too. But, he was covered in grease. His pants, shirt and fingers looked like he'd used it to wash with instead of soap.

"Why are you so dirty?" Meade asked. He'd made no attempt to hug her when he walked in the door, which surprised her, but considering the way he looked, it was just as well. She wasn't sure she would ever be able to get that stuff off her clothes.

"I just got off work."

"Where do you work? The dump?" Meade asked, teasing him. The best thing about her relationship with Benji was she never needed to walk on eggshells with him, like she did with her other family members. The two of them were always in sync and never took offense to each other's wisecracks.

That was why Benji's reaction was so puzzling to Meade.

"We can't all have hot-shot jobs like you," he spat at her. "I work at Anton's."

Meade was taken aback by Benji's tone. Never, in their entire relationship as brother and sister, had she heard him speak harshly to her. His response sounded so much more like Nick—at least, the old Nick— than the Benji she knew and loved.

"Anton's Garage?" Meade asked.

"No, Anton's Bank. Of course the garage."

"Oh." Meade didn't know what to say. She was scared to ask too many questions for fear of irritating him anymore, but she didn't know how he'd gone from medical school resident to mechanic. "What about school?"

"I still go," Benji said, taking a seat on the ground, across the room from Meade and leaning against the wall. "Take a course or two every semester at ACC."

*ACC? The community college?*

"Of course," Benji continued. "At the rate I'm going, it'll take fourteen years to get my Associates."

*Associates?*

Meade had been surprised a lot over the last couple of months. Daniel being alive had nearly blown her mind. But, the difference in Benji—his attitude, his career, his lack of a degree—they were coming a close second in shock value.

And where was their bond? The unbreakable bond they'd always shared—like it was the two of them against the world? Even in the brief time she'd had with him so far this evening, it was obvious that connection was missing.

*Where had it gone?*

"Want to go out to dinner?" Meade asked hopefully. "I'm starving. Mom has crap in the fridge."

"Mom always has crap in the fridge. Some things never change, huh?"

Meade nodded but inwardly wondered what those things would be. It seemed everything changed these days.

"Where to? My treat."

Benji shrugged. "Up to you. You're the visitor."

Meade sensed a hint of bitterness in Benji's tone, but chose to ignore it. Maybe he'd had a bad day at work and was taking it out on her.

"How about the Oasis?"

"The Oasis? That's far."

"I know."

"Can't we go to a food truck on South Congress?"

"I'd like to see the lake."

"It's dry."

"I'd like to see where we used to have a lake."

Benji rolled his eyes. "Whatever."

"Do you want to shower before we go?"

"No."

"Want to do it anyway?"

Benji glared at her, but he got up off the ground. "I keep some clothes at Mom's. I'll be ready in fifteen minutes."

"Thanks," Meade said. Benji grunted and left the room.

Her brother was true to his word. Fifteen minutes later, on the dot, he was dressed in clean clothes and standing in front of her. His hair was wet and his fingers were still covered in grease—Meade guessed they were now a permanent part of his look—but he looked much more like her little brother and not the grease monkey who'd walked into the house a half hour earlier.

If she could only do something about the uncharacteristic scowl on his face.

"Let's go," he said, without a smile.

Meade hopped off the couch and grabbed her purse. Benji locked up the house and they headed to his car. A big, old, beat-up Chevy pickup. Not the small car he'd been driving last time they were together— the one they'd joked and laughed about.

Meade climbed into the passenger seat and they headed across town. Neither of them spoke. It seemed so odd to sit in silence with Benji. Meade couldn't remember the last time the two of them had been quiet in each other's presence. Usually, they had so much to say they tended to talk over each other. But, not tonight. Benji didn't say a word to Meade and she was scared to say anything to him—out of fear that the wrong words coming out of her mouth, would further contribute to his sullenness.

Benji cut across downtown, turning onto Eleventh Street. Meade leaned against the headrest and was about to close her eyes, when they drove past the Capitol building. She sat up, a bolt of electricity running through her body.

*The Capitol.* A memory flashed through Meade's mind. What was it? Something about the Capitol. The inside of the building. The six seals on the floor of the rotunda. A tour?

Just as quickly as the memory came, it vanished. Meade tried to pull it back, but there was nothing there. She turned in her seat, as Benji turned down Congress Avenue, craning her neck for a better view of the building.

What was that memory? She hadn't been on a tour of the Capitol since she and Daniel were kids. *But...*

Meade suddenly had a sick feeling in the pit of her stomach and she wasn't sure why.

"What are you doing?"

Meade turned back around at the sound of Benji's voice. He sounded irritated. "Looking at the Capitol. It's so beautiful, lit up at night."

"Yeah, I guess." That was the last of their conversation until they arrived at the Oasis. And for once, Meade was happy for the silence between them.


"Is this the Oasis?" Meade said, startled, as they pulled into the parking garage.

"The one and only."

"It's huge! When did it get like this?"

"They rebuilt it after the fire a few years ago."

"Looks like they did more than rebuild the restaurant," Meade said. When Meade was growing up in Austin, The Oasis had been a much smaller, yet still beautiful, restaurant on Lake Travis. Known for its seating on its multilayered outdoor decks, every table had a breathtaking view of the lake.

That is, when there was a lake. Texas was in a drought, and had been for years. Every year, the lake's levels had dropped and, though not completely dry, there were islands of land in the center of the lake where only water had been visible before.

A few years ago, the Oasis caught on fire, burning much of the restaurant and wooden decks. Meade had heard it'd been rebuilt, but never imagined they'd not only re-created the restaurant, but what seemed like a whole little village, complete with parking garage, shops and an additional restaurant. It was certainly no hole-in-the wall establishment. It seemed this was now a tourist destination all to itself.

They made their way inside and were seated outside on one of the higher decks. Benji ordered a margarita and Meade did the same. She had a feeling it would be essential to get through tonight.

Benji sat across from her, as sullen as when they'd left the house. Meade was going to need to turn this ship around if she was going to have any fun tonight. "So, tell me about you. I want to hear all about your life. Your job. Your friends. Have you seen anybody from high school?" Meade also wondered if he preferred to go by "Ben" in this world, but since he hadn't yet corrected her, she assumed he didn't.

"I see everybody from high school. Most everyone still lives in town."

This was news to Meade. The old Benji had broken ties with nearly all of his high school buddies the minute he left for college and rarely saw any of them, especially the ones who didn't leave home to make a name for themselves in their careers. His life revolved around his college friends and medical school buddies—and work. Benji was always working.

"What about a girlfriend?" Meade said, winking, as the waitress brought their drinks. "Any special lady?"

"Is this Twenty Questions?" Benji asked. "Why are you so nosey?"

Meade did her best not to take offense to the question. She had to remember this was not the same little brother she knew. Something was different about him. He'd changed. And she wasn't sure why, but she was going to do her best to change him back—or, at least change back their relationship.

"I'm not nosey. I'm curious. I'm interested in your life."

"Since when?"

*Since when?*

"I...what do you mean?" Meade had always been interested in Benji's life. In fact, she was more than interested. She was *invested*. His successes were her successes. His failures hurt her as much as they hurt him.

"Since when do you care what I do? Since when do you care about anything but yourself and Daniel?"

Meade felt like she'd been punched in the gut. "That's not true."

Benji took a big gulp of his margarita.

"Of course it's true. I'm not insulting you. You are who you are. And you, Meade, care about you and you care about Daniel. And I guess those two things are all-consuming. There has never been time in your life for you to care about anyone else. Not Mom. Not Nick. Certainly not me."

What was he talking about? This was craziness. She had a lifetime of memories of the things she'd done with Benji—the memories they'd shared. Trips the two of them had taken. Papers she'd helped him write. College applications she'd stayed up until three in the morning typing for him. After Daniel died...

Meade gasped.

*After Daniel died...*

But, Daniel hadn't died. Once again, Meade couldn't believe how those three words had changed everything all over again. Daniel didn't die, so she'd had no need to throw herself into Benji and his life. She thought back to her dreams for her and Daniel when he was ill—all the things she thought the two of them would do together if he got better. Events they'd attend, movies they'd see, places where she wanted to travel...and none of those dreams included Benji.

Meade looked at the surly man sitting across the table from her and suddenly saw the scared, awkward, eager-for-attention little boy her brother had been. He was right. As sure as she was that nothing was certain in this world, she knew she hadn't had time for him. She'd spent all of her time with Daniel when he'd gotten better—invested her life in her boyfriend and their future together—and, in the process, her little brother had gotten left behind. There'd been no one to fully participate in Benji's life—certainly not their mother. No one to guide him, help him succeed, listen to him, spend time with him. Benji had been on his own. And his life and attitude were a reflection of that.

Meade looked her brother squarely in the eyes. She wanted to make sure he understood she meant what she was about to say. She was sincere.

"Benji, I'm sorry. I owe you an apology. You're right. I wasn't there for you. I wasn't there for anyone but myself and Daniel. And you suffered because of that. I can't tell you how sorry I am for that."

Meade could see the surprise register in Benji's eyes. He hadn't been expecting an apology from Meade. He certainly hadn't been expecting her to show how much she cared. For a split-second, Meade saw the sparkle in his eyes that used to be characteristic of him in his younger days. Hoping to grab that glimmer and keep it there, she quickly went on.

"I can't go back and re-do the past, but I'd like us to start again. I want to have a relationship with you. Not just a casual, 'How you doin'?' relationship, but a deep friendship. If you're willing to forgive me and move on, I'd like to get to know you better. I want to be an integral part of your life."

For a moment, Benji didn't move. He gave no indication of what he was thinking. For all Meade knew, he was about to tell her to go to hell. That it was too late. That there was nothing left of their relationship to salvage.

He took a deep breath and, to Meade's relief, said the words she wanted to hear.

"I'd like that."

Meade smiled and, after a moment, Benji smiled back at her.

"I don't know about you," she said, "but I think we're going to need another round of margaritas. We have a lot of catching up to do!"

Benji laughed—the laugh Meade had missed—and raised his hand to get the waiter's attention.

"So now...back to my question about any women in your life..."

Meade smile at her brother and winked and, to her pleasure, he smiled back.

# CHAPTER TWENTY-SIX

"How was Austin?"

Meade tilted her head against her neck to hold the phone in place and began to sort through the papers on her desk. Was it her imagination or had an unusual amount of people died in the time she was away?

"Exhausting. Horrible. Enlightening. Depressing."

"That's all? That doesn't sound too overwhelming," Lori said. "Did you stop by and see my parents while you were there?"

"No! I wish I had. I would've loved to have seen them, but I was too busy spending time with Benji."

In truth, Meade had especially wanted to see Daniel's mom, too, while she was in Texas, but when she got there and realized the shambles her relationship with Benji was in, she'd decided it was best to spend every moment she had of the three days at home with him.

The two of them had gone for long walks around Town Lake—*Lady Bird* Lake, Benji had kept reminding Meade. When the former first lady had passed away, the portion of the Colorado River which ran through downtown Austin had been renamed in her honor. Meade had peppered Benji with so many questions about his life and his dreams that he asked her, on more than one occasion, if he was being interviewed for a book.

"Or maybe you're pre-writing my obituary?" he'd joked.

"Ha. Ha. Very funny," Meade had said, slugging him playfully on the arm.

"You know," Benji had said one morning, as the two of them sat outside a food trailer, eating their breakfast tacos. "You're really different."

"Really?" she'd said, wiping the salsa off her mouth. "How so?"

Benji shrugged. "I don't know. It's hard to describe. More engaged. Not so self-absorbed."

Meade's mouth had dropped open. "Self-absorbed?"

Benji laughed. "I mean that in the best possible way."

"Oh, yeah. It sure sounds like it."

"No. Seriously. You've never been a mean person. You...I don't know... didn't seem to have an interest in anything or anyone that didn't involve you directly." Benji put his head down and began to play with the aluminum foil his taco had been wrapped in moments earlier.

"And that involved you?"

He'd nodded. "I know it seems silly. I'm a grown man now and all. I shouldn't need anybody, but..."

"But it's nice to have a big sister you can depend on?"

Benji had glanced up at Meade and the two of them locked eyes. "It's great."

Meade picked up one of the large piles of papers on her desk and dropped it to the floor. She was running out of room to work in her small cubicle.

"And what about your mom? How was she?" Lori asked

"Well, you could have told me she wasn't married before I got there."

"Married?" The shock was apparent in Lori's voice. "Why would she be married?"

"Because she is in my other life."

She could hear Lori's gasp. "You are *kidding!*"

"Not."

Lori laughed. "You need to tell me all about it. Want to meet for lunch?"

Meade looked at the work in front of her. There was no way she'd be able take a lunch break. "Can't. I'm going to see Pantera around dinnertime. Want to join us?"

"I wish. I have to see clients tonight. We'll figure something out later. I'm dying to hear about your mom and her husband."

Meade looked up to see Marshall standing in the entrance to her cubicle.

"Thanks, Mr. Livingston. I'll check my email to see if the death notice has arrived yet."

Lori laughed. "Talk to you later."

"It should be in tomorrow's edition," Meade said. "Thanks for calling." She hung up the phone.

'Hey, Marshall," Meade said. "What's up?"

"Have a good trip?"

She shrugged. "Family."

Marshall smiled. "You don't need to say another word. No one can stress you out like your own family. I see my parents once a year—at Christmas—when I go home to Cleveland. I immediately start drinking the eggnog so I can survive. It makes you wonder how we ever endured our childhoods."

"Amen to that."

"Listen, I heard a rumor that Randy Johnson might not make it through the night."

"The basketball player? What happened to him?"

"Geez. Do you not have the news in Texas? He was in a serious car accident two nights ago. Head-on collision. He's apparently on life support."

"Oh." Meade wasn't a particularly big sports fan, but she knew who Randy Johnson was. Everyone in New York did. He was one of the stars of the Knicks. "That's sad."

"Yep. And, because he's so young, we don't have anything written on him. Could you get moving on that, so we're ready?"

Meade scanned all the work she already had on her desk and did a mental calculation. She'd be lucky if she got out of here at all tonight. "Sure."

"Great. Thanks, Meade." Marshall tapped the wall of her cubicle twice and headed toward his office.

Meade picked up her cell phone and quickly sent Pantera a message. *GONNA BE LATE TONIGHT. KEEP THAT COFFEE BREWING.*

Meade rocked back in her chair and stretched her arms toward the ceiling. She wondered if she knew a good chiropractor. Her back was killing her. She hadn't once gotten up in the past four hours, not even to pee. Who knew so much work went into the obituary section of the newspaper?

She glanced at the clock. Daniel would be getting ready to leave for work at the hospital soon. He was working the evening shift. She picked up her phone and dialed his cell number.

"Joey's Pizza," he answered.

"I'd like to order a large pepperoni with extra cheese. Can you deliver it to my office?"

"Sure," he said. "I'll get right on that. You might have to wait until tomorrow, though. We're very busy here."

"Tomorrow? What kind of business are you running?"

"Not a very successful one." Daniel laughed. "How's work?"

"Awful. How are you?"

"Good." He sounded distracted. "Do you know where my keys are?"

*Again?* How could he lose them every single day?

"Did you check the pants you had on yesterday?"

Meade heard a jingle.

"Oh, here they are."

"So, what's new?"

"Since you left this morning? Nothing."

Meade sighed. This was how most of their conversations went these days. The two of them seemed to have very little to say to one another. Meade could still remember how'd they been as teenagers, spending hours on the phone with each other, long after they should've both been sleeping. Meade would hide under her covers and hope her mom wouldn't hear her as she'd whisper into the receiver. She and Daniel would talk until neither of them could keep their eyes open, and, on more than one occasion, they'd both fallen asleep with the phone line still connected.

Meade wondered where all those words had gone? Had they used them up over the past twenty years? Were they now like an old married couple? Minus the being married part, of course.

"Okay, then. Have a good day at work."

"You, too. See you tomorrow."

"Yep. See you." Meade heard him hang up the phone. "Love you, too," she said into the silent receiver.

"Where's my coffee?" Meade said, as she walked into the café and Pantera rushed up to give her a big hug. "I'm about to fall over!"

"I think you need an espresso!" Pantera said, grabbing Meade's hand and pulling her over to the counter. "Long day?"

Meade glanced at her watch. It was nearly nine o'clock. She'd gotten to work at six this morning, with the hope of catching up on things before most people arrived. It had been a long and exhausting day. "I thought I'd be there until past midnight. If the new intern hadn't helped me finish up on the Randy Johnson stuff, I would've never gotten out of there."

"Oh, yeah," Pantera said, pouring Meade's drink. "I heard about him. So terrible."

Meade nodded and took the steaming small cup Pantera handed her. Taking a sip, she looked closely at Pantera. "Nice hair."

Pantera smiled and pushed her bangs out of her eyes. "You like?"

*Like? Hmm.* That was an interesting question.

"It's you."

And Meade wasn't lying. The bangs, which were now cut even shorter than usual, were bright teal in color while the rest of Pantera's hair was still jet-black. Meade didn't know anyone else who could get away with that look—or want to—and not look completely ridiculous.

"Why don't you take your drink to the back table? I'm not off work yet." Pantera nodded to the back of the café.

Meade looked in that direction and let out a little gasp. She turned back to her friend. "What did you do?"

Pantera shrugged. "I don't know what you're talking about." She picked up a tray of drinks and sandwiches. "I need to get back to work. Have fun."

Meade took a deep breath. She momentarily debated walking out the door and not toward the back of the café, but as she was about to make her move, the man at the back table looked up and spotted her. A wide smile crossed his face and he waved.

*Damn you, Pantera.*

Meade waved back and headed over to him. She was surprised to find her heart begin to pick up speed as she got closer. He stood as she reached the table.

"Hi, Tanner."

"Hi. It's nice to see you again. Pantera said you were going to be stopping by tonight."

*Oh, she did, did she?*

"What are you doing here?" Meade glanced down at the table. He had a host of papers spread out in front of him.

"Work. It's much nicer to work here than in my stuffy office."

"You're a lawyer, right?"

He nodded. Meade figured he assumed Pantera had told her that.

"Would you like to join me?"

Meade glanced back to the counter. Pantera was busy waiting on customers. Tanner must know she'd been planning to hang out with Pantera tonight and so leaving would seem to be directed toward him and rude. And, truth be told, Meade had a strong desire to sit down across from Tanner—to relax, to laugh with him, to engage in their familiar banter. Despite her best efforts to push him from her mind, he'd been creeping into her thoughts much more than she wanted to admit.

"Sure. That sounds great." Meade sat down as Tanner pushed aside some of the papers, stacking them neatly off to the side. He sat down across from her.

"Are you going to eat anything or inhale a whole lot of caffeine?"

"Only the caffeine for now."

"It's gonna keep you up all night."

"I doubt it. I had a rough day at work. This will barely keep me awake for the next hour."

"Okay, then I'll need to be extra witty to keep your attention. A challenge. I like that."

Tanner smiled at Meade. She couldn't help but relax as she stared at him.

"So, what are you working on?" she said, eyeing the mound of papers.

"Nothing that would interest you. Or me, for that matter. Let's skip the small talk and take ten steps forward?"

"Ten steps forward?" Meade acted as if she didn't know what he was getting at, but she did. She couldn't help but remember how, on their first date, he'd wanted to delve in deeper. There was no chitchat. They immediately began the business of getting to know each other.

"Yes. Let's talk about more important things."

"Like my most embarrassing moment in life or my worst habit?"

Tanner's face lit up. "Exactly!"

"Can I ask you a question?"

"Shoot."

"Do you do this with all women?"

"I don't think I understand the question. Do I do what with all women?"

"Do you tell them that you want to skip the pleasantries and leap straight into more profound topics?"

Tanner took a sip of his coffee. "Actually. No. I've never said that to anyone else before."

Meade smiled inwardly. She was hoping he'd say that.

"So, you don't want to make just small talk with me?"

Tanner paused and looked carefully at Meade, as if he was examining her face. She saw him chew the inside of his cheek right before he took another sip of coffee.

"I have a confession to make," he finally said.

"You do?"

"Yes. And I hesitate to make it, because I'm going to sound crazy. And, frankly, I'm not crazy."

"You're sure about that?" Meade said with a smile.

"Fairly certain."

"Okay, then. Let's hear it. And I'll do my best to not have you committed once it's out."

Tanner took a deep breath. "I know we don't know each other. We just met a few days ago in the cupcake store. But..." He took yet another sip of his coffee. "This is where the crazy part comes in. I feel like I know you."

*Because you do...*

"Not like, I know you because we've met somewhere before. I'm pretty sure we haven't. And not because Pantera has told me a lot about you, because before the other day, she'd never even mentioned you. What I'm trying to say is...I feel like I *know* you."

"You know me." It wasn't so much a question as a statement—but sounded mostly as if Meade was merely repeating his words.

"I'm going to sound like a hopeless romantic, which I'm not. Until last week, I thought I was a realist. But...do you believe you can look at someone across a room, look into their eyes and see their soul?"

Meade felt as if she couldn't breathe. She felt as if his words should make her nervous. After all, she barely knew Tanner. What kind of man tells a woman, the second time he meets her, that he knows her soul. He sounded like a lunatic.

Except, he didn't. Meade had a series of memories with the so-called stranger who sat across from her. Not memories that existed in his mind. This Tanner had never walked around New York City with her and sat on the steps of the New York library or texted her 200 times a day or eaten dinner with her on her roof deck. But Meade remembered doing all of those things with him. And so, nothing he said sounded ridiculous. He was right. He did know her. And she knew him, too.

"No. I have no idea what you're talking about," she said, instead of saying what was on her mind. The look Tanner gave her was one of such hopelessness, she couldn't help but giggle. "I'm messing with you."

He closed his eyes briefly and shook his head, a small smile on his lips. "I know. It sounds insane. I'm embarrassed to say it. But, this whole time, I've been sitting here, trying to concentrate on the trial I have next week, and all I could think about was that Pantera said you'd soon be stopping by. I was going to ask you what is the scariest thing you've ever done."

"The scariest thing?"

"That was my opening line. Not most embarrassing moment or worst habit. Scariest thing."

"I walked on a tightrope once."

Tanner's head popped up in surprise. "Like, in the circus?"

Meade nodded. "My mom is into all this weird stuff. It's kind of hard to explain. Anyway, when I was about twelve, she decided we should all join the circus. I'm not sure, but I think she was having an affair with one of the clowns."

Tanner chuckled and Meade giggled, too.

"Anyway, we didn't really have any talents to get into the circus, and none of us wanted to travel the country picking up elephant dung, so my mom enrolled us in some class on how to walk a tightrope. She thought if we had some raw talent, we could learn so they'd let us join."

Tanner gaped at Meade.

"I know. It sounded ridiculous to me, too. But she was my mom. What was I supposed to do? We all went along with it.'

"How'd it go? Were you a natural?"

Meade snorted out a laugh. "It was, like I said, the scariest thing I've ever done. I had to climb up this teeny tiny ladder, three or more stories in the air, with no safety harness on. They hooked me in when I got to the top and handed me a long, skinny pole that I was supposed to use to balance. The platform was miniscule.

"There was a guy standing on the ground telling me to step off onto the wire. And I couldn't move. That wire looked like a piece of dental floss and though there was a net below, I was frozen. I couldn't do it."

Meade wiped her hands on her pants. "See? Even talking about it makes my palms sweat. It was that scary."

"Sounds like it! Did you ever do it?"

"I had no choice. Going down that tiny ladder seemed like an equally awful option. I took one step out, very slowly."

"And, could you walk on the tightrope?"

Meade laughed. "No! I fell! I took one step and I fell! And I got whacked with the pole on the way down—needed six stitches." Meade pointed to a small scar above her left eyebrow.

"Did your mom feel guilty?"

"Ha! No! She told me I couldn't balance because my feet were too big for my body."

"She did not!"

"She did." Meade took a sip of her coffee. "Okay, I've spilled my guts. Your turn. Scariest thing you've ever done."

Tanner folded his hands in front of him on the table, and regarded Meade very seriously.

"Telling you what I told you tonight. That was the scariest thing I've ever done."

"No, it wasn't."

Tanner nodded. "It was. I'm not like that. I'm not a person who leads with his feelings. I'm very rational."

"Tanner," Meade sighed. "I'm flattered by all you've said. And I'd be lying if I said that I don't feel a connection to you, too. But...I'm engaged." Meade turned her hand over on the table, revealing her ring.

Tanner looked down at it and then back up again at her. "I know. Pantera told me."

"And so you can see why I can't..." Meade's voice trailed off. What was she supposed to say?

*Why I can't go out with you? Why I can't tell you that I know your soul, too?*

"I know," Tanner said, interrupting her. "I didn't expect you to take off your ring and announce to C U Latte that I was your soul mate."

Meade chuckled, though her stomach was in knots.

"But..." Tanner continued. "I will tell you this and then I'll never bring it up again. I hate Sunday nights. Hate them. There's something about knowing that Monday morning is coming—the work week, the stress, all that. I find Sunday nights so depressing. So, for years, I've made a habit of going to Bryant Park to relax on Sunday evenings. I bring a book. I watch the kids on the carousel. I buy myself a drink and sit at one of the tables. I do my best to enjoy the beauty that is New York and try to forget that Monday is coming."

"That sounds nice."

"I'm telling you this for one reason. I am always in Bryant Park on Sunday evenings. Rain or shine, I'm there. If you ever want to find me—even to talk—I'm there."

Meade nodded.

"And, if you want to show up one week and tell me your engagement is off, that would be even better." Tanner smiled broadly at Meade and winked. She couldn't help but chuckle.

"Thanks. I'll keep that in mind."

Tanner reached for his briefcase, which was on the floor next to him. Opening it, he piled all of his papers inside. "It was good to see you again, Meade. I enjoyed our time together."

"Me, too," she said softly.

He stood up from the table. "I hope that fiancé of yours knows how lucky he is."

Meade nodded, but inwardly wondered if Daniel actually did.

"Bye, Tanner."

"Bye."

Meade watched as Tanner made his way through the crowded café and out the door, onto the streets of New York. She resisted the urge to follow him and instead, twisted the engagement ring on her ring finger.

She was building a life with Daniel—the boy she'd loved since she was in grade school. She was living an existence she'd, literally, only dreamed possible.

Then why, she wondered, staring at Tanner's empty coffee cup still on the table, did watching Tanner walk out the door feel as if she was watching her future slip away, ever so slowly?

# CHAPTER TWENTY-SEVEN

"Hey, sleepy head," Meade said to Daniel as he walked into the kitchen, wearing nothing more than his boxers. "I made you breakfast. Migas. They're in the frying pan on the stove. You might need to reheat them in the microwave, though."

Meade picked up her purse and threw her cell phone inside. "Have you seen my keys?" It was unlike her to misplace them. Living with Daniel was obviously rubbing off on her.

"Where are you going?" he asked. He rubbed his eyes and yawned. He looked sleepy—and understandably so. Meade hadn't even heard him come in last night. He'd worked a double shift at the hospital yesterday—there'd been a big bus accident with a lot of victims—and he'd come in well after she fell asleep.

"I'm meeting Lori for breakfast."

"Today?"

"Yeah. I didn't think you'd mind. I thought you'd sleep away half the day."

Daniel lifted the lid off the frying pan and began to scoop the eggs, mixed with onions, peppers, tortillas and salsa on a plate. "But it's the second Saturday of the month."

*The second Saturday of the month? Shoot. That was supposed to mean something.*

"Oh? Is it? I guess I lost track of time."

"I guess I could go by myself..." Daniel said, opening the fridge and taking out the orange juice container.

Meade was about to say, *"Can you? That'd be great."* She really wanted to see Lori. The two of them hadn't had a chance to get together since Meade had returned from Austin and Meade was dying to tell Lori all about how different things had been from what she'd expected to find. Whatever they did on the second Saturday of the month could wait, couldn't it? But Daniel's next words halted that train of thought.

"I know my mom will be disappointed, though. I think she enjoys spending time with you more than she does with me."

*His mom? Mrs. Spencer? Was she in New York? Had she moved here from Texas?*

"Oh...your mom. Right."

"It's okay. You never miss a visit. I'll tell her you couldn't make it this month."

*It would be really good to see Mrs. Spencer.*

Meade glanced at her watch. "What time do we need to leave by?"

"I don't know. Maybe in about thirty minutes. It's kind of a long drive and I'd prefer not to get home too late. I'm beat."

*A long drive? His mom must not live in Manhattan.*

"Okay. You're right. I don't want to miss seeing your mom." Especially not if they only saw her once a month. What if Meade wasn't still here next month? "I'll text Lori and ask her if we can reschedule."

"Really? You don't mind? I know mom will be happy you're there."

"Nope. I don't mind at all." Meade took her phone back out of her purse. "I love your mom." She typed a quick message to Lori, hoping her friend would understand. Meade still felt like they were on rocky ground after what had happened when Lori had popped by unexpectedly.

"Great." He put his now-empty plate in the sink. "I'll go shower and dress and we'll head out."

"Hey," she said, completing her text and hitting send. "Aren't you forgetting something?"

He looked around the room. "Uhm...no."

"I think you are."

"I didn't wash my dish?"

Meade glanced at the kitchen. It was certainly a mess. Daniel's dish only added one more to the stack in the sink. She had to admit, she was surprised to find he wasn't more helpful around the apartment. She always thought he'd be...well, not a stereotypical man. Mrs. Spencer had made him do chores when he was growing up. And yet...Meade tried to brush the thought from her mind. She didn't like feeling irritated with Daniel. She shouldn't feel irritated with him. She was so thankful he was here. But still...if he was going to be here—*alive and all*—would it kill him to load the dishwasher or fold some laundry?

"Washing the dish would be nice. Really nice. But I was thinking more along the lines of kissing me good morning."

He sighed. "Can we wait 'til after I shower and brush my teeth for that? I have morning breath."

She tried to hide her disappointment. *Morning breath?* What did she care about that? She was thankful any breath was coming out of his mouth. "I guess."

"Thanks, babe." He turned and walked into the bedroom.

Meade sighed and sank down into the couch. That was the biggest thing she found surprising about this new Daniel—how non-affectionate he was toward her.

The old Daniel loved to hold her. Couldn't keep his hands off her—and not only in a sexual manner. He loved to snuggle in bed while they watched movies and hold her hand when they walked through the park. But now? This new Daniel? He certainly wasn't demonstrative in his love for her. If she grabbed his hand while walking down the street, he'd hold hers—for a bit—but then way too quickly, he'd find a reason to let it go again. He'd need to check his phone or he'd have to scratch his head. There always seemed to be some reason—albeit subtle—for him to let go of her hand. He probably didn't notice. But Meade did. And it kind of hurt.

Meade craved Daniel. Craved his touch. Longed to be in his arms—always. She tried to remind herself that it was different for him. He hadn't just spent the past fifteen years apart from her. This wasn't new for him. Their relationship was routine. Old hat. But for Meade? It was fresh...and new. If she could, she'd spend every day, all day, in bed with Daniel—their arms wrapped around each other. But she had a feeling, if she even suggested they do that for one day, he'd look at her as if she had fourteen heads.

"I have work to do, babe," he'd tell her.

Well, she had work to do, too. If nothing else, trying to figure out what she was supposed to be doing at her actual job. But nonetheless...

"Okay, I'm all ready."

Meade's head popped up, startled to see Daniel standing in front of her, fully dressed.

"Wow, that was fast!" She must have been lost in thought. It felt like he'd left the room fifteen seconds ago. She stood. "Do I get that kiss now?"

Daniel smiled at her. "Sure." He walked over and planted one on her forehead.

*Seriously?*

"That's it?"

He bent down and kissed her quickly on the lips. "That better?"

*Not really.*

"I guess," Meade said, picking up her purse. "Let's go."

It wasn't the kiss she'd been desiring. Wasn't the passion for which she longed. But it was still a kiss. And it was from Daniel. A month ago, she would've been happy with any sort of physical touch—no matter how small—from him. She would have cherished it.

After all, it had been fifteen years since his lips had touched hers. And she had missed them. Desperately.

For years, she had lain in bed and thought, *If I could only have one more kiss...feel his lips one more time...*

And here she was, getting that wish. Daniel was standing right next to her. She could reach out and touch him. Kiss him. Wrap her arms around him.

It was what she'd been dreaming about for fifteen years. It was all she'd thought about and longed for and wanted.

It was the one thing she thought she was missing in her life. The one thing she desired most of all.

So why then, when it was finally a reality, did it seem like it wasn't quite enough?

It turned out Mrs. Spencer lived in Connecticut. At least, that was what Meade figured out once they got on I-95 and reached the Connecticut state line.

Connecticut was a beautiful state. Meade could see why Mrs. Spencer would want to live here. Daniel's mom wasn't really a city person. Although she'd grown up near Austin, she was always more comfortable in the surrounding hill country and rarely ventured into the city. Not that Austin was that big of a city to begin with—at least, not compared to New York.

It was hard to picture Mrs. Spencer outside of Texas at all, if Meade were to be truly honest. Daniel and his mom had never really traveled much and once Daniel died, his mom seemed to travel even less. Meade wasn't sure if the woman had actually ever left the state since she and Daniel had taken that road trip to Duke years before his death.

But Daniel was the woman's only child, and she didn't have a husband. It was logical that if Daniel—and Meade—had settled in New York City, then she'd want to be close by. Meade wished she were closer. Though only about sixty miles away, with this traffic—even on a Saturday morning—it was seeming like an endless drive.

Meade wanted to ask Daniel so many questions about his mom. When had she moved here? Why did they only see her on the second Saturday of the month? Did his mom come to visit them? Surely, if she didn't like fighting the traffic, she could take the train. Did she work? Had she ever fallen in love again?

But Meade sat silently, staring out at the tall trees that flew by the window of their car.

*Texas definitely doesn't have trees like these.*

She couldn't ask any of her questions because she was supposed to know the answers to all of them. She wasn't a visitor in this life— at least, not in Daniel's mind. She'd lived through all of those experiences with him. How could she tell him that she knew nothing about his mom and her life on the East Coast?

She was, however, tempted to ask, "Are we there yet?" She was getting tired of sitting in the car. But, again, she was supposed to know where his mom's home was.

Meade was thankful he hadn't asked her to drive. How would she have explained that she didn't know which direction to point the car?

Meade almost clapped her hands when Daniel finally pulled off at an exit and, after a few turns, began to slow the car down to pull into a parking lot. She hoped this meant they were getting close to his mom's house. She'd begun to doze in her seat and had, without opening her eyes, assumed they were stopping for gas or a drink. She was surprised to see they were pulling into the parking lot of a nursing home.

*A nursing home?* What were they doing here?

Unless...*of course.* Mrs. Spencer wasn't in Texas anymore, so clearly, she didn't run the women's shelter. But, because she'd left the state didn't mean she'd given up on her desire to help others. This must be her new mission—at least, her Connecticut mission. Meade could picture all the good Daniel's mom was doing for the elderly who lived here. She was such a joy—a wonderful person to be around. The residents would certainly love her.

"Do you want me to drop you off while I park the car?" he asked.

"No, that's okay. I'll walk in with you."

*Since I have no idea where I'm going...*

He parked and the two of them walked into the building together.

"Hey, Daniel! Hi, Meade!!" one of the nurses at the front desk called out to them. "Good to see you again."

"Hey, Marion." He paused at the desk. "Good to see you. How was your vacation? Get some rest?"

"Oh, not as much as I would have liked," the nurse replied. "I went to visit my grandbabies and they had me up at the crack of dawn every morning. Still, I wouldn't have changed it for the world."

Meade smiled pleasantly at the woman. She assumed she knew her and wished she had something pertinent to add to this conversation, but...truth be told...Meade had never seen this woman before.

"Your mom's all ready for you. She was so excited this morning when she realized it was your morning to visit. Go on back and see her. There's some coffee and Danishes in the break room if you and Meade would like some."

"Thanks, Marion. You're the best," Daniel said, as he and Meade said good-bye and continued to walk down the hall.

Meade was so busy looking for Mrs. Spencer's silhouette in the hallway—or, at least, an office door with her name on it—that she was startled when Daniel pushed open what was clearly the door to a patient's room.

"Daniel," Meade hissed. "I don't think we should be going in there..."

He appeared not to hear her and walked inside. She stood in the hallway, uncertain of what to do. Should she follow him? Perhaps Mrs.

Spencer was inside, working with the patient. But how would Daniel know that? Meade glanced up and down the hall to see if anyone was around who might stop them. It was empty. She took a deep breath and followed Daniel inside, hoping she wouldn't be embarrassed once she got in there.

Embarrassed was certainly not the word Meade would have used to explain herself.

Horrified. Shocked. Appalled. Sick. Those were words she might have used. But embarrassed was definitely not one of them.

Daniel was squatting down, near the window, in front of a woman in a wheelchair. He was holding her hands in his own and whispering softly. The woman was smiling, a crooked smile, and rocking gently. She turned her head slightly when she heard Meade enter. Meade felt a sudden rush of nausea and for a moment, thought she might pass out.

The woman wasn't simply any patient. The woman was Mrs. Spencer. And it was glaringly clear, right from the start, that something was very, very wrong with her.

"Look, Mom. Meade's here. You remember Meade, don't you?"

*You remember Meade? She might not remember Meade?*

The woman nodded slowly and put out her hand to Meade. Meade's legs were suddenly Jell-O. They didn't move. They only shook.

Daniel looked at her expectantly. *Meade,* his eyes seemed to implore her, *come over here.*

Meade centered herself and somehow managed to find the ability to tell her legs to go forward. She was lightheaded and swallowed a few times so she wouldn't vomit. If she did, how would she ever explain it to Daniel?

She took Mrs. Spencer's hand in her own and bent down to kiss the woman on the cheek. She didn't smell like Mrs. Spencer—not the woman whose scent was always a mix of gardenias and chocolate chip cookies. This woman smelled like old Chinese food.

"I hear you were excited that we were coming today. Marion told us. Is that true?" he asked.

His mom nodded. Meade noticed a bit of drool dripping from the corner of her mouth.

"Do you want to go for a walk in the commons today? We can sit outside. It's a lovely day."

Again, Mrs. Spencer nodded. Meade looked at her closely. This was clearly Mrs. Spencer and yet...she seemed to be at least ten years older—if not twenty. Her hair, normally worn in a shoulder-length bob, was in a short, jagged cut and Meade could see a scar peeking out of an area of thin hair on the left side of her skull. She wore no makeup and, instead of being in one of the cute sweater sets she'd been wearing since Meade was a child, she was in an old Duke sweatshirt and flannel pajama pants. She was thin. Painfully thin.

"Daniel?" Meade looked up and noticed Marion, from the front desk, standing in the doorway. "I'm sorry to interrupt your visit, but Peggy in billing was hoping to talk to you while you were here. Can you stop by her office?"

Daniel breathed a heavy sigh. "Sure. I guess." He seemed to force a smile on his face when he turned back to his mom. "I'll be back in a little bit, Mom. Meade will take you outside."

*Oh, no.* He couldn't be leaving her with his mom. Meade felt the panic begin to rise in her chest.

Daniel turned to Meade. "Take her out to the courtyard. I'll be there in a bit."

*Where was the courtyard?*

Meade nodded. "Okay." Daniel stood slowly and followed Marion out the door. Meade watched him leave, praying he would return quickly. Eventually, she turned back to Mrs. Spencer. The woman was looking at her with huge eyes. They were the same light brown they had always been and still as kind as the first time Meade saw them when Daniel's mom had come into their second-grade classroom to help out on track and field day. But there was something different about them. They looked a bit confused. And simple. Yes, that was it. There was something simple about the expression on Mrs. Spencer's face—as if she had turned into a little child. She was looking at Meade to take care of her.

"Okay," Meade said again. She let out a deep breath. "Well, then, let's see how we unlock this chair."

Meade bent down, and after pushing and pulling a few levers around the wheels, she found the one that released the lock. She stood back up again. "Let's get going."

Meade pushed Mrs. Spencer toward the door. She had to prop it open to get the chair out, making sure to put Mrs. Spencer's hands on her lap so that they didn't get caught between the chair and the door-frame.

Meade walked down the hallway very slowly. With the way Mrs. Spencer was bent over and leaning crookedly in the chair, she was afraid the woman might slide right out.

"Now, which way do we go?" Meade said aloud when they came to a new hallway. She looked down at the older woman. "Do you know which way we turn?"

Mrs. Spencer smiled up at Meade, as if she were a little girl and Meade had just said to her, "Let's have ice cream for dinner tonight."

"Okay, then..." Meade said. "How about left? We'll go left."

To Meade's relief, it turned out left was the correct direction. Half-way down the hall, she saw a door that opened into a courtyard.

"Here we are."

It appeared this door had no stopper to prop it open and so Meade opened the door with her back and then reached down to pull Mrs. Spencer's chair forward, while still holding the door open. It wasn't an easy task. The woman might look like nothing more than skin and bones, but the chair, with her in it, was actually quite heavy. Much heavier to pull than it had been to push.

"Here! Let me help you with that!"

Meade looked up with a grateful expression at the nurse who'd come to her rescue. As she held the door open, Meade got back behind Mrs. Spencer and pushed Daniel's mom out into the fresh air.

"Thank you so much!" Meade said.

"No problem," the woman said. She looked like she was in her late twenties, with bright red hair and so many freckles. "They really need an automatic door there. I don't know why they don't get one."

"You're right. They do. I could have herniated disc trying to get out here!"

"I'm Zoe." The young woman stuck out her hand to Meade.

"Meade."

"I see you're here to see Mrs. Spencer." Zoe turned to Daniel's mom. "Hey, beautiful. Are you having a good day today?"

Mrs. Spencer smiled the same, simple smile up at Zoe. Meade hadn't heard Daniel's mom say a word yet and wondered if she could actually speak.

"Yes. She's my boyfriend's mom." Meade still wasn't used to the word "fiancé."

Lowering her voice, Zoe leaned into Meade. "I'm new here, but Mrs. Spencer's story was one of the first ones the other nurses told me about. It's so sad."

This was Meade's chance to find out what was going on. She quickly looked around the courtyard, but Daniel was nowhere to be found. She didn't know how much time she had before he found her, so she spoke quickly.

"Really?" Meade said, turning away from Mrs. Spencer so she couldn't overhear. "I don't know much about what happened and I don't want to ask Daniel. It seems so intrusive. But I am really curious."

Meade silently prayed Zoe didn't know that Meade and Daniel had been together for well over a decade.

"It is such a sad story. From what I hear, she'd just moved to New

York City to be near her son. She'd found an apartment and gotten a job at a local flower shop and was really, really happy. I guess her husband had died years ago and she'd begun dating some really nice, rich doctor her son had introduced her to. Everything seemed great."

*Until...*

"And then, one night, she was coming home, late, from a concert at Lincoln Center. Your boyfriend was supposed to go with her, but he'd been called into work at the hospital. And so, she'd gone by herself. She took the subway and was attacked by a bunch of teenagers who wanted her phone."

"No!"

"Yes!" Zoe nodded solemnly. "They hit her over the head with a baseball bat, while bystanders stood by and no one helped her. The attackers ran off. They never caught them."

*Oh.My.Gosh.*

Meade felt tears spring up in her eyes. How could this happen? To Mrs. Spencer? She was such a loving woman. So kind. And what must it have done to Daniel? The guilt he must have over not being there with her to protect her.

"How long ago was this?"

"I think about three or four years."

"And this is as good as she's gotten?" Meade looked back over her shoulder at Mrs. Spencer and smiled reassuringly. Daniel's mom was staring, intently, at a bird pecking some bread crumbs off the ground.

"They say this is as good as she's going to get. There was severe brain damage. As you know, she can't talk or walk and pretty much needs complete care. The kicker is, her heart is strong. She could live like this for years and years."

Meade suddenly felt faint. Pulling up a chair behind her, she sat down. "What a horrible, horrible story!"

"I know," Zoe said. "To think she had such an exciting new life ahead of her...in a whole new city. And then this happened."

Meade sighed. *Yes. And then this.*

"Well, I need to get back to work. It was nice meeting you, Meade. I hope I see you again."

"Me, too." Meade gave her a weak smile. She hoped Zoe didn't mention this conversation to Marion or any of the other nurses who might be familiar with Meade and Daniel's long-term relationship. She didn't want them to wonder why she'd ask Zoe about a woman she, herself, had supposedly known for the past twenty-five years.

"Hey, there," Daniel said. Meade turned, startled. Once again, she'd been lost in thought and hadn't heard him approach. He had a big smile on his face, but Meade sensed, by his eyes, that it wasn't sincere. He was carrying a cafeteria-style tray with some bowls on it.

"You hungry, Mama? I brought you your lunch."

Mrs. Spencer looked adoringly at Daniel. It took everything Meade had not to burst into tears. Clearly, no matter what the damage was inside her brain, those thugs had not killed the part of her that loved her little boy.

Daniel pulled up a chair and sat down next to his mom. Meade sat quietly as she watched him, lovingly and with great care, spoon-feed his mom applesauce, cottage cheese and lukewarm chicken soup, gently wiping her chin, as she dripped, with the cloth napkin he'd brought with him.

It reminded Meade of the way Mrs. Spencer used to sit at Daniel's bedside, feeding him when he'd become too weak to lift the spoon. If there was ever a full-circle moment, this was it.

If she sat and watched Daniel and his mom for one more minute, she was going begin to sob. So instead, she reached inside her purse. "I have a brush with me," she said to Mrs. Spencer. "Would you like me to brush your hair?"

The smile Daniel's mom gave her, in between bites, spoke volumes. And the one Daniel gave her said a thousand words, too. Meade had a feeling, though, that they weren't the ones she wanted to hear.

"So, what did the lady in billing want?" Meade asked on the drive home. They'd spent about three hours with Daniel's mom, until the woman had closed her eyes and dozed off in her chair. Daniel had lifted her, like a father carrying his toddler, into her bed, tucking the blankets in around her. It had broken Meade's heart.

"The usual."

*And what would that be?*

"What did she say?" Meade said, hoping to get more details.

"Insurance isn't paying enough. They need a check from me or I'll have to move Mom to a new facility."

"How much do they need?"

"Twenty thousand."

*Dollars?* Meade swallowed hard. "What are you going to do?"

"What I always do. Try to pick up a few more shifts at the hospital. Eat less. We may have to cancel the cable."

Daniel merged onto the highway. The traffic was worse than it had been on the way to the nursing home and it had started to rain, slowing things down even more. Meade stared at Daniel's profile. His jaw was tense. His eyes were dark. It was clear he had an enormous amount of stress in his life. Meade corrected herself. *They* had an enormous amount of stress in their life together.

Daniel fell silent as he drove, seemingly concentrating on the road, but she was sure his mind was on deeper issues.

Meade's mind drifted back to the box of bills she'd found. If her math was correct, with what Daniel owed in student loans and for his mother's care, he was well over $100,000 in debt. Piecing together bits of information, Meade had realized Daniel's full basketball scholarship had never transpired. Though he'd lived, he was never physically the same—especially not on the basketball court. His college tuition had been high. In addition to those bills, he also had credit card bills and a car payment. She couldn't even bear to add all of that in. The number was staggering.

No wonder they lived in that little crap hole.

"I could sell my ring."

Daniel glanced at her quickly and then back at the road. "Of course you can't. You can't sell my mom's engagement ring."

*Oh. It was his mom's?* She hadn't even known that.

"Well, maybe I can get a second job."

"You've been saying that for years."

*I have?*

"Besides," he continued. "I don't expect you to get a second job. You work hard enough at the first one and cover most of our living expenses so I can throw nearly my entire salary at my loans and my mom. It's my mess. I'll get out of it...somehow."

But Meade didn't really see how. They were barely keeping their heads above water as it was. There was no wiggle room for anything "extra." No movies. No fancy dinners. No vacations together. None of the things Meade had dreamed she and Daniel would do together if he'd gotten better.

"It's *our* mess."

"No, it's mine," Daniel said stubbornly. "It's not like we're married."

*It's not like we're married.* Another topic that confused and bewildered Meade. Why weren't they married? They were clearly engaged, though, of course, she had no recollection of the proposal. She liked to think it was beautiful and perfect, but the way things were going, she had a feeling Daniel might have popped the question over the pu pu platter at Wok This Way.

"You know, I've been thinking about that..." Now seemed as good a time as any to broach the subject. "Why don't we go and get married at the Justice of the Peace? We don't have to do anything big. You and me. Maybe a couple friends."

Daniel's sigh was audible. "We've been through this a thousand times."

*Have we?*

"Well, refresh my memory on your objections."

"I don't want to get married until I'm financially stable and secure."

"Daniel! Have you seen your bills? That might not be for the next thirty years!"

"Thanks for reminding me!" His voice rose. "You know I'm doing the best I can to pay them off."

"Well, apparently, I'm doing the best I can to help you pay them off, too. We're in a partnership here. We've been together for close to twenty years. So why am I not Mrs. Daniel Spencer yet?"

"I gave you a ring."

"You gave me a ring?" Meade's voice began to escalate. "You *gave* me a *ring?* Was that supposed to tide me over? Hold me off? Take some of the pressure off you?"

"Of course not."

"Then what was it? How long have we been engaged now?"

"Five years."

*Five years? And we're not married yet?*

Meade began to wonder what on earth was wrong with her. Why was she putting up with this? If a man proposed, but you never actually saw a wedding, it meant he'd never really meant the proposal. And yet, here she was—five years into an engagement. His mother's ring on her finger and no matching wedding band next to it.

"And, not once in five years, has it seemed like the right time to say, 'I do' to me?"

"Come on, Meade. Why are you picking a fight? You know it's been a tough day for me."

She did know that. And, a part of her felt bad about what she was doing. Still...

"When exactly would be a better time? When you come home at two in the morning from working at the hospital? Or, should I call you from my desk at work, in between writing about dead people?"

Daniel didn't reply, but Meade saw his jaw tense even more.

"And what about kids? We're not getting any younger. If we want kids..."

"I don't want kids," Daniel said softly. So softly that Meade wasn't sure she'd heard him correctly.

"You don't want kids?"

Had she known this already? Was this a new revelation or something they had discussed in the past?

"No. I don't want children. I know that you do..."

Of course she wanted children. She'd always wanted children. She'd always wanted *Daniel's* children.

"But..."

"I know we've discussed adopting since I can't have any..."

*Daniel can't have children?* Meade vaguely remembered the doctors telling them there was a possibility, with all of the chemotherapy he'd undergone, that he'd become sterile.

"You don't want to adopt?"

"Well, first of all, adoption is expensive and we have no money..."

He had a point there. They were broke. Beyond broke.

"What about surrogacy? Or maybe we could get someone to lend us their sperm and I could use a turkey baster..."

Daniel looked over at Meade, his expression a mixture of half disgust and half amusement. "Seriously? A turkey baster?"

"I know someone who did that! The sister of a friend of mine. She agreed to have a baby for two gay men. They mixed their sperm together, stuck in in a turkey baster and nine months later...shazam! Baby Kendall was born!"

"We are not using a turkey baster with some stranger's sperm to have a baby."

"Do you have a better option?"

"No, I don't have a better option, because frankly, I don't want to have kids at all."

Meade was speechless. *Not at all?* Daniel had always wanted kids.

Always. Two girls and a boy. They'd even picked out names when they were teenagers. Rebecca, Lindsey and Brandon.

"You don't want kids?"

"No."

"But...why? You're great with kids. You've always loved kids."

"And I still do...love them. I don't want my own. Or, maybe it's more that I don't want to bring kids into this world. It's a horrible world. Terrible things happen. People get beaten with baseball bats and kids get cancer and there's a new school shooting on the news every week. Why bring a child into that?"

"But, Daniel...there's so much good in the world, too. So many wonderful experiences to have with a child."

"With what money? We couldn't go on vacations. We can't buy a house. If we stay where we are, the baby would have to sleep in the closet and go to some sketchy schools 'cause we couldn't afford anything private. And, our child would pretty much have no grandparents."

"But we'd love him."

"Love isn't enough to survive in this world."

"Of course it is! Daniel, how can you say that?" Meade was beginning to panic. Who *was* this man? Not the Daniel she'd loved since she was eight. Not the one she'd held in that hospital bed when they were eighteen—the one who'd been so full of hopes and dreams and joy. This Daniel was hardened to the world. Cynical. Dare she say it... bitter.

"Meade, of course it's not. You can't live on love. You can't eat on love. You can't pay your rent or the car payment or my mom's nursing home bills on it. I'm glad we have love. But it's hardly going to help us get anywhere."

They were in the city now. While the trip to Connecticut had seemed to take a year, the ride home had flown by—and not because they were having fun.

Daniel pulled up to the parking garage and entered the code. Meade opened her car door.

"Where are you going?"

"I need to go for a walk."

"Now? It's raining."

"Yes. Now. I need to think."

"About what?" Daniel seemed genuinely confused.

"Us. This life. What are we doing?"

"We're surviving, Meade. That's what people do. They survive."

"Well, maybe I want to do more than survive. Did you ever think of that? Maybe I want to live and thrive and love."

A car honked behind them. Daniel looked in the rearview mirror.

"I'll see you later."

"When will you be home?" Daniel seemed to be getting nervous.

"I don't know. Don't wait up." Meade got out of the car and slammed the door behind her. She began to walk down the block, in the opposite direction of their apartment. By the loud, repetitive honking, she was pretty sure Daniel was still sitting there watching her. But she didn't turn around.

She kept walking, into the rain. She'd thought, since she'd entered this new world with Daniel, she was finally walking toward something—toward the life they were going to build together. But now, as she took each step in the rain, she began to wonder if she'd been wrong. Maybe she wasn't actually walking toward anything.

Instead, maybe...the direction she was walking was away.

# CHAPTER TWENTY-EIGHT

Meade heard Daniel roll over in bed, but she kept her eyes closed, pretending to sleep. When he didn't move again, she assumed he was staring at her back, waiting for her to give some indication she was awake.

"Meade," he said softly. "Are you up?"

She didn't reply. She'd come in late last night, well after midnight. Daniel had been waiting for her, jumping off the couch when she came through the front door.

"Where've you been? Are you okay? I've been so worried."

"I'm fine. I'm going to bed."

"Can we talk?"

"Not now. I'm tired." Meade had walked by him, not even looking at his face. He'd probably been frantic. And part of her felt guilty for letting him feel that way. But most of her was weary.

She'd spent the first few hours wandering the city in the rain, the falling droplets intermingling with the tears pouring down her face. She'd had no plan when she stepped out of Daniel's car. She'd known she needed to get away from him. It had all become too much. This life was too overwhelming—the uncertainty of everything, coupled with the bills, Daniel's lack of affection toward her, the changes in Benji and her mother, a job she loathed. When Daniel told her he wasn't sure when they'd ever marry and that he certainly never wanted children, Meade had thought she might explode with agony.

This wasn't the life she'd thought she and Daniel would have together. Not even close.

When she was about all cried out and soaked to the bone, she found herself on the stoop of Lori's townhouse.

"What on earth?" Lori said, opening the door and finding her friend looking like a drenched subway rat on her doorstep. "Get in here. Try not to drip on my new rug, though."

Meade stepped inside as Lori hurried to the bathroom to grab some towels. She threw them at Meade. "Dry off as best you can and then go take a hot shower. I'll get you some of my clothes and I'll put on the coffee. We'll talk when you're dry."

Meade wanted to thank her friend, to tell her that, after the way she'd treated her so badly for so long—even if Lori didn't remember it—she didn't deserve such kindness. But instead, all she could do was stand in her friend's hallway and cry.

"Shower!" Lori ordered. "You can weep over coffee."

Thirty minutes later, Meade was sitting, cross-legged, on one of Lori's kitchen chairs, dressed in her friend's sweatpants and T-shirt.

Lori placed a hot mug of coffee—black—in front of Meade, along with a blueberry muffin. "I'll bet you haven't eaten all day."

"What time is it?"

"Seven."

*Seven? Really?* She had been walking around the city much longer than she'd thought.

"Daniel called here, looking for you."

"What did you say?"

"I told him I didn't know where you were. And, I didn't. He called a few hours ago."

"Did you call him when I was in the shower?"

Lori shook her head. "No. I thought that was up to you."

Meade nodded her head in gratitude. "I didn't ruin your evening, did I? You didn't have a date..."

Lori practically snorted out her coffee. "A date? Me? I never have a date. Nice thought, though."

"I'm sorry."

Lori shrugged. "Such is life. So, want to tell me what's going on?"

Meade put her head in her hands and began to sob again. She'd thought she was done crying—twice now—but the tears continued to fall.

"Oh, sweetie," Lori said, gently resting a hand on her friend's shoulder. "It's gonna be okay. What's going on?"

"We went to see Daniel's mom today."

"Oh."

Meade looked up at Lori, her eyes blurry from the tears. "You knew, didn't you?"

"Knew what? About the accident?"

Meade nodded.

Lori's shoulders dropped. "Then I'm guessing you didn't?"

Meade shook her head sadly. "I had no idea. I thought she was still in Texas. I didn't have time to try to see her when I was home. In my other life, she runs a woman's shelter. And she's dating Mr. Barker."

"The school principal?"

Meade couldn't help but smile as she nodded. "I know. I couldn't believe it, either."

"Isn't he kind of old for her?"

Meade shrugged. "They seem happy."

"So you must have been in shock when you got to the nursing home."

"I had no idea. I thought, when we pulled up, maybe she worked there. Have you seen her?"

"Yes. I've gone with you a few times. It's devastating to see her like that."

"And then Daniel and I had a huge fight on the car ride home."

"Over his mom?"

"Over everything. Our bills. The fact that we're apparently never actually going to get married." Meade glanced at Lori, who didn't seem at all surprised by that statement, confirming Meade's own concerns even more. "Did you know he doesn't want kids?"

Lori shook her head. "No. But I'm not surprised."

"You're not?"

"No."

Meade was going to ask why, but then decided she didn't really want to know. "Can I ask you a question?"

"Of course."

"Was I happy?"

"Were you happy? When?"

"Before. Before all this. Before I came back into this world from my other one. Was I ever happy in my adult life?"

Lori thought about that for a moment. "I don't know. That's an interesting question. I guess I never thought about it before. We never really talked about it. I don't think you were unhappy, per se."

"Just not giddy in my life?"

Lori chuckled. "Who's giddy in their life?"

"Good point," Meade said. "Did I express my frustration over the lack of a wedding?"

Lori nodded. "Yes."

"Did I like my job?"

Lori shook her head. "No."

"So, it's not only the new 'me' that's disenchanted by this life?"

"No, it's not only the new you. But, I do see a difference between the new you and the old you."

"And what is that?"

"The new you knows the difference. The new you knows a whole other life is possible. She knows she's capable of writing more than obituaries and that she's the type of woman who can support herself, all on her own, with no debt. This new Meade knows that relationships with the people in her life really and truly matter. And she knows what it feels like for a man to make her feel like a woman and not simply continue on with a high school love."

Meade looked up at her friend in surprise. "Daniel loves me."

"I know he does."

"And I love him."

"I've never doubted that."

"So, I don't understand what you're saying."

"It's not what I'm saying, Meade. It's what you're feeling."

Meade rested her elbows on Lori's table and dropped her head in her hands. "What am I going to do?"

"I can't tell you that. But we only get one life, Meade." Lori giggled. "Well, in your case, you seem to get two."

Meade looked up and smiled, despite the pain in her eyes.

"And I get the feeling that in both of your lives, you're deeply in love with the same man."

Meade sighed and nodded. Lori was right. And Meade knew it.

"So, the question isn't really were you happy? The question is, what are you going to do to ensure your happiness?"

Meade kept her eyes closed, as she thought about what Lori had said. She and Daniel were due for a long talk, but she wasn't up to having it now.

"I have to leave for work," Daniel said.

"Okay."

"Will you..." his voice faltered, as if unsure he wanted to finish the sentence. "...be here when I get back?"

After a moment's hesitation, Meade replied, "I'll be here."

She heard him breathe a sigh of relief. "Good."

The two of them didn't say another word to each other as Daniel got ready for the day. Meade ignored the three texts he'd sent her and the two voicemails he'd left throughout the day. Meade spent most of the day in bed, watching reruns of *Friends* and *Everybody Loves Raymond.* By the time she heard Daniel coming in the front door, she realized she'd only gotten up once to pee and she hadn't eaten a thing all day.

He was standing in the doorway as she picked up the remote to change the channel to the evening news. She glanced up at him, but said nothing.

"Did you move all day?" he asked.

"Nope."

"Want to go out to dinner?"

"Not really."

"Come on, Meade," Daniel said, crossing the room and sitting on the end of the bed. "We need to talk."

He was right. They did. There were a million things they needed to say to each other—things Meade needed to say to Daniel. But, she didn't know where to begin, so pretending she was still mad at him was easier than facing the truth of the conversation ahead of them.

And she was pretending. She wasn't mad at Daniel. Not at all. None of this was his fault. He hadn't done anything wrong. She glanced up at his face and melted. He looked so sad and confused. He didn't understand what was going on. To him, their life hadn't changed. It had always been this way—or, at least, it had in recent years. He certainly didn't understand the change in her.

Meade sighed and threw her legs out of bed. "Okay. Let's go eat. I am kind of hungry."

She felt guilty when she saw the smile that brought to his face. It reminded her of the millions of smiles she'd seen on his face when they were kids and she felt guilty that, for once, she hadn't earned this one.

Maybe she was making too much of the situation. Things weren't terrible. She still loved Daniel. He was a good person and he wanted to make her happy—even if he seemed incapable of giving her what she really wanted in life. She needed to remind herself that, if asked in her old world if she'd want Daniel back, but that with him would come debt and a different job and a whole new life, she would've said, "absolutely" with enthusiasm. There wouldn't have been even a second's hesitation.

*So what was her problem?* Maybe she was the type of person who could never be truly happy. Perhaps she'd always find something to bemoan.

Meade pulled on a pair of jeans that were laying on the floor beside the bed and began to zip herself into them.

"Great. Let me change," he said, disappearing into their closet.

A news story showing the Texas flag caught Meade's attention and she picked the remote off the bed and turned up the volume.

"In other news today, the little boy shot at the Texas State Capitol last month has died of his injuries," the reporter said.

Meade squeezed her eyes tightly and then opened them again. A memory flashed through her brain.

*What was it?*

"Max Barnes was visiting the state capitol from New Jersey, with his mom, when a gunman broke through security and opened fire in the rotunda of the Capitol building..."

An image of the gunman flashed through Meade's mind. *Had she seen him on the news earlier?*

"The eight-year-old boy has been in a coma since the shooting. He was taken off life support earlier this morning and passed away shortly afterward."

An image of an adorable little boy, with perfect black curls, suddenly flashed across the screen. Meade gasped. She knew him. And not because he looked so much like Daniel as a child. She *knew* him.

*But how?*

She quickly pulled on the hoodie that was thrown on the top of the chair next to her nightstand and slipped on her sneakers.

She needed to get out of here. She needed to figure it all out.

*She needed Tanner.*

Picking up her phone, she saw it was Sunday evening. Sunday. She knew exactly where he'd be. Meade glanced out the window. It was raining again, but he'd said "rain or shine."

She couldn't wait one more day—one more moment. Nothing was right in this world and the only road that seemed clear to her at the moment was the one that led to Tanner.

"I need to go out," she said frantically, as Daniel emerged from their closet.

"Out? I thought we were going to dinner."

In a frenzy, Meade grabbed her purse, throwing her phone inside and a baseball cap on her head. Ducking to look under the bed, she searched for an umbrella, but found none. She hopped up and pushed past Daniel, flinging open the door to their hall closet. "Do we not own any umbrellas?" she snapped.

"I think they're all broken."

"Figures. And I imagine we have no money to buy new ones."

"Meade, what's gotten into you? You were fine five minutes ago."

Had she been? *Fine,* that is? Or had she been resigned? Resigned to this life she was now leading. Resigned to the fact that there was no more for her. Resigned to the realization that this was as good as it gets.

Well, she wasn't fine. And she wasn't resigned. There was a whole other life out there—and she'd been living it. And it didn't include worries about money or a wedding that would never happen or a lack of affection from the man she loved. It certainly didn't include a little boy dying in the Capitol. She wasn't sure how she knew this, but she did. Somewhere, in her subconscious, that little boy, Max, had survived the shooting.

Meade flung open the front door and raced out into the hallway. Daniel was at her heels as she flew down the stairs.

"Meade! Stop. Talk to me. What's going on?"

"I can't talk, Daniel. There's somewhere I need to be...before he leaves."

"Before *who* leaves?" Daniel asked, clearly beside himself with confusion. Meade could see, out of the corner of her eye as she wound her way down the stairs, he'd thrown on a polo shirt, but was still in his scrub pants.

Meade reached the entrance to her building. "Go back upstairs," she barked to Daniel.

"Not until you tell me what's going on. Where are you going?"

Meade pushed open the front door and ran out outside. The rain was coming down hard now—"in buckets," her mother would've said, if it ever rained in Texas. She pulled the hoodie over her baseball cap and ducked her head to keep the water off her face.

Spinning around, she saw Daniel standing outside, too. He was barefoot.

"Go back inside. You'll get sick."

"And you won't?!" he yelled, over the sound of the rain and the thunder and the honking cabs that flew by their building. *Didn't they know to slow down in the rain?*

"It doesn't matter. I have to be somewhere."

"Where?" Daniel pleaded with her. *"Where,* Meade? What is going on?"

"Please, let me go, Daniel."

"Go where?" he begged her.

"Go."

Daniel became very still, the rain falling down his face, soaking his clothes. If he still had his long black curls, they would've been clinging to the side of his face right now.

"You're leaving me."

Meade pursed her lips together. She didn't know what to say, so she nodded. Tears sprang to her eyes.

"You're leaving me?" Daniel said, more as a question this time. "Really?"

Meade nodded again. Even she couldn't believe this was happening, so she could only imagine his shock at the notion. It had always been Daniel and Meade. Meade and Daniel. In this world, they'd always been one—not two. Neither could imagine a life without the other.

Except, Meade could. She'd lived a life without Daniel. She knew it could happen. It needed to happen.

"But why?" His eyes were so sad. So mournful. Meade almost grabbed hold of him and pulled him back inside the building—back where it was warm and dry. And safe.

But it wasn't safe. At least, not in the way she needed it to be. She didn't feel secure in her life with Daniel. She didn't feel love—not the way a woman her age should feel love from a man. There was no passion. No romance. Somewhere along the way, perhaps when she hadn't been paying attention, that had all evaporated. And what was left was a love like she felt for Benji or Nick. Deep and true, but not the kind that makes your heart race at the thought of the other person. Not the kind of love that withstands all hardships of life. They'd withstood cancer—an enemy more ferocious than any other—but that fight had taken everything from them. Meade had nothing more in her. She'd fought for Daniel—*with* Daniel—through the cancer. But the rest? The battles they now faced. They were too much. She was done.

"I need to go, Daniel," Meade said, the tears falling as fast as the rain now. "I need to go. Please let me go."

"I can't, Meade. I love you."

Meade pulled her hands inside her sleeves and brought them up to her face, wiping her nose. "I love you, too," she said. "I promise, Daniel. I love you, too." She looked down the street. It was getting dark. If she was going to catch him, she needed to leave now. "I'll come back. I promise. I'll come back and explain everything. But right now, I need to go." She began to back away from Daniel, toward the street.

*Maybe she could catch a cab...*

"Meade, don't go. Please."

"I'll be back. I promise, Daniel. I'll be back. We'll talk then, okay?"

Meade took one more step backward and found herself falling. She hadn't realized she was so close to the curb. She threw out her arms to brace herself and as she did, something slammed into her side.

The pain...it was staggering. She looked up at Daniel. His face was a mix of horror and fear.

"Meade!" he screamed.

She turned her head, just in time to realize she was flying over the roof of a yellow cab. Her body landed on the wet, black asphalt road. She tried to get up, but everything hurt and nothing moved.

"Meade!" she heard Daniel scream again, but this time, his voice sounded very far away. She could still hear the horns honking, no doubt annoyed she was blocking the road, but even they began to fade in intensity.

"Daniel," she said softly. "I'm sorry."

He was crying. Daniel was next to her and crying.

She wanted to tell him it would all be okay—that he'd find someone new—someone better for him than her. Just as she'd found Tanner, but the words didn't come. "I'm so sleepy."

"Stay with me, Meade. Stay with me," Daniel pleaded with her.

"I can't," Meade said, her head falling to the side. Her eyes were getting heavy. It was hard to keep them open. "He'll leave. I need to get there before he leaves."

"Stay with me, Meade. Stay with me."

"I love you, Daniel. I promise. I love you," Meade said. And she did. She loved Daniel.

But, she loved Tanner more. And that was her last thought as she closed her eyes, letting the rain fall on her eyelids and down her face.

# CHAPTER TWENTY-NINE

Meade's head was killing her. It felt as if she'd been shot fifty feet out of a lead canon, landing squarely on her noggin. She tried to open her eyes, but they were apparently glued shut. Making an effort to pry them open, she moaned with the effort.

"Meade, sweetie. Are you waking up? Open your eyes, baby. We're all waiting to see you."

*Mom? What was her mom doing in her bedroom?*

Meade tried again to open her eyes, but they wouldn't budge. She attempted to shift in the bed and a sharp pain cut through her back, as if someone had a knife lodged in there and was yanking it toward her chest.

"Ow," she cried. In reality, she thought she'd screamed it, but the little squeak produced by her throat was no louder than a sick cat's meow.

"It's okay, baby. Open your eyes. Please," her mom pleaded with her.

Meade made one more attempt and, as she was about to give up, certain someone had applied some sort of epoxy to her lids, she was able to open them the tiniest bit. Through mere slits, she saw a fuzzy version of her mom next to her. "Mom," she whispered.

"Yes, baby. It's me."

"Where am I?" It hurt to talk. Her throat was as dry as if a fluid hadn't dripped down it in a week. Her eyes opened a bit more and began to clear. She couldn't see much past her mom, but what she did see made it clear she wasn't in her bedroom.

"You're in the hospital, honey. We've been so worried."

*The hospital?* Meade tried to rack her brain for what had happened? Was she sick? Had she fallen? Was there a car accident?

*A car...*that was it. Meade had a vague recollection of being hit by a car. In the rain. While she was arguing with Daniel.

*Daniel?* Where was he? He must be so worried.

She was about to ask her mom, when she heard a male voice enter the room.

"She's awake. Meade's awake!" her mom cried with joy.

"Thank God." Relief flooded the man's voice. "We've been so worried, young lady. You gave us quite a scare."

Meade felt a big, strong hand lift her own. *Jimmy.* This was Jimmy. What was he doing here in New York? What was her mom doing in New York? And why were they in New York *together.* They weren't married in this world. Had they somehow met through her accident?

Meade tried to smile up at him, but only a tiny bit of drool came out of the side of her mouth.

"Oh, here," her mom said. "Let me get that." And she wiped Meade's mouth like she used to when Meade was a baby and she'd made a mess with her oatmeal.

"Katie's going to be so happy to hear you're okay," her mom continued. "She just left. She was here all day."

*Katie'd been here, too?* What on earth had happened while she was unconscious?

"Be thankful you're in the cool air conditioning," Jimmy joked. "It's unbearable out there. I think they said Austin is setting some sort of record today."

*Austin?*

Meade looked at her mom. This time, really closely. Her mom's eyes sparkled. She looked good and healthy and fit. *And her hair...*it was cut in a short bob.

If Meade had been able to gasp, she would have. She felt her eyes fill with tears. Jimmy was here because he was married to her mom. And Katie had been here because she was Meade's stepsister.

"Where's Benji?" she asked.

"He had to get back to the hospital, but he's driving back tomorrow night. And he said he can stay for a few days."

"He's a doctor?"

"Of course he is. What did you think he was?" her mom teased. "A mechanic?"

*Well, actually...*

She was back. In her other life. Meade didn't know if she should laugh or cry. As it turned out, she didn't have time to do either. Within a minute, she was surrounded by nearly half a dozen doctors and nurses.

"You're one lucky lady," a male doctor, with a southern twang, said to her. "One inch to the left and the bullet would've gone straight through your heart."

*The bullet?*

"We weren't sure you were going to stay on this earth. It's good of you to join us," he continued.

*She'd been shot?* Surely, the doctor was kidding.

"As soon as you're feeling up to it, there's one very thankful little boy and his mama who'd like to come visit you."

And suddenly, as if she was being hit by a tidal wave of memories, it all came back to her. The Capitol, the tour, the gunman and Max.

*Max.*

She'd jumped on him to try to save him.

"Is he okay?" Meade asked worriedly.

"He's more than okay," Jimmy said. "He's perfect and alive—thanks to you and your quick, albeit reckless, thinking."

"You jumped in front of a bullet, Meade!" Meade's mom said, her voice reprimanding, but also full of obvious pride. "You saved his life."

"And about lost your own," the doctor said. "No more heroic stunts like that. We don't want to see you in here again."

Meade nodded. Her mind was spinning and swirling with everything she was trying to process. It was hard to remember what was true in this world and what had happened in her dream...had it all been a dream? She wasn't sure. It hadn't felt like a dream. It had felt real. Completely and utterly true.

Daniel had been alive. She'd seen him. Felt him. Made love to him. And ultimately, left him.

And what about everyone else? Had her interactions and experiences with all the others been real, too, or nothing more than figments of her overmedicated imagination?

"Is there anything you need?" Meade's mom asked, sitting down by her bedside as the entourage of medical personnel left her room, with orders to let her rest.

"Yes," Meade said fervently. "There is something I need. Or rather, someone."

It had been difficult to decide who to see first, but deep in Meade's heart, she knew who it had to be. "I need to see Nick."

If Meade had said she could now walk on water and read minds, she wouldn't have surprised her family any more with her words. That was obvious from their expressions. Nonetheless, no one questioned her request and, within an hour, Nick was standing in her doorway.

By the time he'd arrived, Meade was feeling a little bit better. She'd been given some water, with the promise that, if she could keep it down, she might get to have some soft food by the end of the day. They'd also increased her pain medication, and the dagger in her back and chest was no longer piercing her quite so sharply.

She was alone in the room when he entered; he appeared uncomfortable. Meade looked at him. Perhaps for the first time in her entire life, she really *looked* at her brother. And what she saw broke her heart.

He wasn't the big, ol' jerk she'd made him out to be. He was a scared young man—someone who'd never been given a chance—by anyone. Certainly not by her.

"Hey, Nick. Thanks for coming."

He nodded, but made no attempt to walk further into the room. He shifted his weight from one foot to the other.

"Can you come a little closer?" she asked. "I don't have much of a voice."

Her brother hesitated, but then made his way over, sitting down by her side. He stared at the IV attached to her arm and not at Meade herself, but she didn't mind. She understood. They weren't close. They never had been. What was there to say to each other?

*A lifetime of things,* Meade realized. And she was about to start now.

"I want to tell you something, Nick. Something I've never said to you before, but should have."

Nick's eyes moved to Meade's face. "Oh yeah? What's that?"

She could hear the sarcasm in his voice and saw he was bracing himself for the worst. "I love you."

The look on Nick's face indicated he was waiting for the punch line. But, for once, there was none. That was what she'd wanted to say and she meant each one of those three little words.

"I'm sorry I haven't been a better sister to you." The conversation was seeming vaguely familiar to Meade, as she'd had one nearly identical to it in her dream—but that time, it had been with Benji. "And I'd like to make up for that.

"But, more importantly, I want to tell you that you are an incredible person. You're smart and you're resourceful and I know..." Meade reached down and grabbed her brother's hand. She thought he might wrestle it away, but he didn't. "...that you are capable of really great things. Amazing things. And, if you'll let me, I'd like to help you reach whatever dreams you have."

Nick said nothing. He sat and stared at Meade. For a moment, she thought he might spit out some rude insult about how she'd clearly lost her mind in that coma and how he didn't need "nothing" from her, but he said none of those things. He continued to stare at his sister.

Then, very carefully, he lifted her hand to his lips, and kissed it.

The next two weeks went by faster than Dorothy's tornado in Kansas. Meade was released from the hospital after a few days with a whole grocery bag full of medication, bandages and antiseptic cleaners, along with paperwork instructing her mom how to help her care for her wound. Meade nearly snorted with laughter when the doctor told her mom she was going to need to be taken care of at home by her parents for a little while. He clearly didn't know who he was talking to. They hadn't even owned a thermometer when she was growing up. And chicken soup, even out of the can, had been out of question. Her mom was not the nurturing type.

But Meade was in for a surprise. Her mom tended to Meade as if she was an Egyptian princess. After three days of being waited on hand and foot—she'd even been given a bell to ring—Meade was waiting for her mother to start feeding her grapes from above her head.

And her mom wasn't the only one to dote on Meade. Jimmy and Katie brought her magazines, her favorite Mexican food, and DVDs of all of the latest hot movie rentals, which Benji was more than happy to lie next to her and watch when he arrived. Even Nick showed up in her room every day, with her favorite Izze drink in hand, to see how she was doing. A week after she was home, he brought home the local community college course book, telling her he'd been thinking of taking a few business courses and wondering if she'd look over their descriptions with him. It was clear he was clean and sober and doing his best to straighten out his life and Meade was so proud of him. She'd never thought he could amount to anything, but if her dream had taught her one thing, it was that she'd been wrong.

Every once in a while, though, when her room was empty or as she closed her eyes to doze, she'd think about Daniel. Not the Daniel who'd died when they were teenagers, but the one from her dream. Even as the days went by, the dream did not fade from her memory, as most dreams do. It still seemed so real. She was tempted to tell someone—maybe Benji or Katie—about it, but she knew they'd never understand. How could they? She didn't feel as if she'd merely dreamt all of those experiences—the conversations she'd had with them and Pantera and Lori and the new friends she'd made—or the days she'd spent at that awful job.

*And, boy, was she relieved to realize she no longer wrote obituaries for a living.*

Meade felt as if she'd truly lived those experiences and it was going to take an awful lot to convince her they'd never actually happened.

When she was feeling a bit better, Jimmy informed Meade that numerous news stations—and not only local ones—were driving them nuts for an interview. Apparently, a shooting in a state capitol was big news.

"Do you want to do an interview?" Jimmy asked. "You don't have to. I can tell them all to get lost."

Meade smiled at this big man who'd become the father she'd never had. She sure did love him. She'd always known that, but never more so than when she'd dreamt he'd never married her mom. He wanted to protect her—like no older man ever had.

And Meade needed that protection. She didn't feel up to an interview. Didn't know what she'd have to say, other than she did what anyone else would have done in her situation. So, it was decided she'd release a statement to the media and hope they'd eventually all stop hounding her family for a story.

Max and his mom, Rachel, came by the first day Meade made it down to the living room couch. Rachel was carrying an enormous bouquet of sunflowers while Max plopped a large, stuffed armadillo on her lap. They'd made a special trip back from New Jersey to see her.

"Did you know an armadillo can hold his breath for six minutes?" Max asked.

"I had no idea," Meade said, pulling the little boy down on the couch next to her. She kissed the top of his head. He smelled so good. She remembered how she'd been so devastated to learn he'd died—at least, in her dream, he had. But, here he was, living and breathing right next to her, telling her the armadillo is one of the only animals that can eat fire ants.

Meade smiled up at Rachel, who burst into tears the moment their eyes met.

"I'm sorry. I'm sorry," Max's mom said, pulling a wad of tissues out of her back pocket and wiping her eyes. "I don't know how to thank you. I've felt so guilty ever since that day. It should've been me. I should have been the one who'd been shot protecting my child. How can we ever repay you?"

Meade held up the armadillo and smiled. "Like this." She smiled at Max. "I've never had my own armadillo."

The boy beamed up at Meade and she was once again reminded of how much he looked like Daniel did when they were kids.

Daniel was never far from Meade's mind. She couldn't sleep at night thinking about him. She knew he was dead. She didn't need to ask anyone to understand that. But, she'd just seen him last week. He was alive and well. So how could he be gone?

"Where are you going?" Benji had asked her one morning when she came downstairs, clean from a shower, asking him if she could borrow his car. He was drinking a cup of coffee at the kitchen table. "I can drive you," he'd said. He'd gotten in the night before. Anytime he had a break from work, he came home to see Meade.

"No, that's okay. The doctor said I'm okay to drive."

"I don't mind," Benji had said hesitantly. It amused Meade to see how, since her injury, he'd taken on the role of "big brother," though he was so much younger than she.

"No, really. I'm fine. There are a few things I need to do on my own."

He'd pulled the keys from his pocket and threw them at her. "Don't wreck it."

"Promise."

It felt so good to be alone in Benji's little car. Meade couldn't remember the last time there'd been no one around her. Someone in her family always seemed to be hovering—sure every sneeze or cough was going to rip out her stitches and cause massive internal hemorrhaging.

Meade turned on the radio and sang along to Willie Nelson at the top of her lungs. It felt good to be alive.

She turned the music down, though, and mentally braced herself when she turned onto the small driveway at the cemetery. She'd been down this road a hundred times over the years. Sometimes, she'd come here to think. Other times, she'd show up to tell Daniel about her day. On occasion, she'd drive down this road in a fury, her rage over Daniel leaving her alone evident the moment she stomped up to his headstone.

But never before had she approached his grave with uncertainty as to whether or not he was really buried here—or maybe was living an alternative life in New York City.

She could see the grave with the big oak tree the moment she turned the corner. It was the only heart-shaped headstone in that section of the cemetery. She and Mrs. Spencer had picked it out together. Meade parked the car and got out slowly. Walking over the grass, she knelt down and touched the engraved writing.

*Daniel Jonathan Spencer*
*March 25, 1980—June 5, 1998*

He was gone. Daniel was really and truly gone and all her memories of him—the little crappy apartment, their dinners at Wok This Way, making love, snuggling in bed, arguing over the bills—they were all part of a dream.

Daniel was dead and he was never, ever coming back.

*How could she have thought any differently?*

Meade gently laid her body down on top of the grave of the boy she'd loved so deeply, resting her face on the grass. She could almost hear him say to her, "You're going to get bit by a fire ant," but she didn't care. She needed to lie next to him. And cry.

Even in her annoyance with Daniel in the other world—even with her frustration over the way their lives had turned out—she had loved him. She'd never stopped loving him. The mere thought of him had always brought a smile to her face and caused her heart to beat a little bit faster.

Their love had never been in question.

It was, she had learned, simply not enough. Never had she thought their love wouldn't be enough. But, as it turned out, it wasn't.

"I'm sorry," Meade whispered, the tears falling onto the ground. "I still love you. I'll always love you."

She wasn't sure how long she stayed there. A soft breeze, unusual for this time of year in Texas, brushed through her hair and swept it onto her cheek. With her eyes closed, she felt Daniel lying next to her—as he had been last week—gently rubbing her back, whispering his love for her.

When she finally sat up, her back was aching again. It was, no doubt, time for more medicine. And Meade knew she couldn't stay here all day. It was also time for her to leave. She and Daniel were over. This time, forever.

Standing up, she gently touched the top of the headstone.

"I love you," she said one more time. She didn't need to hear him say the words back to her. He loved her as well and nothing would ever change that. Not in this world or any other.

Meade took a deep breath as she turned the corner onto the small road in South Austin. She rarely came to this part of town and was thankful for the GPS on her phone or she would've been lost five miles ago. Finding the correct house, Meade parked the car and put her hands in her lap. She took a deep breath. This wasn't going to be easy. If she could have, Meade would've restarted the car and headed straight home to her mom and Jimmy's house. But, she couldn't do that. She knew what needed to be done and it needed to be done right now.

Meade stepped out of the car and made her way to the front door. She knocked three times and then waited. She could feel the sweat dripping down her armpits and her chest, running between her cleavage. She was unsure, for once, if it was the result of the unbearable Texas heat or her nerves.

The door opened, and for the first time in fifteen years—in real life, at least—Meade saw her childhood best friend in person. She looked great. Her hair was shorter than it had been in Meade's dream, and Meade thought she saw a few more wrinkles, but she'd clearly aged well. Meade was so happy to see Lori, she wanted to pull open the screen door and hug her.

"I'm so sorry," both women said at once. And then, startled, they started to laugh.

Lori opened the front door and Meade threw her arms around her friend.

"I wasn't expecting this!" Lori said.

Meade laughed, hugging her friend tighter. "Me, neither!"

When the two women finally let go of each other, Meade could see Lori had tears in her eyes.

"Why are you crying?" Meade asked.

"I'm so happy. I never thought you'd forgive me."

"There's nothing to forgive. Can you ever forgive me for the way I treated you?"

Lori nodded, tears streaming down her face. Suddenly, two little blond boys ran into the hallway. They stopped when they saw Meade.

"Mommy, who's that?" one of them asked.

*Mommy?*

"This is Mommy's good friend, Ms. Meade. She and Mommy have been friends since we were little girls. Can you say hi?"

One boy waved while the other one hid behind Lori's leg.

"You're a mom," Meade said. It was more of a statement than a question.

"I am. And I have another one on the way," Lori said, patting her slightly rounded belly. "This one's a girl."

Meade shook her head in disbelief. She'd imagined this reunion a dozen times over the past few weeks, but never did she expect Lori to have children.

"Come on into the kitchen," Lori said, motioning to the back of the house. "I was making banana bread. It should be almost done. You hungry?"

Meade smiled. "Actually, I am."

The boys ran ahead of them into the kitchen, eager for the treat their mom was baking.

"Danny," Lori said sternly to one of the boys. "I told you there'd be no snack if you didn't pick up all your toys."

"Danny?"

Lori turned to Meade, a blush rising up her cheeks. She nodded as both boys ran to pick up their Legos and throw them into a large bin.

"He was my friend, too," she said softly.

Meade looked lovingly at her old friend and smiled gently. "He was."

And then, in an attempt to change the tone of the conversation, she asked lightheartedly, "What's your other son's name?"

Lori laughed. "Eddie, after their daddy. I married Ed Magee."

"Ed Magee," Meade said with disbelief. "From high school?"

Lori nodded.

"Wasn't he the nerdy one who..." Meade stopped before she embarrassed herself.

Lori laughed again. "The nerdy one with the thick glasses who wore his pants too high and barely ever said a word to anyone?"

Meade nodded, embarrassed.

"That's the one," Lori continued. "We met again after college. He'd gotten contacts by then and his pants fit much better now, though he's still kind of quiet. There's a family photo on the fireplace mantel over there." She gestured with her chin as she put on two quilted mitts and opened the door to the oven. The aroma of the bread was heavenly.

Meade went to the mantel and picked up the framed photo. She had to hold in the gasp that formed in her chest. "Wow!"

Lori laughed once more. "He didn't look like that in high school, huh?"

Meade stared at the hottie in the photo. He was drop-dead gorgeous—and tall, from what she could see.

*Hadn't he been a little shrimp when they were growing up?*

"And the moral of this story," Meade said, "is pay attention to the geeks in high school because they grow up to be *fine.*"

"And successful," Lori said proudly. "He owns his own computer software company."

Meade put the frame back and smiled again at her friend. Lori turned the bread pan over and a delicious-looking loaf flipped onto the plate. Meade sat at the kitchen counter as Lori served her a steaming slice.

"I'm happy for you, Lori."

"Thank you. And I want to hear all about the shooting and how you've been—before and after. What's New York City like? I've always wanted to go there!"

This news startled Meade. "You've never been to New York?"

Lori shook her head. "Nope. Never. We have so much to catch up on!"

Meade nodded as she blew on a piece of the bread and then gingerly placed it in her mouth. Perfection.

"Absolutely," she said, her mouth full of the warm treat. "But, first, let's talk about what a nice name Meade would be for your baby girl."

# CHAPTER THIRTY

Meade had never been so happy to be back in New York City in her life. She'd loved her time in Austin—minus the getting-shot part, of course—but there was nothing like The Big Apple. It was truly the city that never slept and she'd done enough sleeping over the past few months to last a lifetime. She was ready to, once again, wake up in the city she loved.

She stood at the bottom of the steps of the building which housed Brownsbury Press and tilted her head to look all the way to the top of the skyscraper. It was a beautiful sight. To know she worked there—even better.

And this time, Meade was certain this was her place of employment. She'd found her ID badge in the side of her laptop bag, right where she always kept it. Searching for it had been the first thing she'd done when she'd entered her apartment two days ago. That is, after she stood in the doorway and took in the beautiful sight that was her home. It was meticulously decorated and organized and, most importantly, affordable. In this world, Meade had no outstanding debt. She'd never before realized what a wonderful a feeling that was—but she'd never forget it now.

Realizing she'd need to keep working, though, in order to maintain her financial security, Meade walked up the steps to her building and pushed her way through the revolving door. The effort stung her back. She wasn't fully healed yet, but she was definitely well enough to return to work.

She immediately saw Cedric, sitting behind the front desk and was flooded with a sense of déjà vu.

*What if he doesn't know me?*

Her fears dissipated as quickly as they arose, though, the moment she saw the enormous grin spread across his broad face. He immediately stood and came around the corner, wrapping her in an enormous bear hug.

"I am so glad you're back. You have no idea how much I've missed seeing your smile every morning!"

Meade had tears in her eyes as Cedric held her by the forearms and examined her closely.

"You don't look too much the worse for wear. A bullet can't keep you down."

Meade shook her head. "Not me."

"You need to come over to the house for dinner. Sylvia wants to cook something special for you now that you're home. How about this Sunday night?"

"Sunday sounds perfect. I'll bring the wine."

Cedric slapped his hands together in delight. "Oh, Sylvia's going to be so happy to see you. We've been so worried. We had our prayer group at church praying for you."

Meade smiled warmly at this loving man. "Thanks, Cedric. Tell her I can't wait to see her and the girls. I bet they've gotten so big."

Cedric sighed deeply. "You have no idea."

Meade gave him another hug before heading up to her office. She could have given him fifty hugs—she was that happy he knew who she was—but stopped herself at two. She didn't want him to think she'd lost her mind while in the coma.

"Surprise!"

Meade jumped a bit when she opened her office door and saw forty of her colleagues crammed into her relatively small office.

She'd been surprised there'd been no one to greet her when she'd stepped off the elevator. And she couldn't believe Pantera hadn't been at her desk to greet her with a big hug and some black roses— Pantera's favorite.

"What kind of friend is that?" Meade had moped silently.

As it turned out, the best kind of friend, who had insisted Cedric call her the minute Meade headed for the elevator so she could herd the entire office together to welcome Meade back.

For the next hour, Meade was hugged and patted on the back— which hurt a little bit—and kissed on the cheek. Everyone wanted to hear about the shooting and the coma and her recovery. It was clear they'd all been sincerely concerned about her for many weeks. If she hadn't felt love from her colleagues before, she certainly did now. By the time the last employee had trickled out of her office, Meade was exhausted—and the work day hadn't even begun. She plopped down in her chair as Pantera went to answer the phone. She glanced around her office—thinking about the small cubicle she'd had in her dream. She'd never appreciated these four walls and her big window so much.

"Knock, knock."

Meade looked up to see Ian standing in her doorway, an enormous bouquet of lilies in the crook of his arm.

*A sight for sore eyes.*

"Ian!" Meade cried in glee. She stood up from behind her desk and practically knocked him down in her rush to embrace him.

"Whoah!" Ian said, startled. "If I'd known that all I had to do was get you shot so you'd throw yourself at me, I would've hired a hit man years ago."

"Ha, ha," Meade said, squeezing him one more time before backing away. "Very funny."

He leaned down and kissed her on the cheek, placing the flowers in her arms. "It's good to see you, too. I was pretty scared."

"That seems to be the theme with everyone I know."

"If you'd wanted attention, you could've tried pole dancing. It's a lot less dangerous, I hear."

"I'll keep that in mind," Meade said as she gently laid the bouquet on her desk and went back to her chair. Ian took the seat across from her. "So, please tell me you have a best seller out right now." She couldn't help remembering the shock of her dream when she'd realized Ian was not only missing from the *New York Times* Best Seller List, but hadn't even yet published a book.

"Of course, I do," Ian said, his cocky nature still intact. "I am still breathing, aren't I?"

This was the Ian she loved.

"So, let me ask you," Ian continued, leaning forward on his knees. "Did that coma knock any sense into you?"

"Excuse me?"

"Is there any chance you woke up wanting me? You know, because you dreamed about me?"

Meade burst out into laughter. Oh, she'd dreamt about Ian, all right. And part of her thought it was a shame he'd remained fully clothed during her dream. He was even sexier than she remembered him.

"You know what? I'm not sure you and I were hot and heavy in my dreams, but I did come up with a book character idea for you while I was sleeping. Have you ever thought about writing about the life of an obituary writer?"

By lunchtime, Meade was exhausted and achy. She'd planned on going back to full days as soon as she returned. She'd been gone from the office long enough and the work that her colleagues hadn't handled for her was stacked high on her desk. It felt like it would take a year to get back to where she was, professionally, before the accident. But Meade also knew her limits and she had reached them.

"I'm going to head home," she said, peeking her head out the door of her office. Pantera looked up from what she was working on at her desk. Her hair was as jet-black as it had been before Meade got shot. Meade momentarily wondered if she should ask Pantera if she'd ever considered dying her bangs teal blue, but then decided she didn't want to give Pantera any ideas. She could imagine how that look would go over with the other editors.

"It's about time. I thought you should've left two hours ago," Pantera scolded.

"Thanks, Mom."

Pantera rolled her eyes at Meade. "Want me to stop over tonight with some dinner? We have a lot to catch up on."

"Oh, why? Do you have a new man since I've been gone?"

"Of course not. Remember. I have a very particular picker."

Meade smiled. Pantera's picker. She'd forgotten about that expression.

"Speaking of my picker," Pantera said, spinning around in her chair and kicking her legs up onto her desk. "Have you called Tanner?"

Meade shook her head. "No. I know I should."

"Uhm...yeah, you should. He flew all the way to Texas to see you."

"He did?" This was news to Meade.

"He sure did. I wanted to go with him, but someone had to hold down the fort here while you were being all Sleeping Beauty on us." She winked at Meade.

"No one told me he'd been there."

"He asked your family not to. He didn't want you to feel pressured by his visit when you woke up. But he was there for three days—and from what Benji told me, he was a real lifesaver—relieving your mom and Jimmy from sitting by your side all night so they could go home and get some sleep."

Meade was stunned. She knew he'd sent her flowers. They'd arrived at her parents' house the day after she was released from the hospital. And, she'd been meaning to text him. It was...she didn't know what to say. Everything involving Tanner was so confusing—the real Tanner and her experiences with him and the Tanner from her dream and the way she felt about him. Meade was having a hard time wrapping her head around it all and so, for now, she'd avoided contacting him.

But hearing he'd visited her in Texas, and sat vigil by her bedside, made her feel incredibly guilty. She needed to sort through her emotions—and quickly. She couldn't keep taking her sweet old time over it.

"Wow," Meade said. She couldn't come up with any other word. Then, blinking her eyes and shaking her head, she changed the subject. "Come over for dinner. Whatever time you're done here will be fine. I'll be working from home," she said, stepping back into her office and picking up a stack of books from her desk.

"Oh, no you won't," Pantera said, suddenly standing next to Meade. She took the books right out of Meade's arms and put them back on the desk. "You're going home to rest. No one—except for you—expects you to work a full load until you're better. And that's an order."

Meade was about to argue, but then realized she'd never win against Pantera. It was a good thing Pantera hadn't been on one of the opposing debate teams when Meade was in high school. The girl would have terrified Meade.

Meade decided to take the subway home. She could walk from her place—and usually did—but she didn't really feel up to it. She needed to sit down and the faster, the better.

She reached the nearest subway entrance and saw the sign for the lines heading to Canal Street. In a split-second, she changed her mind and headed toward that train.

The smell of Chinatown hit her the moment she came up the subway staircase. Simply the effort, though, of hiking the seemingly countless steps had winded her and she needed to put her hand on the nearest building and lean against it to catch her breath. Getting shot wasn't for wimps.

After she felt like she had the strength to walk farther—and knowing Pantera would kill her if her assistant knew she wasn't home lying on her couch—she turned and headed toward the smell of egg rolls.

It had been months since Meade had walked down these streets—quite possibly, a year or more—but it felt as if she'd strolled down them yesterday. The newspaper stand on the corner—the one with the sign advertising chocolate egg creams on the big chalkboard sidewalk sign—was where she knew it would be. And the word "chocolate" was misspelled, like it had been in her dream. The same knock-off handbag guy, with the long red beard and pierced nose, was selling imitation wares out of his blue sedan on the corner. She remembered him, too. Meade's pace quickened. It was all there. All her memories—except, they weren't memories; they were part of a dream. But there they were, right in front of her. The McDonald's that looked like it belonged in Beijing; the restaurant with the row of ten or so headless, plucked ducks hanging in the window; and the French sandwich shop that looked completely out of place in this Asian neighborhood. Meade reached the door she was looking for and threw it open.

"Welcome to Wok This Way," Li greeted her. "How many?"

*Li.* She was here. Not in her dream. Meade was certain she'd never met her before, and she'd never eaten in this restaurant, and yet...here she was. Meade looked to the back of the restaurant and saw the table she and Daniel had sat at each time they dined here in her dream. It even had the same red tablecloth and Chinese Lantern centerpiece.

"Uhm..." Meade said, backing out the door. "Sorry. Wrong restaurant."

She turned quickly and headed toward the apartment she'd shared with Daniel in her dream. It wouldn't be here. It couldn't be. Not the building. Certainly not that specific apartment.

She was less than a block away when her heart began to beat faster. She could see it. The ugly brick building that had been her home in her dream. It couldn't be. She'd never seen it before in real life. Or, if she had, it wasn't anything she would've noticed and remembered. It was such a crap hole. So nondescript. She would have walked by without a second glance.

As she reached the entrance, someone opened the main door and walked out. Meade rushed up and grabbed hold of it before it closed. She slid inside the building. It was as she knew it would be. Cracked stairs. Mailboxes to her left. Rent box to her right.

She slowly headed up the stairs and was completed exhausted by the time she reached the fourth floor. She knew the apartment number she'd find at the top, before she even looked at the door—452. This was it. Her and Daniel's apartment.

Quickly, before Meade lost her nerve, she raised her hand and knocked. She needed to know. Had to know.

*Was he here?*

It seemed to take forever, but eventually, she heard the deadbolts, all four of them, being unlocked.

"One sec," a male voice said from within.

*Was it him?* Meade couldn't tell.

Eventually, the door swung open and Meade stood facing a short, bald man, wearing nothing but boxers and a white T-shirt.

"I'm not buying anything," he said gruffly.

"Oh, I'm sorry," Meade said, trying to see past the man into the apartment. Same kitchen counter. Same peeling window sill and frame. Same ugly carpet. "I'm looking for someone. I thought he might live here. Daniel. His name's Daniel."

"Never heard of him," the man said tersely, closing the door in Meade's face.

Meade wanted to knock again and ask the man if he was sure. Did he really not know Daniel? Was he a former tenant? Could she get the name of the landlord?

But she stopped herself. This was insane. Daniel didn't live here. He'd never lived here. He was dead and had been gone for fifteen years. All of the memories were part of some crazy, surreal dream Meade had experienced while in the coma.

*But they were so accurate.*

Suddenly, Meade had a thought. She looked at her phone. It was Wednesday. Quickly, she typed in a number.

"Pantera, it's me. Have you had lunch yet?"

"Are you in bed?"

"Never mind that. Did you take a lunch break?"

"Of course not. Who has time for a break? Didn't you hear? My boss was shot. I'm kind of busy these days."

"Okay, smart aleck, I need you to meet me somewhere. Grab your purse. Be there in twenty minutes," Meade said, rattling off the address. "Don't ask me any questions." She hung up the phone.

She might be wrong about this, but she had a feeling she was actually very, very right.


"When I left this place, I had no intention of ever coming back," Pantera said, as Meade held the door of CU Latte open for her friend. "Once you quit a job, you should never go back."

"You're not here to work," Meade said, scanning the restaurant. "You're here for lunch."

"We live in New York City. There are millions of restaurants. Why on earth would you pick this one?"

Meade spotted them in the back, where she knew they would be. "Oh, I have my reasons," she said, smiling. "Follow me."

Meade made her way through the crowd to the tables at the back. She was happy to see the one next to where she wanted to be was free. Hanging her purse over the back of a chair, she turned to Henry and Leighton.

"Hi, gentlemen," she said. "How are you today?"

Both men looked up at her, surprise in their eyes. They clearly didn't know who she was, but Meade had expected that. She knew who they were and that was all that mattered.

"Oh, not too bad for two old fuddy-duddies," Henry said, smiling back at Meade.

"This is going to sound like a crazy question," she said. "But, are you retired teachers by any chance?"

Now the men really looked startled.

"Why, yes," Leighton said. "We are."

"I knew it. My dad's a retired teacher and you give off that educational vibe."

Meade could see Pantera's puzzled expression out of the corner of her eye, no doubt caused by the fact that Meade's dad had been an electrical engineer—at least, the last time she'd heard from him he was.

Henry stood up and put out his hand. "My name's Henry. This is my friend, Leighton."

Meade shook their hands happily. "I'm Meade. This is my friend, Pantera." If either man seemed surprised by Pantera's appearance, it didn't show on their faces. Maybe, being schoolteachers, they were used to eccentric kids.

"Hey, I remember you guys," Pantera said, suddenly brightening. "I used to work here. I think you started coming in regularly right about the time I quit."

"Panty!" Leighton said. "I knew you looked familiar."

"She's not easy to forget, huh?" Meade said, laughing.

"She certainly isn't," Henry said. "In fact, we used to joke she'd be perfect to introduce to Leighton's grandson. We even brought him in here once, hoping to make the introduction. But, by that time, you were no longer working here."

Meade could see the relief in Pantera's eyes. She knew her friend hated the thought of being set up on a date, but that was only because Pantera hadn't met Cory yet. Today, though, would set that plan in motion. As far as Meade was concerned, it was going better than she could have ever dreamed—and, truth be told, she did dream it.

"Would you ladies like to join us? We'd love to have some company. We get bored with ourselves," Henry said.

Meade could see Pantera was about to object, so she jumped right in. "We'd love to!" Quickly, Meade pulled up a chair. "Come on, Panty," Meade said with a wink, knowing how her friend must be squirming with disgust over the nickname. "Have a seat."

Pantera once again gave Meade a questioning look, but did as she was told. There would be time to explain all of this to Pantera—and did she ever have a lot to explain—but, for now, all Meade needed to do was to allow Pantera to find Henry and Leighton delightfully charming. They'd win her over. And somehow, they'd get her introduced to Cory.

Then Meade's dream—or at least, part of it—would become reality.

# CHAPTER THIRTY-ONE

Meade stood by the big fountain in the center of the park, her eyes scanning the crowd. Her biggest fear, at this moment, was that he'd spot her before she saw him. She didn't want to be caught unaware by his presence. Meade wanted to be the one to approach him—to make the first move.

He'd made all the plays up until now. It was her turn to deal.

He'd told her he spent every Sunday evening reading, in Bryant Park. That was why she was here. In her heart, she knew he'd told her the truth. It didn't matter that the Tanner who gave her this information was not the real one, but the one in her dream. If she'd learned anything from her time in Chinatown and at the coffee shop with Pantera, it was that her dream wasn't actually a dream at all. At least, not the kind most people have when they close their eyes.

She didn't know what to call it. Daniel had never actually survived the cancer. But, she also knew that other things—like Henry and Leighton being in the café on Wednesdays and the places in Chinatown actually existing—were truly real.

And that was why she was certain, at the deepest part of her being, Tanner would be here tonight. That part of her other world was real, too.

She'd barely completed that thought when she saw him. She wasn't even surprised to learn her instincts had been correct. He was here. *Of course he was.*

Meade's heart leapt at the sight of him, as it did every time he came into view. Her soul relaxed, as if finding solace in the presence of its mate.

This was her love. The man she was meant to be with—spend her life with.

She'd awakened from that coma knowing this fact. It was truth like the heat of the sun or the waves of the ocean. Day after day, year after year, it would exist. More, though, it was *meant* to exist.

She was made for Tanner. And he was made for her.

Now she needed to tell him that.

Meade's breathing became more rapid as she took her first steps toward Tanner. He was sitting at a small café table, hunched over his book. He was dressed casually, in shorts and a polo shirt. She couldn't see his freckles, but she knew they were there.

"Is this seat taken?" she asked, as she approached him.

Tanner looked up and, upon seeing her, a startled expression crossed his face.

"Well, I'm sort of waiting for someone."

Meade's heart sank. Had he moved on already? Is that why he hadn't contacted her once he knew she was awake from the coma? She'd thought he was giving her some time and space.

"Someone beautiful?" she asked, hoping he was playing a game with her, remembering their first encounter.

"Most definitely." He winked. A wink that spoke a thousand words in a million different languages. "She's the most beautiful woman I've ever seen."

Meade looked at the chair across from Tanner and then, without a second thought, she pushed his shoulders back and placed her bottom on his lap.

"I woke up."

"You woke up." Their eyes were locked on each other. The whole park could have been looking at them, or perhaps running away from an ever-present danger, but neither of them cared. Nothing mattered at this moment except the connection between them.

"I dreamt of you."

"You did?"

Meade nodded.

"Was I naked?"

Meade chuckled and ran her fingers through the back of his hair.

"Were *you* naked?" he asked hopefully.

"Neither of us was naked. At least, not yet. As I said, I woke up."

Tanner put his arms around Meade and gently rubbed her back. "How do we get you back into that coma?"

"I don't need to go back into a coma. We can make all my dreams come true right now."

"Oh, can we?"

Meade nodded.

"And what about my dreams?" Tanner asked.

"I'm sure we can do something about those, too," Meade said softly, lowering her face closer to his.

"My dreams are pretty raunchy," Tanner said, his lips a breath away from hers.

Meade giggled. "Why does that not surprise me?"

"I'm just that kind of guy."

"Tell me again what kind of guy you are."

"The kind who wanted to kiss you on the lips and wake you up from the coma, like a prince in a fairy tale."

"And why didn't you?"

"I thought you needed to wake up on your own and come to the realization you needed me, not because I saved your life, but because I'm a part of you."

"And I'm a part of you."

"Precisely. I'm glad you finally figured that out."

Meade had figured it out. It had taken a bullet and a coma and the end of her relationship with her deceased boyfriend, but she'd finally figured it out. Most people would have come to the realization a little bit easier. But not Meade. No, she always had to do things the difficult way.

"And now that I have," she continued. "I'm never going to forget again."

With one final, slow movement, Meade put her lips to Tanner's and kissed him. It was glorious and beautiful and true. Everything she'd always hoped for and more.

She couldn't have dreamt a better one.

# EPILOGUE

"Hey, hon, I'm going to run down to the hotel gym for a quick workout while you shower and take a nap, okay?" Tanner said, as he popped his head in the bathroom door. "I have my key."

Meade pushed back the shower curtain. She could barely see the outline of Tanner's face through the steam-filled bathroom. She'd been enjoying her time in the shower and, by the looks of it and without even realizing it, had been doing so for a long time.

"Okay, sounds good. I think I may be awhile in here. It feels so good. See you in a bit!"

"You might want to get out soon. You're reaching prunish levels."

"Don't worry," Meade said, laughing as she put the shower curtain back in place and allowed the hot water to beat down on her chest. "My skin will be perfect by the time you crawl back into bed next to me. Just make sure *you* shower before you join me!"

"Don't appreciate me ripe from a workout?"

"No," Meade said firmly. "And remember, don't pull any muscles I may need later...*husband.*"

She heard Tanner chuckle. Neither of them was used to that word yet. Or *wife*, for that matter. Husband and wife. That's what they were now. Tanner and Meade Dale.

Meade could hardly believe it.

The wedding had been beautiful. Perfect. And simple. Just as they wanted it. They were married at a small vineyard in Texas with only a few family and friends present. Meade's mom and Jimmy were there, as were her brothers and Katie. Lori and her husband also attended, holding their new bundle of joy—Alexandra Meade—in their arms. Pantera had flown in with Cory. Meade wanted to pat herself on the back every time she looked at the couple. She'd done a good job as matchmaker. Perhaps her picker wasn't so bad after all.

Henry and Leighton had surprised her by accepting the invitation to her wedding and flying all the way to Texas. Neither of them had ever been to the state before and said they planned to road trip to Dallas and then Houston before heading back east. Even Cedric and his wife had made the effort to be there. They'd told Meade they wouldn't have missed it for the world.

Daniel's mom had been there, too—with Mr. Barker. Meade was so pleased she'd accepted their invitation and had been able to get away from the women's shelter for the day, which Meade had been relieved to hear she still ran. Such a special day would not have felt right, or complete, without Mrs. Spencer. She was an integral and important part of Meade's life—of her life story. Meade needed her there. It had been difficult, however, not to shed a tear as the two women's eyes met on Meade's way down the aisle. Meade knew, instinctively, the older woman's thoughts. *This should have been Daniel's wedding day, too.*

But Meade knew the truth. The absolute and undeniable truth. This was never meant to be Daniel's day. Even if he had lived, nothing would have changed that. This day was always meant to belong to her and Tanner—and to no one else.

Meade took one last moment to enjoy the heat and the quiet of the shower before turning off the water. She opened the curtain and grabbed one of the large, fuzzy, white hotel towels beckoning her to snuggle into them. *Why are towels never so inviting at home?*

She took her time drying her body and wrapping it in the hotel bathrobe hanging on the back of the door—the one with *Hers* on the breast pocket. Tanner had left the *His* robe on the floor next to their bed the previous night. In actuality, it had slipped to the ground once Meade untied the belt in her pursuit of what was underneath.

Meade smiled at the memory of their lovemaking. She and Tanner fit together—in every way possible. Sexually, of course. But also, emotionally and mentally. And physically, now that the two of them had both begun working out regularly. Meade had informed Tanner she needed him around, for a long time to come. No more of his "deceptively fit" body. She wanted him *actually* fit. As part of the deal, she agreed to work a little bit less and exercise with him a little bit more. They'd even begun toying with the idea of entering a marathon together next year. But it wasn't the thought of running a marathon that put a smile on Meade's face. No, it was the image of the long relationship they had ahead. This relationship, unlike her others, wasn't a sprint she was quickly rushing through, eager for the next one to make itself apparent. Their bond was, in every sense, a marathon. One she planned to run carefully and beautifully—with Tanner by her side—matching her, step for step.

Meade quickly ran a brush through her wet hair and glanced in the mirror. Looking back at her was a radiant woman. She'd never seen herself look so happy and relaxed—and content. Yes. That's the word that suited her best. *Content.* It was a feeling she hadn't known since high school and it felt incredibly good to be in that place in her life again.

She was still smiling to herself when she opened the bathroom door. The fresh, clear air of the bedroom, in contrast to the steamy bathroom, felt cool on her face. She would have paused to enjoy the sensation if she wasn't suddenly overcome by the feeling she might pass out. She felt the blood leave her head and the room begin to spin.

*This can't be real. She must be seeing things.*

Meade quickly grabbed the doorframe to brace herself.

Seated on the chair—the one she was certain she'd left her dirty clothes on only a half hour before—was Daniel.

Meade took a deep breath. This could not be happening—*again*.

She closed her eyes tightly and then opened them again. He was still there—smiling at her. As she began to catch her breath, she took a good look at him and gasped. Even more surprising than finding him sitting in her hotel room was that this was not the Daniel she'd left in New York City. This was not the thirty-something Daniel she'd lived with and loved and ultimately left. This was *her* Daniel. The one she'd said goodbye to at the age of eighteen. The one she'd seen run up and down the basketball court a thousand times. The one she'd watched take his last breath as her tears fell on his cold, thin arm.

Except, he wasn't that Daniel, either. He was healthy and fit. His skin had the olive tone she'd always loved and not the pasty one he'd left this world bearing. He was muscular, not painfully thin. And his hair. *Oh, Daniel,* Meade almost said aloud. *Daniel.* He had a head full of hair. Those beautiful curls that had reminded her of an angel's locks when she was eight years old, framed his face as they did before she and he had shaved them off in his upstairs bathroom so many years earlier.

As the first tear fell from her eyes, Daniel rose from the chair and slowly moved closer to her. Silently, he took her hands in his own and led her to the bed. She sat on the end, as he pulled over the chair and sat in it, so they were facing each other, their knees touching.

"Hi," he said softly.

"Hi," Meade said. She couldn't take her eyes off him. *What was happening?*

"I didn't mean to scare you. I thought you might pass out there for a moment."

Meade laughed nervously. "I think I almost did."

They sat there, lost in their own thoughts, for what seemed like a very long time.

Finally, Daniel spoke. "I had to come say goodbye to you. I didn't like how we left things."

"Which time?" she asked, wondering if this Daniel even knew about New York. "The time when I watched you die or the time when you watched me almost do the same?"

"Either time," he said, full of understanding. "I didn't like either time."

Meade didn't know what to say. This was all so confusing. So... *much*. This Daniel was not a day over eighteen and yet...he knew about New York. He knew what had happened there. He knew how things had ended.

"I don't think I understand," Meade said. "I don't understand."

Daniel let go of her hands and sat back in the chair, stretching out his legs next to hers. He smiled at her. That glorious smile. Gosh, she'd missed that smile. It wasn't until this moment that she realized older Daniel hadn't had that same grin. Oh, he'd still had a beautiful smile—one that would make any woman melt, she imagined. But it hadn't been this same, carefree, silly, I-know-something-that-is-going-to-knock-your-socks-off type of smile.

"I answered your question," Daniel said.

"What?" Now she was even more confused. *What was he talking about?*

"I answered your question. It's as simple as that."

"My question?"

"Yes." Daniel crossed his arms in front of him—the way he'd always done when he had a point to make and wanted to make sure she got it.

"Did I ask a question?" She was confused. "I didn't ask a question."

For a moment, Daniel was silent. He looked deep into her eyes— the way he used to look at her when they'd lie together in his hospital bed. The way he'd peer deep into her soul, without either one saying a word. She knew then, though neither of them would ever say it aloud, that he knew she was scared. That he knew she was worried she'd lose him. That he knew *she* knew he was frightened, too.

"But didn't you?"

His words floated between them, slowly gliding their way through the air until they reached Meade. She looked up at Daniel, startled.

"What if?" she said quietly. "I asked, 'What if?'"

Daniel nodded gently. *Yes,* his eyes said silently. *You asked, what if?*

Meade gasped and closed her eyes. "That was you? *You?*"

Opening them again, she saw Daniel nod.

"Yes," he said. "It was me."

"But how? Well...how? I don't understand," Meade said again.

"Some things can't be explained. Someday you'll understand. For now, all you need to do is accept them."

Meade didn't know what to say. She was truly speechless—something that, before the past year, she could safely say she'd rarely ever been. Lately, though, with all that had happened to her, she seemed to regularly be finding herself without words.

"I had to answer you," Daniel continued. "I saw you going from relationship to relationship. Never happy. Never satisfied. Always wondering what if I'd lived? Would your life have been better if I were still in it? Your whole life was based around the question, 'What if?'"

Meade's eyes filled with tears again. *He'd seen her? He knew?*

"And it was my fault."

"What do you mean it was your fault? Of course it wasn't. You had no control over dying, and you fought as hard as you could to stay with me. I knew that."

Daniel shook his head sadly. "That's not what I mean. It wasn't my fault that I died. It was my fault that you felt you couldn't really live."

Now Meade was getting angry. What was he talking about? She was the one who'd made such a mess of her life—not him. She was the one who'd been stuck in the past, unable to move on.

"If I hadn't insisted you make that promise to me..."

Oh. Now Meade understood. *The promise.* She'd promised Daniel he'd always be the one love of her life. Yes, she'd made it. And she had meant it with all her heart. She might not have spent her life thinking about that vow. She might not have consciously thought the promise she'd made to Daniel was the reason she was never able to give her heart to someone else along the way. But it was always with her—never completely out of reach. Always on the horizon of her mind.

"I couldn't let you live the rest of your life like that, especially knowing I had caused your unhappiness. At first, I thought you'd figure it out on your own...you'd understand it was okay to move on and make a new life for yourself—that I was a scared eighteen-year-boy who didn't understand the implications of what he was asking, but..." His voice wandered off.

"But, I didn't," Meade finished for him.

"No." Daniel sighed. "You didn't. It was killing me...no pun intended."

Meade smiled. Even in the worst and most difficult situations, Daniel had always been able to make her smile.

"And so you made sure I figured it out."

"Yes," Daniel said wearily. "I made sure you figured it out."

Suddenly, a thought occurred to Meade. "Did you make sure I got shot?"

"What?!" Daniel nearly jumped out his chair, horrified. "Of course not! I would never do such a thing to you!"

"But then...?" She was even more confused.

"I had nothing to do with what happened that day in the Capitol," he said. "I promise. Things like that...well, those who are like me have no control over things like that. Having said that, let's say I saw an opportunity and I took it."

"You took it?"

"I saw a way to make you see...to answer your question...and I took it."

"Oh," she said. "Oh."

Once again, the two of them fell into silence.

"Are you mad?" Daniel asked.

Meade had to smile at him. He was still her Daniel. So innocent. So concerned about her and what she thought of him.

"Of course I'm not mad. I'm not mad at all."

She took his hands in hers. "I promise," she said, looking deep into his eyes.

"I wanted you to be happy. And you weren't. Day after day, year after year...you weren't happy..." he trailed off.

"No, I wasn't happy. You're right. I definitely wasn't happy."

"And you are now."

It sounded like a statement, but Meade wondered if it was really a question.

"Yes, Daniel," she said reassuringly. "I'm happy now. Very, very happy."

Daniel smiled. "You did good, babe. You did really, really good."

Meade thought she saw a tear in the corner of his eye, but she wasn't quite sure.

"This doesn't mean I loved you any less," he said. "I loved you with all I had in me. Just because..."

He didn't finish what he was saying. Meade sensed he couldn't.

"I know. *I know.* You loved me in a way I had never experienced before. What we had was so incredibly special. So unique. No other love of mine can take the place of that. What you and I had...it's still all ours. Nothing changes that."

Daniel nodded again. Then he reached up and wiped the corner of his eye, pushing away the tear Meade realized had really been there.

Daniel stood slowly, pulling her to her feet with him. "I need to go," he said solemnly. "I don't want to, but...I need to go."

Meade was so torn. She wanted him to stay. She never wanted to let this Daniel out of her sight. But, she knew that she must. It was time she let go. Of this Daniel...of the older Daniel...of that part of her life.

Meade moved close to him and put her head on his chest. He was still so tall. She felt him put his hand on her hair and stroke it softly.

"I love you," she said. "I've always loved you."

"I know, babe. I know. And I will always love you." He kissed the top of her head and then gently pushed her back, away from him.

With his big, teenage hand, he wiped the tears that were now running down her face.

"Remember," he said, looking deep into her eyes. "I got your back. I will *always* have your back."

Meade smiled through her tears. "I'm counting on that."

She leaned into him again, as he kissed the top of her head once more. Her eyes closed. She hugged him tightly to her and then, with all the strength she had, she let go and pulled away.

When she opened her eyes, he was gone.

Meade scanned the room quickly. *Daniel*...she almost said aloud and then stopped herself. He wasn't here. He was gone. And this time, he wasn't coming back.

She expected a feeling of sadness and grief to overcome her, but it didn't. Instead, she felt happiness. And joy. Yes, definite joy.

She had loved. And been loved. If there had ever been any doubt of that, there was no more.

And that love was over...but her new love, the one that was now struggling to get his key to open their honeymoon suite door, was not.

That love was beginning. It was full of promise and hope and a future...not the future she'd always thought she'd have...not the one she'd dreamed of and lost...but a new future. One that was bright and lay stretched ahead of her like a million wild flowers on a grassy field.

"I'm back!" Tanner called, as he finally got the key to work and entered their room.

Meade ran to him and threw herself in his arms.

"Hey! Hey! I'm all stinky!" Tanner said, laughing. "I thought you didn't like to touch me when I'm all sweaty."

"Kiss me," Meade said. "Kiss me like you love me."

"I do love you," Tanner said, putting his lips to hers. "I will love you always. You're my forever."

"While you," Meade said, with more certainty than she'd ever had before, "are mine."

And somewhere, a teenage boy with the blackest curls of any angel, breathed a sigh of relief, and smiled.

# About The Author

Kelly Bennett Seiler is the author of *What if?* A former high school English teacher and school counselor, Kelly has written articles for such websites as *eHow, Livestrong* and *Answerbag*, in addition to creating test questions for nationally standardized tests. She's been featured in *Woman's Day* magazine and was on the cover of *Military Spouse* magazine and *Hobby* magazine. Kelly has edited numerous books, including a *New York Times* Best Seller. She currently serves as the social media agent to a well-known surgeon and author, working with producers at NBC, ABC, CBS, CNN, FoxNews and *HuffPost Live*, as well as editors at the *Wall Street Journal* and *Newsweek*. She has a Bachelor of Arts Degree in English, a Bachelor of Science Degree in Education and a Master's Degree in Educational Counseling, all from Bucknell University in Lewisburg, PA. Kelly currently lives in Austin, TX, with her husband and three young children.

If you liked "Shifting Time," we invite you to try books by these other Infinite Words authors.

# THE

# TROUBLE

## *With*

# THE

# TRUTH

by Edna Robinson
Available from Infinite Words

Set in the 1930s, this poignant, funny, and utterly original novel tells the American story of one lost girl's struggle for truth, identity, and understanding amidst her family's nomadic, unconventional lifestyle.

What's the right way to behave, to think, to feel—if you're always the new girl? How do you navigate life when you're continually on the move? Do you lie? How do you even know if you're lying? What's the truth anyway?

It's 1928 and nine-year-old Lucresse Briard is trying to make sense of life and the jumbled, often challenging family it's handed her: a single art-dealer father who thinks nothing of moving from place to place; her brother, Ben, who succeeds in any situation and seems destined for stardom; and their houseman, Fred, who acts like an old woman. As Lucresse advances through childhood to adolescence, she goes from telling wild lies for attention to desperately seeking the truth of who she is as a sophistication-craving teenager in the 1930s.

Told from Lucresse's perspective as a grown woman, *The Trouble with the Truth* transcends its time in the late 1920s and '30s, and weaves the story we all live of struggling to learn who we are and the truth behind this human journey.

# PATIENCE, MY DEAR

by Bower Lewis

Available from Infinite Words

In this quirky, romantic novel, in the irreverent spirit of Christopher Moore's national bestseller *Lamb*, a young woman is getting texts from an iPhone-obsessed God, and she's not okay with that. Her handsome new neighbor tries to intervene in the dispute, but is he on her side, or the Almighty's?

Patience Kelleher doesn't want to be a soldier of the Lord. She doesn't want His voice in her head, and she certainly doesn't want Him texting her emoticon-laden messages about boy band singers and sinister solar power corporations. What would a cranky, twenty-three-year-old waitress know about preventing the Apocalypse? He's got believers for that sort of thing, or the Army. All Patience wants is to keep a job she actually likes, and to avoid falling for her confounding new neighbor, if at all possible. When the Lord enlists said neighbor to convince her to step up, it doesn't brighten her mood. That was dirty pool.

Zane Grey Ellison doesn't particularly want to be a soldier of the Lord either, but he's keeping an open mind. His world's been pretty skewed since he abandoned his father's estate, and his preoccupation with the waitress across the street hasn't helped him regain his equilibrium. The messages she's receiving from a text-happy God don't seem all that much more wondrous to him than his discovery of diner food, or the realization that not every girl in the world can be impressed by a Bugatti Veyron. In fact, if Patience would just stop bickering with the Lord for a minute, he believes they might even get the job done.

Patience fights to keep her sanity as Zane fights to keep the peace, determined not to let the world die...not when it's just getting good.

# CONTRITION

by Maura Weiler

Available from Infinite Words

In this sweeping, heart-wrenching and inspiring tale, twin sisters separated at birth reconnect through art, faith, and a father who touched the world through his paintings.

When journalist and adoptee Dorie McKenna learns her biological father was a famous artist, she also learns that she has a twin sister, Catherine Wagner, who inherited their father's talent. Dorie hopes to introduce her sister's genius to the public, but Catherine is a cloistered nun who refuses to show or sell the paintings she dedicates to God.

The sisters' shared biological past and uncertain futures collide as they clash over the meaning and purpose of creativity in this beautifully detailed journey of the heart.